"BANDITS AT TWELVE O'CLOCK . . . FIRE AT WILL!"

Nelson stumbled against a bulkhead as the *Tigress* shuddered with the first hit.

The ship swayed as gunners activated missile launchers and unleashed their own clouds of missiles. The *Tigress* started to spin slowly and Nelson realized that it was doing so to bring all its weapons into play. *We're too close to the* Lioness *for a full sphere of fire.*

As a MechWarrior, Nelson felt a mixture of joy and dread concerning fighters. He knew they could easily devastate ground-bound forces and even cripple DropShips. Though such an action would mean his death, it would also bring the Red Corsair's predations to an end. That fed into the optimistic feelings in his heart, and spawned a desperate plan.

I don't have to die. Nelson knew it was true with the conviction of a madman or a prophet, and he knew two other things without a doubt. The first was that he would survive whatever happened at Zanderij.

The second was that he would finally be free of the Red Corsair!

BATTLETECH®
#5

NATURAL
SELECTION

MICHAEL A. STACKPOLE

A ROC BOOK

ROC
Published by the Penguin Group
Penguin Books USA Inc., 375 Hudson Street,
New York, New York 10014, U.S.A.
Penguin Books Ltd. 27 Wrights Lane,
London W8 5TZ, England
Penguin Books Australia Ltd, Ringwood,
Victoria, Australia
Penguin Books Canada Ltd, 10 Alcorn Avenue,
Toronto, Ontario, Canada M4V 3B2
Penguin Books (N.Z.) Ltd, 182–190 Wairau Road,
Auckland 10, New Zealand

Penguin Books Ltd, Registered Offices:
Harmondsworth, Middlesex, England

First published by Roc, an imprint of New American Library,
a division of Penguin Books USA Inc.

First Printing, July, 1992
10 9 8 7 6 5 4 3 2 1

Series Editor: Donna Ippolito
Cover: Bruce Jensen
Interior illustrations: Elizabeth Danforth
Mechanical drawings: FASA art staff

To Dave Arneson,
gentleman, scholar and friend.
He proves that intelligence, creativity,
wit and generosity can be wrapped up
in one package.

The author would like to thank the following people for their contributions to this book: J. Ward Stackpole for medical research; Kerin Stackpole for free legal advice (the best of which being that if she didn't get mentioned, it wouldn't be free); Liz Danforth for tolerating my cackling madly while working on this book; John-Allen Price for the continued loan of a Cox; Dennis L. McKiernan for the challenge; Sam Lewis for editorial advice; Donna Ippolito for translating it into English; and the GEnie Network over which this novel and edits passed from the author's computer straight to FASA.

A short story of Nelson Geist's early career appears as part of the MechWarrior manual for the interactive BattleMech game by Kesmai and offered on GEnie.

MAP OF THE SUCCESSOR STATES
CLAN TRUCE LINE

1 • Jade Falcon/Steel Viper, 2 • Wolf Clan, 3 • Ghost Bear,
4 • Smoke Jaguars - Nova Cats, 5 • Draconis Combine,
6 • Outworlds Alliance, 7 • Free Rasalhague Republic,
8 • Federated Commonwealth, 9 • Free Worlds League,
10 • Capellan Confederation, 11 • St. Ives Compact

Map Compiled by COMSTAR.
From information provided by the COMSTAR EXPLORER SERVICE
and the STAR LEAGUE ARCHIVES on Terra.

© 3054 COMSTAR CARTOGRAPHIC CORPS.

Prologue

Kooken's Pleasure Pit
Federated Commonwealth
15 February 3054

Kommandant Nelson Geist started to bark at his grandsons as he once would have yelled at his troops, but then thought better of it. The twin boys, both just turned five, knelt in the dust and marched little plastic BattleMechs into position for a battle. Their blue eyes glittered and the tips of their tongues peeked from the corners of their mouths as they concentrated on their play. So much did they resemble the Kommandant's son that it made his heart heavy to watch them.

Joachim shook his head violently, spraying his fine blond hair over his face. "No, Jacob, this time *I* get to be the Kell Hounds. *You* be the Tenth Lyran Guards."

Jacob sat back on his haunches, a defiant grimace settling on his face. "I always have to be the bad guys, Joachim. It's my turn to be the Kell Hounds."

Nelson Geist made sure his left hand had a solid grip on the coffee cup as he set it down on the porch steps. "Boys," he said, "the Kell Hounds and the Tenth Lyran Guards are on the same side. They're allies."

"But mommy says Victor Davion killed daddy. The Guards are his." Joachim and Jacob both looked troubled as the contradictions slammed together in their minds for the first time.

Nelson stepped forward and dropped into a squat at the edge of their battlefield. He picked up one of the little plastic miniatures of the ten-meter-tall death machines that were to warfare in the thirty-first century what cavalry had been to Napoleon. "Your father piloted a *Phoenix Hawk*, just like this. He was part of Prince Victor's unit, the Revenants, when they went to Teniente to rescue Hohiro Kurita. It was the Clans, the Nova Cats, who killed your father, not Prince Victor."

The boys remained solemnly quiet for a moment as Nelson set the miniature *Phoenix Hawk* down, then Joachim grabbed it and added it to his army. "Daddy is now part of the Kell Hounds."

Jacob protested and Nelson would have tried to adjudicate the dispute, but he heard the screen door slam shut behind him. Turning toward the house, he saw Dorete standing there, hugging her skinny arms around her waist. The expression in her eyes was distant, but her mouth was set in the thin, grim line that had become so familiar since his return from the Clan war. She still showed some of the youthful beauty that had attracted Jon, but two years of mourning had changed her.

"I should never have let you give them those things, Kommandant." Her voice cut at him like a knife. "Those are demonic toys. They seduce our youth with thoughts of glory, then betray them."

Nelson forced himself to look away as he reached down for his coffee cup. Scars crisscrossed the back of his left hand, which he forced open, ignoring the phantom sensations of the two missing last fingers as he made his half-hand grasp the cup firmly. By shunting all his anger into that action, he brought himself under control.

"You cannot protect them from life, Dorete. They must learn. They must be proud of their father."

Her blue eyes flashed like a PPC beam. "Proud, Kommandant? Proud of a man who foolishly followed a princeling on a mission to save the spawn of our greatest enemy? Don't bother bragging about how he died to save Victor from a Clan attack. I've viewed the holodisk the Prince sent, and I know every syllable of his message by heart. Victor is no different from his father—may he burn in Hell—raping the Lyran Commonwealth and killing our men. Jon died a sacrifice on the altar of Victor's ego, and you know that as well as I do. Didn't you lose half your hand as a sacrifice on that same altar? How can you defend the man who murdered your son?"

"The Prince did not kill Jon!" Nelson's shout brought

a look of shock to Dorete's face and even made the boys look up from their play. "Jon died defending the Inner Sphere from the Clans. I lost my fingers and more good young men and women like Jon doing the same thing." He looked down at his grandsons. "Those warriors died to keep their families from becoming slaves to the Clans. These boys need to know and understand that because the day will come when they too must take up arms to defend their homes."

"Never!" Dorete's eyes sharpened. "The Clans have given us peace."

"But only for ComStar, and only for thirteen more years. Besides, we're located above the truce line. The Clans have already been carrying out limited attacks and raids into Federated Commonwealth space, and they'll be back in full force when the truce is over. When that day comes, your sons will be of an age to fight."

"Old enough to die, you mean."

"No, not if they're prepared."

"Preparation did not save Jon."

"Dorete . . ."

"No, Kommandant, no. You don't understand, do you?" She looked away, her eyes glistening with tears that threatened to spill down her pale cheeks. "Your universe has been swept away. Things are changing. Takashi Kurita is dead. Hanse Davion is dead. Jaime Wolf is out of the picture. Morgan Kell is retiring. The old ways are no more. I will not have my sons trained to preserve old ways that have killed billions."

Nelson's nostrils flared. "They are Jon's sons, too, Dorete. Think of him."

Her lower lip trembled. "I do, all the time." She whirled and retreated into the house, her shoulders already beginning to heave with silent sobbing.

"Grandfather, why is mommy crying?"

Nelson choked down the lump in his own throat. "Because she misses your father very much." He knew that Dorete hated relying on him, but she had suffered a breakdown after Jon's death. Nelson had gladly taken her and the boys in, but Dorete's feelings of helplessness and abandonment fed on each other. He was the only object for venting her frustration and he accepted the role. As much as her actions hurt him, he knew they were motivated by her love for his son and he could dishonor neither that nor Jon's memory. "She loves your father very much and it hurts her that he is not here."

As he dropped his body wearily onto the porch steps, the twins approached him. Joachim planted the tiny *Phoenix Hawk* on Nelson's left knee and set another 'Mech beside it. "You had a *BattleMaster.*"

Nelson nodded. "Just like that one there. A BLR-3S *BattleMaster.*" In the background he heard the bleat of the visiphone, but ignored it. "I captured it while still a cadet at the Nagelring and kept it all during my service in the Armed Forces of the Federated Commonwealth. Now I'm here with you, and my 'Mech is in Dobson, with the First Kooken Reserve Militia."

"Can we see it?" The twins looked at each other, their eyes widening in anticipation. "Please?"

The creak of the screen door hinges cut off Nelson's reply. "Come inside now, boys," Dorete called.

"Mom," they pleaded in tandem.

"Now."

They obeyed but only reluctantly, leaving the toy 'Mechs balanced precariously on Nelson's knee. Bracing himself for another stinging blast of Dorete's venom, Nelson didn't turn around. "I would have said no, Dorete."

"That was the duty officer in Dobson," she said coldly. "You're being called up, Kommandant."

"What?" As Nelson turned and stood up, the plastic 'Mechs spilled off his knee and onto the ground. "What's happening?"

"Need to know, Kommandant." She stared straight through him. "You're to report immediately, and it's not a drill." She tossed him the keys to the aircar. "Go."

He looked at the house. "The boys . . ."

"I'll tell them." She pressed her lips into a thin line. "Go."

Nelson Geist nodded and moved quickly away from the house, barely aware that the heel of his boot had ground the toy *BattleMaster* into the dirt.

These are no ordinary bandits. Riding high in the forward seat of his *BattleMaster,* Nelson Geist looked out over the battlefield. Once-green meadows had been churned into a black and brown quilt of smoldering grass and torn sod. In the valley below him the shattered remnants of the Kooken Reserves fought a delaying action. In theory, the Robinson Rangers were somewhere behind them, re-forming after a brutal battle that had lasted more than twenty-four hours.

During his briefing, Nelson had learned that bandits had been spotted coming in fast toward Kooken's Pleasure Pit. The Grave Walkers and the Robinson Rangers were the Pit's active garrison, but the Grave Walkers could not reach the Rangers' location in time because they were stationed such a distance away on the southern continent. That was how the Rangers had happened to call up the Reserves, for the bandits arrived with ships enough for a regiment or more of BattleMechs—though the possibility that *all* those ships could contain 'Mechs had seemed inconceivable. No bandit group had that many 'Mechs.

Coming in, the bandits boldly announced themselves. An audio-only message from a woman who identified herself as the Red Corsair challenged the Rangers to come out and prove themselves. By itself, such bravado would not have been unusual—Nelson knew that most bandit leaders had a loose board or two between their ears—but the gesture was a chilling reminder of the Jade Falcon challenge that had preceded the fighting on Wotan.

Nelson made a call to the *Catapult* on his left. ''Spider, suppress the *Vindicator* over on the right flank. Two barrages.''

''Roger.''

Slowly and reluctantly the Reserves gave ground. The bandits came on hard, surprising Nelson by pressing their attacks even after his command lance began a barrage of long-range missile fire against them. It made no sense for the bandits to keep on coming once the command lance had spread its missile umbrella. *Unless* . . . A sinking feeling tugged at Nelson's heart.

A 'Mech appeared over the hilltop on the other side of the valley, instantly attracting his attention. But for its bright scarlet paint scheme, it looked remarkably like his own *BattleMaster*. The main difference was that the red 'Mech mounted a particle projection cannon in each of its massive hands. In a show of incredible skill, the pilot pointed each PPC at a different target and then fired.

One azure lightning bolt drew a broken line from the weapon muzzle to a war-worn *Locust,* hitting one of the 'Mech's birdlike legs. The particle beam boiled the leg's armor away, then melted the ferro-titanium bones. The *Locust* spun about before crashing wildly to the ground.

The second PPC bolt flogged a humanoid *Dervish.* The blue beam whipped away what little armor remained on the 'Mech's right arm, devouring a medium laser and a short-range missile launching pod. Unbalanced, the *Dervish* fell, too, then stayed down as another bandit 'Mech flogged it with laser fire.

Nelson flipped his holographic display from vislight to infrared. The computer compacted the 360-degree circle around his *BattleMaster* into a 160-degree arc in front of him. He expected to see the red *BattleMaster* shining bright as a beacon in a black night, but the 'Mech showed very little heat after having fired two PPC beams. *That 'Mech should be white hot!*

That the other *BattleMaster*'s heat profile remained a cool blue gave Nelson a real fright. In the three hundred years that the Clans had lived apart from the Inner Sphere, their weapons technology had progressed well beyond what the Inner Sphere knew or could produce. The Clans had weapons and advanced heat sinks that made their 'Mechs run cooler and hit harder than could their Inner Sphere counterparts. It was just that technological edge which had let the Clans overwhelm the forces of the Inner Sphere on almost every world they deigned to attack.

Nelson dropped his golden crosshairs onto the scarlet *BattleMaster*'s dark outline. The dot in the center pulsed fast, confirming a target lock. Nelson tightened down on the trigger of his right joystick, sending a line of twenty long-range missiles streaking out, one after another, from the launcher in his right arm.

The LRMs hammered the bandit 'Mech. Virgin armor cracked and splintered amid the fireballs, the explosions running across the torso and left leg. Armor plates dropped smoking to the ground, but the pilot rode out the assault as if it were little more than a hailstorm.

Nelson nodded to himself in acknowledgment of the

skill that let the enemy pilot shoot at two targets while keeping his 'Mech upright after being attacked. Meanwhile a blinking light on his command console told him he had just used the last of the LRM ammo against his red counterpart. *All I've got left is shorter-range stuff.*

"Spider, take command. Pull out all you can. Run for it." He glanced at his left hand and tightened his grip on the joystick. "I'll buy you some time."

"Don't do anything stupid, Skipper."

"That's an order, Spider." Nelson started his *BattleMaster* down the hill toward the red 'Mech. "Besides, if these bandits were really any threat, do you think anyone would send a one-handed Kommandant after them?"

Without waiting for Spider's reply, Nelson opened his radio and sent a widebeam broadcast out to the bandits. "I am Kommandant Nelson Geist of the First Kooken Reserve Militia."

The red *BattleMaster* stopped and raised both of its PPCs in salute. "And I am the Red Corsair. Your troops were pitiful."

"Then pity them." Nelson kept his crosshairs on the Corsair's *BattleMaster* as he stepped his 'Mech around the blackened carcass of the Dervish. "They have a half-handed commander and cast-off equipment. They're not prey worthy of the likes of you."

"What would you know of what I am?"

"It's obvious you are a warrior." Things began to click together in Nelson's brain. After the battle of Tukayyid, in which the Clans had been defeated and forced to accept a truce of fifteen years with ComStar, there had been rumors that some Clan warriors had angrily renounced their Clan ties. It was also said that others had revolted and repudiated the truce agreement, setting off minor internal battles within the Clans. Still others had gone renegade, taking their equipment and heading out on the bandit trail. With Kooken's Pleasure Pit so close to the border of the Clan Jade Falcon occupation zone, it had been a convenient target for raids by some of these bandits, but the Rangers had been more than able to handle them. Even when two of the groups had actually made landfall, the Reserves had not been called up.

Nelson kept his 'Mech heading in toward the bandits, with each step closing the distance between him and the Red Corsair. Her troops had stopped their chase, waiting for some sign or signal from her. But Nelson knew that each step he took deeper into danger was one more his troops could take to escape. "I would surmise, from your voice, that you were once Clan."

"I do not recognize your name, Kommandant. Should I?" She spoke the question almost as though it were an order, yet her tone also carried a hint of curiosity.

"I doubt it. The Jade Falcons took half my hand at Wotan." Assuming her equipment *was* Clan standard, Nelson knew that it would take a series of solid hits to breach her armor. And that would only be possible at pointblank range. "My son, Jon Geist, died on Teniente, in service with the Revenants."

"The Revenants." A harsh burst of brittle laughter echoed through the speakers built into Nelson's neurohelmet. "The Revenants seriously shamed the Nova Cats when they liberated Hohiro Kurita. Your son died in a glorious battle."

At that moment Nelson saw the rangefinder at the top of his display telling him he was in close enough. *Here goes.* "Yes, it was. Almost as glorious as your defeat at Tukayyid."

Nelson started his *BattleMaster* off on a tangent, then twisted the upper body so that the weapons continued to track the Red Corsair's 'Mech. He hit the thumb button on his joystick, launching an SRM flight at her *BattleMaster*. The missiles shot out from the left side of his 'Mech's chest, spiraling down at the Red Corsair's 'Mech. Fireballs blossomed all over her machine, shredding armor across the chest and arms, then hitting the left leg.

A wave of heat washed up over Nelson as his medium pulse lasers next drilled energy darts into the red 'Mech. One beam sliced huge chunks of armor from the *BattleMaster*'s left leg, enlarging the hole made by the missile hits. Melting armor oozed from a hole in the 'Mech's chest, and more ran from the gashes made by hits to either arm.

Glancing at his secondary monitor, Nelson saw that he'd failed to pierce the *BattleMaster*'s thick hide. His heat registers had spiked up into the yellow range, but his 'Mech's heat sinks had just as quickly brought it back under control. He headed straight at her, swiveling his weapons around even as she also brought her weapons to bear against his machine.

Twin PPC beams leaped from the pistol-like weapons on each of the red *BattleMaster*'s arms. One missed, but the other wreaked havoc. Crackling static into his earphones, the artificial lightning peeled armor off the left side of his 'Mech's chest. With his auxiliary monitor reporting a 55 percent reduction in protection on that side, Nelson instinctively knew that her one shot had hurt his 'Mech more than all his assaults combined had hurt hers.

It was then he noticed the squat muzzle of a weapon just about where the *BattleMaster*'s navel would have been if it had one. The muzzle let loose with a blast of green energy darts that stitched their way up the left leg of his 'Mech. The large pulse laser left the armor with steaming pits in it, but the armor held and prevented more serious damage to the 'Mech's internal workings.

As the left leg wobbled, Nelson had to fight both the pull of gravity and the 'Mech's shifting weight to keep the machine upright. Favoring the damaged leg slightly, he pivoted to the right and triggered his weapons. Six more SRMs shot out, but only four hit the target. Armor crumbled on the other 'Mech's left arm, left chest, and right leg, but still showed no breach.

Those four lasers plus the missile damage further burned away the armor protecting the bandit 'Mech. Two sets of ruby needles slashed armor from the chest while the other two sliced half-melted shards of armor from the *BattleMaster*'s legs. Heat pulsed into his cockpit and the hot air dried his throat. Sweat dripped into his eyes, stinging them, but his gaze never left the image on the projection before him.

"Not bad, Kommandant, but I tire of this game." The Red Corsair's PPCs swung out of line with his 'Mech, but the weapons built into the shoulders and torso all oriented on him like sharks scenting blood. As the Corsair triggered every one of her lasers, Nelson knew in an instant that these bandits were very, very unusual. Her *BattleMaster* was configured with nothing but energy weapons, which made it ideal for long campaigns where resupply could be a problem.

The pulse laser in her 'Mech's torso boiled more armor off the left torso of Nelson's, which still boasted a thin layer of armor there, but now had a huge hole in the mid-chest. With her next shot one PPC withered the armor on his machine's left arm, while the other plowed a furrow through his right-leg armor.

Again Nelson struggled to keep his 'Mech standing, but it was no use. As the *BattleMaster* began to fall, the most he could manage was to twist it around so that it would land on its back. He winced as his helmeted head smashed into the back of his command couch, the hot sting of sparks shooting across his bare legs.

Lying there he looked up and saw clear air above his cockpit canopy. With a sudden jolt the truth about these bandits hit him like some kind of divine insight. The next instant came the urgent necessity to escape so he could warn his superiors. *They've got to know!* "Eject, now!" he commanded the computer.

Nothing happened.

With a glance, Nelson saw that his auxiliary monitor had gone dead. "Have to do it manually." *This ejection seat will get me clear and then I can get a message out through ComStar.*

With his left hand he reached over to flip the small lid over the manual ejection control. It popped up, but before he could hit the red button, it snapped shut again. He did it again, but once more gravity made the casing close. *If my hand were only quicker.*

Suddenly the sunlight from outside his cockpit died. When he looked up he saw one of the bandit's PPCs eclipsing the sun.

"Your fight is done," she said. "Surrender. You can no longer hurt me."

Nelson worked the lid up with his left middle finger and slid his index finger in over the red button. "I could eject. The chair would destroy your PPC."

The Red Corsair's voice filled the speakers in his helmet. She sounded surprised. "That you could. Surrender or die—your way or mine."

Nelson looked at the button and back up at the muzzle that would kill him. *Is this how futilely Jon died?* He swallowed hard and remembered his grandsons playing in the yard. *Was Dorete right?*

"Your decision, Kommandant?"

Nelson's half-hand slid back into his lap. "I surrender."

The Red Corsair's voice turned cold. "You disappoint me. A real warrior would have chosen death."

"Part of me has." His left hand tore ineffectively against the buckle of the straps holding him into the command couch. "Perhaps someday my body will catch up with it."

BOOK I

The Best of Times

Arc-Royal
Federated Commonwealth
12 April 3055

Prince Victor Ian Steiner-Davion turned toward the elevator in the waiting area as its door opened. Tugging down at the hem of his dress jacket, he smiled and nodded at the two security men flanking the elevator. Those two remained motionless, yet Victor knew from long years of experience that their eyes were alert behind the mirrored glasses and that their guns were near at hand.

The Prince's smile broadened as a tall, robust warrior in the red and black dress uniform of the Kell Hounds stepped from the lift. The warrior's long hair brushed the shoulders of his jacket, but it had changed over the years from black to almost white, matching the equally snowy field of his beard. The crow's-feet around the man's dark eyes deepened as his face creased with a warm smile.

"I'd not expected to find you up so early, Highness," said Morgan Kell, cocking his head toward the windows giving a view of the the dark spaceport. "Having the DropShip arrive this early in the morning was meant to keep the idle curious away."

Victor's laugh was good-humored. "I am hardly the idle curious, Morgan." Knowing that the leader of the Kell Hounds was well-aware of his secret reason for being on Arc-Royal, Victor played along with the banter, assuming it was for the benefit of the elevator's other passenger. "I suppose I still haven't adjusted to Arc-Royal's time. And then after we got the news of the bandit strike at Pasig, I was up all night studying the preliminary reports.''

''I heard about that—not good.'' Morgan turned back and looped his left arm around the shoulders of the young man who had trailed him out of the elevator. Tall and gangly, the youth had the black hair of a Kell, but his eyes were an unusual blue-green. He was still blinking away sleep.

''Highness, this is my grandson, Mark Allard. Perhaps you remember seeing him when we came to greet you on your arrival.''

The Prince of the Federated Commonwealth extended his hand to the young man. ''Victor Davion.''

Mark smiled as he looked down at Victor and shook his hand. ''I am honored to meet you, Highness.''

''Just call me Victor, cousin.'' Victor frowned slightly as he glanced at Morgan. ''I have tried, repeatedly, to get your grandfather to do that, but he insists on formality. I could order him, I suppose, but everyone knows that the Kell Hounds can't follow orders.''

Morgan laughed, but Mark's eyes became distant for a second. ''Like Phelan.'' The words, heavy with contempt, hung in the air like a foul vapor.

Morgan's eyes narrowed slightly. ''I thought it would be good for Mark to see his uncle again in a less formal situation than what all the receptions are likely to be later this week.''

The younger man tried to shrug off his grandfather's arm. ''Why you want to save that traitor embarrassment, I don't know.'' Mark looked over to Victor. ''You must be suspicious of him, too. You have all your bodyguards here.''

Victor hesitated a moment before replying. ''Actually, these men go everywhere that I do. Were I really worried, I'd have asked Kommandant Cox to come along. And, yes, I am here in my official capacity as Prince of the Federated Commonwealth to welcome a Khan of the Wolf Clan. I am also here as myself to welcome my cousin.''

Mark's hands balled into fists as the frustration all but shimmered off him. ''How can you two be so blind? Phelan got himself expelled from the Nagelring, then went over to the Clans. He's a hero to them, a hero to the same people who have tried to destroy the Inner Sphere. The Wolf Clan, the one he helped, has been the most successful in attacking us, and they rewarded him by making him a Khan. He shouldn't be welcomed, he should be shot on sight.''

Victor folded his arms across his chest. ''I think you have that a bit wrong, Mark. Phelan *was* expelled from the Nagelring, but it wasn't exactly what you're suggesting. Phelan saw a job that had to be done, and he did it. The Honor Board, as I understand it, believed he had violated the honor code. I was at the New Avalon Military Academy that year, so I only know what I read in the files, but Phelan's action saved lives.''

Even as he spoke, Victor shifted uneasily. He didn't like having to defend Phelan because, despite being cousins, they had never been close. Victor had tried to get to know him while at the Nagelring, but Phelan had rejected the overtures. *Actually, I thought he was a big waste at the Nagelring, and it didn't surprise me in the least when he got bounced. I was relieved when he was gone.*

Mark clasped his hands behind his back. ''Forgive me, Prince Victor, but I remember about Phelan. He was my idol. I was hurt when he left the Nagelring, but happy at his return to the Kell Hounds. When he was reported killed in what turned out to be the first engagement with the Clans, I was crushed. I took heart, though, because I believed, like so many others, that he had died a hero. Then it turned out he'd become a full-fledged member of the Wolf Clan, had rejected the Kell name, and even become one of their leaders.''

Victor shook his head as he noticed several of his bodyguards nodding ever so slightly. ''There is no faulting your logic, Mark, but I wonder if you have all the facts.''

''Such as?''

Victor smiled at the younger man's fiery enthusiasm. ''Well, for one, ComStar has just released the casualty figures for the worlds the Clans have captured. Of all the Clans, the Wolves have been the easiest on the indig population of the worlds they've taken. And they say Phelan captured the planet Gunzburg without a shot being fired.''

Mark nodded curtly. "Sure, he wanted to save his troops from being killed."

"More important, Mark, Phelan saved countless lives among a people who had treated him monstrously while the Kell Hounds were trapped on Gunzburg. He could have insisted that the planet be razed. And I'm sure more than one person in the Inner Sphere would have been happy to see Tor Miraborg get his arrogant head handed to him when the Wolf Clan hit Gunzburg."

"You can put me at the top of that list," Morgan said softly, and Victor felt for the dilemma his uncle was in. The Kell Hound commander obviously loved his son, and respected what he had done on Gunzburg and elsewhere, yet Phelan's membership in the Clans had just as obviously compromised that love and respect. *I would not like to find myself in Morgan's position, ever. It must be devastating having to choose between family and nation.*

Mark frowned as both Victor and Morgan nibbled away at the corners of his argument. "But Phelan is one of their leaders, a so-called Khan. So is Natasha Kerensky, that other traitor."

Victor shook his head. "No. Natasha was always of the Clans. In spirit that may also have been true of Phelan. You've managed to build him up into a monster, though I admit you're not the only one who thinks that way. Many people believe that what Phelan has done is a crime, an act of treason. But for all we know, Phelan's rise to power among the Clans may only reinforce the fact that the Kell Hounds beat the Clans on Luthien and on Teniente. So did my Revenants. The Clans may produce great warriors, but that doesn't mean they produce the *greatest* warriors."

Morgan gently squeezed the back of his grandson's neck. "I have been among the Clans, Mark. I've met with Phelan and ilKhan Ulric. Give your uncle a chance."

Outside the waiting area a silvery shimmer lit the sky like a magnesium flare, lighting up the ferrocrete landing area like white moonlight over a placid lake. Little dust clouds billowed up and away from the center of the DropShip as it slowly descended. The ship's ion jets continued to put out millions of pounds of thrust and Victor felt the heat radiating through the windows.

The spherical K-1 Class DropShuttle hovered over the ground as its landing gear descended and locked into place barely seconds before touching down. Victor grudgingly admired the pilot, knowing how much daring and skill it took to pull off such a maneuver. *Every Clanner I've ever seen displays phenomenal skills. How we managed to even slow them down astounds me.*

When the ship finally landed, the docking gantry was rolled into place. Victor saw the huge docking arm move out to cover the door of the craft, then felt the vibration as the arm set itself firmly against the DropShip. From within the docking corridor one of his bodyguards opened the doorway into the reception lounge, then headed down toward the Clan ship.

Victor frowned to discover that his palms were sweating. He wiped his hands surreptitiously against the sides of his navy blue trousers, then pulled at the gray-trimmed cuffs of his jacket. For half a second he wished for a mirror, then snarled at himself for that momentary spark of vanity.

With the frown still on his face, he caught sight of his cousin, the man once known as Phelan Kell, who was now a Khan of the Wolf Clan.

Almost instantly it hit Victor that he'd always resented Phelan for his height, then dismissed the thought as unworthy. Always tall, Phelan seemed also to have bulked out in his time with the Clans. The gray leather uniform hugged his thickly muscled body, and he wore his black hair long, like his father. He did not sport a beard, however, nor did his green eyes glitter with the devilish light Victor remembered. Now they seemed to burn with a deeper fire.

Phelan took everyone in with a glance, then saluted his father.

"Thank you for your invitation to visit, Colonel."

"Thank you for accepting, Khan." Morgan returned the salute, and then opened his arms to embrace his son. Victor found Morgan's acceptance of his son exactly what—if he'd thought about it—he would have expected from the Khan.

After returning his father's embrace, Phelan turned to Victor. "I thank you for permitting this visit, Prince Davion."

Victor nodded, his wariness returning at the cold formality with which Phelan addressed him. "We are happy to honor Colonel Kell's wishes. The Federated Commonwealth owes him much. Despite recent raids originating in Jade Falcon territory, I could not refuse his request to see you."

"One should not be surprised that bandits come from the Jade Falcon area, *quiaff?*" Phelan hesitated as if wanting to add something. Victor nodded, knowing they would have a chance to discuss the raids later. A smile tugged at the corners of Phelan's mouth as he extended a hand toward Mark. "You have grown quite a bit, Mark. It is good to see you."

Mark made no attempt to take Phelan's hand. "You look well, *Uncle,*" he said, managing to infuse the word with so much contempt that it sounded like a curse. Victor looked to Phelan for a reaction, but the Khan had not even flinched.

Phelan slowly withdrew his hand, then gestured to the people in the corridor just beyond the room. "Colonel, Highness, nephew, please allow me to present those who accompanied me here."

Phelan took the hand of a tall, slender woman with very short white hair, and brought her forward. She wore gray leathers similar to Khan Phelan's, which made her not at all hard to look at. Her blue eyes might have struck Victor as cold, but the way she looked at Phelan dispelled that impression. *She looks at him the way I imagine Omi looking at me.* Victor also found something disturbingly familiar about her, but he could not place it.

"This is Star Captain Ranna. She is of the Kerensky bloodline. She is, in fact, Natasha Kerensky's granddaughter."

Morgan Kell took her hand and kissed it. "It is good to see you again, Ranna."

"And you, Colonel Kell."

Victor nodded a salute to her and she returned it, along with a smile. Mark held himself ramrod-straight and tried to ignore her.

Following her came two others, also wearing Clan leathers. One, apparently a woman, filled the doorway. Victor immediately assumed that the giant woman was an Elemental. Flinging her long braid of red hair back over one shoulder, she studied Victor's bodyguards for a moment. Apparently confident that she had nothing to fear from them, she entered the room.

The man coming up behind her might have been her opposite. Thick blond hair capped a head two sizes too big for his small, slender body. Victor was short, but this man actually stood a couple of centimeters less, which made him tiny by any standard. His physical size and his large green eyes also made him ideal for an aerospace pilot. The grin on his face suggested he was the commander who had so skillfully brought the DropShip in.

"These are Star Captain Evantha Fetladral and Star Captain Carew. He is of the Nygren bloodline. Evantha is an Elemental and Carew is a pilot."

Amid the general exchange of nods and mumbled pleasantries, Mark remained stoically silent. Victor frowned at him, then noticed one final person in the entryway. The man looked taller than the last time they'd met, and, like Phelan, he had also filled out. He did not wear leathers, but rather a dark gray jumpsuit. His blond hair was cropped short, as befitting a MechWarrior.

"Prince Ragnar?" Victor looked hard at the man with whom he had trained on the planet Outreach. "I had heard you'd been taken by the Wolves, but. . ."

Phelan nodded at Ragnar, who responded by extending his right hand to Victor. "Greetings, Prince Victor. It is good to see you again."

Victor took the man's hand and shook it, noting that Ragnar's grip had grown stronger. He also noticed the bracelet of white cord on his wrist and the mechanical note in his voice. "Are you well, Prince Ragnar?"

Ragnar's serious expression lightened, as did his tone. "I am just Ragnar now, Prince Victor. I am a bondsman of the Wolf Clan, though I hope one day to be accepted as a warrior."

"And you shall be, Ragnar." Phelan smiled confidently. "Ragnar served valiantly during the battle for Tukayyid. He was assigned to an evacuation battalion, but actually saw combat when a Com Guard squad raided the area where his hospital stood."

Victor smiled. "That's no surprise. On Outreach Ragnar was always more than game." Victor shook his head.

"Looking at him, and looking at you, Phelan, I am impressed at the loyalty the Clans can inspire in outsiders."

Ranna smiled and squeezed Phelan's hand. "Forgive me, Prince Davion, but neither Phelan nor Ragnar were outsiders once they became bondsmen. Your people equate our bonding with slavery, but that is incorrect. We value all the castes."

"I see. I intended no slight, Star Captain." Victor smiled as charmingly as he could. "I am struck, though, by the changes wrought in both men. It makes me wonder that we ever managed to defeat the Clans."

"You did not defeat us, Victor." Phelan's voice took on an edge that the Prince did not like at all. "We beat ourselves because the ilKhan chose that it be so. Yes, you had your victories over the Jade Falcons, while the Combine and some elite mercenaries were able to beat the Smoke Jaguars and the Nova Cats. Those were great triumphs for the Inner Sphere, and you have the right to be proud. Even so, to think of the Clans as defeated is an error."

"But ComStar has made a truce." Victor raised his head. "The Clans have agreed not to advance beyond the truce line toward Terra. Having lost the chance to win that objective, your comrades seem also to have lost the ability to coordinate their operations. What happened to the massive invasion, with simultaneous strikes against multiple worlds? Last year my troops dealt handily with the Falcons' invasion of Morges and the Steel Viper strike at Crimond. And this year it seems to be only raids."

"Yes, the ComStar truce has somewhat diluted the single-minded unity among the various Clans. But no matter how well either you or the Draconis Combine are able to repel the limited attacks and raids launched against your worlds above the truce line, the truce will not last forever."

Victor arched an eyebrow. "And?"

"And," the Wolf Khan breathed quietly, "if certain elements of the Clans have their way, neither will the Inner Sphere."

2

Christian Kell reached forward around the headrest of his pilot's command couch and tapped her on the helmet. "Nice landing, Caitlin. Thanks."

"My pleasure," crackled back through the speakers in his helmet. Caitlin hit the release button and the canopy slid back into the body of the aerospace fighter. "I needed to log the hours on this *Stingray* anyway. With all the traveling we've been doing, I came close to losing my certification."

As the swept-wing fighter rolled to a slow stop in the Kell Hound hangar, techs began almost immediately to fit aluminum ladders to the sides of the cockpit. Chris mumbled *"Arigato,"* as he dismounted, then quickly remembered to append the word "thanks." The tech standing at the bottom of the ladder smiled.

"You're welcome, Major. The Old Man wants to see you and Lieutenant Kell pronto. Has your cousin with him."

Chris nodded and removed his helmet. The hangar's cool air soaked through his sweaty black hair and raised goose bumps all over his body. Chris handed the tech his helmet, then gave the man a quick nod. "Thank you, Mr. Hanson. Cait, did you hear that?"

Pulling off her helmet, Caitlin freed a cascade of black hair that splashed over the shoulders of her cooling vest. They looked enough alike, Chris had repeatedly been told, to be more than cousins, though Chris's brown eyes were a marked contrast to the green of Caitlin's. Looking at her, Chris could see the similarities, but having been raised outside the Kell Hound environment, he saw even more the differences.

"Message received," she said with a smile. "I wonder if Colonel Allard is angry about my using a pass around the small moon to decelerate."

Chris shook his head. "I do not know." *What I'm wondering is if the cousin mentioned is* our *cousin, or* your *brother.* Chris waved Caitlin toward the door into the base facility, then followed behind, still lost in thought. He tried to examine which he would prefer: meeting Victor Davion or Phelan Ward.

He knew Victor from their days in the training cadre on Outreach, where Wolf's Dragoons had tried to teach Inner Sphere warriors the ways of Clan warriors. Both Chris and MacKenzie Wolf had trained Victor and the other sons and daughters of the ruling houses of the Inner Sphere. Victor had showed great promise, and realized far more of it than Chris or Mac—had he lived to see it— would have thought possible. Still, Victor had a prickly attitude that alienated potential allies as much as it bedeviled his enemies.

Phelan was, for Chris, an even trickier proposition. In 3042 Chris had presented himself to his uncle, Morgan Kell, and was acknowledged as Patrick Kell's son. Morgan left the Hounds at that point and brought Chris to the Dragoons' world of Outreach for training. Chris had drilled there for the next three years, then joined the Hounds as a lieutenant in command of a lance.

Before leaving for Outreach and in the brief time before his assignment to the Kell Hounds Second Regiment, Chris had sensed some resentment from Phelan. At first he had put it down to Phelan's rather logical dislike of a newcomer who had as much of a blood claim to the leadership of the Kell Hounds as did Phelan himself. It later occurred to Chris that Phelan's resentment might likely have been due to his fear that Chris would damage the legend of Patrick Kell and the Kell Hounds as a whole by not being able to live up to it.

By the time Chris had proven himself in combat, assuming the leadership of his company after the death of its commander, Phelan had left for the Nagelring. Then came the battle on The Rock, in which Phelan had been believed killed. Chris was pleased for Morgan's sake when he'd learned that Phelan had not died on The Rock, but he was angry to learn that Phelan had gone over to the Clans. Not only were the Clans the greatest threat the Inner Sphere had ever faced, but the invasion had been devastating to the Draconis Combine—the nation of his birth.

Chris still had not decided between Victor Davion and Phelan Ward by the time he reached the briefing office. The huge oak meeting table dominated the far end of the room, making the whole enclosure seem small. Two men had already taken seats opposite each other at the near end of the table and had turned on the lights only at the door-end of the room.

As Chris and Caitlin entered, Lieutenant-Colonel Daniel Allard stood, saluted both pilot and passenger, then also shook hands with each one. "Good to see you both again. Caitlin, so nice of you to buzz the moon base to let us know you were coming."

Caitlin blushed just a bit, and glanced down in mock penitence for a moment, then smiled. "The decel saved some fuel, Colonel."

Dan nodded, a wisp of white hair flopping down over his forehead. "I appreciate that, but I would prefer you kept such tactical details quiet in front of a potential employer." The Colonel raked his hair back into place with his fingers, then smiled at the other man in the room. "You both remember Prince Victor Steiner-Davion."

"Cousin!" Caitlin stepped forward and embraced Victor as the Prince rose from his chair. Victor returned the hug with a laugh, then released Caitlin and looked at Chris. "Good to see you again, Christian."

Chris bowed formally. "Greetings, Highness."

Victor aped the bow with crisp precision. *"Gomen nasai, shitsurei shimashita."*

Chris straightened up, a smile slowly curling up the corners of his mouth. "There is no reason to excuse you, Highness. You have not been rude. I must say, though, that your Japanese has greatly improved."

Victor smiled. "I spent some time with Shin Yodama and Hohiro Kurita after Teniente. Though reluctant, they proved able teachers."

"I was pleased to hear they both survived the Clan war. When Mac and I were training the lot of you, we never dreamed your group would survive intact. Both Ragnar and Kai gave us a scare, but they made it, too."

Dan cut in quickly. "I know you and Caitlin want a chance for some racktime after coming in. Despite your economy measures, the trip must have been exhausting. I just wanted to get you here for a report before I try to sort out base gossip. How does Deia look?"

Chris clasped his hands at the small of his back. "Deia is in good shape. Zimmer's Zouaves were able to bring their 'Mech battalion up to full strength with the supplies we sent them. They've got a great working relationship with the Deia Volunteers and have attached scout lances from the militia to each company. Using a force-in-being strategy, they've scattered supply depots over some of the nastiest territory on the world. Hit by anything this side of a Clan Galaxy on a surprise drop, they'll hold them off for over a month."

"Good." Dan paused, then frowned. "What did they do about Hauptmann Sagetsky?"

Chris smiled. "Kommandant Zimmer sacked him while he was still in the hospital."

"Hospital?" Dan's blue eyes glittered. "What happened?"

Caitlin scowled. "He heard about my birthday before heading out on the inspection tour with Chris. He said he had a present for me."

"You didn't. . . ."

"No, Colonel, I didn't." Caitlin let a slow smile light up her face. "He made the remark at a reception and within earshot of his wife. He was drunk at the time, as usual, and she christened him an idiot with a bottle of champagne. Cracked his skull."

Chris nodded. "Kommandant Zimmer agreed that Sagetsky needed to retire. They brought an officer over from the militia to take his place and the Zouaves seemed to welcome the change. Morale was good when we left." The young mercenary officer looked at the Prince. "Your frown betrays concern, Highness."

Victor blinked, then forced a smile. "I do not doubt your report, Major, but I've been wondering about your program of sponsoring these little mercenary units. Your subsidies have been most generous, which, it seems to me, has prompted all sorts of people to create units just to get them.''

Chris raised his head. ''I am not certain I understand your concern.''

''Take these Zimmer's Zouaves, for example, Victor said. I recall seeing a readiness assessment of them—and, granted, it was before your recent trip there—but it said the Zouaves were two parts AgroMech drivers, one part retirees, and one part cashiered officers. Though some of their equipment is very good, I hear they've got two full lances of *Locust*s whose parts come from more than thirty-five different machines.

''You can't take untrained warriors, stuff them into BattleMechs, and expect them to come out a fighting unit. Officers like Sagetsky will ruin potential warriors in training, and get them killed in combat. I know you have spare equipment and are on a sound financial footing—both because of the Kell family money and with what Justin's Solaris corporation is sending Dan—but I wonder if you aren't wasting money on a hopeless situation. This is, what, the fifth unit you have sponsored this way?''

''Fourth. The Legion of the Rising Sun has instituted a similar policy and has also sponsored a unit.'' Dan Allard folded his arms and leaned back on the briefing table. ''We have been very pleased with the results of the program, in terms of both the military and collateral benefits.''

Chris nodded. ''The program was based on the work your father started when he created training battalions.''

Anger flashed over Victor's face as he waved Chris' comment off. ''I do not think you can consider short-term contracts for a rabble the same as a full-fledged training program, can you? Your little battalions do not have the facilities, supplies, and personnel the AFFC can offer.''

''True, Highness,'' Dan countered, ''but the training battalions start with raw recruits drawn from a pool of people who have already had 'Mech training of one sort or another. Perhaps you believe that our instructors are inferior because they are retired MechWarriors, but look what good use the Clans make of their old warriors by turning them into instructors for those who are up and coming. I would also point out that citing an officer like Sagetsky as indicative of a trend is a canard. Sagetsky was fired.''

Caitlin also wanted to have her say. ''We're doing a bit more than just forming a training battalion, Victor. We're giving the people of Deia some security.''

''Security? I hardly think Zimmer's Zouaves will be much of a match for the Jade Falcons. I doubt they'd even be able to stop the bandits who hit Kooken's Pleasure Pit and are now apparently in the process of attacking Pasig.''

Chris frowned but said nothing. He heard in Victor's voice a resistance to what did not conform to his idea of the universe. This did not surprise Chris as much as it disturbed him. Having lived his life on Murchison under the shadow of the powerful Federated Suns, he understood the fear of people on border worlds like Deia. Local organizations like the militia or the yakuza *Ryu-no-inu-gumi* gave those populations a sense of security that let them live on a day-to-day basis with the overwhelming threat they faced purely because of the location of their world.

''But, Prince Victor, their purpose is not to *defeat* such forces. Their job is to tie them up long enough for us to respond.'' Dan Allard twisted around and sat in his chair. ''You and Kai, when facing the Clans, successfully pointed out that in space there are no borders. The key to meeting and defeating an enemy is forcing him to attack you at a point where you are strong.''

''Yes, Colonel Allard. That's why we hit Twycross with a huge force. The Zouaves are not that sort of force.''

''But they don't have to be. On Tukayyid, the ComStar forces showed that the Clans were not set up to fight long campaigns. The Com Guards strung them out and ground them down. You spotted that situation right off the bat on Trellwan, and the Combine also used it when Hohiro went into hiding on Teniente.''

Victor nodded, then leaned forward on the table. ''True, but the Clans have also been known to shift their tactics to face a new threat. The Wolves did it.''

''Agreed, but the Wolves are not the Jade Falcons, and the Falcons have shown themselves to be one of the more traditional Clans out there. That aside, the key to what we are doing is this: Zimmer's troops can hold a force off for at least a month. It will take us less time than that to mobilize the Kell Hound Regiments and deliver them to Deia. By letting the Zouaves occupy the Clan unit, we pin it in place and then deliver the kind of overwhelming force used on Twycross.''

The small Prince nodded, but the concern had not left his expression. ''Your strategy is sound. We did the same thing on Morges, where the Skye Rangers and Arcturan Guards stayed alive just long enough for us to get the Dragoons in and smash the Jade Falcon force. But the Kell Hounds are operating without a contract. Deia isn't even in the Donegal March. Morgan would only accept a garrison contract for Tomans, nothing more. Perhaps, when he steps down, you will see the wisdom of having steady employment.''

Dan laughed heartily. ''Highness, you know the Colonel refused any more contracts because we were in the process of rebuilding. We got hammered on Luthien, and though the Combine permitted us *very* generous salvage rights, putting the unit back together has been a long process. This is yet another reason for sponsoring the smaller units because they have given us some excellent pilots and MechWarriors. If war were a sport, these units would be our farm teams. Perhaps we are ready to accept your contract, but we will only do so when we feel comfortable.''

Chris heard the hesitation in Dan's voice that Victor seemed to have missed. *How can we make Victor understand that by refusing his sponsorship we get more cooperation from the people of what was once the Lyran Commonwealth? Having Morgan Hasek-Davion as the Marshal of all the armies and Victor's using the Tenth Lyran Guards to free Hohiro Kurita from a deathtrap has created a negative impression here in this part of the Federated Commonwealth. If his mother, the Archon, were not so adept at appeasing Ryan Steiner and not so well-loved among her people—despite the fact that it was her marriage to Hanse Davion that sealed the unification of the two nations—Victor would have serious political troubles here.*

Victor seemed to accept Dan's explanation. ''You know, of course, that I believe you will respond valorously to any attempts the Clans make to advance. I also know you would never accept a contract that would put you in conflict with the Federated Commonwealth.''

Chris arched an eyebrow. ''But?''

''But I would like to be able to reward such loyalty with the sort of contract a unit like the Kell Hounds deserves. You and the Dragoons helped win the battle that otherwise would have ended the Inner Sphere's chances for survival. Since then both units have dealt with internal problems and I suppose I just don't like to think of the Federated Commonwealth facing an enemy without its strongest allies alongside.''

Dan winked at the Prince. ''We're here, Highness. This is our home and all the money in the universe couldn't make us fight any harder to defend it.''

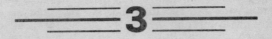

3

Pasig Pirate Point
Federated Commonwealth
15 April 3055

Nelson Geist felt thankful to be out of the hellhole of a hold in which he had been confined, but, unlike other members of the work detail, he avoided making himself conspicuous. It wasn't that he didn't understand what the others were trying to do. By showing that they were co-operative workers and not troublemakers, his comrades obviously hoped that the bandits would not send them back to the crowded, stinking confinement bay once they'd finished the job of offloading the DropShip *Tigress*.

Nelson wrapped his half-hand around the edge of the noteputer and tucked it tightly into his left elbow. Holding the stylus in his right hand he hit the appropriate icons as the crew pulled crates from the DropShip's hold. Despite the very light gravity aboard the nearly motionless JumpShip, the bandits had decided that Nelson's injury made him useless for hauling boxes. And after noticing that a couple of captured reservists treated him with deference, a bandit had made him supervisor of the work party.

Nelson kept to himself, answering questions and acknowledging comments with only a grunt or a nod so that the rest of the loading crew would not think he was basking in the glory of doing no work. Soon, though, he became absorbed in the job he'd been given as the disturbing nature of the loot attracted all his attention.

The steel manacle on his right wrist clicked against

the plastic case of the noteputer as he continuously punched in the icons. His mutilated hand had almost gotten him shot when the squad of bandit infantry pulled Nelson from the cockpit of his 'Mech because they assumed it would make him useless. But then an order quickly came through that he was to be taken alive, no matter what his condition. The bandits had shoved him and a number of other survivors into a DropShip, which then delivered them to the JumpShip, where they were stripped, deloused, dressed in sleeveless olive jumpsuits, and manacled at the wrists.

Nelson knew, from the first, that the manacle served no practical purpose, for it had no link for attaching it to a chain. When another of the prisoners suggested that the seamless band of steel might conceal listening and tracking devices, the prisoners began to limit most communication in the holding pen to crude sign language. Nelson half-smiled as he recalled Spider whispering that "the Kommandant has a bit of an accent," because of his mutilated hand.

Nelson glanced up and saw that the offloading was proceeding very well. Because the JumpShip was moving very slowly, acceleration gave it only a hint of mock-gravity. It was no problem for even the leanest prisoner to move huge boxes of loot, each with a code stenciled in black on the wooden slats. As each box left the DropShip hold, Nelson punched the icon with the appropriate code. Though his screen gave him no totals, he knew very well what they were.

Munitions, though they were not identified as such, were stored in one area of the DropShip bay. He'd seen enough similar arrangements throughout his career as a MechWarrior. A fair amount of explosives and ammunition had come aboard, but Nelson noted that most seemed suitable for small arms or demolitions. The distinctive and mammoth crates for BattleMech missiles and autocannon ammunition were definitely not part of the boxes being unloaded from this ship.

By far the most numerous items were foodstuffs. The stenciled codes on those boxes were equally uninformative, but the cardboard cartons were emblazoned with the manufacturer and product names. The food he had been served while a prisoner was easily recognizable as stuff taken from Kooken's Pleasure Pit.

It had been easy to figure out the stencil code for miscellaneous items. As rarely as he hit the Miscellaneous icon, Nelson noticed that none of those crates appeared to be the same size or shape or weight. The bandits had apparently struck swiftly and scattered the battalion of Twelfth Deneb Light Cavalry defending an industrial complex. They'd had time to loot the complex before reinforcements arrived, but the high-tech machine tools, computers, lostech, industrial grade gems, and other traditional spoils of such a raid were nowhere to be seen. Instead they'd taken only a smattering of jewelry and art objects, which now dotted the ship's hold. Nothing of value compared to the expense of conducting such an operation.

With what I'm thinking, I'm praying *more treasure or something of real worth comes up.*

Out the corner of his eye Nelson caught the motion of the bandit guards straightening up, but it wasn't until the work party suddenly fell silent that he turned to look. When he did, Nelson was as transfixed as the rest of the prisoners by the sight of the woman standing to his right on the catwalk overlooking the DropShip bay.

There was no question that she was beautiful. Red hair fell to her shoulders and down her back. With her long limbs and lithe figure, even the bulky cooling vest could not make her look dowdy. Her sharp features made him mindful of a fox, and her violet eyes shone with animal cunning.

Yet it was more than her physical attributes that drew his attention. It was true that the skintight shorts revealed her legs and the shape of her buttocks to good advantage, but her stance cut off any glimmering of sexual fantasies that might arise. She stood with one elbow cupped in the hand of the other arm, pulling softly on her lower lip with the thumb and index finger of her free hand. Her eyes flicked from man to man in the work crew, evaluating and dismissing each one in an instant. As her gaze wandered from one prisoner to the next down below, each seemed to shrink away, his dreams and hopes dying with her judgment of them.

Then she looked at Nelson. He felt a jolt as their stares

met, an electric ripple that crystallized as fear in his gut. At the same time it ignited in him a lust unlike any he had ever known. He had loved Jon's mother deeply, passionately, but he had never *desired* her in this way. He felt as if, cell by cell, his DNA screamed for union with this woman's genetic material.

He waited for her to look away, but she did not. With every second that her gaze continued, Nelson feared she would pass him by, and at the same time, he desperately wanted her to dismiss him as she had the others. Mechanically, he punched icons as crates began to move again from the DropShip.

She walked toward him. Coming closer, her steady military tread devouring the distance between them, she let her boots click sharply against the catwalk grating. She was as tall as he was and must have been about half his forty-seven years. She did not smile, but the way she eyed him brought self-conscious color to his cheeks.

"You were the one in the *BattleMaster, quiaff?*"

Nelson nodded.

She took the noteputer from him and set it down. Grabbing his left hand, she forced it open and pressed it against her own right palm. The last two fingers on her hand curled down and around over the scars. Her flesh seemed unnaturally pale against his, and the scars on his hands looked almost like tendrils curling out from her fingers.

She kept his hand in hers for a bit longer than he felt comfortable, then she released it. "How long?"

"Almost four years."

She pursed her lips for a moment, then stared at him like a cobra. "I could get you repaired. You could regrow those fingers."

Nelson tried to suppress a reaction, but a thrill shook him. All the things he had lost since his maiming in the Clan invasion, everything he had blamed on the loss of his fingers, flashed before him. He could have his command back. He would be respected again. *Even Jon . . .*

He realized his error as her lips peeled back in a cruel smile. "I would have done that, were you a warrior."

Nelson swallowed hard and straightened up. "Were I a warrior, I'd be dead, *quiaff?*"

His use of a Clan word seem to surprise her, but her

smile did not change so he could not be sure if that was good or bad. She looked him up and down again, then turned and pointed at the next-nearest prisoner on the bay deck below. "You, replace him."

In one leap Spider bounded up the ladder to the catwalk. He picked up the noteputer, and Nelson silently passed him the stylus. Spider gave him a wink, the silent prison argot sign for "things are looking up." Nelson nodded, then looked at the Red Corsair and waited.

She let him wait. She raked him with her gaze, letting it linger on his loins and then his maimed hand, clearly seeking a reaction. He fought to keep his face impassive, and computed mentally the exponential values of 2 to distract his thoughts. His effort, though successful, only seemed to heighten her interest.

"Follow me." She turned and walked back to the hatchway.

He trailed behind her, his concentration flagging for an instant as he noticed the sensual sway of her hips as she walked. *Two times 32768 is 65536. Two times 65536 is 131072. . . .* He refocused his eyes on the mass of red hair trailing down to the middle of her back and kept multiplying numbers in his head.

The Red Corsair stepped through the hatchway, then closed it behind him. She turned to a communications monitor and opened a line to the bridge. The commtech sat straight up in her seat when she saw who it was in the monitor. "Yes, Captain?"

The Red Corsair tucked a stray hair behind one ear. "ETA for the last DropShip?"

"One minute, sir."

"Good. When it attaches, increase our velocity to 1.2 gravities. When we reach the jump point, we will go out."

"Understood. Helm out."

Nelson frowned. Increasing the acceleration would make unloading the DropShip far more difficult than it currently was. It made no sense to increase speed unless there was some sort of in-system defense or pursuit.

"You are concerned for your friends, *quiaff?*"

"As you are for your people."

"Good, some of your spirit returns." She reached out

and took his maimed hand in hers, then led him down the corridor to a central core of elevators. The doors opened when she pressed the button on the wall. They both entered the box and she selected a deck.

The box started to move and Nelson's legs almost collapsed. His weakness surprised him, then he realized the ship had begun its acceleration. Grabbing the elevator handrail, he pulled himself erect. He glanced at the Red Corsair, but saw no reaction, no sign that she had even noticed his problem.

The elevator stopped at an upper deck and they exited when the doors opened. Nelson followed her to a cabin door, then into the cabin. The door slid shut behind him and she used a wall switch to bring up the lights.

He felt a moment's surprise when he realized she had brought him to her private stateroom, but that died fast. The instant the lights went on, Nelson felt as though he had wandered into a set designed for a bandit leader in some potboiler holovid. Lurid reds, golds, and purples dominated the room, with the gold coming mostly from chains and lamps and little items that were beautiful but probably chosen at whim while stalking through a shattered enemy's stronghold. Brocaded and embroidered scarves hung from lamps, staining the light with red tones. Crystal bottles half-filled with multi-colored liquors stood racked in a sideboard.

The room was the Red Corsair and yet it was not. From all that Nelson had observed during his two months with the bandit band, he knew that most of them were Clanners—probably members who had gone rogue. What struck him now, however, was the fact that such gaudy but rich surroundings were totally out of character for someone born of the Clans. Mementoes of battles, trophies from past victories, he could have accepted, but not this self-indulgent and extravagant display. Again he had the same vision of a holovid director creating these quarters to emphasize the romantic side of the Red Corsair for a cheap mini-series.

Suddenly the truth hit him right between the eyes. All the prisoners had long since agreed that *this* Red Corsair must have named herself after the legendary pirate who, almost fifty years before, had cut a bloody swath through Free Worlds League planets near the Periphery and the

Lyran border. Some had argued that the original Red Corsair could have stayed young by maintaining her ship's travel at a significant percentage of the speed of light, and thus could, in fact, be *this* Red Corsair.

But seeing this room, Nelson saw that fanciful idea exploded faster than a back-shot *Rifleman*. He couldn't prove it, of course, but this room bore too much resemblance to those he'd seen in many a late-night holovid he'd watched while stationed up and down the Federated Commonwealth. Granting that this Red Corsair *was* Clan, and that the role had been specifically chosen for some reason, it made sense that whoever had put together the sham would use holovids as source material. Where else would a Clanner go for information about the ways of people of the Inner Sphere?

And that, he decided, was why the picture didn't fit the frame.

The Red Corsair looked at him. "You think too much."

"Does it matter what I think?"

She grabbed him by the right wrist and twisted the manacle until it bit into his flesh. "Do you know what this is?"

"I had heard that when the Clans take a bondsman, they bind his right wrist with a bondcord."

"And when a bondsman is accepted into a different caste, the bondcord is cut in a ceremony." She let his hand fall down to his side, and he felt blood begin to rush back into the flesh. "Steel does not cut."

"Then I am a slave?"

She shook her head. "You are a prize of war. If I thought you had value, I would ransom you."

"It appears, then, that I will remain a prize. No one will pay for a maimed warrior."

The Red Corsair's eyes flashed with a light that might have been amusement. "Oh, I know they would not pay for your hand." She reached out and lightly cuffed his right temple. "On the other hand, they would pay handsomely for your thoughts. Tell me what you have decided about us. Do not lie. I will know if you do."

"You have more loot in this cabin than was offloaded from Pasig." Nelson glanced away as she began unlacing the cooling vest. "The equipment, the personnel, and the speech of everyone I have met here tell me that you are all Clan. All the slaves in the group with me are from Kooken's Pleasure Pit, so I assume you took no slaves before that. The supplies you bring up from the world are enough to feed the slaves, so I also assume we can be jettisoned into space as situations demand it.''

She shrugged her way out of the cooling vest. Muscles rippled on her stomach and a droplet of sweat coursed down between her breasts. ''Your powers of observation are to be commended.'' She turned away from him—not out of modesty, he was certain—to reach into a closet for a short kimono of amethyst silk. ''You have drawn conclusions about us, *quiaff?*'' she asked, pulling the kimono closed and knotting it with a golden sash.

''I have.''

Her hair rippled down in a veil as she bent to unfasten the clasps of her boots. ''Tell me.''

''Your 'Mechs are configured with energy weapons and made to look like those a bandit group would use. Your demands for munitions are low. You are prepared for extended operations in areas where resupply could be a problem.''

She stepped out of the boots and put them in the closet. Reaching under the kimono's hem, she snaked off the thigh-length spandex shorts she had been wearing and tossed them into the closet before closing it. ''From this you have decided. . . ?''

Nelson shook his head. ''I know only that you are engaged in raiding.''

The Red Corsair looked hard at him. Then her eyes narrowed as she allowed herself a self-satisfied grin. ''Very well. You know too much to be freed, but not enough that I must kill you. I will keep you until I break you.''

Nelson suddenly felt himself the mouse to her cat. ''Breaking me will not be hard.''

''You underestimate yourself.'' She focused distantly for a second, then nodded. ''I will begin by having them regrow your fingers, I think.''

Nelson frowned but said nothing.

''Do you know why? Not so I can take them again, I assure you. If it was at Wotan that you lost them, I might have been the one who did it to you.'' She smiled broadly at that thought, but Nelson restrained his immediate angry response. "No, I will start the regrowth because it is something you desire and for which you will be grateful, but it is me you will have to thank. But with all the rest I will do to you, that sense of gratitude will strike sparks off your hatred for me until someday it will burn you alive."

Later, when he returned to the holding pen, Nelson flopped down on his bunk. From across the narrow aisle, Spider tapped him on the shoulder and drew a question mark in the dimly lit air.

Nelson stabbed a thumb into the center of his chest, described a quick circle with a flick of his wrist, then pointed with two fingers at the external hull. He nodded once, confidently, then let his head sink back against the mushy pillow.

Spider winked at him and nodded twice, letting Nelson know he'd gotten the message, even with the accent problem.

Nelson stared up at the black bulkhead above him. *It's decided. When the opportunity presents itself, I'm out of here.*

Victor Davion did not take it as a good sign that he arrived at the small meeting room only to find Phelan already seated behind the computer terminal at the far end of the table. Hovering over his shoulder like a ghost was a white-robed ComStar Precentor, who nodded to the Prince. They had not yet met, but Victor knew this was Special Liaison Klaus Hettig, the official representative of Anastasius Focht, Precentor Martial of ComStar. Focht was the one who had issued the actual invitation to the meeting, Victor's true reason for coming to Arc-Royal.

The Prince stretched, then headed directly for the insulated pitcher of coffee on the table beside the door. He glanced at a sweet pastry while pouring himself a cup, but his stomach flip-flopped at the thought of that much sugar so early in the morning. He was tired, the toll of travel finally catching up with him, but even the promise of an energy boost could not make the idea of food appealing.

Phelan looked up from the keyboard, his green eyes bright. "Good morning, Highness. I've been reviewing some of the reports from Pasig. Your sources are *very* thorough. My compliments."

My sources? Victor frowned. "That information is in files that your father assured me would be secure."

The Clan Khan smiled far too easily. "And they probably are, from most people. But, remember, I spent most of my youth here.'' He patted the computer console. ''I know ways into this computer system that no one else even dreams exist.''

The ComStar Precentor moved away from Phelan and checked the room's door. ''Khan Phelan is correct. Your information is excellent—up to a standard to which ComStar might also aspire.''

Right! ComStar controls communication between the stars and actually sent *the messages that provided the data in the files Phelan has cracked. I'd be a fool if I thought ComStar had not already gone over them and supplemented them with their own material.* The Prince nodded and sat down at the opposite end of the table. He dimly recalled that the charges against Phelan during his honor trial at the Nagelring had involved his using the Nagelring's computers to break into the Department of Defense's computers to steal information. Victor sipped his coffee and immediately felt the weight of sleep lifting from his brain. ''Having the Kell Hounds' computer system compromised by a member of the Wolf Clan is not comforting, though your assessment of our data does soften the blow, Precentor.''

Hettig did not react to the sarcasm in Victor's voice. ''Please, Prince Victor, do not take offense. You would have showed the Khan the data any way. After all, you did agree to cooperate when you came here.''

Victor shrugged, then frowned. ''Why *am* I here? Why is he here?''

The Precentor smiled benignly. ''The reason *we* are here is to discuss our mutual concern over bandit raids—specifically the Red Corsair.''

Victor set his cup down. ''She is strictly nuisance material. I have *military* units to worry about coming from Clan space to hit our planets. Morges got hammered by the Clans harder than Kooken's or Pasig.''

''Jade Falcons and Steel Vipers, Victor, not *all* the Clans,'' Phelan corrected him.

''There's a difference?'' As Victor began to feel more awake, he found Phelan's calm superiority and ComStar's passive manipulation irritating.

Phelan nodded slowly. ''Perhaps the next time the Combine strikes from Wolcott you will want the ilKhan to complain to you about it. The Jade Falcons are distinct and quite separate from the Wolf Clan.''

"Point taken,'' Victor allowed, then he looked accusingly at Hettig. "Why is ComStar concerned about bandits when they've let the Jade Falcons and the Steel Vipers raid the Federated Commonwealth above the truce line? Why the need for this meeting? I'm taking a lot of heat from Ryan Steiner and his mouthpieces for guaranteeing a Wolf Khan safe passage here, and it doesn't help matters that he's dragged Ragnar with him.''

"ComStar appreciates your difficulties and your efforts on our behalf.'' The ComStar Precentor smiled. "We would not have asked you to go to these extraordinary lengths were the problem not so grave. These are not ordinary bandits, Prince Victor.''

"They got lucky.''

"*Twice*, they got lucky, Victor.'' Phelan leaned back, but Victor saw concern flash through his green eyes. "Hear the Precentor out. The Precentor Martial was able to convince the ilKhan that enough was at stake to have us meet here under cover of my father's retirement celebration.''

Victor nodded, knowing the Precentor Martial's reasoning had been sufficient to convince his mother to send him to Arc-Royal. "To what are these bandits such a threat?''

"The truce, Prince Victor, the truce between ComStar and the Clans.'' Hettig folded his hands together, but the movement was so stiff that Victor knew it was a deliberate effort by the man to maintain his placid façade.

"How can bandits threaten the peace?'' Victor looked down into his nearly empty coffee cup and waited for the caffeine to clear up his fuzzy thinking. "They are just bandits. They raid and they run. If the Grave Walkers could have gotten around from the other side of Kooken's just two hours sooner, we would be talking about the Red Corsair in the past tense.''

Phelan shook his head. "You have been looking at the reports of bandit raids and been dismissing them because what you see jibes with what you believe about bandits. Your experience with them is not personal. Perhaps I see matters differently because I once hunted bandits in the service of the Federated Commonwealth. What I'm trying to say is that our information shows that a very lucky bandit group got away with some spoils, most of it not terribly valuable. By any analysis, Kooken got off light—it lost no industrial assets, damned little in the way of loot, and was not conquered.''

The Prince nodded. "I remember the numbers. The raiders took food and some slaves. You can't shoot enemies with cans of soup.''

Hettig nodded. "But you also remember another old saying, Prince Victor, 'An army marches on its stomach.' ''

"But those bandits are hardly the armies of Napoleon, Precentor Hettig,'' Victor snapped, then downed the last swallow of his coffee to give himself a chance to calm down. Having heard enough whispers that he had a "Napoleon complex'' because of his small physical stature, he couldn't help but wonder if the allusion was meant as a subtle rebuke. *ComStar is nothing if not subtle.*

"That is true, Prince Victor, but to date they have not found a Waterloo.''

The Prince snorted. "Then I will play Wellington for them.'' He glanced at Phelan. "If you can persuade the ilKhan to keep the Jade Falcons in line, I will bring my Revenants up and we'll pound the Corsair.''

Phelan shook his head. "The Jade Falcons would ignore that sort of request, even if the ilKhan were foolish enough to make it.''

"Does the ilKhan even want the bandits stopped?''

The ComStar Precentor and Phelan both looked at him quizzically. "What do you mean, Prince Victor? The ilKhan sent Khan Phelan to Arc-Royal precisely for the purpose of discussing the means to do just that.''

"Really?'' Victor put down his empty cup. "You both agreed that my information was good. Do either of you dispute the fact that the Red Corsair retreated into Jade Falcon territory after the strike on Kooken's? That would have been a perfect opportunity to resupply a covert force.''

"Unworthy, Victor. We have had raiding on both sides and no unit has seen the need to strike from behind a false identity.''

Hettig nodded in agreement with Phelan. "Determining the unit's identity is also immaterial at this point because the perception of its origins is doing more harm to the peace than anything else."

"I do not understand, Precentor." Victor stood and refilled his cup. "How can perceptions do more damage than the fighting?"

Hettig drew in a deep breath. "There are elements within the Tamar and Skye communities who believe that the Red Corsair bandits are a covert unit in the employ of the Federated Commonwealth government. They say the bandits are actually a death squad whose mission is to destroy those who oppose the union between the old Steiner holdings and House Davion."

"Ryan Steiner again works overtime to manufacture rumors." Victor shook his head. "That whole idea is, of course, preposterous."

"Of course, but humanity's fascination with conspiracies makes it intriguing. In this scenario, which is helped by the fact that the Kooken's raid damaged facilities owned by a Ryan Steiner supporter, the raids will continue until you or your brother Peter can be positioned as the hero who stops them. It would be a replay of the role Ryan himself played in the 3034 uprising."

The Prince nodded. "And, I suppose, others think the Red Corsair is a unit being funded by Ryan Steiner to build up the tensions along the border. As he champions the cause of the oppressed people out here, and uses a mercenary unit to destroy the bandits, he gains a great deal of popularity."

The Wolf Khan smiled. "Ryan calls the bandits a Clan unit running covertly, and uses the fear of the Jade Falcons to keep his people united and dependent on him for security. He isolates you as someone who does not care for the people. Should your mother ever step down as Archon, he will be a viable and powerful rival opposing you."

Victor chewed his lower lip. "And all this infighting will sap our strength and make us look very vulnerable to the Jade Falcons, who might then decide to launch multiple strikes over the line, destroying the peace."

The ComStar Precentor nodded appreciatively. "You two have distilled in minutes what it took weeks for ComStar's analysts to conclude."

"And the solution is to kill the bandits." Victor again

sat down. "Despite your worries about Ryan, my Revenants can do the job."

"There is no doubt about that, Prince Victor, but ComStar has something else in mind." Hettig looked up and his eyes focused distantly. "As I indicated before, this is an atypical bandit unit. If you look beyond the battle-damage assessments for Kooken, what you find is that the bandits are using energy weapons almost exclusively."

Victor shrugged. "Bandits work with what they can get."

"You're missing the point, cousin. I pilot a *Wolfhound*. When my father designed it, he armed it with lasers. He did so because he wanted to create a scout lance of 'Mechs able to operate beyond the line of supplies, in the enemy's rear area. Because the 'Mech has no need for missiles and autocannon ammo, the only limitation on its operation was the pilot's need for food and water."

"As the Khan says, the Red Corsair has her bandits configured for a campaign in which food will become the most important factor for success."

Hence the Napoleon quote. Victor felt a shiver run down his spine. "I see what you're saying. But I can mobilize enough force to track her and kill her."

"ComStar knows and appreciates that, but we have another suggestion." Hettig looked at Phelan. "Khan Phelan?"

Phelan nodded, and Victor got the distinct feeling he had been set up. "The ilKhan has authorized me to offer you the use of a Clan unit to hunt these bandits down."

Victor blinked. "What?"

"We have units devoted specifically to dealing with bandits." Phelan smiled complacently. "The ilKhan will impress upon the Jade Falcons the need to destroy these Corsairs."

"That is most generous." Victor again gulped coffee to recover from his surprise. "Does he make this offer because he doesn't want Inner Sphere troops going after bandits in Clan space?" *Or because ComStar is holding some sort of gun to his head?*

"Partly. With the Red Corsair operating from Jade Falcon space, he could not guarantee the safety of any

Inner Sphere units that crossed the line." Victor's tall cousin got up from his end of the table to refill his coffee. "More important, though, the Jade Falcon Clan is very much against the truce. They believe it robbed them of the chance to regain the honor they lost in the early fighting."

"On Twycross and Alyina, right?" Victor smiled because his Tenth Lyran Guards had worked with the Kell Hounds to pound the Jade Falcons on Twycross. His escape from an ambush on Alyina had further frustrated the Jade Falcons.

"Among other places. The ilKhan hopes that by gaining victories and honor while *defending* the Inner Sphere, he can make the Jade Falcons look a bit more favorably on the peace."

"Slim hope of that, it sounds."

Hettig smiled. "On that point we can all agree, but as the resumption of the war is the only logical alternative, it is a chance worth taking. More important, though, is that the success of our plan will help defuse the power Ryan Steiner is gathering. Keeping the Federated Commonwealth strong will act as another caution to the Jade Falcons to think long and hard before breaking the truce."

Hettig's remark sent shivers down Victor's spine. He turned around to look at his cousin. "Is the peace so fragile on your side of the line?"

The tall MechWarrior shrugged stiffly. "The people of the Clans are warriors. Peace does not suit them. The ilKhan hopes that finding an acceptable outlet for their aggressive potential will keep them in check for the period of the truce. If you agree to let a bandit-hunting unit operate in Federated Commonwealth space, I will send word out immediately and the ilKhan will assign someone to deal with the problem. We can see if this grand experiment will work."

"If I don't, we will likely be at war by year's end." Victor frowned. *And ComStar will likely punish the Federated Commonwealth by raising the cost of sending messages between our worlds. It's been such a relief not to be in a continual covert war against ComStar the way my father was for so long. But I don't like feeling coerced into an agreement, especially one like this that I would probably support anyway.*

Victor looked over at Hettig. "This is what ComStar wants?"

The Precentor nodded. "It is ComStar's truce, and ComStar deems this the best way to preserve it."

The Prince glanced at his cousin. "The ilKhan believes this effort is important enough to risk Clan personnel and materiel?"

"That is my understanding."

Victor nodded. "If this works, Ryan Steiner loses, and I am in favor of that. I would prefer that one of my units be the one to get the bandits, but I can see the wisdom of having the Jade Falcons hunt them down. There seems little to object to."

Hettig nodded. "So it does. Then you agree?"

This must have made sense to my mother, or I would not be here. It seems sound to me and prevents my people getting killed. If I did not agree, I could still be overruled. And even if my mother did not agree, ComStar could probably use its control of communication to successfully screen a Clan force operating in FedCom space.

"All right," Victor said. "I agree. If you get me the designation and make-up of the force that will be coming in, I can communicate the same to our units in the areas where the Red Corsair is likely to strike." Victor smiled at the ComStar Precentor. "There, you have your agreement. The threat to the peace is over."

"One of them is *lessened,* in any event." Hettig turned to Phelan. "The presence of Ragnar has attracted attention . . ."

Victor shook his head. "I have taken steps to help defuse that situation, Precentor Hettig. I have already vetoed any schemes to covertly or even overtly rescue him. However, if Ragnar wants his freedom, all he has to do is ask."

"I know that, Prince Victor, and I appreciate it." The Precentor did not even glance in his direction as he spoke. "There have been communications, *other* communications, in which Ragnar has been mentioned. Unfortunately for the senders, those communications were misrouted and will not reach their intended recipient until *after* you and Ragnar have left Arc-Royal. Still . . ."

The Wolf Khan nodded. "I understand. I will keep Ragnar on the base unless he is with an escort that can ensure his safety."

"ComStar is in your debt."

"ComStar *mis*-routed a message?" Irony coated Victor's words like wax. "I cannot believe that happened."

Irritation passed over Hettig's face. "The senders were hasty and did not clearly address the messages. Haste makes waste."

"And desperation makes haste."

"True enough, Prince Victor, as we all know." The ComStar Precentor folded his arms into the sleeves of his white robe. "But then we also know that proper planning precludes desperation, and proper planning is what this meeting was all about. ComStar thanks you for your cooperation because, in this matter, desperation would mean a haste that wasted humanity."

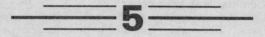

5

Victor Davion smiled politely as the dowager Baroness de Gambier introduced her niece, Charity, to him. "No, it is *my* very great pleasure to meet you, Lady de Gambier." He kissed the gloved knuckles of the young woman's hand and gave her fingers a surreptitious squeeze. "Your aunt is quite right. Your father's service with the Second Royal Guards has been very important to the Federated Commonwealth."

"Thank you, H-h-highness," stammered the young woman.

"I mean that very sincerely," Victor added hastily as he released her hand. He had little doubt that the tall and gangling young woman would have been decidedly less nervous if her plump old aunt were not hovering close enough to hear their every word. Victor—who had learned long ago to be very polite to the young women thrust at him as possible brides by ambitious relatives—felt especially sorry for Charity.

"Lady de Gambier, you are preparing to enter a university, *ja?* I believe that is what your aunt mentioned."

Charity nodded as she collected her thoughts. "I am hoping to go to the New Avalon Institute of Science after getting my first two years at the Gambier Technical Institute. If I can transfer to the NAIS, Dr. Riva Allard's neurocybernetic regeneration projects interest me. I could help my father and others recover from battle wounds."

"You are a visionary, as is Dr. Allard." Victor said,

at the same time reaching out to catch Mark Allard by the arm as the young man was passing by. Spinning his cousin around, Victor inclined his head toward Charity. "In fact, this is Dr. Allard's nephew, Mark. Mark, this is Charity de Gambier. Her father is Marshal Richard de Gambier."

Mark's face lit up as he took in the pretty young woman, lifting a great pressure from Victor's chest and brightening Charity's expression considerably. "Mark is thinking of going to the Nagelring in a few years, but I was hoping to convince him that another Allard should go through the New Avalon Military Academy. That would put you both on New Avalon at the same time. Having friends in new places always makes the transition so much easier."

Taking some personal delight in the darkening expression on the Baroness' face, Victor let the couple drift away in conversation as a slender blond officer a bit taller than himself approached. Like Victor, the man wore the blue-trimmed dress gray uniform of the Tenth Lyran Guards. Because both of them were members of the Revenants, the Guards' large reinforced battalion, their epaulets were black and trimmed with a white ghost embroidered on the flat surface.

"Galen, you look amused."

Victor's aide, Galen Cox, nodded and let his smile broaden. "Some of the Hounds have been swapping tales of Luthien, and the Khan has just joined the circle. I thought you might be interested."

Despite Galen's light tone, Victor caught his concern. Phelan had never been known as one who could control his anger. It wouldn't hurt to keep the peace here and now, given the extraordinary agreement Victor had just made with ComStar and Phelan, but neither did he mind letting his cousin twist a bit in the wind. Victor realized he was still smarting some from Phelan's superiority during the morning's negotiation, but he resolved to put that behind him as he followed Galen toward a growing circle of warriors.

One woman, a Kell Hound company commander, was using her hands to indicate the relative positions of 'Mechs as she recounted a fight. ". . . So there the Colonel was, standing alone on the hilltop. The Nova Cats kept coming at him, but they never even got close. I was in my *Blackjack,* hanging back where the Colonel had placed us. I popped them with my autocannons as they came in, then burned them down with my medium lasers. There was this one Clan moron who had been strafed, leaving the whole right torso of his 'Mech open. He cruised right past me and I went internal on him with all my shots.''

As she spoke, the Inner Sphere warriors gathered around her chuckled and nodded sagely. Most of the warriors were from the Kell Hounds, but Victor saw a scattering of other units represented, including the Fourth Donegal Guards and a half-dozen militia units from worlds where the Hounds had pulled garrison duty. The Tenth Lyran Guards, as represented by Victor, had seen the most action against the Clans, but the majority of those present had also tangled with the Clans at one point or another.

Arrayed against all these warriors, Phelan and Ragnar stood alone at the circle's edge. Phelan again wore his gray leathers, plus a long gray cloak whose shoulders were covered in fur that could only be that of a wolf. Standing beside him was Ragnar, wearing the bondcord on his right wrist and dressed in a gray jumpsuit. He held an elaborate wolf's-head mask that looked as though it was made from enamel.

The dark-haired Kell Hound nodded her head. ''Yeah, we kicked Clan butt on Luthien that day.'' She grinned around at her comrades, then glanced up at Phelan with a look of challenge.

''I have no doubt you did, Captain Moran,'' he said evenly. ''I recall the day your father turned the *Blackjack* over to you, saying he hoped it would do as much for you as it had for him. You are to be commended for your action.'' Phelan inclined his head toward her in a silent salute, yet the smile on his face still made him look superior.

Victor frowned. *The old Phelan would have fought back. The Clans have matured him, but not changed him so thoroughly that he can't help being smug.*

Michelle Moran looked puzzled. ''I hadn't thought a Clanner—especially one of their leaders—was the type to admit defeat so easily.''

''Defeat?'' Phelan shook his head, and would have appeared calm if Victor had not noted the tightened flesh around his eyes. "You would expect me to dispute what you have said? The Smoke Jaguars and Nova Cats have been reluctant to share the battle ROMs from the Luthien debacle, so I have not seen them. But what you describe rings true. Those Clans were defeated without taking Luthien. That is truth. That is fact."

"The whipping ComStar gave you on Tukayyid is likewise *fact,*" Moran countered in a voice loud enough to attract some attention. Victor saw Star Captain Ranna look over from her conversation with Phelan's parents, but a slight shake of the head from Phelan apparently satisfied her concern. He saw no other Clansfolk in the room, but did see several other MechWarriors join the circle.

Victor turned and whispered to Galen. "Why is the name Moran so familiar?"

"The Twelfth Donegal Guards, sir. We lost Damien Moran. They may have been related."

The image of Damien's smiling face came back to Victor. He'd not known the young man before the Jade Falcons hit Trellwan, but he'd learned all about him after being forced to evacuate that planet. As with all the other warriors who had given their lives so he could escape the Clan trap, Victor had memorized the man's face and service record. "Yes, he was from Arc-Royal. I should have seen the resemblance earlier. Thanks."

Phelan nodded slowly. "It is a *fact* that ComStar won the battle for Tukayyid. They bargained well and when all was done, they were the victors. I would point out, however, that the Wolves gained their objectives. I would also note that the ComStar victory won only a truce, not a war."

"But you Clanners were beaten."

"Captain Moran, you do not seem to understand that it is folly to lump all the Clans together."

Michelle glared at Phelan, but he said nothing more. "What is that supposed to mean, Khan Phelan?"

Phelan glanced at Ragnar and the bondsman cracked a bit of a smile. With a bow of his head to Phelan, Ragnar then turned to face Michelle Moran. "What Khan Ward means, Captain, is that lumping the Clans together is as foolish as suggesting that all parts of the Inner

Sphere be treated as a single group. You and the Kell Hounds are Steiner loyalists with a long history of opposing the Draconis Combine. Prince Davion here is heir to both the Steiner and Davion thrones, yet he and his Revenants traveled to the Combine to rescue Theodore Kurita's heir from the Nova Cats."

Ragnar pointed to a man in the uniform of the Morges Militia. "You come from the last of the Tamar worlds in the Federated Commonwealth, so your loyalties lie with Ryan Steiner. He and his Skye separatists are known to be in opposition to Prince Victor and the Davion domination of the Federated Commonwealth. The Inner Sphere, as a lump, also includes the Draconis Combine, the Free Worlds League, the Capellan Confederation, the St. Ives Compact, and what little remains of the Free Rasalhague Republic. All of these have different goals and different means for achieving them."

"What, then, is your point, Ragnar?" Victor let a predatory smile tug at the corners of his mouth. "Must we think less of what we have done to hold the Clans back because it was the Jade Falcons or the Smoke Jaguars we defeated and not the Wolf Clan?"

Phelan rested a hand on Ragnar's shoulder. "Ragnar's point is this, Prince Victor: attempting to pillory a member of the Wolf Clan with your victories over other Clans is useless."

"Then you, of the Wolf Clan consider our victories inconsequential?"

"No, cousin, we do not. We applaud them." Phelan looked around at the Kell Hounds. "You cannot know the pride I felt when I heard that the Kell Hounds had been part of the force that stopped the Smoke Jaguars. When I was called upon by the ilKhan to argue in the Grand Council in favor of abiding by the bargain struck with ComStar, I pointed to your victory. I used Prince Victor's stunning raid on Teniente and Kai Allard-Liao's exploits as yet more examples of what the Inner Sphere could do. Those achievements, when brought forward, made the Clan Khans pause to consider the wisdom of pressing the invasion.

"And do not doubt, not for a moment, that some of the Clans want to continue the war, now. Just as Ryan and you, Victor, can differ on what should be the course for the future, so the Clans have their factions. The Crusader faction wishes to conquer the whole of the Inner Sphere. The Warden faction believes that is not the vision General Kerensky had for the Clans. It is your good fortune that the ilKhan and the Khans of the Wolves are all Wardens who want to protect the Inner Sphere. Were we not, this would be a wake and not a celebration.''

Michelle Moran shook her head. ''If what you have done is supposed to be protecting the Inner Sphere, I don't think having Crusaders coming through would be much worse. And I'm not overly certain I want my victories touted by a Clan that managed to kick the weak legs out from under a fledgling nation, then pulverize a bunch of pacifists. Why, the Wolf Clan didn't even enter the fight for Tukayyid until a week after the other Clans had softened up the world for you.''

Victor saw fire spark in Phelan's eyes. ''Captain Moran, do not even hint at cowardice within the Wolf Clan. Our delayed entry into the battle for Tukayyid came as part of a bargain forced upon us by the other Clans. The Precentor Martial held back his best troops for us and we beat them.''

''So you say, Khan Phelan, but there is no proof of that.'' Michelle Moran folded her arms across her chest. ''ComStar's history of the battle could easily be one big political whitewash to maintain the truce.'' Her face darkened. ''After all, Khan Phelan, one has to wonder at the skill of the warriors in a Clan where a man expelled from the Nagelring can rise to leadership inside three years.''

Victor saw Phelan begin to tremble with anger, but marveled at how he brought it under control. ''Were you of the Clans, Captain Moran, we would settle this difference in a Circle of Equals. You have made a mistake, but I dismiss it because you do not know our ways.''

Moran shrugged. ''Talk is cheap.''

''I will not have the blood of one of my father's officers on my hands.''

Victor smiled. ''Why spill blood? I think Captain Moran would like to test how good you Wolves really are. The Kell Hounds have simulator facilities.''

Phelan smiled with real pleasure. ''Very well. I will

take a Star of BattleMechs against whatever you wish to offer.''

"Captain Moran, you have a company?'' Victor smiled when she nodded. "I will add a command lance to it, if that is permitted. That would put us sixteen on your five, if that is acceptable, Khan Ward.''

Phelan nodded. "I will require two pilots to join Ranna, Ragnar, and me in our Star. If you will allow it, Prince Victor, I would take your Galen Cox and my cousin Mark as the other two pilots.''

Victor nodded. "Done.''

Phelan nodded. "Bargained *well* and done.''

Victor smiled. "Now all I need do is find three pilots to fill out my lance.''

"Make that only one more, Victor, if you'll have the two of us.''

Victor turned at the sound of the familiar voice and he smiled. "Bargained *very well* and done.'' He glanced at Phelan and nodded. "These two, Khan Ward, will do splendidly. Khan, let me present *Chu-sa* Shin Yodama of the Draconis Combine and the current champion of Solaris, Kai Allard-Liao.''

6

Arc-Royal
Federated Commonwealth
15 April 3055

"What do you mean I'm acting like Vlad?" Phelan whipped off his cloak and tossed it over the back of a chair. "Ranna, if Vlad were here, he would be insulting people and picking fights."

Ranna folded her arms across her chest and arched an eyebrow at him.

Phelan winced. "You can't count this little simulator battle I've set up for tomorrow. There was no way out of that fight. Moran was waiting for me on that one." He shook his head. "How can you think I'm like Vlad? He's arrogant, insensitive, annoying, obtuse, and worships the ground on which Crusaders like Conal Ward walk. I'm not like that at all."

"Not right now, you are not." A smile softened Ranna's expression as she removed her cloak. "Right now you are being yourself. You are talking with contractions and you are letting your emotions vent through your words. Out there, at that reception for the guests arriving for your father's retirement celebration, you were stiff and unnatural. As your sister put it, you needed to 'loosen up.' "

Phelan opened his mouth, but shut it before words came out. *Is that how I've been?* A quick mental review of the party's high points brought a flush to his cheeks. "Accepting—for the sake of argument only—that there is some validity to what you have said, how bad was I?"

"For the sake of argument, not as bad as Vlad would

have been, my love. But you have angered your sister by not choosing her to fight with your Star. She was offended that you selected your nephew over her.''

"But Caitlin's a pilot. We were bidding in Stars of 'Mechs.''

"I know that and I explained that to her. It would have been more politic to have chosen your cousin Chris or your father instead of Galen Cox to fill out your Star.'' Ranna sat down on the white leather couch that dominated the suite's living room. "I know your father did not take offense at having been left out, and I believe Christian would have been uneasy had you chosen him, but I think the Kell Hounds consider it a sign of contempt that you chose a Revenant and a half-trained boy to hold off one of their companies.''

Phelan shook his head and also settled down on the couch. "But the Revenants fought well against the Nova Cats. I thought I was honoring them by choosing Galen.''

"That you might have been, Phelan, but did you not sense the unease when the subject of the Revenants came up?''

"Huh?''

Ranna smiled and drew her legs up on the cushions. "Apparently not. The fact that Prince Victor and his people rescued the heir to Theodore Kurita is not particularly popular. People appreciate the bravery it took to accomplish the deed, but many think Victor has been bewitched by a Kurita sorceress named Omi.''

Phelan nodded as he pulled off his boots. "Omi is Theodore's daughter. I've heard all the stories that she and Victor fell in love during the time spent training on Outreach.'' His boots flew across the room and landed next to where Ranna had stepped out of hers. "That cannot be, of course. Victor and Omi come from Houses that are mortal enemies. Such a love is impossible.''

Ranna kicked Phelan playfully. "Is it? More so than a warrior and a bondsman falling in love?''

As her foot flicked out again, Phelan caught her ankle and kissed it. "As always, Ranna, you know far better than I what is possible and impossible.''

"Had I visited this place before you won your Bloodname and became a Khan, I would have said it was impossible for this environment to produce a warrior such as you.''

"Why?'' Phelan allowed himself a wry grin. "The Hounds may not be Wolf's Dragoons and Arc-Royal may not be Outreach, but the Kell Hounds were always considered one of the top mercenary units in the Inner Sphere.''

"As you have said on more than one occasion, my love.'' Ranna reached out with her right leg and tickled his stomach with her toes. "It is just that this place is so different from the kind of sibko in which I grew up. The caretakers assigned to us were very conscientious about their jobs, but they never showed us the degree of love and affection that your parents show you. I see it in your mother's eyes and hear it in your father's voice. It is why they try to accept me and my place in your life.''

Ranna's voice dropped off. Phelan squeezed her knee gently. "Yes, this is much different than the way the Clans select their warriors even before birth. Your very genetic makeup is determined according to the past performance of your sires, the way thoroughbred bloodlines are maintained to produce great racing horses. You are raised in a sibko and constantly tested to winnow out the losers in the genetic lottery. You are focused on attaining the goal of becoming a warrior—an admirable goal, yes—but your training and testing almost preclude the development of strong interpersonal attachments.''

"It is something more than that, Phelan.'' Ranna frowned. "In the sibko everyone watches for errors and failures. They plot ways to test for weaknesses. Everything is designed to maximize the potential for failure. If one of our blood kin dies, it casts aspersion on both the bloodline and the individual.

"Here, though, the opposite seems true. I went to the cemetery where you bury and honor your dead. The Kell Hounds provide housing and schooling for the dependents of those who have died in battle. They do things for the offspring of the fallen that the Clans would never consider because of the stigma of failure those offspring bear.''

Ranna's teeth raked across her lower lip. "The Hounds' attitude is so alien to me. Though most of those I have met obviously consider you a traitor, they still admire your willingness to engage in a simulator battle. They want to hate you, yet are willing to grant you respect. They want to integrate the person you are now with what they remember of you from before your capture.''

"You're right, and I want them to be able to do that." Phelan sighed heavily and shook his head. "That's why I chose Mark to be in my Star. As a boy he was always a bit of an annoyance because he followed me around a lot. When I left for the Nagelring, I promised to keep a slot open for him in whatever lance I ended up commanding. I knew I'd face resentment when I came here, but it hurts having it come from a member of the family." He looked over at her. "You're not getting the same sort of thing from him are you, *quineg?*"

Ranna shook her head, suppressing a yawn with her fist. "No, not at all. In fact, your family has been more than friendly to me." Ranna plucked at her leather uniform skirt. "In fact, Caitlin suggested that this uniform was hardly suitable for the banquet and has offered to take me shopping tomorrow after this battle you have arranged. I told her I would think it over, though I do not understand what is wrong with my present kit."

"I think that you should go, Ranna. Steiner royalty has always placed an inordinate value on high fashion, even for its military officers. We should attempt to respect their customs. ''

"Fine. I will suggest to Evantha Fetladral that she also attempt to honor these customs."

Visions of the two-and-a-half meter tall Elemental being loaded down with boxes after an expedition to the shops of Old Connaught flicked through Phelan's mind. Smiling at the thought, he patted Ranna on the leg. "Tomorrow we will shoot up their 'Mechs, then you'll be free."

Ranna looked warily at Phelan. "I gather you assume we will defeat them?"

"Your question borders on treason, Star Captain."

"Does it? Apparently you underestimate our foes. Captain Moran's company may be only medium weight, but they pack mostly missile boats. Besides that, they have already fought against the Nova Cats and Smoke Jaguars, so they are familiar with our tactics and equipment.''

"Michelle Moran does not worry me. She is, and always has been, a tenacious fighter, but she never withdraws from a fight until a bit too late. She believes that one more exchange will win the day, and it tends to cost her."

Ranna mulled that fact over for a moment, then nodded. "What about Prince Victor? He and Shin Yodama were both on Teniente."

"I expect Galen Cox to give me the measure of Yodama. As for Victor, well, getting his goat was never much of a problem when we were children. Once Victor is angry, he stops thinking at all. You can take him easily."

Ranna bowed her head. "My Khan is so gracious." She slipped her leg off the top of his, eluding his attempt to grab and tickle her foot. "What of Kai Allard-Liao? Even if what we heard from the Jade Falcons has been grossly exaggerated, his position as the reigning champion on Solaris does suggest that he is a foe more than worthy of respect."

Phelan nodded slowly. "It's odd, but when I was a child I heard lots of speculation about who would have won in a battle between my father and Kai's father. Justin Allard had also been the Solaris champion, and my father, well, he is a very rare pilot indeed. Someone once did a computer projection of the battle, arranging it under Solaris-type conditions."

"Who won?"

"Depended on which time the battle was run. All the fights ran for a *long* time and both 'Mechs were hammered by the time one could not continue. I think a series of a hundred bouts resulted in Justin Allard winning 53 to 47. Some folks pointed out that if the situation were reversed and the battles were in the field—the way my father fought most often—the results would have been reversed as well. Both men were offered money to actually fight it out in a simulator battle, but they refused. On the other hand I heard a rumor that at Dan Allard's wedding to my half-sister Megan, Justin and my father did actually use simulators to test each other."

"And?"

"Replacing the computer's burned-out logic boards was expensive."

"I see, I think. So, in your parlance, the sins of the fathers will fall to the sons?"

"Right, Kai's mine." Phelan cracked his knuckles. "Once I've dealt with him, I can start to make amends for having offended people tonight."

"A wise plan, my Khan," she teased.

"Have you any ideas in that department, Star Captain?"

Ranna pursed her lips, then nodded. "You could start by giving me a kiss."

Phelan scooped his arms under her knees and pulled her toward him. Leaning forward, he rested his hands on either side of her head and used his body to press her flat on the couch. "And after that?" He kissed her.

She kissed him back. "Another kiss and another. The rest of my ideas can wait until morning."

7

Arc-Royal
Federated Commonwealth
16 April 3055

Victor slid himself around on the vinyl seat of the simulator's command couch. The restraining belts held him in place, but his bare flesh was also sticking to the couch. In real combat, of course, he would have been perspiring enough from nerves to slick up his skin. In the simulator he just wasn't as anxious.

He couldn't fault the equipment because the Kell Hounds had invested in the best. The simulator cockpits were mounted within a three-dimensional movement matrix that rested on a bed of hydraulic pistons. Each lumbering step his simulated *Daishi* took in the virtual-world projected on the screens before his 'Mech's viewports was reflected in the realistic pitch and roll of the cockpit pod. Victor knew, from other exercises, that enemy hits and their effects would be simulated as well.

The simulation also included heaters built into the cockpit to inject heat whenever weapon-firing or other activities would normally create heat buildup in an actual 'Mech. He even wore a special cooling vest that functioned exactly as if he were really piloting his 'Mech, the *Prometheus*. The coolant snaking its way through the tubes in the vest pulled excess heat away from his body and kept him alive in the cockpit.

I've had little enough use for it so far. Victor watched the holographic projection of the simulated landscape. Off to his left Kai marched Yen-lo-wang, his modified *Centurion*, across an open meadow toward a low line of hills. On the right and slightly back, Shin Yodama's *Griffin* watched their back and the flank. *As it's been all day— nothing!*

Daniel Allard and Morgan Kell, who had come up with the battle scenario, had decided that the sides were not even enough. Both Mark Allard and Galen Cox were using Inner Sphere 'Mech simulations while operating as part of a Clan Star, and Victor was using a Clan-based OmniMech that dwarfed anything in the opposition. By sheer tonnage of war machines on the battlefield, the Clan forces surrendered a four-to-one disadvantage.

Victor knew that tonnage was not entirely indicative of advantage, but he had to concede that the Clans were underpowered. To even up the odds, the Kell Hound leaders suggested that Victor's three-'Mech lance could become the prize. In the new scenario, the Clans would be hunting him on a huge, circular battlefield intended to honor the Clan tradition of the Circle of Equals. The Kell Hound company was there to help Victor get away from the Clans. It made the exercise into an elaborate game of Capture the Flag, but one in which the flag could shoot back.

To further complicate matters, Victor's group could not radio the Kell Hounds because they lacked the proper codes to unscramble the messages from their rescuers. Kai, however, had quickly figured out that by using a simple system resembling the send and break of Morse code, increasing the pace as the Kell Hound signals got stronger, his team could guide them in. He knew that it would pull the Clans in as well, but having everyone together should be Phelan's worst nightmare.

Problem is, Phelan and his folks don't seem to be sleeping badly. As he had the morning before, Phelan arrived bright-eyed and ready to go. He even wore his pistol into the simulator cockpit, giving Captain Moran and her people cause for amusement. Not Victor, though, for the gesture told him Phelan was very serious about the simulation and was treating it exactly as he would a real-world analog.

The Flag group, as Victor had come to think of their trio, had heard a *lot* of radio static, apparently coming from the Kell Hound company. Though they could make no sense of it, the messages seemed to be coming quickly while the number of people involved in the conversations slowly began to drop off.

The Flag group had begun to move in the rough direction of the radio transmissions, but things fluctuated too rapidly to be certain they were on the right track. Victor knew that meant the Kell Hounds were involved in a running battle, which should have been good for them. *Hit-and-run has been the tactic* de jour *to use against the Clans. If Phelan's turning it back against us, though, we could be in trouble.*

As if the other side had been reading his mind— *dammit, only Galen could have set this trap*—three 'Mechs moved up over the crest of the hills. The first, a thick, squat *Masakari* spread its birdlike legs wide to establish a stable footing among the hill's crumbling rocks. The arms ended in twin barrels and the two left-arm PPCs flashed even before Victor could call out a warning to his companions.

The twin bolts of blue lightning crackled through the air. Both hit the *Prometheus'* right leg, reducing its armor to virtual vapor. A pulse laser in the *Masakari*'s right arm drilled a series of green bolts into the same limb. That hit ripped away all but the very last bit of armor as far as the computer was concerned.

Victor had a nanosecond to take in how much damage the *Masakari* pilot's uncanny accuracy had done to his 'Mech. As soon as the computer controlling the exercise determined what that amount of damage meant, Victor felt the cockpit begin to pitch up and to the right. The savage attack had blasted away almost two tons of the ferro-fibrous armor on his 'Mech, unbalancing it severely.

Twisting his body to the left, Victor struggled to keep the 'Mech upright. The computer read the input from his neurohelmet, but even his utmost effort could not defeat the combined forces of physics and gravity. The computer-created landscape blurred into a confused palette outside the *Daishi*'s viewports, then the cockpit spun and tipped way up. Victor braced himself and groaned as panels in the command couch slammed into his back when his 'Mech crashed to the ground, destroying some armor on its right flank.

Momentarily stunned, Victor could do nothing but

watch his holographic display as the two lightest BattleMechs on the field headed after each other. Kai's *Yen-lo-wang* turned toward the slender Clan 'Mech that looked like a mechanical avatar of the ancient Egyptian god Anubis. Victor knew without a doubt that Phelan was the *Wolfhound*'s pilot.

The *Centurion* struck first. Its right arm came up, its Gauss cannon spitting out a silver projectile amid a brilliant flash of energy. Streaking up the line of the hills, the ball hit the *Wolfhound* in the left chest. The 'Mech dropped armor like a snake shedding skin, leaving the ferro-titanium skeleton open to view. Victor saw a puff of smoke curl up out of the gash and the Wolfhound staggered a bit. *Lost a medium laser and maybe took engine damage! Way to go, Kai!*

The twin lasers mounted beneath the left arm also assaulted the *Wolfhound,* their hail of red energy darts shredding the armor on the other side of the 'Mech's chest. The skeleton beneath the lost armor glowed red and the *Wolfhound* again appeared to shudder, but Phelan managed to keep it upright despite the vicious pounding.

Then the *Wolfhound* bit back with a vengeance. The large laser that made up most of its right arm sent a green spear of coherent light into the *Centurion*'s right arm. Armor fragments rained down over the simulated hillsides, starting little brushfires. The three pulse lasers mounted in the *Wolfhound*'s chest focused their fire on that same limb. The first burned through the rest of the armor and the others stitched fire up and down the arm. Myomer muscles snapped apart and the ferro-titanium bones glowed white-hot before they melted away.

More important, the lasers blasted into the Gauss cannon's mechanism. The capacitors exploded, shredding the armor on the right side of the *Centurion*'s chest. The 'Mech's internal structure looked warped and twisted by the explosion. The round silver balls that the 'Mech used as ammo for the Gauss cannon spilled out, bouncing off the 'Mech's right thigh, to roll down the hill.

On the left Victor saw Shin's *Griffin* get hit by one of two long-range missile flights from Galen's *Crusader*. Most of the missiles flew right over their target as Shin ducked his 'Mech forward and cut to the left. Explosions peppered the center and right side of the chest, chipping away at armor. The *Griffin*'s left arm caught a number of missiles, but suffered no more than a few lost armor plates.

From the *Griffin*'s right chest a flight of LRMs tracked back toward the *Crusader,* hammering into the center of the *Crusader*'s chest, crushing armor. In return the *Griffin*'s pistollike particle projection cannon shot out a jagged line of azure fire, flaying half-melted armor from the *Crusader*'s right arm, but failing to breach the protection.

Victor brought his *Daishi* upright, turning to present his left side to the *Masakari.* He knew he was facing Ranna in the other Clan OmniMech, and his admiration for her skill outweighed his outrage and fear. Again her PPCs and a large laser tried to finish the job they had started on the Prometheus' right leg, but Victor's maneuver kept the limb hidden and her shots missed.

Victor swung the Omni around and smiled. *This time it will be my turn.*

Before he could bring his weapons to bear on her, the *Centurion* and the *Wolfhound* went at it again. The two 'Mechs closed and Victor's auxiliary screen reported that both were grossly overheating. In a normal battlefield situation the 'Mechs would have been so damaged that retreat would be the first thing on either pilot's mind, but not so here. *A Khan of the Wolf Clan fighting against the Champion of Solaris. A bootleg battle ROM of this fight would be worth a fortune in broadcast rights.*

The *Centurion* fired its two pulse lasers at the same time that the *Wolfhound* used its remaining pulse laser and the large laser in its right arm. The *Centurion*'s lasers bored in through the open right side of the *Wolfhound*'s chest. Victor saw the computer project pieces of skeletal structure flying out through the greasy black smoke that marked another hit to the engine.

The *Wolfhound*'s two lasers shot through where the *Centurion*'s right arm should have been, the beams surgically carving away at the Edasich 200 XL engine that powered the 'Mech. The ruby bolts from the medium laser in the *Wolfhound*'s chest coaxed a puff of dense smoke as it cored into the controller maintaining the magnetic shielding around the *Centurion*'s fusion engine.

Like mirror images, both 'Mechs showed an unholy white light igniting in the hollow cavities of their chests. The computer faithfully displayed how the fusion reaction, freed of its shields, expanded and consumed any and all available fuel. The boiling plasma spheres swelled, then exploded up through the head and shoulders of the 'Mechs they had powered. With black roiling clouds marking the fireballs' subsequent explosions, the 'Mechs' legs fell into a mutual tangle at the base of the hill.

Victor saw the flash of weapons and knew that both Galen and Shin had inflicted more damage on each other, but neither of their 'Mechs went down. That helped ease the loss of Kai and his *Centurion,* but not much because the *Masakari* fired on him again. Victor knew he'd only have one chance coming back, so he let the *Masakari* have it with everything in the *Daishi*'s arsenal.

The Gauss cannon sent a silvery slug sizzling into the *Masakari*'s chest, gouging out a huge chunk of armor over the 'Mech's heart. One of the three large pulse lasers in the *Daishi*'s right arm missed its target, but the other two hit hard. One scored a glowing scar in the armor on the *Masakari*'s left breast, while the second punched straight through the armor in the middle. Flame shot out of the flamer muzzle, and Victor's auxiliary screen reported heat rising in the enemy 'Mech.

One of Victor's two Streak SRM systems failed to lock onto the target, but the other succeeded and fired a full spread of missiles at the *Masakari*. They peppered it with fiery blossoms, battering the armor and dropping it in steaming chips onto the ground. Though the SRMs did not seem to do much damage, they helped further unbalance a 'Mech already hammered by the Gauss cannon and large pulse lasers. Victor smiled as the *Masakari* began to topple, but his joy died as he realized that soon he would be joining it.

Both of the *Masakari*'s PPCs and its large pulse lasers successfully hit the *Daishi*'s damaged right leg, evaporating the last bit of armor like a water droplet on a hot griddle. The four energy beams combined to melt the leg clean away. Myomer muscles bubbled and exploded. The ferro-titanium femur glowed white-hot before it became transparent and insubstantial.

Their energy insufficiently spent, the beams tracked upward. Burning through the remnants of armor on the *Daishi*'s right side, they touched off an explosion of the anti-missile system's ammo. The concussion panels in his command couch smashed into Victor's back and neurohelmet, momentarily disorienting him. The cockpit whirled him around as if his 100-ton war machine were a rag doll caught in a cyclone, then unceremoniously bashed him again as the 'Mech pounded into the ground.

Victor shook his head to clear it and found himself hanging from the restraining straps of the command couch. Focusing beyond the holographic display that showed the *Masakari* getting back to its taloned feet, he saw only blackness through the viewports. His eyes confirmed what gravity had already told him—that his 'Mech had landed face-down in the dirt. *With only one leg and my right-side armor breached front and back, there's no way I can continue the fight.*

Glancing at the approaching *Masakari* in the display, he mentally amended that idea. *And there's no way Ranna is going to* let *me continue the fight. I can't even punch out!*

Leaving no doubt as to why the BattleMech had ruled warfare since its creation six centuries earlier, the *Masakari* concentrated all four of its guns on the downed *Daishi*. Aiming in deliberate and well-practiced moves that showed Victor why the Clans had so easily swept through the Inner Sphere, the *Masakari* opened the *Daishi*'s back like a coroner doing an autopsy. The PPC bolts fried structural stabilizers while the lasers sliced through ferro-titanium ribs.

The lasers freed the *Daishi*'s fusion engine from its mountings. It dropped down, the safeguards in it snuffing the reaction before it could explode. As if the *Masakari* had pulled the *Daishi*'s heart out, Victor's 'Mech shuddered once, then all the monitors died, leaving him hanging in a hot, dark cocoon.

The deathly stillness pressed in on him, then he shook his head. *The only advantage we ever had in fighting the Clans was that they always played by a rigid set of rules that gave us a tactical edge. If they ever come to embrace the flexibility that Phelan and the others showed here, Ragnar won't be the only Prince of the Inner Sphere sporting a bondcord.*

8

Arc-Royal
Federated Commonwealth
16 April 3055

Though he knew better, Phelan couldn't resist a cocky smile as he entered the reception room. He raised Ranna's left hand in his right and kissed it, then winked back at Ragnar. "The Wolves have done well this day. We have good reason to be proud."

Ranna nodded and tugged at the hem of her black jacket. "That is true, my Khan, but were our opponents Smoke Jaguars or Snow Ravens, we would not lord our victory over them, *quiaff?*"

"Aff, but they are not Clan, are they?"

"Your point being?"

Phelan winked at her. "It's an old Kell Hound tradition called 'bragging rights.' "

Ranna shook her head and disengaged her hand. "As they are not Clan, neither are you a Kell Hound. Do not be surprised if they react poorly to your effort to teach them humility." She arched an eyebrow at him. "And, my love, your speech is deteriorating."

Phelan winced. "And your grandmother isn't—I mean, is not—here to accept the blame, is she?"

"No, nor is she here to tell you to be careful." Ranna nodded toward Captain Moran and the knot of people near her. "We already have many enemies, Khan Phelan, both inside the Clans and out. There is no reason to make things worse."

Phelan started to tell Ranna not to worry, but her words resonated with truth. The familiar surroundings of Arc-

Royal and the perverse delight he took in annoying people he regarded as pompous had made him slip into old patterns of behavior. He was glad for the chance to recover some of the esteem he had lost by joining the Clans, but he knew Ranna was right in reminding him, subtly, that he was now more than he had been when yet a member of the Inner Sphere. He was still the son of Morgan Kell, but now he represented more than just his family. The Wolf Clan had made him one of their two Khans, and with that came responsibility for more than just himself.

"Your wisdom is taken to my heart, Ranna." He let his gratitude to her burn the smugness out of his smile. "I will comport myself as befitting a Khan."

"I had never thought you would do otherwise, Khan Phelan Ward." Her head dipped as she acknowledged a wave from Caitlin Kell. "If you will excuse me."

"Of course." He smiled at her, watching her walk away gracefully in spite of the black woolen skirt clutching at her legs in what a Clan warrior could only experience as an awkward and binding way. "You will join me, Ragnar?"

"As my Khan wishes."

"Good." Phelan noticed that others had joined the circle of losers from the morning's game. He fought down his desire to gloat and, surprisingly, found it not so hard to banish. Instead he felt a sense of shame at having entertained so petty and unworthy an emotion.

Standing beside Victor and Galen were the other two members of Victor's command lance. Both men were of oriental descent, though Kai's lighter skin and the softer tilt of his almond-shaped eyes made his mixed blood obvious. Their gray color also contrasted sharply with the dark brown of Shin Yodama's. The Draconis Combine officer stood a few centimeters shorter than Kai and looked a decade older. Phelan thought he saw the edges of a black and gold tattoo peeking out from the neckline of his shirt.

"Good evening." Phelan nodded to Galen, then smiled at Kai. "I can see easily why you are the Solaris champion." He shifted his gaze to Shin. "And why the Coordinator still has an heir."

Shin stiffened and then executed a short bow. Phelan

read a hint of shame on Shin's face. Coordinator Takashi Kurita had been murdered only a few months before, and Shin had been in charge of Takashi's bodyguards.

Kai nodded at Phelan, the hint of a blush coloring his face. "Considering that my modified *Centurion* out-massed your *Wolfhound* by fifteen tons, you would be a favorite on Solaris. It would have taken many other fighters months of plotting to do what you managed on the fly out there."

"Lucky shots," Phelan shrugged. "I do not think you have anything to fear from me. Even *if* I were allowed to travel beyond the treaty line to Solaris, I would not welcome a rematch with live ammunition. As I recall, neither one of us would have survived our fight."

"Point well taken."

Michelle Moran tossed off the last of the beer in her mug. "I wouldn't think that your getting to Solaris would be that difficult, Khan Phelan. His Highness seems to be quite adept at getting all manner of hostiles anywhere he wants them."

"That may well be, Captain Moran, but for Khan Phelan to travel to Solaris would be an abrogation of the agreement the ilKhan made with ComStar." Ragnar kept a half-smile on his face. "The Precentor Martial has been reluctant to grant any Clan personnel the right to cross that line."

Victor nodded. "At this point things are so touchy that even a *rumor* of a Clansman crossing the line would set off the war again."

Moran waved that comment away with an empty mug. "Was there ever really an end to the fighting, Highness? Look at Morges and Crimond invaded last year, and now the raiding going on in the Lyran holdings. Anything this side of the line, including Arc-Royal here, is open season. The old Federated Suns seems to be intact, though."

Victor stiffened and clenched his jaw. "*Ja*, Captain Moran, the Federated Suns *seems* intact, but it is not. It participates in the defense against the Clans by sending its men and women here to die. It supplies materiel for war and assistance for recovery."

"But no one in the Suns is under the threat of invasion!" Moran handed the beer mug to one of her men and used her freed hands to help express her anger. "The

Federated Suns never loses worlds. In the Fourth Succession War your father managed to increase the size of the Federated Suns by a fourth, then relied on the Lyran Commonwealth to foot the bill for his conquests. Never mind the fact that we lost worlds to the Combine. Now we suffer the brunt of the invasion and the Federated Suns offers us a band-aid to staunch an arterial wound.''

"Captain! Remember who you are talking to!" Galen Cox barked.

"It's all right," Victor said quietly, folding his arms across his chest and turning back to Moran. "We are doing all we can."

"No you're not." Moran pressed her fingertips to her temples, then brought her open hands down. "We opposed the Clans with one hand tied behind our backs. If all the troops in the Federated Commonwealth had been used to fight the Clans, we could have driven them back."

"You don't seriously suggest that we should take all the troops from the Federated Suns and bring them here, do you?"

"Why not?"

The Prince looked surprised. "Because the Clans are not the only threats to the Federated Commonwealth. Romano Liao would have attacked if we had stripped troops from the border with the Capellan Confederation."

Moran shook her head vehemently. "Nonsense. Besides, the St. Ives Compact, a nation that the Capellans still claim is legally part of their nation, devoted a greater percentage of its troops to opposing the Clans than the old Federated Suns did. And please don't say that the Free Worlds League was a threat. As long as you have Joshua Marik there on New Avalon as a hostage, Thomas won't do anything that could jeopardize his son's life."

"There's something you're forgetting here, Captain Moran. It is that I am Victor Ian *Steiner*-Davion. I was raised right here, in the Lyran half of the Federated Commonwealth. I went to the Nagelring and graduated with honors. And all my service has been here. My only trip back to New Avalon came at the time of my father's death."

Victor's voice began to rise and Phelan began to feel for him. "Captain Moran, I feel the pain of the losses we have suffered here in the Federated Commonwealth precisely because of who I am. I regret your brother's death on Trellwan, but I also rejoice in your skill. I am pleased and proud to have done all I could to defeat the Clans, and I wish I could do more. Yes, my father was Hanse Davion, but my mother is Melissa Steiner, and that ties me as closely to the Lyran Commonwealth as you can imagine.''

"Does it?'' Moran's eyes narrowed. "There are times I wonder.''

Phelan took a moment to read the group. Michelle Moran and her people seemed more relaxed toward him and Ragnar than they did Victor and Galen. That only made sense if their heated discussion had traveled entirely out of the realm of the morning's exercise, or even the conduct of the war against the Clans. Phelan smelled politics and wondered what was really going on. When he noticed it, a second later, he could have kicked himself for missing something so obvious.

Victor and Galen—both members of the Tenth Lyran Guards' elite Revenants—had abandoned their uniform jackets and instead wore exquisite green silken robes with black trim at the cuffs and hem. The crest embroidered in red on the sleeves and breasts of the robes looked like the Revenants' insignia, but the border around it showed little Kurita dragons chasing each other.

The robes Shin wore were identical in design, though the crests on his kimono were appropriate for the Dragon's Claws. It did not strike Phelan as remarkable that Shin Yodama was a member of the Combine Coordinator's bodyguard unit—by all accounts of the war, Shin had served the Kurita family faithfully and well. What did surprise Phelan was that Victor would wear a garment that so clearly resembled a Kurita uniform.

Phelan sensed instantly that Victor's choice of clothing was not what had angered Michelle Moran, but what his wearing it meant. He had no doubt that many of the Kell Hounds had shared a smile when Victor rescued Hohiro from Teniente in the same way that the Hounds had helped save Luthien. That would have struck them as justice. Somehow, though, things went deeper.

Watching Victor chafe beneath Moran's anger made Phelan uneasy. It was true that Michelle might have had a beer or two more than wise, but Victor was hung on the tree of politics. If he agreed with her and word of it got out, certain forces in the Federated Suns section of the Commonwealth would immediately pounce on him for leaving them open to predation by the Capellan Confederation.

Just as the Crusaders have been hounding the ilKhan to repudiate the truce. Hearing the echoes of Ranna's words in his head, Phelan laughed lightly. "I assure you, Captain Moran, that from my point of view, Prince Victor acted, as did the rest of you, exactly the way I expected Steiner troops to act. After all you had done to harass the Smoke Jaguars and the Nova Cats, I had expected better."

Moran, her eyes flashing, turned on him in a quiet rage. "You died quickly enough."

"And because of it, Captain Moran, your company took only marginally more time to die. I set a bondsman and my nephew, a youth who has still not even been accepted into one of your military academies, to the task of drawing you off and leading you on a wild goose chase. You took the bait and your troops were scattered."

Phelan brought his hands up to chest-height and deliberately pressed them fingertip to fingertip in a sign of superiority. "We let them pick off stragglers while we crushed those you hunted. And though I did die in that exchange, I died at the hands of the only member of your company—save *Chu-sa* Yodama—who had the least claim to Steiner blood or training."

Moran raised her head. "It was Star Captain Ranna who killed most of us. It took a *real* Clanner to do that."

Phelan's nostrils flared. "Very good, Captain Moran, but hardly a killing shot. I have been ridiculed for my extra-Clan origins by the best in the Wolf Clan, hell, by the best of *all* the Clans. They hate me for what I am, and probably for the same reason you do. They hate me because they're afraid of me. They hate the fact that I, a *freebirth* from outside the Clans, could rise to the top of one of the most powerful Clans. They fear me more completely and totally than they know."

"I'm not afraid of you," Moran scoffed.

"Oh, but you are, Captain Moran." Phelan looked around the group, touching each of them with his frank stare. "You all are. You are all afraid you couldn't do what I did. You're afraid that when the Clans come again I will use what I know to guarantee that no force, no matter how huge, will ever stop us."

Phelan smiled a predator's smile. "When I see you bickering like this, I marvel that anyone in the Inner Sphere was even able to slow us.

"Next time?" He shook his head. "Next time you'll be lucky to even see us coming."

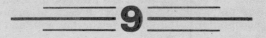

Arc-Royal
Federated Commonwealth
16 April 3055

You arrogant son of a . . . Victor's hands balled into
fists as he glared at Phelan. The adrenalin jolt he felt as
his cousin returned the stare deflected him from immediately snapping out a furious reply. *I am not afraid of
him!*

"I can see your time with the Clans has not changed
you at all, Phelan."

Victor turned around as he recognized the gentle voice
that mildly rebuked the Clan Khan. Standing eight centimeters taller than him, but sharing the golden blond
hair they had both inherited from their mother, his sister
Katherine leaned down and gave Victor a peck on the
cheek. "Are you surprised, Victor? I hope so."

"Katherine? I thought you were on Tharkad with
Mother. No one told me. . . ." Victor felt himself whip-
sawed as his anger shattered against the anvil of surprise,
then melted away into happiness at seeing his sister again.
"When did you arrive?"

Katherine ignored the question and extended her left
hand to Shin Yodama. "*Komban-wa, Chu-sa.* Thank you
again for letting me hitch a ride aboard your DropShip."
She squeezed his hand, then let it drop.

"And you for permitting me the use of your shuttle to
get here ahead of the *Taizai,* Duchess Katrina."

"You came in on the Combine DropShip?" Victor
blinked in surprise. "Duchess Katrina?"

Katherine glanced down at her brother, then laughed

lightly. "Yes, Victor, I came in on the *Taizai*. I was on the *Jadbalja*, hoping to transfer to another ship as it headed from Tharkad to Morges. We ran across *Chu-sa* Yodama—Shin—at Hamilton and I invited myself aboard. He was polite despite the utter breach of protocol. I begged him not to tell you I was on my way, and use of the shuttle sealed the deal."

Victor raised an eyebrow at Shin. "You could have told me."

The yakuza from the Draconis Combine shook his head. "Once sworn to a secret, I keep my word, no matter the consequences."

Katherine's cool blue eyes glittered mischievously. "And it is a good thing for you that he does, Victor. But to answer your question, we got in this morning while you and your friends were engaged in that combat exercise." She pulled her hands up and wiggled her fingers as if the wargame had been a long-dead creature left to molder and rot. "You were preoccupied, so we decided to plan a surprise for you. Morgan agreed, so our operation remained covert."

The lilt in her voice made Victor grin. "But Duchess *Katrina?*" Victor voiced the question in a tone he knew would get her attention. "When did this happen?"

Katherine knitted her brows with concentration and Victor sensed the urge on the part of the males in the circle to offer her any help they could. Because she was his sister, he had some difficulty understanding their reaction. If pressed, however, he'd have been forced to admit that the teal blue jacket and skirt complimented her slender figure. With its cleric collar, shoulder pads, and diagonally cut double-breast, the gold-buttoned jacket looked to him to be state-of-design for the current fashion season.

Katherine, he recalled quite easily after a moment's reflection, had always been adept at beguiling even the sternest of courtiers and tutors with her innocent confusion. She claimed to have inherited the ability from their mother, but Melissa protested that she'd been too shy to flirt in her youth. The Archon freely acknowledged Katherine her superior in that area.

"The news of Morgan's retirement got me thinking about our grandmother. As my middle name is Morgan

in his honor, I decided to return to the original form of
my name in *her* honor.'' She smiled and Victor felt the
heat in the circle go up a degree or two. ''After all, Katherine is the kind of name one gives a dowdy old empress
with a taste for horses. Katrina is much more to my lik-
ing.''

Phelan nodded confidently. ''And it suits you well,
cousin.''

Katherine winked at him. ''Is it the Clans who have
taught you flattery, Phelan?''

''No, merely to rationally assess situations and report
on them.''

''You should instruct my brother on such things, then.''
She turned back to throw a smile at Victor. ''By the way,
I like the robes. You and Kommandant Cox look quite
dashing.''

From beyond Phelan, both Caitlin and Ranna approached the group. Caitlin's look of happiness found a
twin on Katherine's face. ''Katrina, you look wonderful!''

Victor frowned and turned to Galen. ''Does everyone
know of this name change except for me?''

Galen blinked, then looked down at Victor. ''Beg your
pardon, sir?''

''Never mind,'' Victor grumbled.

''And you are Ranna?'' Katherine cooed as she took
the Clanswoman by the hand. ''Caitlin said you were
pretty, but she woefully underbid, didn't she? I would
have started at 'divine' and then might have been talked
down to 'absolutely gorgeous,' *quiaff?* I did that right,
ja?''

Victor took refuge in Ranna's momentary look of surprise. He rolled his eyes as the Wolf Clan warrior stammered out a reply. *Katrina—Katherine—is a magician!
The next time I bid a battle against the Clans, I want her
with me.*

He watched his sister work the crowd. Though he always thought she went too far, no one else seemed to
think so. Her combination of compliments and wit en-
chanted everyone she met. Even Kai and Galen had
drifted forward to keep Katherine the center of the circle.
As she linked her arm through Ranna's and whispered

something to her, the circle drew tighter, leaving Victor a step back and forgotten as it squeezed him out.

Not a little disgusted, he started the long away around the outside of the crowd in the reception room. He plotted a course to the refreshments table and wished he could have teleported there like a JumpShip making its way between stars. So fixed was he on becoming invisible as he skirted the assembly that he was two steps beyond the doorway when he actually translated the whispered sound into his name.

Spinning about, he saw her, and his jaw dropped open. She wore a jacket and skirt similar in style to his sister's, but different enough to save them the embarrassment of arriving in the same outfit. Unlike his sister's clothes, however, hers had been cut from white silk embroidered with pink cherry blossoms.

"Omi?" Victor recovered his wits, and swallowed hard. "I mean, *komban-wa, Kurita Omi.*"

Omi bowed her head to him in return, her long black hair falling forward over one shoulder like a velvet curtain. "Your Japanese is flawless, Victor. You have been practicing."

Victor nodded, unable to speak as his racing heart lagged a second or two behind the pace of his thoughts. To save her brother from the Clans on Teniente, Omi had been forced to enlist Victor's help. In exchange for allowing her to invite Federated Commonwealth forces to perform the rescue, her father had made Omi promise never to communicate with Victor again. Her grandfather, however, had overridden that command in gratitude for her role in saving Hohiro. He even appointed her head of the foundation that provided money for the education of the children of the Revenants, a job that required a regular exchange of messages with Victor.

When leaving Outreach four years ago, Victor had thought he would never see Omi again. She had thought so, too, which may have made them feel freer to express themselves in the messages they sent back and forth. Their relationship had deepened to the point that Omi's promise to her father became a form of torture to them both. Still, the distance that separated them helped keep things in check.

Seeing her again, Victor wanted to take Omi in his

arms right here, but he refrained. He must have been staring at her, though, for she blushed suddenly. Averting his eyes in embarrassment, he felt the heat rising on his own cheeks.

"Sumimasen," he said. "I did not mean to embarrass you. It is just that it is so hard to believe you are really here."

Omi smiled carefully. "The Draconis Combine owes a great debt to the Kell Hounds. My father would never allow us to be disrespectful. I have come to honor a great warrior. I also impressed upon my father that the foundation had urgent business that was best conducted in person here on Arc-Royal."

"I see." Victor tugged nervously at the loose ends of the sash holding his robe shut. *Another secret mission— one of which I knew nothing, but one I welcome wholeheartedly.* "I had not thought I would ever see you again. I thought you might have been offended that I was unable to attend your grandfather's memorial service. I was grieved at your loss."

She looked down at the white marble floor. "Takashi's passing was so unexpected, but he wanted no public spectacle to commemorate him." Omi looked up and met Victor's gaze for a moment before her eyes flicked down again. "That is not to say you would not have been welcome."

"Thank you." Victor smiled at her and his chest felt like it would explode. "Come, I must introduce you to my sister."

She held up one hand. "No, Victor, I have already met her. She helped my staff create this dress while the *Taizai* was coming into the system. Your Katrina is very nice."

Victor sighed audibly. "But a bit much, yes?"

"She is very *vivacious*, I think." Omi politely stifled a yawn. "I came here this evening because I promised her I would. I should have followed my own counsel and gone to bed early."

"Yes, no, I mean, I understand, but I am happy you decided to come." Victor glanced back at where his sister still had the crowd enthralled. *Of course they won't notice me.* Captain Moran did look over, scowling instantly, but that fact barely registered in Victor's mind. "Would you like me to escort you to your quarters?"

Almost immediately he realized how the question sounded. "I mean, I would consider it an honor to be sure you made your way back safely."

Omi's blue eyes sparked for a second, but her face remained politely expressionless. "I can find my way from the garden. If you would accompany me that far, I would be in your debt."

Victor pointed her back down the corridor. While on his way to the party, the same hallway had seemed to go on forever, but now, escorting Omi back the same way, it seemed so pitifully short. They did not speak, nor did they touch, even by accident, but it didn't matter. Even keeping his eyes forward, Victor could feel her beside him. The rustle of her dress whispered seductively and the hushed sound of her breathing sounded like music in his ears.

Opening the door at the corridor's end, he ushered Omi into the cool evening air and the garden the Kell Hounds maintained so carefully.

Victor remembered how much the spot had impressed him on his first morning on Arc-Royal. Over the years the Kell Hounds had managed to bring back specimens of the various plants native to the many worlds where they had served. Little greenhouses dotted the large compound, providing the appropriate atmosphere for flora from planets entirely dissimilar to temperate Arc-Royal. The rainbow display had been impressive enough by day, but the perfume of night-blooming flowers more than made up for what it lacked in color by night.

A sparkling riot of stars filled the black sky overhead. The Milky Way slashed across the sky, north to south. Victor tried in vain to spot a constellation he recognized and could point out to Omi, but he saw none.

Looking back toward her, he saw her shiver. "Are you cold?" He deftly unknotted the sash of his robe and had it half off even before she shook her head. "Are you sure?"

"Quite, Victor." She looked around and then smiled. "I was just remembering the last time we were alone, at night, in a garden like this."

"Outreach, four years ago."

"You and Hohiro were heading off to fight the Clans. I thought I would never see you again. There was so much uncertainty and fear then.'' She smiled at him. ''And fear now.''

"Fear?'' He looked at her and tried to read her shadowed expression. ''What do you have to fear?''

"I fear that I may succumb to my desires and ask you to guide me all the way to my chambers this evening.''

Victor's guts twisted in on themselves. Knowing she felt as he did made his spirits spike up through the top of his skull, but then they crashed down as her caution and implied warning came through to him. For the two of them to be together would be utterly wrong and hopelessly irresponsible. It could literally fracture the trust between the Federated Commonwealth and the Draconis Combine. That, in turn, could open the way for the Clans to successfully crush the Inner Sphere. What would be a passionate lark for any other two people became, for them, the overture to the downfall of civilization.

You are being overly dramatic, Victor. Not everything leads to Gotterdämmerung. He shook his head as he realized she was asking him to be strong, and yet, at the same time, she was willing to abide by his decision. His heart ached as his personal desire crashed headlong into his sense of responsibility.

"You know there is nothing in this life I would rather do.'' *Victor, what are you saying? No one need ever know!* As part of him screamed at him to stop, the easing of Omi's shoulders told him he was right. ''In a garden just like this, four years ago, we asked each other if we were falling in love. We talked of the problems of such a union. While our answers from that time may have changed—mine has, in any event—the problems have not.''

She reached out and caressed the right side of his face with the back of her right hand. ''There is a legend of a place, a utopia, in which one person is kept in squalid and torturous conditions so that all the others may live lives of peace and plenty. There are times I have wondered, since my answer to our question changed, whether the universe does not require such anguish to keep it viable.''

"And there are times when even the destruction of the

universe would seem a worthy price for a moment of ecstasy.'' Victor reached up and gently pulled her head down toward his. He kissed her lightly on the lips, and then again. She returned his kiss a third time and then a fourth.

Victor's left hand knotted into a fist and he pulled back. "Too close, too fast." He took in huge lungfulls of the night air through his nose, hoping the flower scents would supplant Omi's jasmine perfume. "You and your family trust me far more than you should."

"The Combine owes you the life of the Dragon's heir. If they can trust you with that, they believe they can trust you with my honor." Omi turned away from him. "They are shrewd judges of men. They knew you would be stronger than me."

"Do not rebuke yourself, Omiko." Victor shook his head. "Tonight it was my turn to be strong. I think you will yet have your chance before we leave this world."

"And if I fail?"

"Then the universe can find someone else to make miserable for one night."

10

Arc-Royal
Federated Commonwealth
16 April 3055

As Omi moved off into the darkness, Phelan cleared his throat. ''There are times that love seems to bring as much pain as it does pleasure.''

Victor whirled on him, his left foot spraying out a fan of crushed white stones as it came down. ''How long have you been standing there?'' he demanded. Shadows hid the Prince's face, but the anger in his words was loud and clear.

''I only just came to find you. I heard nor saw anything that you would consider a confidence. Moreover, if I had, I would never use it against you.''

''Wouldn't you?'' Victor folded his arms across his chest. ''You're the one who said we of the Inner Sphere were afraid of what you would do to us when the Clans came at us again. Wouldn't you use privileged information against me if we were to face each other in a bidding war?''

''I cannot figure out what you want me to answer, Victor.'' Phelan ticked the alternatives off on his fingers. ''I could say that you are, of course, correct, but that would only confirm the image you cling to so tightly of Clanners being shallow, single-minded death machines. I could tell you that I would not use the information because you are my cousin and I value our blood ties, but you'd laugh yourself silly with that one. Or, as I already have, I could tell you I saw nothing and will have nothing to report *if* I am called upon to give a report.''

"You have superior officers, Phelan. You *will* give a report."

"I am a *Khan*, Victor. I do what I want. If the ilKhan were to demand a report and I withheld information, no one would know." Phelan held his hands up. "Wait, wait, this is getting out of hand. I didn't come out here to argue with you."

The Prince's head came up. "Then why did you come?"

"To give you a warning."

"It must be an important one if you managed to free yourself from my sister's web." The sardonic note in Victor's voice told Phelan that the Prince was beginning to question why he had let Omi walk off.

"I am like you in that. Because she is a cousin, the incest taboo renders me somewhat immune to her charms. I also seem to remember her at your grandmother's funeral, when she dyed her hair to appear more adult."

Victor's silhouette hunched over as he laughed. "Yes, she went for red hair, like Natasha Kerensky, but ended up with orange. She did look funny."

"And she turned it to her advantage. She turns all disadvantages to advantages. She is very good." Phelan sat down on a concrete and tile bench, and the chill in the tile worked its way straight through his clothes. "I think, if she were a Wolf, I would have her shot."

"If that is your warning, forget it." Victor combed his hair into place with the fingers of one hand. "The death of Romano Liao will be the last regicide in the Inner Sphere if I have anything to say about it."

"Good. I agree." Phelan rested his hands on the bench and leaned back. "That was not my warning, however. I had been wondering why Captain Moran was going after you so hard back at the party. After you walked away, but before you left with the Coordinator's daughter, Michelle caught sight of you. Her face closed snap-shut."

"Her brother died on Trellwan and I didn't. I was ordered off even though I didn't want to go. Galen slugged me and put me on a DropShip."

"That could be the core of her resentment, all right. I think it runs deeper, though."

Victor came over and sat down beside him. "What?"

"I am probably mistaken, and you might not want to hear it."

"Tell me."

"Are you sure?"

Victor nodded silently.

Phelan took a deep breath, then started. "You and I have never really seen eye to eye. I've always resented authority figures who assumed they knew best because of their rank. You know I had a friend at the Nagelring who died when she got her commission because some moron Kommandant had her lance working by the book. Free Worlds League troops killed her, but that Kommandant escaped. I hope one of the Jade Falcons got him.

"Tor Miraborg, on Gunzburg, is another case of someone who had authority because of what he had once been. When I met him, he was just a bitter old man intent on breaking me. In me he saw something to hate, and that was fine because I hated him right back. That hatred cost us both a lot—me my life as a member of the Inner Sphere and him his daughter."

Phelan leaned forward, resting his elbows on his knees. "You were like my nemesis. You had authority purely because of an accident of birth. At the Nagelring I stayed away from you because I didn't want courtiers kissing my butt just to get close to you. I took great pains to antagonize those who thought they could use me to get to you. There were times I hated you so much I could have wrung your little neck."

Victor smiled. "The feelings were mutual, Phelan. I saw everything you did as a personal affront to me and my family and the memory of our kin. Part of me thought you were pushing things just to see how far I would go to protect you. I was also disgusted to see you wasting your potential, which was so much greater than what others had, precisely because of your position of birth. I was glad you got bounced when I was at NAMA for that year because I didn't want to have to put up with you begging me to let you remain at the Nagelring."

"Figures you were conceited enough to think I'd come asking you for anything."

Victor picked up a handful of the stones lining the garden walkways and started pitching one after the other out into the darkness. "You're projecting your own worst fears onto me. You would have hated to beg, so you figure I wanted you to. You don't understand something really basic here, Phelan.''

''And that is?''

''And it is that I *hate* being accorded privileges and rights that I've not earned. I hate being bound by who I was born to be, not what I have made myself.'' One stone arced far into the darkness. ''If I was just a soldier in the AFFC, I wouldn't be sitting here on a cold bench talking to you. I'd be somewhere very warm and cozy with someone I love.''

''Maybe so, but it wouldn't be *her.*'' Phelan picked up his own little handful of stones and also began tossing them into the shadows. ''And I do know you hate the honors and rigors of being the Prince, the heir. Because I know that—or knew it deep down back at the Nagelring—I didn't strangle you. I saw how you tested everyone to see if they were seeking an advantage. I guess I kept distant because I didn't want to see you look at me as though I *was* just another sycophant using my tie to you. Truth be told, that is.''

''Honesty. That's different.'' Victor clapped his hands together to get rid of the pale dust on them. ''Outside of Omi, Galen, and Kai, I don't see much of that.''

Phelan smiled. ''I have a little larger circle of critics, but that's because I work differently than you do. See, for you, the fact that both you and Omi are royalty sort of cancels out and you can be yourselves. I don't know what Kai or Galen have going for them, but I'll take it as given that each is special in his own way.''

''They are. When I first met Kai he was so down on himself that I felt compelled to help build him up. He wouldn't have dreamed of asking for a favor or any other thing because he was so sure he wasn't worthy of it.'' Victor moved his jaw back and forth and laughed. ''Galen, well, I got saddled with him so I couldn't accidently kill the Twelfth Donegal Guards. I managed to do it anyway, but he stuck with me.''

''My people are like that, too. Each of them saw me and my worth when I was just a bondsman. Evantha . . .''

''The Elemental?''

''Right. She saved my life even though I had stunned her with a punch in front of the Clan Khan and some other Elementals. That punch mortified her, but she decided a warrior like me shouldn't be wasted. If not for her training, I'd have died long ago."

"Phelan, how can you survive in a culture that is hyper-authoritarian when you hate authority?"

Good question, that. Phelan shrugged, giving himself time to think. "I guess it is because Clan society so clearly distills conflict that I always have a very direct route toward resolving a problem. For example, if your mother thought a new tax should be raised throughout the Commonwealth, she would have to get the legislatures to agree to it. That means power chits would be exchanged and deals would be cut. Everything would have to balance and someone who disagreed would do his best to destroy that balance."

"That *balance* is politics, cousin. You can't tell me the Clans are without politics."

"Not at all, but the Clans have a swift court of final arbitration. If someone disagreed with something I had done, I would be challenged to settle the dispute in a Circle of Equals. There, fighting according to odds determined by the Khan or a vote by the Clan Council, we would have it out. Often even the hint of a good battle or two being put up to defend an issue will forestall a fight."

The Prince laughed aloud. "So, if you don't like something, you get to hit someone!"

Phelan shifted uncomfortably on the bench. "Crudely put, but accurate."

"Had we a Circle of Equals at the Nagelring, you'd never have been tossed out." Victor scratched at the back of his neck. "Still, you must agree that politics is a necessary evil."

"Stress on *evil*."

"Stress on *necessary*. As satisfying and cathartic as the Clan way might be, it doesn't work outside the military." Victor looked over at Phelan. "What does your scientist class do to settle disputes—draw a circle, then challenge one another to prove theorems?"

The Clan Khan shook his head. "Their disputes can be solved through repeating an experiment. I agree that compromise is part of life, and our bidding process does that nicely, but being able to put your life on the line for what you believe is a good way to cut through a lot of hot air and posturing for position.''

"And what is decided in a Circle of Equals is final?"

"Final. What goes into the Circle stays in the Circle." Phelan smiled. "It's almost as good as confession for relieving guilt."

"Guilt I don't mind, it's the feeling that others see me as guilty that bothers me." Victor shook his head. "And yes, I know that sounds like the beginnings of clinical paranoia, but it isn't. I understand why Captain Moran doesn't like me and I accept it. But it's the others seeming to chime in with her so fast that has me a bit worried."

We come full circle. "That is what I came to talk to you about, Victor. Because you're always judging people, evaluating them to determine what they want, you put up a wall between you and them. Sure, there are going to be people who want to get to know you because, to them, you're a larger-than-life figure. You are a symbol to them, a bona fide hero. All the public images of you make you seem vibrant, alive, carefree, and very attractive."

"It's all propaganda concocted by scandal-vids that want to make money."

"Yeah, but the reason it is propaganda is because it works." Phelan sat up straight and gently slapped Victor's right shoulder with the back of his left hand. "Coming in-system I saw dozens of news reports about you. Arc-Royal was going nuts because you are here. You're the Inner Sphere's most eligible bachelor, *quiaff?* You're not half bad-looking and you're a war hero. You are a *somebody.*"

"But I don't *like* it."

"The hell you don't."

"I don't."

"Victor, you're afraid to like it. You are afraid you will begin to believe the courtiers and then you'll isolate yourself in a world of sycophants. You're afraid you'll end up as out of touch as Maximilian Liao and be overthrown. So you insulate yourself from that possibility, which means you insulate yourself from a lot of normal folks." Phelan chewed his lower lip for a second. "For all her show, do you think Katrina believes half the things she's told?''

''No.'' Victor shook his head confidently. ''She knows that the second she's out of earshot some of the women are going to start sniping and she knows that many of the men are complimentary in hopes of one night they can build memoirs around. She's no fool.''

''No, she isn't. She comes in and befriends everyone. She manages to be kind to them, making each one think they are important to her. If she has to refuse an invitation to dance or spend the night or visit an estate, it's always with deep regrets. If Katrina detested someone, he'd never know it, he'd never have a clue. You, you'd take him out and shoot him.''

''Yeah, or send him up against the Wolf Clan,'' the Prince chuckled. ''And her name is Katherine.''

''There you go again.''

''What?''

''What difference does it make if she wants to change her name to that of your grandmother? It's a nice gesture and one that was received quite well back there at the reception.'' Phelan glanced toward the building behind them. ''In fact, it played much better in the trenches than your exit.''

Victor stood and kicked at a stone. ''Meaning?''

Phelan shrugged. ''Meaning the Lyran Commonwealth and the Federated Suns have spent a lot of money and a lot of blood fighting the Draconis Combine. I don't think anyone would begrudge you and Omi happiness, and folks are enjoying the heck out of peace between the Commonwealth and Combine. Some people are bound to resent your rescue of Hohiro, but that's because they're remembering the past, not thinking of the future. They will come around, but you have to give them time.''

''I know, I know. Wags already have it that we've got one 'love child' stashed on Terra. The Galactic *Insinuator* even put together a holovid with actors.'' Victor slammed his right fist into his left palm, then turned back to Phelan. ''A Circle of Equals would have been a wonderful way to settle that problem.''

The Wolf Khan stood and stretched. ''Fighting with the press is like wrestling with pigs: you *may* win, but you *will* get dirty. I feel the same way in dealing with the Smoke Jaguars. Look, let some people in. Learn from Katrina. Open up a bit, let people see what you are like. Let them get to know you, so they can sympathize with you. Let them like you so they can root for you and Omi to have a chance at cementing a peace that is, right now, fragile.''

''Wise words.''

''Thank you.'' Phelan pointed at Victor's robes. ''Better do up that sash, or folks will assume you and Omi were discovered in *deep* conversation.''

The Prince nodded and reknotted the sash. ''Why did you tell me all this, Phelan, really? If I succeed in doing what you suggest, when the truce is up we will be stable and ready for you.''

''I'll give you two choices—you pick one. First, we're cousins and I don't want to see a nation and a people I care deeply about suffer because no one will speak frankly to you. Second, I'm from the Clans, and a strong, stable Federated Commonwealth will give me the greatest chance to cover myself in martial glory.''

''How about I choose 'all of the above.' ''

Phelan threw his arm around Victor's shoulders and steered him back toward the party. ''Bargained well and done.''

11

Arc-Royal
Federated Commonwealth
17 April 3055

Christian Kell rubbed his chin with his right hand. "I like it, but I'm not certain I'm the sort of person who should be advising you on fashion." He glanced up from the computer screen to Evantha Fetladral's face and back down. "Katrina is really the one to make decisions like this."

Evantha studied the screen intently. She looked to Chris as if she were treating it like a battlefield puzzle she could solve with superior tactics. "I just do not know. This is entirely outside my realm of experience."

The shopkeeper, a small man with a thin moustache and thinner hair, clasped his hands together at his breastbone. "You must trust me, mademoiselle. This is perfect for you. Because you have such height, broad shoulders, and such a trim waist, we want to use this strapless bodice to emphasize your figure. The black velvet bolero jacket helps soften some of those arm muscles. The flowing gown is really the sort of thing that is de rigueur this season, and the scattered rhinestones throughout hint at the more exotic and wild side of your nature."

Evantha looked at the man, then back at the screen where the garments had been painted over a video-sample of her body. "But this is going quite far afield when what I want to do is wear my uniform." She frowned. "Bondsman, your opinion?"

Ragnar studied the screen for a moment, then nodded.

"It will do very nicely for it really is like your uniform, only feminized in keeping with current fashion."

Chris nodded in agreement. "*All* of the Kell Hound women officers have made the change to something more stylish for the banquet. It might be impractical, but who can understand the world of fashion?"

Ragnar tapped the computer screen. "Perhaps you would feel less naked if they added two stars, right here and here, on either side of the jacket collar, just like insignia."

Evantha slowly smiled. "You are very observant, Ragnar. Very good." She nodded to dressmaker. "You will have it ready by sixteen hundred hours today?"

"Today?" The man started to shake his head no, but Chris nodded confidently and the dressmaker aped him. "Ah, yes, anything for a friend of Major Kell." He glanced at Chris again and added, "And I will deliver it personally, just in case we need to tuck it in or let it out a bit."

"Bargained well and done." Evantha clapped the man on each shoulder, and for a half-second Chris feared the dressmaker would collapse like a ship with its keel smashed in.

"Thank you, André. Send the bill to me." Chris smiled as the man rolled his eyes. He ushered the two Clansfolk back out into the narrow, cobbled streets of Old Connaught, and pulled the little shop's door closed behind him. "André does very good work. You will be pleased."

Evantha nodded and the sunlight gleamed from her nearly shaven head. Her long braid of red hair started back near the crown, roughly where a samurai would have located his top-knot, and hung down her back, even beyond the waist of the Kell Hound jacket she had borrowed for the outing. "I find this curious. I am more nervous about wearing these clothes than I have ever been about entering battle."

"I can understand that—the unknown is always forbidding." Chris smiled broadly. "Which means I will not inflict *fugu* or haggis on either of you for lunch. And I would not worry, Star Captain. You will look wonderful."

"You are kind, Major Kell."

"Chris. Formality is fine in its place, but not among friends."

"Evantha, then. And I thank you for using your influence with André to arrange for tailoring so quickly."

"Oh, he would have delivered. He has a warehouse full of machines that take the design from the screen and turn it into something you can wear. The stall was just a first step in negotiating the price up through the stratosphere." Chris shoved his hands into the pockets of his black woolen trousers. "André and I have a working relationship that encourages him to make me happy. I have certain ties to the Draconis Combine that make obtaining certain fabrics a bit easier than through normal channels. Had he tried to make you pay, he knew one source of supply was going to dry up on him."

"I do not know which is harder to imagine," Evantha said, unable to hide her scorn, "a member of the merchant caste daring to cheat a warrior or a warrior like you dabbling in merchant affairs."

Chris shrugged. "Things are not as stratified here in our world. It keeps life interesting and full of surprises."

"I also think, Star Captain, that more mixing goes on than you believe." Ragnar smiled slyly. "There has been quite a traffic in war spoils heading back out to the Clan homeworlds. And, yes, warriors are merely bartering things they have with the merchants for goods they want, but the exchange rate has been very good to the warriors."

"As I said before, you are very observant, bondsman." Evantha frowned as they walked past a shop displaying all manner of shoes. "I supposed I will need a new pair of footwear to go along with my gown?"

Chris glanced down at the combat boots she wore. "Yes, I think that would be appropriate, but not right now. I am beginning to get hungry. Ragnar, did you know that a Rasalhagian refugee family has opened a restaurant in the Oslo district? It's called Callas. We could try it if you like."

Ragnar looked up at Evantha. "If the Star Captain approves."

She nodded and Chris started them down the twisting street. Two blocks further and they turned north, heading up a hill. The whitewashed brick and thatched roofs of the Irish section of Old Connaught did not change that much moving into the Oslo district, but the difference was still readily apparent. Street and shop signs included the unique calligraphy of the Swedenese language spoken by most of the refugees. The citizenry began to look decidedly more like Ragnar, making Chris a dark-haired standout.

"Leaving Luthien, we ran across a Rasalhagian JumpShip that had blown the seals on its liquid helium tanks. We managed to patch the ship up and brought it with us here to Arc-Royal. My grandfather, the Grand Duke, subsidized the expansion of the tourist district in the city and encouraged the Rasalhagians to settle here. They first comers contacted other refugees and eventually a whole community grew up." Chris pointed to a tall building in the distance. "Your people have done well here, Ragnar. Ryan Steiner financed that tower and dedicated it as your father's home in exile if he ever decides to leave the Free Rasalhague Republic."

Ragnar stared at the white tower but said nothing.

Evantha frowned. "Ryan Steiner did that *here,* on Arc-Royal, a world belonging to the political camp that most opposes him?"

Chris held a hand out, palm down, and waggled it back and forth. "Not quite, but close. My grandfather embarrassed Ryan into sinking the money into the project by once saying in public that Ryan was long on talk but tight on the purse strings. My grandfather also doled out money in no-interest loans to the refugees, even though that wasn't the most popular gesture here at home. Ryan paid out his cold, hard Kroner and the refugees benefitted. We're here, by the way."

Chris held the door open while Evantha stooped to enter the building. Two steps down into the common room and she was able to straighten up again. A massive wooden beam running the length of the restaurant supported a dark-stained pine ceiling. Similar deep brown planking covered the floors and rose halfway up the walls. Plaster walls connected the paneling to the ceiling, with various pictures, paintings, and other artifacts of lost Rasalhague decorating the room. Blocky handcrafted tables and chairs of various sizes and shapes also lent an antique charm.

Chris shut the door behind them, then greeted the owner with a smile. *"God morgon,* Olaf. Three for lunch."

The heavyset man had white hairs threading his moustache and goatee and a big smile splitting his face. "Greetings, Christian." He looked the party over, then surprise swallowed his smile. "It cannot be." He dropped to his knees and kissed Ragnar's hand.

Ragnar looked stunned and Evantha shifted uneasily. Chris wanted to kick himself for being so unbelievably stupid. *For so many of the refugees, Ragnar is a symbol of what the Clans have taken away from them. How could I have brought either Evantha or him here?*

Olaf turned to him. "You have no idea how much this means to me, friend Christian. I will make you all a fine meal. I will call friends and we will celebrate. I . . ."

Ragnar stooped and helped the man to his feet. "Goodman Olaf, you cannot do that. I mean, yes, please, make us a meal." Ragnar sniffed the air and smiled. "The entire Kell Hounds force could not move me before I have eaten here today. Unfortunately, a celebration is not in order."

The heir to Rasalhague's royal line held up his right wrist and tugged at the white bondcord surrounding it. "I am now of the Wolf Clan. I am here as a guest of the Kell Hounds, but this day belongs to Colonel Kell. Another time we will celebrate."

Olaf brushed away the tears brimming in his eyes. He started to speak, but his lower lip trembled and no sound came out. He swallowed once, then again, and finally just nodded. His voice then returned in a hoarse whisper, "I will tell my wife, *ja?* And my children, and they can help serve?"

"Ja, varsagod."

"Tack sa mycket." Olaf guided them to a round table in the center of the room. He held the chair out for Ragnar, placing him in the seat of honor, then sat Chris on his right and Evantha on his left. After patting Ragnar on the shoulders, he headed back toward the kitchen, where they heard him shouting orders over the clanking of pots and pans.

Chris felt not a little conspicuous at the large table. "The only time I've been seated at this table is when I treated one of my companies to dinner. I hope that's not an omen for how much food we'll be getting because you know we'll have to make a sizable dent in all of it.''

"I know." Ragnar sighed and lightly tapped his right thigh. "And look, I forgot to wear my hollow leg today."

Evantha smiled at the joke, then glanced over toward the table nearest the door. Two men seemed to be watching them them avidly. Her smile turned into a scowl, and the two men finished their beers before hastily departing.

That made her smile return.

"I'm not certain scaring off Olaf's customers is a good thing to do." Chris squinted his eyes. "On the other hand, that look is one I'd like to see some of the womanizers in my unit encounter from time to time."

She shook her head. "This is perhaps what I find so bewildering about the Inner Sphere. This gown I have ordered, these shoes I will buy, they are designed to make me appear sexually attractive, *quiaff?*"

"Yes."

"And the ultimate sign of success would be attracting someone with whom I would be willing to couple, *quiaff?*"

Chris nodded slowly, dreading the direction of the conversation, though not sure why. "Yes."

"Yet men and women who succumb to the snares laid by others are labeled with derogatory terms like gigolo or slut." Her brows nearly touched beneath her furrowed forehead. "So you punish those who succeed at the game that you all play, and you torture yourselves by withholding satisfaction in the face of mutual attraction."

The Kell Hound nodded. "That's about the size of it."

"I did not understand it with Khan Phelan, nor do I understand it now. Life is too short for pleasure to be denied when it is available."

Chris started to say something, then closed his mouth and looked over at Ragnar for help. The bondsman shook his head and leaned back, taking himself out of the conversation. Chris reluctantly began his defense of Inner Sphere ways. "I think, Evantha, you are generalizing from limited data."

"Am I? Last night I met Duchess Katrina. She had obviously made herself attractive to many of the men there. The men were not wholly unattractive, either. I watched her deftly turn aside any number of openings for coupling, which, given the way she dressed and acted, was what I thought was her goal. As she is a leader among you, I assumed this was a societal norm."

Wait, I see now what's going on. "Evantha, I think you are mistaking biological urges and their resolution for courtship."

"Courtship?"

"You said life was short, and within the Clans, I suppose this is true. Here, however, we look at establishing a relationship in which each partner can nurture the other and in which children can be raised and loved. I know the Clans raise children in sibkos, so that sort of family unit is not necessary."

"Even our breeding comes independent of physical attraction." Evantha raised her head proudly. "Since I won my Bloodname seven years ago, my genetic heritage has contributed to three sibkos. Though it is far too early to know if my progeny will prove themselves, whispers are quite favorable. I also assume that if I am killed honorably, my genes will still be utilized well after my death."

Chris gave her an encouraging nod. "That is wonderful, Evantha, but breeding is not courtship, either. Courtship is a process of showing another how much you care."

"As when the Khan gives Ranna a gift, or she touches his arm in passing?"

"There you have it."

Evantha waved it way. "Highly impractical."

Chris winked at her. "True, but fun nonetheless."

Chris had noticed various people coming and going from the restaurant during the conversation, but it wasn't until he felt the pistol's cold barrel pressed into the back of his neck that he realized how crowded it had become with young men and women. Chris flattened his hands out on the table. Across the way he saw a shotgun slide from beneath an overcoat to cover Evantha.

A man pulled Ragnar's chair away from the table. "Highness, we have come to rescue you from the Clans."

Ragnar looked very surprised. "Who are you?"

"We are part of the underground," the man said, indicating the half-dozen people nearest the table. "We call ourselves Ragnarok. We will get you to safety."

Chris shook his head. "You know you cannot get off this world."

"We have resources you know nothing about." The man tugged Ragnar to his feet. "We must hurry." He pointed to Chris and Evantha. "Shoot them."

"No!" Ragnar grabbed the man's thick sheepskin coat with his right hand.

"It is for the best, my Prince."

Ragnar frowned. "Not that, give me a knife." He flicked the bondcord with his left hand. "I need to cut this, then. . . ." His words trailed off as he looked at Evantha.

The man from Ragnarok smiled. "Of course, Prince Ragnar." From within the folds of his coat he pulled out a trench knife and presented it hilt-first to Ragnar.

The bondsman slowly slid his fingers through the brass-knuckle grip. Holding his right arm out at waist height, he bared his forearm and slipped the knife under the cord. Grinning, he rubbed the blade back and forth on the cord, beginning to fray it, then he pulled up on the knife and pushed forward. The taut cord parted with a snap.

His left-handed lunge plunged the knife straight into the chest of the man who had given it to him. With his right hand Ragnar shoved the ringleader into the woman holding the gun on Chris. As she fell, she jerked the trigger. Powder burned his right ear as the thunder of the near-miss deafened him.

The adrenaline kicking into his system made Chris feel he had the strength of hundreds. Shoving the heavy table forward, he spilled Evantha back and out of the way of the shotgun blast aimed at her. Leaning on the table, Chris rose out of the chair and sidekicked the woman who had nearly shot him. She partially blocked the strike with her gun arm, but the kick drove the arm back into her chest, shattering the ulna and crushing two ribs.

The second his right foot touched the ground again, Chris spun. His other foot came up in a roundhouse kick that snapped a Ragnaroker's head around. As that man went down, teeth and blood spraying from his mouth, the man who had fired at Evantha finished reloading his shotgun and clicked the barrel shut. The gun swung into line with Chris's stomach.

Roaring like a lion, Evantha tipped the huge table up on its edge and threw it at the gunman. The table's edge hit the ceiling, deflecting it from its target, but the thick slab of wood managed to interpose itself between the shotgun and Chris. The mercenary saw the flash of light and felt the spray of splinters that accompanied the gunshot, but the table stopped most of the pellets.

Evantha leaped up from the floor and at the gunman. The table rolled on past just in time for Chris to watch an overhand right fist crush the shotgunner's face. He went down immediately and Evantha snapped his fowling gun across her knee.

Chris kicked the pistol away from the downed woman's left hand and saw Ragnar standing over an unconscious woman. He sucked at his bruised knuckles, then stabbed the bloody knife into the floor between him and Evantha. "One escaped, Star Captain. I will pursue him, if you wish."

Evantha shook her head as Olaf came out of the back. "I have called the constabulary. My Prince, are you hurt?"

Ragnar withheld his right hand from Olaf. "No, it is nothing."

"Easy, Ragnar. Olaf didn't bring these people here. The one with the shotgun was one of the two who were in here earlier." Chris nodded to Olaf. "I have no doubt Olaf's word was good despite his desire to let others know you were here. He's a responsible man, a keystone here in the refugee community."

Ragnar nodded slowly, his stern expression softening only slightly. He knelt and picked up his severed bondcord. "Is what he says true, Olaf?"

"Yes, my Prince."

"Then I believe it." His blue eyes became like chips of ice as he narrowed them. "I charge you with a duty, then, Goodman Olaf. I am hurt, and I require you to aid me."

"Anything, Highness."

"My hurt is not physical, Olaf, but it cuts deep and goes to the heart. To my heart and to the heart of the

Rasalhagian people. Carry this message for me to everyone.'' Ragnar toed the dead leader's body. ''Let it be known that I am hurt to think we believe freedom can be bought with the blood of friends.''

12

Victor grinned unconsciously as he watched Morgan Kell walk across the dais to the podium. The warrior took his place without revealing the weaknesses one would expect of a man who had lived more than two-thirds of a century. Except for the increasing proportion of white in the mercenary leader's hair and beard, Victor would have said Morgan had not aged at all.

The Prince set his fork down beside his half-eaten cake and smiled at Omi, seated across from him at the round table. She returned the smile, then respectfully turned in her chair to face the speaker. Katherine—Victor refused to think of her as Katrina for reasons he could not nail down—whispered a comment to her dinner companion that elicited a polite chuckle, then they both fell silent as Morgan adjusted the microphone up toward his mouth.

"I would like to thank you all for coming here. I know, of course, that the Kell Hounds have been in existence for forty-five years, but it was not until I saw everyone gathered here—Hounds past, present, and future—that the enormity of that time fully struck me. And I am certain all our hearts carry memories of many others we wish could be here tonight. But I think . . . I know . . . they are here in spirit."

Looking around the large banquet hall, Victor was impressed at the number of people who had come to witness Morgan's retirement. Most of the guests were former or current Kell Hounds and their friends and families, but that was not all. Omi Kurita and Shin Yodama were representative of former enemies or employers who had come to honor Morgan. Even Thomas Marik of the Free Worlds League and the Precentor Martial of ComStar had sent envoys, and a number of Brothers from St. Marinus House had left their monastery to attend.

Morgan smiled at his audience and looked a little embarrassed. "As some of you know, this is the third time I have retired from the Kell Hounds. The first time was without this sort of fanfare. My leaving became known as "the Defection" among those who remained with the unit. During that time my brother Patrick took over leadership of the Kell Hounds and further improved on what was already an ace unit. To my eternal regret he died to preserve the Kell Hounds during my time of self-imposed exile."

The white-haired man paused for a moment and Victor felt a sympathetic lump in his throat. Though Patrick Kell had died several years before his own birth, Victor had always hoped in some magical, mystical way that the courage and compassion his mother described in Patrick had somehow been reincarnated in him. As he grew older, he realized the idea was pure fantasy, but it had still driven him to push himself hard.

"Being ever the master of timing, I returned to the Hounds and recalled many of you to us just in time for the Fourth Succession War. The Seventh Sword of Light dulled itself on us and the Genyosha learned they were very good, but so were we. The Third Dieron Regulars paid a price for arrogance that I had hoped, once and for all, would act as a beacon to warn others about the futility of war.

"To my regret it did not. In 3039 we answered yet another call to war, and again acquitted ourselves admirably. Throughout the next ten years, we did the same again and again, which has made me proud that my family's name is linked with the Hounds. However, you accomplished those great things without me because, in 3042, I retired for the second time and took my nephew, Christian, to Outreach for training."

Morgan looked over to where Chris sat at the head table, and sketched a salute to him. Chris returned it, and mild laughter rippled through the group. "I even managed to stay away when the Clans first invaded. Colonel Allard and his staff were more than adept in plotting the course of the Kell Hounds. In concert with the Tenth Lyran Guards and the Ninth FedCom RCT, we handed the Jade Falcons their first clear defeat—and that gave them something to think about as they wandered off to choose their new ilKhan.

"Then I came out of retirement at the urging of Jaime Wolf, who persuaded me that the Clans had to be stopped at all costs. I was there, with you, as we stood side by side with the Genyosha and the Dragon's Claws, fighting to preserve the capital of the realm that has been our long-time enemy. I remember well the loud and long bitch sessions about how our old comrades would be spinning in their graves when we touched down on Luthien. Perhaps they would have been surprised, but I believe those warriors would have given all to help us win rather than be angry at our accepting that assignment."

A number of warriors nodded in agreement. "Why do I believe that? Because I know how warriors think. I know what we hold dear, what we desire, and what we fear. I know our goals and I know what we are willing to surrender to reach them. This is something that each of us who is heart, soul, and body a warrior shares.

"In the popular mind each warrior lives only for combat, like some rabid beast lying in wait for a kill. He is vassal to death, one tooth in the razor-kissed jaws of destruction. Like a vampire, who grows stronger and more savage by sucking up the lives of others."

Morgan took a sip of wine from a glass. "This is what people believe because they never know what it is to live through a battle. They hear us talk about blasting away the head of an *Atlas* with a lucky shot. They hear about flanking maneuvers that rout the enemy, or an air-strike that obliterates a portion of his defense. They hear stirring tales of midair dogfights, of heroic efforts to get friends out of the field of fire, and of sacrifices made so others may live. And they hear those stories because those are the stories we choose to share with them.

"All of us know that cold, clutching feeling that rips through you when the enemy is sighted. All of us know the thick, sour taste of fear when our 'Mech is hit or our wingman tells us we have an enemy in our six. In nightmares we relive the terror of an unanswered support call and the grief of seeing a friend fallen where once he stood.

"What we should let everyone know is the truth of the paradox each warrior represents. Though trained in the ways of death, schooled in tactics, and steeped in strategies, the last thing any of us wants is war. We accept our responsibility and willingly do our duty, but we truly wish it would pass us by. Not because we are cowards, but because no one else so fully and deeply understands the consequences of our actions as we do."

More heads nodded around the room. Morgan's words echoed in Victor's heart and found a home there. *It is not an easy thing to kill anyone, nor should it ever be so.*

"Of all the things I have done with the Kell Hounds there is one act that, were a history of this unit ever written, would only comprise a footnote. On Lyons, in the spring of 3029, we helped to build a small community for refugees from the war. In that action we used our BattleMechs to actually *create* something. Destruction is easy, but *creation* is difficult. That community was called New Freedom and the reason it will never be more than a footnote is because within six weeks of its creation it became collateral damage."

Morgan let that thought sink in for a moment, then continued. "As I said, creation is hard work. In 3010 I created this unit. In 3027 I recreated it, and over the past three years, after the toll Luthien took on us, I have labored to rebuild the Kell Hounds. Several weeks ago Dan Allard and I agreed the job was done. And so am I—after the third try, I think I got it right.

"So, now with Chris and Caitlin readying themselves to one day assume command, and with Dan and his children coming up to ensure continuity, I leave the Kell Hounds in capable hands."

Morgan hesitated and looked over to where his son and the other visitors from the Clans were seated. "I hope that if the Clans someday decide they have had enough of him, Phelan might find a home here—more so if a Galaxy of his Wolves want to come with him. Surely if we can go to Luthien—the home of an age-old enemy—

to defend it against the Smoke Jaguars and Nova Cats, then we can accept a Wolf into our company.''

Victor sensed tension build as Morgan spoke about Phelan. No one in the room would have doubted the Kell Hounds' commitment to opposing the Clans were the war to heat up again, yet Morgan's hope that Phelan might be welcomed on Arc-Royal made his audience uneasy. Morgan obviously loved his son and had somehow resolved the conflict between his heart and his duty. Victor also felt a new kinship with Phelan after their talk. *I think I would welcome him home were he to come back.*

The mercenary leader smiled. ''My job here is done, so now my wife and I can retire to the rigors of planetary government and pestering our children to produce children of their own so we can hopelessly spoil some grandchildren.''

The elder Kell let the laughter from his remark die down before he concluded his speech. ''Let me leave you with one last thought. There are those who would interpret these comments as bolstering their case for utter and total disarmament. They would say that without weapons of mass destruction men would be forced to work with each other to get along. They would urge us to beat our swords into plowshares to give us tools to reverse the destruction/creation problem I have cited.

''As much as I would like to agree with them, this cannot be. Man managed to hurt others before we had swords. In the absence of weapons, fists do damage. In the absence of fists, words do damage, and taking away words would also take away the means for communication we seek as the cure for all mankind's ills.

''In this they are correct: communication, meaningful and respectful communication among equals, is the key to living prosperously and well with one another. This mutual respect can only come when each side knows that it cannot just turn around and take what it wants if it does not get its way in negotiation. When war is the final option that neither side wishes to embrace, communication becomes the only other logical possibility.''

Morgan smiled at his audience. ''So, thank you all for being friends in the good times and bad. What we have shared, the history we have created, is not ended with my departure. It becomes the foundation for what I know will be a viable and vital future.''

Without a thought Victor sprang to his feet applauding, and he was not the first person to do so. The ovation thundered through the hall, and for the first time in all the years he had known Morgan, the mercenary seemed truly at a loss. The applause continued after he sat down and only stopped when Morgan raised a glass in thanks to his guests and shared a wordless toast with them.

The banquet then began to break up. Katherine was doing fine entertaining those at their table without any help from Victor, so he excused himself and left. He debated whether to wade through the crowd of well-wishers surrounding Morgan and his wife Salome, or perhaps head over to the First Regiment's Assembly Hall for dancing, but could decide on neither.

Glancing back at his table, he saw Omi preparing to leave. She pressed Shin back down into his chair as she walked away. Victor caught her eye and headed over in her direction when she smiled at him. *"Komban-wa."*

''And to you, Prince Victor.'' Omi, wearing a black velvet gown trimmed with white lace, had her hair gathered at the back of her head and held in place with a silver comb. ''Colonel Kell is a good speaker.''

''Why is it that the good ones finish before I am ready to stop listening?'' Victor noticed his sister watching him out of the corner of her eye, but he chose to ignore her. ''Had you thought of going to the dance?''

''I thought it would be correct to do so, but I dread it because I am not well-versed in your styles of dance.'' Omi clasped her hands together shyly. ''Which is greater, the embarrassment of dancing poorly or the rudeness of not attending a function?''

''I can sympathize, for I am not terribly graceful on the dance floor, yet I share the same obligations. It strikes me that if we went together, no one would dare to ask you to dance—given protocol and the like. And, if you are not dancing, I certainly could not inflict myself on some unsuspecting woman.''

''That, Victor, is a wonderful plan.'' Omi smiled and slipped her right hand through the crook of his left arm. ''And if it looked as if we might be asked to dance, we could slip onto the dance floor ourselves.''

Victor smiled as he picked a path between tables. "Ah, minimize the damage to others by dancing together. Splendid planning."

They left the banquet hall and retraced their steps from the other evening through the garden. Turning south they walked past the small forest of bonsai trees the Hounds had brought from Luthien. "I have heard that the Hounds brought one bonsai for each pilot they lost on Luthien."

Omi gave his arm a light squeeze. "That is true. We have bonsai masters who created a tree for each of the Kell Hounds who fought in that battle. When one of them dies, another tree is sent here."

"I am certain there was a time, back when Morgan and Patrick started the Hounds, when they would never have believed they'd one day be fighting on Luthien in defense of the Combine. Times have changed incredibly, and so quickly, too."

Omi stopped and kissed Victor. "But they change very slowly as well, too slowly."

"Still they do change." He reached up and cupped her face in his hands. "Right now we cannot be together, but that does not mean that someday we will not."

Omi smiled and kissed the palms of his hands. "I know that, and I will work toward that day. It is just that it seems like forever until it will happen."

Victor again settled her hand onto his arm. "Well, for now we can dance together, which for certain Christian sects within my realm is the equivalent of far greater lusts being sated."

"I will dance with you, Victor, but only on one condition."

"And that is?"

The reflections of stars glittered in her dark eyes. "That our dancing is a promise of what we shall share when the times have changed enough."

13

Arc-Royal
Federated Commonwealth
18 April 3055

Phelan gave his mother a hug. "Yes, I know it's been less than a week, mother, but we must head back." He held her out at arm's-length and gave her a grand smile. "You always told me that the Wards who stayed behind when General Kerensky took the Star League army away from the Inner Sphere wondered if Jal Ward had made a difference. He did, a big one, which has given me the opportunity to do what I have done. Now maybe I can make a difference as well."

Salome hugged her son again. "I know you will, Phelan."

He moved from his mother's arms to his father's, enfolding the older man in a back-slapping bear hug. "There will be great rejoicing among the Smoke Jaguars and Nova Cats when they learn you have retired, father."

"Plenty of Inner Sphere leaders will lose sleep over my not persuading you to stay here, Phelan." Morgan stepped back and took a long look at his son, then shook his head. "I have to say that when I heard the Nagelring had expelled you, I never imagined this."

"Nor did any of us." Phelan swallowed past the lump in his throat. "Thank you for accepting me then and accepting me now."

"No matter what, Phelan, you and your sister will always be our children. We are proud of you both." The older man smiled happily. "No matter what, you have us behind you. If need be, you always have a home here."

Phelan watched his father closely. "Does it hurt you that I choose to stay with the Clans?"

Morgan thought for a moment, then nodded slowly. "Inasmuch as we miss you, yes."

"But you are not hurt that I am not here to help with the Hounds?"

"I had hoped for that, once, but I realize you must find your own way. If you decide that your place is with the Hounds, they will be here. If not, then as long as you are happy, so am I."

Phelan wanted to say, "Thank you," but the words stuck in his throat. He embraced his father again.

Then he looked around at the others in the departure lounge. Carew, in his flight suit, was exchanging a final farewell with Caitlin, while Chris, Ragnar, and Evantha were sharing some joke that made them all laugh. Ranna and his mother were whispering in tones that he found far too hushed and conspiratorial to make him feel at all at ease.

Then, from the back, Victor entered the room and walked toward him. "I didn't want to miss seeing you off, but I had a dinner engagement." Victor didn't elaborate, but Katrina had told Phelan where her brother was when she said goodbye earlier. "I am glad we had our chance to talk."

"So am I, Victor. I know our peoples are enemies, but the Federated Commonwealth and the Wolf Clan have more goals in common than differences to set us apart." Phelan half-smiled. "In fact, I got confirmation that the ilKhan has deployed a solahma unit to hunt down the bandit group that hit Pasig."

"Solahma?" Victor looked confused.

"I should explain. Solahma is a designation the Clan gives to units made up of warriors who are beyond the age for regular units or who have disgraced themselves. More often than not the solahma spend their time hunting bandits. They are BattleMech units—at least this one is— where an old warrior can hope for an honorable death and where disgraced warriors may try to redeem their honor." The Khan shrugged. "This one is a Wolf Clan unit. They will get the job done."

"Why are the Wolves hunting the bandits down? I

thought you said it was a job for the Jade Falcons because the Red Corsair operates out of their space.''

''The Jade Falcons are really a bit prissy and decidedly reactionary. They cling to the *very* old ways, which explains much of their impotence. They will abide by the ilKhan's bargain with ComStar, but they are not pleased with it. They have decided that the bandits actually originated somewhere in the Wolf zone, so it is *our* problem. They are making the ilKhan force our Clan to waste fuel, munitions, and personnel trying to get these guys.''

The Prince smiled. ''I understand his predicament. All messes are to be cleaned up by someone else.''

''Exactly.''

''So this unit, is it sharp?''

Phelan hesitated as he recalled who led it. ''Star Colonel Conal Ward is in charge. He is good.''

''He's a Ward.'' Victor nodded with satisfaction. ''We have that going for us.''

''True enough, Victor.'' *I do not think the fact that Conal sees me as responsible for his disgrace bears mentioning here.* ''The ilKhan is keenly aware of Conal's abiding hatred for bandits. Conal wanted the assignment desperately, so much so that he bid away his air wing to get it. He will do the job well.''

Victor offered Phelan his hand. ''I wish you all the best, cousin.''

''Likewise.'' Phelan shook his hand heartily. ''How much longer have you here?''

''A week, then I'm bound for Port Moseby to meet up with the Revenants again.''

Knowing that Omi would not be departing for another four days brought a smile to Phelan's face. ''Enjoy your time here, then.''

''I will.''

Phelan embraced each of his parents and Caitlin again, then summoned his entourage and headed down the loading arm to the K-1 Class DropShuttle that had brought them to Arc-Royal. As Carew headed up into the cockpit, the other four passengers went to their cabins and strapped themselves into their seats. The hatch closed and the ship lifted off from the spaceport facility.

As it accelerated up into the sky , Ranna turned off the interior cabin lights. Slipping his hand into hers, Phelan leaned over to look out the window beside her. As the spacecraft picked up speed and soared into the air, the tiny lights of Old Connaught outlined the sleeping city.

He shivered.

"What is it, Phelan?"

He forced a smile onto his face. "The last time I saw that view of Old Connaught was when I left to chase pirates in the Periphery. Stars have fused a lot of hydrogen atoms since then."

She stroked his dark hair. "You became a bondsman, then a warrior, won your Bloodname, and became a Khan. Yes, many things *have* changed, yet I do not think you have changed that much."

Phelan sat back in his seat. "What do you mean? I have changed a lot since I left Arc-Royal."

Ranna squeezed his hand. "You have, in that you have grown from a youth to an adult, but the change of venue did not alter the path destiny had chosen for you. If we Clans had never come, or if we had never made you a bondsman, you would still have become the man you are today. You see something you want, a goal you want to attain, and you let nothing stand in your way. You have drive and ambition."

She pressed her free hand against the viewport glass. "Down there, spending time with your parents and your family and your friends, I saw them through your eyes. Some always thought you contrary and contentious, but the perceptive ones knew you did not suffer fools or insults. This I have seen many times for myself. Experiencing the environment that produced you, I more fully understand why you have the gifts you now share with the Wolf Clan."

"Had I remained in the Inner Sphere, I would be, at best, a captain in charge of a scout lance in the Second Regiment of the Kell Hounds. That's not saying much for ambition."

"You sell yourself short." Ranna raised his hand to her mouth and kissed it. "I saw the light in your eyes as you forced Kai Allard-Liao to talk about his career on Solaris. You could have ended up there, and if that skirmish was a true indication of your respective skills, you and Kai would be arch-rivals for the title of champion."

Phelan nodded thoughtfully. "Champion of Solaris, that would not be bad."

"No, but I do not think you would have stopped there."

He looked over and arched an eyebrow at her. "Oh?"

"Your cousin Victor would have found a use for you."

"Never. We hated each other."

"Oh, I think you would have been brought together." She smiled impishly. "Katrina would no doubt have found a way to make you two reconcile. You, as heir to the title of Baron of Arc-Royal, would have your uses. Victor might not have seen them, but Katrina would have. She would have convinced him that his cousin, the young, brash Champion of Solaris, would be a wonderful candidate for the Estates General from the Donegal March. You would have been put into a position where your ambition could have worked to counter that of Ryan Steiner."

As she spoke, Phelan filled in the gaps in her hypothesis. *Ranna plots without knowing that my family has long been involved in Heimdall, a secret organization that works to provide stability for the legal government, and operates as loyal opposition when the government oversteps its bounds. What she suggests could have worked very well if the universe could be rolled back and events allowed to unfold differently.*

"But then, my love, we would never have met." Phelan kissed her hand. "Despite the power and position you give me in your scenario, I would not trade you for it."

She gave him a smile that told him he had been anticipated. "That I know as well, Khan Phelan Patrick Kell Ward of the Wolves. When I saw how much your parents love each other, what we have does not surprise me. In my scenario you would have been married off to one of Kai's sisters, I think, but *my* reality is her significant loss."

He laughed. "You have managed, in six days, to become quite conversant in Inner Sphere politics and the squabbling of the aristocracy."

"I did so out of self-defense. Though I think I like Katrina, she is most adept at interrogation at once subtle, polite, and thorough." Ranna shook her head. "I answered some of her questions, got her to answer some of mine, but mostly helped her get your sister, Captain Moran, and others to talk about themselves. I have no doubt she catalogued far more information than I did, but I know I gave her less than she wanted and much less than she actually thinks she knows.''

''Katrina *is* something. Victor is lucky to have her working with him instead of against him.'' Phelan's eyes narrowed. ''So, despite all that, what did you think of my home?''

''It is a wonderful place, magical even.'' She smiled, her eyes bright. ''I know the Kell Hounds are a military unit, but I see that they make room for so much more than we do. The garden, for example, is a place where the Kell Hound history lives. As your father said, destruction is much easier than creation. I know now, more than ever, why the Inner Sphere was able to oppose us as strongly as it did.''

''Good, I am happy you liked it.''

''Like it, I did.'' She turned his face to hers and kissed him on the lips. ''My love, I want you to know that if ever you should decide to return to the Kell Hounds, you would not have to travel alone.''

BOOK II

The Worst of Times

14

Tharkad
Federated Commonwealth
19 April 3055

Karl Kole, as the assassin had named himself on Tharkad, whistled softly as he strolled through Luvon Park. Passing the skating rink, where the happy laughter of children drowned out his tune, he ducked his chin into his scarf, more to keep out the winter cold than to hide his identity.

Karl Kole had no reason to hide. Karl Kole was no more remarkable than any other person who had come to Tharkad and found work at the Freya Florist Service. In fact, as Karl was rather vain, he often identified himself as a botanist instead of a florist. In reality he was nothing more than an assistant whose employer kept him on because of his strong back and ready smile and not because he ever intended to let Karl work with real flower arrangements.

Snow crunched beneath his boots as he continued his constitutional through the park. Most of the activity there was gathered around the rink and the small concession stand, but stippled tracks across broad expanses of snow also marked the passage of men and beasts. Though most people used the webwork of plowed walkways, some intrepid souls had braved the meter-tall drifts. Ahead of him two children were lying on their backs, working arms and legs up and down to leave angel-impressions in the snow.

Had he truly been Karl Kole, the cold would have made him return to the hoverbus stop and continue on home.

Because he was in reality an assassin, he did not have that luxury. Casually scanning the park he decided that no one would notice his slightly eccentric behavior. Just because Karl worked in an unheated warehouse didn't mean he could not appreciate the beauty of winter.

The morning's news packet on the computer had contained the appropriate advertisement in the Lost and Found section, and that had prompted his trip to the park. "Lost: Alsatian bitch answering to the name Lita. Two years old. Reward offered." He saw it, and though the message was not inventively worded, it contained the key phrases that told him more information would be waiting in one of his dead-drops.

His walk took him out toward the small gardener's kiosk near the edge of the woods that formed the park's eastern border. It had been shut up for the winter, and aside from one set of tracks leading to it from the walkway, the previous night's snowstorm had left the spot undisturbed. Karl Kole would have passed it without so much as a glance.

The assassin stepped over the snowdrift and walked around to the back of the small brick building. He dropped to his haunches and pulled a brick loose from the mortar down around the foundation, where the wind had whipped away the snow as it came around the corner. Behind the brick he found a small slip of paper, which he withdrew, then carefully slid the brick back into place.

The paper had been crumpled and dirtied to make it look like a mere scrap that had been discarded long ago. A jagged tear line showed where the upper left corner had been pulled off, carrying with it half the message. All that was left were two lines:

36-4
A7-22-7-K1H.

He memorized it, then tossed the paper into a waste receptacle.

Despite the inner urgency he felt, he strolled back through the park at the same leisurely pace as before. Haste makes waste, he reminded himself. And in his case, it would be him who got wasted, an outcome of this enterprise that he wanted to avoid at all costs.

Approaching the computerized city directory, he walked past at first, then stopped and turned back as if he had forgotten something. He stared off into space for a moment, then selected item thirty-six from the main menu. That brought up a screen showing the bus, train, aero, and space depots in the city. The fourth item on that menu was the Frederick Steiner Memorial train station.

Using his hoverbus transfer the assassin reached the Frederick Steiner station within an hour of having picked up the note. He passed through the vast lobby, pausing only once to let Karl admire the high, vaulted ceilings and the statuary mounted around the top of the walls. Heading through a small doorway, he veered off from the crowd moving down the escalator to the trains, and wandered back to the storage lockers.

He located locker A7 and punched in the combination 22-7-K1H. The little LED display above the keypad told him that he still owed 1.45 Kroner in storage charges. He pulled the coins from his pocket and fed in one Melissa, a Victor, and two Twycross Memorial coins. The display flashed the word "Open" in red, and he complied with the instruction.

Inside, as he expected, he found a small envelope containing a computer disk. That much he could tell by the feel. He tucked it into the inside breast pocket of his jacket, then headed back out into the cold.

Even though he could afford a taxi—for what he would make on this job, he could afford to buy every taxi on Tharkad—he waited for the hoverbus. It was already dark by the time he descended at the stop near his home to purchase a pound of coffee and a frozen dinner at a corner market. As was Karl's custom, he and the storeowner discussed the fate of Tharkad's Curling Team, then he left after agreeing to a five-Kroner bet.

Upon reaching his apartment, he put the frozen dinner in the microwave and started coffee brewing. Only then did he sit down with the envelope, slitting it open with a thumbnail and putting the disk into his computer. He flicked the machine on, and it booted from the new disk.

An interrogation box came up on the screen with a question mark and a flashing cursor. He typed in the name of the dog for which the reward had been offered, then double-checked the spelling before hitting the Enter key because an error would erase the key disk by writing a zero to every location on it. There was no recovery and no forgiveness for that sort of mistake.

The machine accepted his input and he returned to the kitchen. While he finished preparations for his dinner, the computer fed data from the boot program to another program that lurked invisibly on the computer's hard disk. That program, in turn, went out into the public-access system and downloaded the periodicals the smaller disk had instructed it to find.

It discarded half of them immediately. The rest it scanned, choosing certain words from appropriate pages and paragraphs. When all the words had been chosen, the computer discarded the rest of the magazines. A separate section of the hidden program took input from the key program and scrambled the chosen words. Having organized them, it presented them to the screen with a beep.

The assassin returned to the computer and looked at the message being displayed. Because the first word was five letters long, he ignored everything but the fifth word along in the message. Because that word was seven letters long, he looked for the seventh word following it. Because that word had a circumflex over the fourth letter, he looked up at the previous line and counted back four words from the end.

Slowly and laboriously he put together the true message. Once he had it, he punched a button on the computer that erased the key disk and blanked the message. The computer ejected the disk and the assassin snapped it in half before tossing it into the trash compactor.

He ran the message over in his mind. Two months until he was to hit his target. The manner of her death was left to his discretion, and collateral casualties were acceptable. He smiled because the method he had first selected would work perfectly, especially in the crowded place where he would have to take her.

The microwave dinged and Karl Kole smiled. The assassin inside him smiled as well.

In two months both Karl Kole and Melissa Steiner Davion would be dead.

Zhongshan
Federated Commonwealth
13 May 3055

Nelson Geist looked up as the Red Corsair entered the room he'd been assigned at the temporary raider base on Zhongshan. She wore an olive jumpsuit similar to the one draped over the foot of his bed. Even by the half-light coming through the open window, he could see the red stain already beginning to show near her left shoulder. He could also smell a cooling vest coolant leak.

Her eyes blazed. "How dare you!"

"Dare what?" He tore his blanket back, and despite being naked, stood to oppose her.

"You told people I ordered the diversion of foodstuffs to a ComStar hideout south of here."

"I did." Images of his grandsons hovered in the back of his mind. "The food you take feeds us slaves. That ComStar center was being converted into a home for orphans. I sent the food because we can't use all we have liberated here and you were going to put the rest to the torch."

The Red Corsair struck without warning. Her stinging backhanded slap knocked him back onto the bed. Lunging forward and straddling his chest, she pinned his arms to the bed with her knees. "I am the leader here. You are less than nothing. If you give orders in my name, they will be obeyed. If you give false orders in my name, you will be punished."

Nelson tasted salty-sweet blood from his split lip. "I

understand. Punish me, then, if you want. Make war with me, not children.''

''I do not make war on children,'' she spat out contemptuously. ''We have slain all the warriors worthy of the name on Zhongshan. I would have slain you if you had made the warrior's choice.'' She slapped him again. ''You are a freebirth nothing. I have ordered the orphanage razed.''

Fury pumped power into his muscles. His stomach knotted and he heaved upward. The Corsair leaned forward to use her weight to keep him pinned, but the movement allowed him to slip his right arm free instead. He struck out blindly at her head, but the blow missed, and he ended up driving his steel bracelet into the wound in her shoulder.

Coolant mixed with blood splashed up from the wound. The Corsair slid off his chest and fell back on the floor. She landed hard, with a thump, then lay there with her knees drawn up and her head lolling to the right.

Nelson sat up on the bed, then slid to his knees beside her. He reached up with blood-spattered fingers to snap on the bedside lamp, then tore open her jumpsuit and saw the hole in the cooling vest. A jagged piece of shrapnel had slashed open at least three coolant lines. The fluorescent yellow-green liquid oozed from the tubes and mixed with blood to become the color of a squished caterpillar.

''Stupid warrior.'' Nelson stripped the jumpsuit down to her waist and tied the sleeves around her like a belt. He unlaced the cooling vest and tossed it aside too. Then he tore a chunk of cloth from the sheets, using it to dab away at the wound. It looked fairly clean, but Nelson knew that told only part of the story. While coolant might keep a warrior alive in the cockpit, the stuff was only slightly less toxic than snake venom if taken internally.

He tore off another piece of cloth and wadded it into the wound. The Corsair moaned in pain, and he was half-tempted to make sure it was set in place very well, but he refrained. *She might not think of me as a warrior, but that's what I am. Torture is not part of the job—at least not for me.*

Lifting the Corsair up bodily, Nelson placed her carefully on the bed. Next he stepped quickly into his jumpsuit and boots, then wrapped her in his blanket and picked her up again. He carried her out to the elevator and down two floors to ground level at the Zhongshan Militia base. Back to the right and around the corner, and he reached the infirmary the raiders had appropriated.

A raider doctor looked up. ''What is this, now?''

''The Red Corsair. She took shrapnel in the shoulder.'' Nelson kicked an interior door open and laid her down on a paper-swathed examining table. ''She's been getting coolant in the wound. You'll want to wash it and start chelating agents to get rid of the coolant.''

The doctor, who had followed Nelson into the room, reached for a wallphone. ''I will have to inform Bryan that he is now in command.''

Nelson pulled the man forward with his good hand and shoved him around toward the table. ''I will call Bryan and give him the news. You just take care of her.''

Nelson wasn't surprised when a pair of armed guards came to escort him to the DropShip's infirmary. If she had come for him, Nelson knew that the Red Corsair would have shot him on the spot. He knew she'd never assign that job to anyone else; these two were probably called in just so she'd have somebody to haul his body away. When they came for him, he signed to Spider not to wait up for him, then followed the guards without comment.

The guards stopped at the door to the Red Corsair's private room. She looked up at the sound and nodded for Nelson to enter. He went in alone and the hatch closed behind him.

The Red Corsair looked haggard, the chelating agents having given her flesh a grayish cast. Nelson knew from practical experience that the drugs made the patient nauseous, which was a horrible way to endure the rigors of blasting away from a planet. Moreover, leaving a world under greater than one gravity's acceleration was tough even when a passenger was in the best of health.

Her eyes remained bright even though they had a tendency to linger in one place for too long. ''I trust you do not expect gratitude.''

''What I expect is immaterial.'' Nelson held his head

high and clasped his hands at the small of his back. "A brush with death has not changed you."

"A warrior would have left me to die." She glanced through the viewport and the world receding in it. "You could have been long gone and we would never have found you."

"I did not know, at the time, that the Wolf Clan had a unit on your trail or that they had arrived at the nadir jump point." Nelson kept his voice even and somewhat distracted. "Had I run, your people would have hunted me down on Zhongshan until they found me."

"Had you known you could have escaped, would you have taken that chance?"

"That is a hypothetical question. What's the point in worrying about it now? What is done is done."

She slammed her right fist into the bed. "No! It is not done." Her eyes burned with an angry light and tracked him carefully. "It's not a hypothetical question, Nelson, and I know the answer to it. The answer is no. You would never have left me there."

Is she right? He shook his head, as much in answer to his internal question as to contradict her statement. "Never is too absolute. I could have left you there."

"No." She remained adamant. "It is your weakness, you people of the Inner Sphere. You cling to the warped view that compassion toward the enemy makes you morally superior. If you cannot win by force of arms, you can claim a moral victory by doing something kind and sweet and honest for those who subjugate you. And you can atone for the savagery of your attack by having mercy on its survivors."

The speech left her breathless, but Nelson said nothing to fill the void. The words rang true to him. Compassion to the vanquished and the weak was lauded as a traditional value. Even the fierce martial society of the Draconis Combine held that the wise man could balance *ninjo* and *giri,* compassion and duty. The Federated Commonwealth clung to the same ideals in the twin facets of medieval chivalry embodied by King Arthur, Frederick the Great, and other heroes from millennia before.

It struck him that while the militaristic traditions of the Inner Sphere sought to balance these two concepts, the Clans had stripped away compassion in their drive to create the perfect soldiers. Ultimately, Nelson acknowledged, a warrior who could kill quickly and without remorse would be superior. He would also become a nihilistic machine that killed and killed until he was stopped or until he had reduced everything to anarchy and death.

He realized that this singleness of purpose was what had attracted him to the Red Corsair and also what made her repulsive. By abandoning compassion perhaps she showed him what he might have become had destiny not maimed him, had he never been forced to hold back. She was at the pinnacle of what he had once hoped to achieve when dreaming of glory as a warrior. He thought he had grown beyond those dreams, maturing along with his understanding of compassion, but someone inside of him—the hunter, the *stalker*—hungered for release.

Yet Nelson feared that release. He hated the lack of control and was afraid that he would fail and die. He also feared what he would do in the throes of a killing frenzy. War was brutal enough without any brakes on the savagery. Because he feared the hunter within himself, it repelled him to see his secret desires reflected in the Red Corsair's eyes.

Her voice returned in a harsh croak. "Bryan reported to me that he successfully countermanded my order to have the orphanage destroyed. He commended you on your diligence in passing my final order on to him."

Nelson managed to keep the smile off his face.

The Red Corsair pushed herself higher up in the bed. "I have not told him that you duped him. If I did, he would demand your death in a Circle of Equals. I will not allow that."

"Afraid Bryan would die?"

She laughed hoarsely. "Success makes you cocky, Nelson. No, Bryan would rip your heart out and let it drip blood into your eyes as you died." She closed her eyes and smiled in pleasure at the prospect. "But you have given me a tool to use against Bryan, and you are the sop I can throw him if I need to deflect him."

"That explains why he will not get to fight me." Nelson watched her closely. "Now why will I not get to fight him?"

"Because you would like to die to escape me, *quiaff?*"

She paused and caught her breath. "You saved me so I would be in your debt, then you disobeyed me so I would have you destroyed. I can read you too well, Nelson."

"You assign me motives you would like to see in yourself." Nelson shook his head. "I saved you for the same reason I countermanded your order. When a warrior takes life, it is to prevent an even greater number from losing theirs. You may live for war, but I live to guard against the necessity of war."

"Did you think to educate me by saving me?"

"No, for I did not think at all. You were wounded and could have died. I acted to deny death another victory." He looked down. "I acted because I did not want to see you die."

Her smiled broadened in a most disquieting manner. "You will think better of such impulses in the future, I believe."

Though she tried to put her words coldly, Nelson heard a hesitation that he could not put down to fatigue. He looked up and caught her watching him. In an instant he knew what she was thinking and it gave him a glimmering of a future he did not like at all.

She is as much intrigued with my ability to be compassionate as I am with her capacity to be utterly ruthless. We are matter and anti-matter locked in a spiral course down a gravity well. Things will move faster and faster until we come together and mutually annihilate each other.

"You don't own me." Nelson hardened his eyes. "You never will."

"I've owned you from the first moment we saw each other." Her eyes focused distantly. "We are soul-mirrors, Nelson Geist. In one another we will each live out our destinies and greet our fates."

DropShip Barbarossa, *Zenith Recharging Station*
Garrison
Federated Commonwealth
17 May 3055

Victor watched the screen as the Clan *Masakari* came in at his *Prometheus*. He winced—which he told himself was better than flinching—as the image shook and his 'Mech went down. *Ranna is not even Bloodnamed yet. The Wolf Clan is nastier than all hell.*

Galen paused at the hatchway and rapped on the bulkhead. "You will want to see this, sir." He held up a holodisk and its mirrored surface split the light into rainbow fragments. ComStar got some homemade h-vid off Zhongshan. Besides, you'll go blind if you watch those battle ROMs anymore."

"Wouldn't do any good. I'd still see Ranna coming after me in my dreams." Victor punched the Eject button and the holovid disk made from the battle ROMs on Arc-Royal came out. He slipped it back into a protective sleeve while Galen put the next one into the viewer.

"I don't think I'd mind too much having Ranna come after me in *my* dreams, but we're probably not working from the same basic premises, Leftenant-General." Galen hit the Play button. "ComStar here on Garrison sent this our way because they thought you'd want to see it. Their people shot most of it, but it's unedited and a bit rough."

The gray static on the screen melted away into a black scene lit only by a view of distant fires burning in a town. Flames guttered up through window casements, and white streaks of tracer rounds shot into the hills from out of the darkness of the town. Most died on the way, but a few hit something that made them ricochet into the sky.

The return fire was devastating. Beams, both PPCs and lasers, answered the light autocannon fire. Lancing indiscriminately through the town, the beams touched off strobing explosions whose light showed buildings melting. Big fireballs launched themselves into the sky, and yet more houses and shops were set ablaze.

Victor glanced at Galen. "Not too concerned about keeping the fighting away from noncombatants, are they?"

"No, sir. It looks like they hammered a militia unit in the field, then closed on the town of Nyrere somewhat quickly. Scattered resistance incited this sort of pounding."

The scene shifted to morning. A thick gray mist hung over the town, as viewed from the heights where the fighting had been recorded the night before. Leaking smoke, fire-blackened buildings stuck up out of the dirty fog like weathered gravestones. Except for the seemingly random movements of five BattleMechs patrolling the streets, the entire town looked dead.

Another shift and the recorder appeared to be in the middle of the city. Victor could tell from the shadows and the white ball the sun projected on the fog that a goodly chunk of time had passed since the camera had last showed the town. Now the camera was on the ground, moving through the ruins, showing images that confirmed the earlier graveyard scene.

Victor had a hard time believing that so small a town could produce so much rubble. Torn and bloated bodies clogged the streets. Water geysered up out of shattered fire hydrants, and lakes formed where bodies choked off the sewer outlets. Dogs ran in packs through the streets, while frightened-looking people sat dazed on stoops with no buildings. Others picked through rubble and repeatedly called the names of those they must have believed trapped within.

The scene shifted to another broken city, and Victor turned to Galen. "Looks like the bandits did on Zhongshan what they did on Pasig and Kooken's Pleasure Pit."

"Yes, but not as bad. They left prematurely and only

took foodstuffs and some other basic supplies. The water purification plant had a six-month supply of spare parts laying around. Stuff worth millions, but the bandits didn't touch it. They didn't even take time to loot the World Treasury Archives.''

The Prince shrugged. ''Would it have mattered? The stuff they took from the Pit and Pasig was junk. Pasig reported that the bandits looted a display of counterfeit works, labeled as such.''

''I'm not an art critic, sir.''

Victor smiled. ''So why do you think they headed out early?''

''ComStar reported that the Thirty-first Wolf Solahma arrived in the system on the thirteenth. That was three days into the attack and a day after the first footage. The Clan troops beamed a challenge directly to the raiders, which ComStar monitored. It seemed to be a straight challenge, but the raiders decided not to fight.''

The Prince raised his left eyebrow. ''That's a good sign.''

''Yes and no.'' Galen pointed to the footage playing across the screen at that moment. ''This may have been the reason. It looks like the Red Corsair got hit.''

The holovid showed a woman with long red hair being carried on a stretcher to a DropShip. An obvious member of the Corsairs held the stretcher at her feet, but a man dressed in an olive jumpsuit was holding the other end. He lifted the stretcher up into the DropShip, and Galen froze the frame on him as he turned away from it.

''This guy here is a real enigma.'' He tapped the screen at the man's right wrist. ''He has a steel band, which ComStar estimates is the pirate equivalent of a bondcord. It confirms the suspicion that a significant number of them are Clan renegades.''

''Okay, they're taking bondsmen or slaves. What's so enigmatic about that?''

''Well, ComStar identified this guy as the one who gave the orders that a shipment of food be diverted to one of ComStar's orphan relief centers. A bondsman doesn't give orders, much less have them obeyed, unless he works for someone very important. After putting the Red Corsair on the DropShip, this guy got out a message to the local ComStar rep to move that center fast because it had been ordered destroyed. He said he had bought them some time, but couldn't be sure the order wouldn't be reinstated.''

"Was it?''

"Not as of the time the raiders left.''

Victor stared at the man's face. "Any ID on him?''

Galen nodded. "I looked through the pictures of the folks listed missing after Kooken's and Pasig. He looks like Nelson Geist, who was maimed on Wotan four or so years ago. He recovered on Kooken's Pleasure Pit and joined their militia. He was reported missing after the raiders hit there.''

"Geist.'' Victor looked down. "Was this guy any relation to Jon Geist? Jon died on Teniente.''

"Yes, sir. Jon was Nelson's son.''

The Prince shook his head. "There's no way a man like Nelson Geist could be working with the raiders, is there? The Clans maimed him, they killed his son, the raiders attacked his home.''

Galen shifted his shoulders uneasily. "On one hand, given the number of Clanners we suspect to be raiders, I would say no to your question. On the other hand, though . . .''

"What?''

"Well, sir, I'd have been the last person to suggest someone like Prince Ragnar would go over to the enemy, much less Phelan Kell.''

Victor felt his stomach begin to knot up. "I see your point. This Geist lost a lot to the Clans. Maybe his spirit was broken.''

"And if it didn't happen like that, there'd be other ways to accomplish the same thing.'' Galen started the holovid moving again. "It could be that he resented his maiming and the loss of his son and somehow blamed his troubles on you and the Federated Commonwealth. Many of those who fled the Tamar Pact worlds resettled on Kooken's Pleasure Pit, so there would be plenty of people there to help nurture such a view.''

"It's unfortunate, but what you're saying makes sense.'' Victor watched Geist walk back toward the building from which the Red Corsair had been carried. "I still don't know if I buy his working with them, though. His action with ComStar shows he has some feeling for the refugees displaced by the fighting.''

"There's not a soldier in the Revenants who would make war on children, Highness.''

"Point. So, worst case, we have a man with considerable experience in the Inner Sphere military who has the ear of the Red Corsair.''

"Right.'' Galen nodded solemnly. "And, best case, we have an experienced warrior watching how the Red Corsair works.''

"No, the best case is that he'll get fed up and kill her.'' Victor rubbed a hand over his jaw. "The Wolf Clan didn't even engage them with aerospace fighters as the raiders left?''

"Not possible. The Wolves came in at the nadir jump point because it had a recharge station. The raiders had come in at a pirate point above the plane of the elliptic and another day beyond the planet for the Wolves. At best they could have chased after them and possibly inflicted some damage, but that would have involved sending DropShips out at three gravities and not recovering them for two more weeks. The fact that the Solahma bid away their fighters really hurt them in this situation.''

Victor studied another combat sequence shot from far above a battlefield. The raiders obviously controlled the battle and forced the militia back with ease. Still, as Victor watched it, he saw the raiders make some mistakes. *You're good, but you're not invincible.*

"Galen, you've been reviewing the information we've gotten from Kooken's Pleasure Pit, Pasig, and now Zhongshan. What's your guess on these raiders? Could the Revenants take them?''

Galen sat back and sank deeply into the thickly padded chair. "That's a hard call. The raiders rely heavily on beam and energy weapons. That means they can hang on for a long time in a campaign. Of course a long campaign is the last thing they want when they're so far from their home base and when we're in such a good position to bring heavy numbers of troops against them. Still, it means they aren't tied to supplies the way we can be.''

"So, are they using OmniMechs?''

"Not that I can see. It looks as if they're just using refits of our Inner Sphere designs. But they do employ

Clan-type technology. The Kell Hounds have some similar 'Mechs built out of salvage from Luthien. That gives them some added punch *and* makes them look deceptively soft. Even so, we're fighting close to even on that account.''

Victor frowned. "As always, they have the advantage because they know where they're going to hit. The lithium-fusion batteries in our JumpShips give us increased mobility, which lets us jump in on them from a long range. But if we jump in when they arrive, they might be able to jump right out again.''

"And if we wait until they commit to an attack, we find ourselves in the same position as the Wolves did.''

"Right." Victor pounded his fist against his leg. That hurt and he stared at his offending hand. "Someday I will learn.''

"Yes, Leftenant-General.''

Victor ignored Galen's sarcasm. "It seems rather obvious that one unit alone isn't going to be able to catch these bandits. If we deployed the Revenants forward, we could coordinate with the Wolves and catch them.''

Galen shook his head. "I think that assessment is premature. The Wolves *did* manage to find the bandits, and forced them away from Zhongshan. Another two days or a little more piloting intelligence and they could have had them.''

"You don't think I should bring the Revenants up?''

"It's not that at all, Victor. Yes, get us into position to help out, but we have more than military considerations here, don't we? Didn't Phelan tell you that the Jade Falcons are just waiting for the ilKhan to fall flat on his face in this? If we use one of our units to destroy the bandits, we flaunt his help. If, God help us, we have to chase them back into Jade Falcon territory, it could serve as a rallying call to unite the Clans against us again. The ilKhan would be forced to side with them against us, too. Boom, we've got full-scale war once more.''

"As always, you tend to think a bit more about the auxiliary concerns than I do. Thank you, Galen.''

"My pleasure and duty.''

Victor sat back and pressed his hands together, fingertip to fingertip. "I think we need to learn as much as we can about the bandits. Let's run some computer sims between their apparent strength and that of the Revenants.''

Galen stood and nodded. ''Works for me. Anything else?''

''Yes.'' Victor chewed his lower lip. ''Get me a file on Nelson Geist. If he's close to the Red Corsair, I want to know how he thinks and what makes him tick. If he's still loyal to the Federated Commonwealth, we can use him. And if he isn't, we'll know who to notify when we kill him.''

=== 17 ===

Christian Kell gladly accepted the snifter of brandy from Dan Allard. He raised his glass to his commanding officer. "The Kell Hounds are operational once again."

"May they always remain so." Dan tossed off the amber liquid and Chris followed suit. It burned its way down to his stomach, but after two weeks in the field, it felt good.

Dan dropped himself into one of the briefing room chairs and put his feet up on the table. Watching him, Chris decided that Dan looked the way he felt. Both men were worn out. After the transfer of the regimental cadres back from garrison duty on Tomans, there had been a full week of integrating the new trainees into their units and then two weeks of exercises and war games. Even so, pleasure at the unit's successful showings took the edge off their fatigue.

"I was especially pleased with the way Akira's Second and Third Battalions were able to configure themselves like the raiders that hit Zhongshan." Dan clasped his hands over his chest. "We handled them fairly effectively, don't you think? Your battalion flanked them perfectly and we nailed the lot."

Chris appropriated the chair across from him. "We had a lot of practice against Clan tactics on Luthien. Yes, we did handle them well, but we also outnumbered them two-to-one. Granted, they were using Clan equipment, but in many cases so were we."

Colonel Allard frowned. "What is it, Chris? That exercise went by the book—hell, it was better than that."

The younger man shrugged. "Intangibles, Dan. There is too much we don't know about the raiders. Our exercise was based on their latest attacks, and though Zhongshan didn't show us anything they hadn't done before, their withdrawal in the face of the Solahma's sudden appearance was damned orderly and organized."

"More so than you would expect from a band of renegades?"

"I think so, yes." Chris rested his forearms on the table. "For bandits, their equipment is way too good. And the way they attack, it's all wrong."

"What do you mean?"

Chris' face twisted into a frown as he tried to find words to express his thoughts. "Raiders usually pick LZs that are sparsely defended so that they can get away with as much loot as possible. They try to avoid direct confrontation because they're generally using second-rate equipment and running low on supplies. These raiders go straight for their targets, and straight at any forces standing between them and their objective. They fight in an organized manner and are able to withdraw in good order."

Dan tapped one index finger against his lips for a moment. "You're suggesting that they fight like a military unit. I buy that, but the explanation is nothing more sinister than that they're Clan renegades."

"Maybe, Dan, it just may be." Chris balled his hands into fists, then forced himself to open them again. Though Dan's explanation made perfect and logical sense, it still did not feel right. Chris understood the value of empirical evidence and logic, but he also knew that his survival had depended on his responding to gut feelings in many a tight situation. Concerning the raiders, his guts were telling him something just wasn't right.

"Besides, Chris, it doesn't matter what their motive is. What *is* important is that we nailed them." Dan smiled slyly. "Now that the Wolves missed their shot at them on Zhongshan, the Archon will be pressured into sending another unit out there. I'll send a message to Morgan that we're ready, and he can let that slip to Melissa when he sees her at the library dedication next month.''

"It won't happen, Dan. We're not 'politically correct.' ''

"Meaning?''

"Meaning that Ryan Steiner will use his influence to make sure it's one of the old Tamar or Skye loyalist units that gets activated to hunt down the raiders.''

Dan laughed lightly. "I think you have Ryan Steiner on the brain, Chris. The local constabulary still has no solid evidence that Ragnarok was or is backed by Ryan.''

Chris stood and folded his arms across his chest. "They'll find it, Dan, because Ryan is not all that bright. Face it. Ragnarok has his prints all over it. Most of the Rasalhague refugees have fled to worlds well away from the border, into areas like the Donegal March here that were formerly immune to his influences. For a miniscule amount of money he manages to build up a great deal of support.

"When Ragnar showed up with Phelan, Ryan's people must have been overjoyed. I suspect we were being watched in hopes there'd be some incident involving the Clanners that could be used against the Hounds or to embarrass Victor. When I was foolish enough to bring Ragnar into the city, they decided to snatch him.''

Dan stared off past Chris, then nodded. "As you said before, Ryan could have traded Ragnar to the Free Rasalhague Republic in exchange for recognition of the right of the Tamar Pact worlds to remain together. Ceding them would cost Prince Haakon nothing because the Jade Falcons have captured almost all the Tamar worlds from both sides anyway.''

"And that move would build up all sorts of good will for Ryan. Liberating Ragnar would make the Rasalhagians happy, and it would win him support here from the forces that believe the ceasefire was a bad move.'' Chris shook his head. "Ryan can muster enough support to force Melissa to use his choice of units to fight the bandits.''

Dan smiled broadly and leaned forward. "But can Ryan gainsay Victor a shot at the bandits? If Ryan presses Melissa for action, she can trump him by sending Victor and the Revenants.''

"Victor is game and will want to go, but would she be willing to risk him? The Prince is not terribly popular within Ryan's sphere of influence. If Hanse Davion were calling the shots, Victor would be the point man, but Melissa is not that vindictive." Chris smiled. "Best case would be to send Katrina. She would charm the bandits and talk them into becoming a House unit."

He pressed his lips together, then looked up at his commanding officer. "What is your read on the Thirty-first Wolf Solahma?"

Dan shook his head. "Don't really know, Chris. They were unlucky and the bandits escaped. What's the matter?"

"I don't know, really. It's just that I heard they jumped out of Zhongshan without recharging or accepting a charge from the charging station there."

"So?"

"So if they had another charge in their lithium-fusion batteries, why didn't they jump out to the pirate point, then disable the bandit JumpShip and trap the bandits?"

"Good question." Dan watched Chris closely. "Does your suspicion of the Wolves extend beyond this incident, or is it isolated?"

Dan's question made Chris stop. During the whole time Phelan had been on Arc-Royal, Chris had found him cordial but never really open. Chris realized he had never taken Phelan aside to ask if they had a problem, yet he could have cited a dozen little things that suggested that there was. Phelan had not invited Chris to fight with his Star in the game. Choosing Mark *had* helped Mark's attitude toward Phelan and the Clans, but Chris wondered if it was also because Phelan thought him less important than a nephew.

Even as he framed that question in his mind, he was able to come up with a dozen different and valid answers to it. He also remembered the very enjoyable time he had spent in Evantha's company. It occurred to him that he was letting whatever difficulties he had with Phelan bleed over into how he thought about the Clans.

Chris pulled the sleeves on his tunic up to the elbows, revealing a portion of a brilliantly colored tattoo on his left arm. "Perhaps my growing up within the yakuza culture of the Draconis Combine makes me overly suspicious. And it is equally possible that my feelings of discomfort and mistrust of Phelan color the way I see the Clans. Though I do realize the ilKhan has risked much by sending a unit into the Federated Commonwealth to hunt these bandits down, the lack of action by the Wolves still looks pretty curious.''

Dan frowned. ''You've got no reason to be suspicious about Phelan.''

''Don't I? Am I not in his place within the Kell Hound infrastructure?''

''You may see it that way, but I doubt he does,'' Dan said. ''I don't know what or where Phelan would be if he had stayed with the Kell Hounds, but I can bet it wouldn't be as a major leading a battalion. If he *was* in that sort of position, he would be the head of an independent action unit, like the Black Widows way back when with Wolf's Dragoons. He's a good warrior, and even has a solid grasp of strategy, but he's a wild card. He's unpredictable, which makes him hell on the other side, but also gets the ulcers burning when you're on *his* side.''

Chris acknowledged the wisdom of Dan's words with a nod, but still raised a protest. ''That could be, Dan, but I've always wondered if he accepted me as a Kell. I know that must sound odd to you, but there is no way to explain it otherwise.''

Dan got up and poured each of them another brandy. ''Let me tell you a story, Chris. A long time ago—well, about the time you were born, actually—my brother Justin left the service of the Federated Suns. He started working for Maximilian Liao, and I saw him at Hanse Davion's wedding. He introduced me to Candace as 'the son of the man who *was* my father.' That was a shot to the gut if there ever was one. Last I'd known, we were still brothers.''

Chris sipped the brandy. ''But at that time Justin was a deep agent working for Hanse Davion and your father.''

''Right. Two nights later Justin killed an assassin who was gunning for our father.''

Chris narrowed his eyes. ''I'm missing your point.''

''It's an old saw, Chris: actions speak louder than

words. Has Phelan ever been anything but friendly to you?"

"I wouldn't call it friendly, but he's been polite."

"Considering the two of you never got to know each other, that's not bad." Dan smiled and sipped some brandy. "You're wondering why he hasn't tried to clear the air between you. Well, how would he act if he didn't feel there was a problem to be cleared up?"

Chris chuckled lightly at himself. "Touché, Colonel. Where I grew up, polite manners hid all sorts of ugly emotions. I suppose I attribute malice where none exists."

"There you go." Dan nodded. "But your original point is well-taken. Believing that nothing is odd with the Thirty-first Wolf Solahma just because we trust Phelan is like assuming that Ryan Steiner is benign just because we trust Victor."

"*Hai!*" Chris swirled the brandy around in his snifter. "So, given all this discussion of politics, are we still going ahead with our deployment plan? Ryan won't like it at all."

Dan shrugged. "It will give him something else to worry about, which may distract his attention enough to frustrate the rest of his plans. We go ahead. Everyone gets two weeks' R and R here on Arc-Royal, then we head out for Deia and give Zimmer's Zouaves a break."

18

DropShip Tigress
D2342.221G
Federated Commonwealth
15 June 3055

Nelson Geist kept his hands on the treadmill's railing despite the desire to tug at the collar surrounding his neck. The heavy goggles he wore made it seem like he was standing in a fully dimensional world, while the earphones brought the sounds of that reality to him. In the artificial world, even the treadmill's handrail appeared as the edge of an old man's walker.

Nelson knew the computer construct was not real. The graphics, though close to perfect, failed from time to time as the program ran through rough patches. The aesthetics of the world it created were not important to him, and he was certain the Red Corsair had forced her technicians to load in anomalies to distract him.

The speed with which she'd recovered from her wound surprised him. Sooner than he would have thought possible or even prudent, she had used the simulators on the ship to prove she could still pilot a 'Mech. Shortly thereafter Bryan challenged her to a fight in a Circle of Equals and she gladly accepted the challenge.

She had allowed Nelson to watch the fight, and seeing her square off against Bryan made him fully realize just how close to death she had been on Zhongshan. Wearing a green leotard that covered her from throat to groin but that left her arms and legs bare, she engaged Bryan in a bout of unarmed combat. He out-massed her by at least ten kilos, but her speed and length of limb gave her all the edge she needed to defeat him.

As Nelson had expected, Bryan came in at her from the left, aiming a kick at her head that she had to parry using what should have been her weak arm. She dropped beneath the kick, then lashed out with her left leg, catching Bryan's left foot with a solid blow that knocked him over.

Bryan scissored his legs through where she had been crouching, but she leaped up above his feet. She landed on one leg, then spun around, her left foot clipping Bryan hard above his left eye. The blow split the skin and dropped him to the deck hard.

It took the Red Corsair about a half-second to see that Bryan was dazed and all but out of the fight. She pounced on him, pinning him to the deck the way she had pinned Nelson barely two weeks before. Bryan instinctively tried to heave her off, but he could not. She glanced over at Nelson, as if to say "this could have been you," then administered the *coup de grace* with her left hand.

If he had imagined she would feel any jubilation at her victory, the Red Corsair quickly disabused him of the notion. "It's your fault I had to go through that, you know," she told him as two raiders carried the unconscious Bryan off to the sick bay.

"And you showed compassion by not killing him." Nelson gave her a smile that he knew would further kindle her anger.

"That was a practical consideration. Bryan is my second-in-command and only did what any other responsible officer would have done in his place." She grabbed his jumpsuit front and bunched the material up under his chin with her fist. "Now it is time for you, a slave, to learn what you will be doing for the rest of your life."

She hauled him off to a cabin that adjoined hers. Aside from the treadmill and some equipment lockers, it was featureless. For a moment Nelson thought it might have been a private gymnasium for her, but he had never known her to use anything but the communal facilities on Deck Twelve.

She fitted him with the goggles and gloves, and stuck little electrodes on his knees, ankles, elbows, and shoulders. "These will allow the computer to track you and determine where you are and how you are standing."

He turned toward her voice because the goggles turned his world into a sphere of static. "Why?"

"Why?" He heard her laugh heartily. "Because, slave, you will learn your duties. I have decided that when I return from this mission it is time for me to have children. I have also decided that you will care for them." He felt her hand start at his knee and slowly begin to caress its way up to his groin. "Perhaps I will even let you father them."

That prospect shot a jolt through him and she laughed. "Perhaps I will *make* you father them."

The edge in her voice got to him and elicited a shudder that seemed to satisfy her. Nelson said nothing and told himself it was to deny her the satisfaction of hearing his protests. Deep down, though, he knew that part of him wanted her desperately.

As much as he wished to deny his attraction to her, he could not. Every time he tried to push it way, it came back, stronger and stronger. It fed on his denial. He found himself thinking about her, fantasizing about her, and all the multiplication tables in the world couldn't snuff out his ardor.

He felt her fasten something around his throat. It felt heavy at the front and had two cool spots where it pressed against the flesh over his Adam's apple. She tightened it and he felt the thing snap shut at the back of his neck.

"This exercise will be simple, Nelson. You will see a clock and a schedule in a corner of the world the computer will create for you. You must get to the appropriate places at the correct time or you will be disciplined."

A small shock trickled through the electrodes on his throat. It hurt, but not enough to incapacitate him. "That is the mildest shock the system offers. If you do your work well, you will never feel even that much. Make a mistake, and depending on how bad it is, you will hurt a great deal."

The twin monitors in front of his eyes stopped displaying static and instead filled his sight with a world of walls and floors. Off to his left sunlight poured reddish glory through a window. Straight ahead he saw one corridor extending the length of the building. To the right he saw a door to the exterior. He moved toward it, and as he raised his hand to where the doorknob seemed to hang in space, he felt a jolt at his throat.

"You may be allowed out later, if you are good. For now, do what is on the schedule."

"Where am I?"

"Where are you?" The Red Corsair laughed airily. "This is a construct of my true home, Nelson. It is the place where you will spend the rest of your life."

The virtual world became a game for the two of them as the environment became more and more complex over the next two weeks. Nelson had two sessions per day, each lasting six hours realtime. That would comprise a whole day in the computer world, with an hour passing every fifteen minutes. As he became proficient with the system, the Red Corsair started giving him more complicated assignments.

For the first four sessions he had been alone in the computer world, but after that, new and interesting people and creatures started to show up. Nelson suspected that idle crew members were being invited to program little distractions into the world for him while everyone waited for the ship's jump drive to fully recharge its coils and for the JumpShip's lithium-fusion batteries to load up.

At first the other creatures bothered him, but he quickly became able to discriminate between what the Red Corsair was making him do and what the others did to interfere with him. It was not that the others had a trademark that allowed him to distinguish between them or discover who the realworld author was. Instead he found that their simulation tricks lacked one key element that was the trademark of the Red Corsair's work.

What she did was always cruel. He remembered very well the first time the assignment "Tend the children" had showed up on his schedule. He searched all over the base for a nursery. The shocks to his throat, building in intensity and duration the further he got from the children, helped herd him back toward the Red Corsair's private domain. Finally, when he searched the house, he found a new addition to it that was jam-packed with tiny children.

Most of them had a surreal quality because they were constructed from spheres and cones and other easily generated geometrical shapes. They looked more like toys come to life than real children. Yet whenever he came close and focused on one, the child changed from the awkward and ridiculous construct to a wriggling, crying child.

Worse yet, when the computer resolved the child in such exquisite detail, he would recognize the child. This one would have the Red Corsair's hair, or her eyes or nose, and it would always have some part of him there as well. He tried to draw away from those children, but when he did the shocks drove him to his knees. If he refused to move his hands in caring and careful ways, more shocks would follow, fast and painful.

He hated the part of him that could look at those children through the haze of pain and still find them beautiful.

He forced himself to settle into a routine that would make the Red Corsair work as hard as he did at the game. He learned shortcuts that allowed him to accomplish his tasks quickly. He moved through the base like a guided missile, always seeking out a new and faster way to get somewhere. He explored for unlikely connections between buildings, and used them like tunnels and skyways when he found them.

At night, when the evening's tasks were behind him, he would spend time outside the home. He watched the night sky and smiled when the program shot meteors through the world's atmosphere. He did not recognize any of the constellations, so he started grouping them into his own little mythology. He named one after his son Jon and a pair of twin stars after his grandsons. Dorete didn't rate a constellation, but the Red Corsair did.

He called it "The Witch," and made it the first one the sun would eat up in the morning.

Of late the Red Corsair had taken to blocking off his skyways and tunnels. This added time to his cross-base runs, but he didn't mind, despite the shocks. As he moved through the base, searching out new shortcuts, he found certain places where he was not allowed access. On the off-chance that his ability to enter them was time-dependent, he tried again and again at different points during the simulated day.

Nelson steeled himself for the shock as he turned left down a corridor in the basement of the base's main building. The time was close to twenty-three hundred hours, which made this the latest foray he had ever attempted on this particular area.

No shock accompanied his first step into the area. He smiled. He took another step and another down it. The red doors at the far end loomed closer. He reached out to push them open and at his touch they flew back.

The jolt that hit him in the throat staggered him. The treadmill whipped his feet away and his chin smacked into the padded crossbar. He flopped to the ground and the treadmill's belt whipped him back, dumping him on the floor in a shaking heap.

He heard her sure tread on the decking, followed by a click and the death of the treadmill's hum. Still unable to move, he felt her kneel next to him and pull the goggles off. The artificial hallway was whisked away, and his eyes took a second or two to focus on her face. He blinked once, but in the time it took him to do that, the look of concern he thought he had seen on her face had vanished.

"There are places you are not supposed to go, Nelson. I trust that was a lesson to you." She propped his head up on her arm and unfastened the shock collar. "It might have seemed brutal, but were we actually there, you would have been shot dead." Her voice grew distant. "I did that for your own good."

He tried to reply, but his voice would still not work. She pressed a finger to his lips. "Do not even try to speak." She reached down and pulled the datagloves off his hands. "It will take you a few minutes to recover."

She sat back on her haunches and Nelson noticed for the first time that she was wearing the same robe she had donned the first time he had met her. "You have made this quite a game, Nelson. You have done very well. You have mastered the distractions and overcome the obstacles we have thrown at you. I am pleased with your progress."

Nelson nodded to her and found his head and neck actually worked. He flexed his fingers and toes, and though they still tingled a bit, they responded to his commands. His arms and legs felt leaden, but they showed signs of returning use.

She took his right hand in hers and he could feel warmth flowing from her flesh to his. "In fact, so pleased am I with your performance, I thought I would reward you." Her glance darted toward the doorway into her cabin. "You perform so well to avoid pain, I thought I would see what you will do for pleasure."

He rolled over onto his right side. "Why torture yourself?" he croaked out.

"Torture myself? Hardly." She smiled hungrily at him. "I am rewarded for training you so quickly and so well and . . ."

"And?"

She stood and pulled him to his feet. She steadied him and helped him walk toward her cabin. "And tomorrow we jump into Deia. On the eve of what I expect to be a confrontation with the Wolves, I do not choose to sleep alone."

Tharkad
Federated Commonwealth
19 June 3055

The day Melissa Steiner-Davion was to die dawned like all others for Karl Kole. He chose a breakfast pack from his freezer and tossed it into the microwave. The assassin looked at the box he had chosen and smiled because it was pancakes with sausage, one of Karl's favorites.

After breakfast he turned his computer on and scanned the headers on the newsfax, then took a shower. He conserved on water, despite knowing he would never have to pay the bill. As usual he hung his wet towel on the bathroom door. Dressing in jeans and T-shirt, he bundled up in a parka and pulled a watch cap onto his head to protect himself against the cold.

Leaving his computer on, Karl carefully locked his apartment, then left the building at the usual time and caught his normal bus. Seated there, his breath steaming the air, he nodded to the other regulars. Most ignored him, but one old lady smiled. Karl returned her smile and sat back.

The ride to Freya, as per usual, passed quickly and uneventfully.

Mr. Crippen's heightened state of agitation was no surprise, but Karl had not expected his boss to be waiting for him at the door. "Where have you been, Karl? Have you forgotten what day this is?"

"No, sir, I haven't." Karl smiled innocently. "I left the house so quickly I didn't even bring a lunch. Sir."

Crippen patted sweat from his bald head despite the chill in the air. "Well, do this correctly and I will buy you lunch. You have the most important job in preparing for this banquet, you know. You need to repot four *mycosia pseudoflora* and make sure they are in place at the reception center by noon."

"Yes, sir. I'll do a good job, sir."

Crippen angrily waved him away. "Then get to it, man."

Karl Kole nodded and made his way into the warehouse. He headed further back than he might normally, but the rest of the staff had become used to his idle explorations of the warehouse. Besides, everyone was busy trying to turn out a hundred centerpieces for the Frederick Steiner Memorial Library banquet. If anyone had actually had the time to notice him, they would have ignored him.

When he got way to the back, where old goods and broken pots were shoved, the assassin knelt down. He took a careful look around the area and decided no one had disturbed it. Moving aside an old advertising sign, he pulled out a box with four rubber-sealed ceramic flower pots. Carrying them as if they were no more important than any others in the building, the assassin became Karl again and went directly to his workbench.

Melissa Steiner-Davion's security people were very good. From the moment he'd decided to take the job of killing her, he'd begun to study films of her. Her bodyguards insulated her so well from people that only a madman could ever get close enough to kill her. Those opportunities only occurred when Melissa plunged into crowds to greet her subjects, but such forays were rare and random. Shooting her from pointblank range would be a way to kill her, but it was also a way to get caught, so he had rejected it instantly.

A long-range sniper-shot might have worked, but, again, Melissa's security people made that difficult. They covered the high points around any public appearance she was to make. Her routes of travel were never publicized beforehand. And if there was any rumor about where she would be and how she would arrive, her security changed the plans at the last minute. There was no way to count on a window of opportunity to shoot her.

The Archon's security forces knew that the one thing that could kill her was predictability. If she developed any sort of routine, she could be assassinated. The only events they allowed her to commit to in advance were those where she would be surrounded by a low-risk audience in a venue they could control.

The dedication banquet was such an event. All the people invited were royalty—of blood, the arts, or industry—and all could be checked out well in advance. Everyone would be screened for weapons at the door and the room itself would be swept for explosives and lurking murderers several times before the banquet took place.

At first, in studying Melissa, the assassin almost thought the job called for a suicide attacker, but he was not one of those and did not like working with that kind of fanatic. He saw no pattern in how she traveled, what she ate, or where she spent her time. She looked as impossible to kill as rumors about an impending Clan assault on Tharkad.

Then, in watching a documentary about her life, he found the key. He began to make notes, double-checking sources and doing research. All he learned confirmed the one weakness in her defenses. It gave him the one weapon to use against her. It gave him *mycosia pseudoflora*.

When Melissa Steiner married Hanse Davion in 3028, the Prince of the Federated Suns had paid vast sums to supply true *mycosia* blossoms for the bridesmaids' bouquets. The green flowers grew successfully on only one world, Andalusia, and blossomed only once a year. Hanse Davion had the flowers harvested and conveyed up to a string of JumpShips to carry them to Terra in time for the ceremony.

That romantic gesture created a demand for *mycosia* the like of which had never been seen in the annals of mercantilism. Hundreds of scientists began to work on breeding a version of the plant that would flower more often, in different colors, and on worlds other than Andalusia. This proved difficult, but the race was won by the New Avalon Institute of Science in 3038. *Mycosia pseudoflora* entered the commercial market two years later and thereafter became Melissa's trademark flower.

If she wore a corsage, it had at least one *mycosia pseudoflora* blossom in it. For important affairs, like the dedication banquet, nothing less than several flowering plants would do.

The assassin aped Karl's work style as he set each pot out on the workbench. He made sure they were evenly in line, then pulled his trowel out of a drawer and picked up a plastic bucket from beside his table. Working quickly he went to the peat pit and filled the bucket. He returned to his bench and used the peat to line the base of the pots, spreading it out evenly to hide the matchbox-sized lump on the bottom, beneath the rubber coating.

He walked to the greenhouse and picked out the four plants he wanted. Each was in full bloom because he had added some flowering compound to their water two days ago. He took one in each hand and transferred them to his workbench, then returned for the other two. That left another four *mycosia pseudoflora* displaying their brilliant green blossoms, so he told Mr. Crippen that he should probably sell them.

Back at his workbench he diligently worked the plants out of their small plastic pots and placed them in the rubberized ones. He packed peat around them and then topped each pot with some white stones, just to be decorative. Finally he placed each of the rubber pots in a decorative gold pot and presented Mr. Crippen with his handiwork.

His boss seemed pleased, then stuck a finger in the peat. "Too dry. Wet them down at bit, but not too much."

Karl frowned. "I thought I would do that when I got them in place. If I do it now, they could get frosted on the drive, couldn't they?"

Crippen hesitated for a moment, then nodded. "Yes, yes. Go. Take them over there now so we can get the truck back to deliver the centerpieces."

"Yes, sir."

Karl covered each plant in a black plastic bag to insulate it, and carried the lot of them out into the delivery truck. He climbed in and started it. The hovertruck rose up on a cloud of air as a snow-curtain curled up and away from the skirts. Driving carefully, Karl headed the truck into traffic and out on the short trip to the reception center.

The dedication banquet was not the first time Karl had delivered flowers to the reception center. The security guard there greeted him warmly and let him into the underground garage. He brought up a rolling cart, and Intelligence Secretariat agents descended like locusts on both of them.

The Archon's security men wore dark glasses and conservative suits. They sent the center's man back to his post, then checked the cart, the truck, and patted Karl down. Opening the back of the truck, one of them produced a chemical sniffing device and waved it around. "Clear."

The assassin didn't let his internal smile make it to Karl's face. The plastic explosive that had been shaped and baked into the flowerpots was double-sealed in a coat of acrylic and then rubber. Though the rubber was semipermeable, it had its own scent that would have masked anything from the explosives. The sniffer didn't get anything, as he'd expected.

"Strip the plastic off the flowers."

Karl looked hurt. "If I do I may burn the flowers. Can I do it upstairs, after I get them in place?"

One security man looked at the other and they exchanged nods. "Seven, flowers coming up," one announced into the small radio microphone on his jacket lapel.

Karl dutifully loaded the four pots and a watering can onto the handcart and let the security men escort him to the freight elevator. They said nothing. Because Karl would have done it, the assassin whistled a popular tune, then stopped when the security men looked at him. "Sorry."

The elevator halted and they rolled into the reception hall from behind the podium where Melissa would deliver the keynote speech for the dedication. Karl smiled as he saw the iron stand already in place in front of the podium. It had four hoops set in a diamond pattern. Mr. Crippen knew his stuff—the display would look perfect.

Karl stripped away the plastic, and the security men used the chemical sniffer again. They nodded and Karl placed one pot in each of the rings. He twisted them around until all the triangular flowers were oriented in the same direction. He looked hopefully at the security men and one of them finally nodded his approval of how they had been arranged.

Karl smiled and picked up the plastic watering can. He raised it toward the flowers.

"Wait."

The assassin forced himself to turn slowly. "What?"

"What's in there?" The security man pointed to the can.

"Water." His heart started pounding in his ears.

"Just water?"

Karl nodded and took a drink out of it. "Just water."

The man smiled. "I told my wife you didn't have to use anything special to keep those miksos thingers."

"Just water and a lot of love." Karl nodded sagely and watered the flowers. As the peat drank the water in, his heart rate dropped back to normal. *It is done. One more step and it is all over.*

He glanced at his watch and nodded. "Good. I can even stop for an early lunch on the way back." He looked at the security men. "I will be back with the centerpieces later. Do you want me to bring you anything?"

They shook their heads and Karl blushed. "Okay, see you later."

They accompanied him back to the truck, took possession of the plastic bags, and continued to watch him until he left the garage.

Karl finished out the rest of the day and, in fact, did help deliver the centerpieces. He refrained from checking his earlier handiwork. He did, however, take stock of the names on the place cards at each seat within the blast radius. *This will be a major blow to Tharkad society, but it will raise the general level of acting on a couple of holovid dramas.*

As he expected, Mr. Crippen did not buy lunch, but Karl didn't protest. Karl wouldn't protest. Karl was a nice, quiet man who kept to himself. He didn't cause trouble.

That would be how they would remember him, and how they would talk about him to the news media. Karl

Kole: assassin or dupe? Historians would debate that question for years.

The assassin left Karl's place of work and walked on past the bus stop. The regulars on his bus home might notice he was not with them, but Karl regularly missed that bus. Sometimes he treated himself to dinner, but more often he took in a holovid at a local theatre. If anyone had noticed him and actually remembered, they would have seen him head toward the Tharkad Theatre on Chase Street.

He stopped at the theatre and bought a ticket to see The *Immortal Warrior Returns*. Glancing again at his watch, he saw he had half an hour until show time. He smiled at the girl in the kiosk and said, "I'll be back."

He lied.

The assassin walked down the street to the Argyle Hotel. At the desk he asked for the key to room 4412, which he had rented two weeks before and guaranteed with a credit card in the name of Carl Ashe. The clerk gave him the key and said there were no messages.

Carl thanked him and took the elevator to the room, where he showered and used colorant to bleach his hair bone-white. He changed into the tailored suits Mr. Ashe had ordered from a nearby tailor earlier in the week. Packing some clothes and a few toiletries into an overnight bag, Carl Ashe donned a long parka and some copper-tinted glasses, then left the room.

He had the doorman summon a taxi and ordered it to take him to the spaceport. He gave the man a miserly tip and demanded a receipt. Once inside the terminal, he went to the storage lockers and pulled out a larger suitcase and retrieved his ticket from it.

He returned to the check-in counter with the two cases and waited in line. Things moved slowly, but not so slowly that he began to worry. Glancing at his watch, he saw he had plenty of time. The clerk at the Odinflight Transport counter checked him in efficiently and whisked his bags away.

"The shuttle to the outbound Tetersen ship leaves from Gate Fourteen at seven-thirty. That's half an hour from now."

"Thank you."

He found the gate with no trouble and no delay. Nearby

was an empty chair with a holovid viewer grafted onto it. He pushed a Kroner stamped with Melissa's face into the slot and changed channels until he got the public access station. He heard applause from the tinny speaker as Morgan Kell finished introducing the Archon, then returned to his seat on the dais.

The camera tightened in on the Archon as she started to speak, also catching one of the *mycosia pseudoflora* blossoms in its frame. The assassin ignored Melissa's words, but drank in her beauty. He could see why she was beloved by billions. She was intelligent and gorgeous. *It would be a pity to let her descend into wrinkles and senility.*

He turned from the holovid viewer and walked over to a visiphone booth. He dropped two Hanse Memorial coins into the slot and punched up Karl Kole's apartment. The phone rang four times before the computer answered it. The assassin punched in the numbers 112263, then hung up.

He was on board the outgoing shuttle when the computer dialed another number. Having done that, it hung up and dialed yet another number. Once it had a connection there, it downloaded a suicide note written by Karl Kole. That note would show up in Mr. Crippen's electronic mail within a day. The computer then wrote zero to every segment on its hard disk, effectively destroying its usefulness.

The computer's call was the second crucial step in the assassin's plan. The first had come when the water he used on the flowers reached the semi-permeable rubber coat. Enough moisture got through in each pot to allow a timer to use it to power up. These timers, which were set for seven hours' elapsed time, counted down faithfully, and by six-thirty all had opened a circuit that fed power from a small battery to radio-phone circuitry.

The computer's call to the cellular number that all four detonators shared came at 7:21 P.M. When the circuits detected a signal, they sent out an electric impulse that would normally have rung a buzzer. Instead, the circuits pulsed energy into the magnesium firestarters to which they had been connected. Within two seconds of the call going out, the magnesium started to burn. It, in turn, lit a small thermite charge. The thermite burned through the acrylic and ignited the molded ceramic explosive.

The explosives did not quite detonate simultaneously, though the assassin had hoped they would. The lowest one went off a half-second before the others, boosting the stand into the air by thirty centimeters. Next, the top and right ones exploded in tandem, and the last one exploded a second after that.

The fact that things did not go perfectly did not matter to the success of the assassin's mission. The bombs converted the decorative pots into lethal shrapnel. The fire and metal literally vaporized the wooden podium, killing Melissa before she ever felt any pain.

As the shuttle rolled down the runway and pulled up into the night sky, Mr. Ashe could see the flashing lights of ambulances gathered around the reception center. "Looks like some excitement downtown," he said to his seatmate.

By the time the shuttle reached the DropShip *Columbus*, Archon Melissa Steiner Davion had been declared dead. By the time the Intelligence Secretariat had begun a worldwide dragnet for Karl Kole, Carl Ashe and the *Columbus* were a whole star system beyond their grasp.

20

Deia
Federated Commonwealth
19 June 3055

Feeling a BattleMech lurch forward with him in the cockpit filled Nelson Geist with more happiness than he had known since his capture. The cooling vest circulated fluid through its tubes and the neurohelmet sat heavily on his shoulders—deliciously familiar sensations to a man who thought he would never experience them again. Being seated high up in the navigation and gunnery seat of the Red Corsair's *BattleMaster* brought back memories, and he was smiling in spite of what his presence there meant.

She will spoil it. She will use it against me. Nelson reached out and took the joystick sighting controls in his hands and moved them around. As he expected, the gold crosshairs burning on the holographic display before him did not move. *She is not so foolish as to let me to have live weaponry to play with.*

Her voice crackled gently through his earphones. "How does it feel to be a warrior again, Nelson?"

"It feels *right.* " The second he spoke he wished he'd said nothing at all, and her laughter told him his caution was correct.

"Good."

He heard a click and other voices came on line. "We have a concentration of enemy two klicks south of your position, Red Leader. We count twelve, repeat one-two, 'Mechs. We will drive these Zouaves toward you. Blue Leader out."

"Red Leader acknowledges, Blue Leader. Red out." The Red Corsair half-turned back toward him. "Ready for battle, Nelson?"

Outside, through the bubble canopy that covered the enlarged cockpit, Nelson saw smoke and fire from Blue Star's initial engagement with the enemy. He saw several flights of missiles head out away from him, but the alpha point of the salvos moved inexorably closer to the Red Corsair's Star of 'Mechs.

Nelson clenched his teeth. "I assume you want me to keep score for you?"

"Quaint, Nelson." She moved her hands, and the crosshairs centered themselves on the display. "What do you know about Zimmer's Zouaves? They are mercenaries, *quiaff?*"

"Don't know. Never heard of them."

"They are supposed to be sponsored by the Kell Hounds. You have heard of *them?*"

Nelson allowed himself a smile. "Yeah, they kicked the Jade Falcons around on Twycross, then busted up the Nova Cats and Smoke Jaguars on Luthien. I've heard of them. They're so tough that the son of their leader became a Khan of the Wolf Clan."

"So, you would expect these Zouaves to be better or worse than you, as Inner Sphere MechWarriors go?" Her radio clicked open. "Red Star, hold your fire until I shoot."

"Not as good."

The running battle kept getting closer. If not for the thick jungle between Red Star and the Zouaves, Nelson knew the raiders could have used their superior Clan technology to pick them apart. He could feel the Red Corsair holding back until the mercenaries were at point-blank range. It was not that she was afraid of missing them, but that she wanted to see the devastation up close.

"Then you would be able to defeat them?"

"With a lance or even-up in firepower, yes."

The Red Corsair hit a switch down below and Nelson's auxiliary and secondary screens started scrolling weapon-readiness data for him to inspect. His hand brushed one of the joysticks and the crosshairs responded to it. "What are you doing?"

"You are my gunner, Nelson."

"No!" Nelson shoved both joysticks forward, making all the 'Mech's weapons point at the ground. "No, I won't do your killing for you."

"If you do not, we will die."

"Then we die."

The Red Corsair's sigh told him he was doomed. "If we die, so do your friends. Spider, Jordan, the lot of them. If we die, I have given orders that they are to be ejected into space."

"You can't. . . ."

"I can and have, Nelson." Down below she raised her hands and folded them behind her head. "The weapons are live. The targets are yours. Fire at will."

Nelson looked from the consoles to the holographic display. The Zouaves were falling back in good order, but they were stumbling back into a trap. Attacking them would be a slaughter. Not attacking them would kill his friends. But even fighting against the Zouaves wouldn't guarantee the Red Corsair's survival.

"Think about this, Nelson. For each kill you get, I will release one of your friends."

"And if I kill them all? What is my reward then?"

"A chance to kill more, and if the Wolf Clan arrives in time, a chance to kill some of them."

Nelson sent the *BattleMaster* crashing forward through the brush. Both arms came up, and the sights tracked with his hand movements. The crosshairs settled on a retreating *Griffin*. Nelson hit the right trigger and sent a sizzling bolt of azure lightning out from the pistol-like PPC in the 'Mech's right hand.

The particle beam boiled all the armor off the *Griffin's* right arm and started to work on its ferro-titanium bones. When Nelson hit the left trigger, another PPC bolt ripped away great chunks of armor on the *Griffin's* chest. Armor vapor wreathed the afflicted 'Mech as the war machine staggered back. The pilot managed to keep it upright, but only just barely, winning both admiration and pity from Nelson.

Two things surprised him in his first attack, and he hated himself for reveling in both discoveries. The first was that the Clan weapons did more damage than even the best weapons manufactured in the Inner Sphere. The devastation wrought on the *Griffin* was easily half again as much as he would have expected from a comparable Inner Sphere weapon.

The second thing was that the Red Corsair's *Battle-Master* cycled heat better than its Inner Sphere counterpart. A normal *BattleMaster* boasted only one PPC, a weapon prone to running hot. After two PPC blasts he still felt no heat building up. Glancing at the heat monitor, he saw it had not risen past the cautionary yellow zone.

"You are in a *real* 'Mech now, Nelson. You can do more."

Nelson tracked the Griffin again and fired. Both PPCs hit the 'Mech square in the chest. The armor over its heart melted away to nothing, exposing the ribs and internal structures to the particle beam's incendiary caress. A gout of black smoke shot out, followed by a spike of silvery fire. Nelson unconsciously cataloged those as an engine hit and the death of a jump jet, respectively.

The large pulse laser in the *BattleMaster*'s center torso spat out a storm of green energy darts, which peppered the *Griffin*'s naked right arm. Chipping away at the ferrotitanium shoulder joint, they filled it with fire and it evaporated. The arm dropped off, flames trailing from the glowing end, and started a brushfire.

The *Griffin,* reeling from the hammering it had taken, tottered and spun. It landed flat on its back, its head tipped back and staring skyward. The canopy shattered as a string of small explosions around its perimeter blew it away. Up out of that dark hole the pilot blasted free, riding his command couch on a jet of argent flame. Nelson couldn't see the man as he shot up through the dark treetops, but he hoped he had gotten clear.

There, now Spider's free.

All around him Red Star had joined in the fray. Trapped between two opposing forces, Zimmer's Zouaves fought gamely, but the raiders ground them down. With an almost careless pair of shots, Nelson melted a *Hermes* from breastbone to spine, then turned and dueled with a *Hunchback*. The other 'Mech did some damage, but went down after two exchanges, leaving Nelson with unbreached armor and a hunger for more targets.

As the radio reported all resistance ended, Nelson stared out at the war-battered, early morning landscape.

What had been jungle now resembled a garden plot in which a robotiller had gone mad. Trees that had once stood tall were snapped like so many little twigs. Fires burned everywhere and BattleMech corpses littered the ground like armored knights fallen in some ancient battle.

The Red Corsair shifted control of the 'Mech back to her section of the cockpit, then stood and looked up at him. "Perhaps you were a warrior after all, Nelson. I am impressed. You have done well."

Her tone was patronizing, yet tinged with respect. Nelson at first took pride in her praise, then remembered what he had done to earn it. *Those were people on* my *side. Not only did I destroy them, but I enjoyed it! This is what it is to lose your compassion.*

The Red Corsair resumed her seat in the command couch and refastened the restraining belts. "However, there are more mercenaries to kill. I will show you what a true warrior can do, Nelson, and you will understand why the Inner Sphere can never stop us."

Her arrogance irritated him. "But you said there are Wolves coming after us. The Inner Sphere won't have to stop you, will they?"

"We will see, Nelson. The Wolves are not here yet, nor are they invincible."

Twelve hours later Kommandant Israel Zimmer stormed into the communications wagon that had become his command post. He wanted to be out in the field, but when his *Marauder* lost a leg in the losing battle for Shasta, he was left waiting for either his 'Mech to be repaired or a 'Mech whose pilot no longer required use of it. Though the latter would likely happen well before the former, he did not look forward to getting back into the battle that way.

"Leftenant, have you got a secure line to those incoming DropShips yet?"

The young commtech nodded and vacated his chair in front of a patched-together visiphone set. He pointed to a button. "This one will activate the link, sir."

Zimmer winked at the boy. "I've used them before, Leftenant."

"Yes, sir." The young officer blushed, but Zimmer

waved it away. The boy still wore a shirt with corporal stripes on it, and the Leftenant's bars on his lapels showed a spot of blood. "It's ready now, sir."

Zimmer hit the button and got a picture of a stern-looking man. "This is Kommandant Israel Zimmer of Zimmer's Zouaves. We could really use your help."

The man on the screen frowned ferociously. "You are mercenaries, *quiaff?*"

Zimmer narrowed his eyes. "Yes, we are. To whom am I speaking?"

"I am Star Colonel Conal Ward, commander of the Thirty-first Wolf Solahma. We will be grounding ourselves to engage the bandits. Our landing zone is in your Sector 3342. Please vacate it."

"Say what?"

Conal stared straight out of the visiphone screen. "Sector 3342, I want it vacated. This is where I have agreed to meet the bandits."

"Star Colonel, I have my battalion dug in throughout that sector. If I move them, I will lose them. If you land in 3244, you will ground yourselves to the northwest of that position and catch the bandits between us. We're not too mobile, but we can still shoot."

"Kommandant Zimmer," the black-haired Clanner began coolly, "if you do *not* move your troops, you will lose them. I will not have your people interfere in our battle."

"*Your* battle?" Zimmer hammered the arm of his chair and made the Leftenant jump. "You listen to me, you son of a bitch, my command is now what is left of my mercenary battalion and the local militia. We've fought these raiders for sixteen solid hours and have just now managed to regroup under cover of darkness. We're good troops and we won't be dismissed."

"Very well." Conal lifted his head up. "With what are you defending 3342?"

"What are you, a moron?" Zimmer thumped his fist against the screen. "I just told you, I'm defending it with every last frigging thing I have."

"Excellent!" Conal smiled at Zimmer. "I shall look forward to meeting you, Kommandant. We land in an hour. Bargained well and done."

The screen went blank and Zimmer stared at it for a

second before he realized the conversation was over. "What the hell just happened there, Leftenant?"

"I dunno for sure, sir." The younger man shook his head ruefully. "But isn't 'bargained well and done' what the Clans say when they've offered a battle challenge and had it accepted?"

"I hope you're wrong, Leftenant." Zimmer left the chair and looked out the doorway toward the sky. High up, like a constellation shifting its position, he could see the Clan DropShips burning their way into the atmosphere. "Unfortunately, I'm afraid you're not."

21

Victor Davion hit the space bar on his computer keypad, and the holographic display of a battlefield froze above the black briefing table. On it an inordinate number of red BattleMechs had succeeded in surrounding a blue force. "This is not good, Galen."

"I agree, sir." Galen glanced at some numbers on a console in front of him. "Unfortunately, this is the most probable outcome of the Red Corsair feinting toward the Zouave position at Rupert, then hitting Shasta. Zimmer could bring in the Zouaves to lift the siege and try to defend the city, but it would be folly. The long march will leave his troops open to ambush, especially here in the Livingstone jungle reserve."

"The key question is this: Can they hold out until the Wolves arrive?"

Victor's aide shrugged. "Assuming Zimmer can put together a defensive position that will take the raiders a while to crack, yes, I think they can. The Thirty-first Wolf Solahma were reported burning fast to the planet."

The Prince shook his head almost absentmindedly. "Coming in at 1.25 gravities is not *fast.*"

"Not fast enough for you, you mean, sir." Galen brushed a lock of blond hair back from his forehead. "To be prepared for combat, we never go in at better than 1.5 gravities."

"But the Clans are supposed to be such bloody hotshot warriors." Victor slammed his right fist into his left palm. "Dammit, they could hurry so our people can live."

Galen's head came up. "I thought you told me you had disparaged the Zouaves in front of the Kell Hounds back on Arc-Royal."

Victor waved the comment away. "I was young and stupid then." He looked at the time being displayed in the corner of the battlefield. "Where *is* that ComStar Precentor? He says he has a Priority Alpha message for me, then takes his own sweet time about getting here. No wonder the Clans decided they wanted to take Terra."

His comment prompted a momentary guffaw from Galen, and after a moment Victor joined in, bleeding off some of the tension. "The bitch of all this, Galen, is that even going as fast as we could, the Revenants couldn't make it to Deia in near enough time to save Zimmer. It would take us a month to get out there. . . ."

"But only with you commandeering every JumpShip in sight."

"That's why it's called a command circuit, Galen. If you're in command, you make the circuit." Victor started the simulation moving again. "We can't get there to stop them this time, but we can be there for the next time."

A gentle knock at the door of the briefing room made Victor stop the simulation again. "Enter."

An older man wearing the simple white robes of a ComStar Precentor slipped through the crack between the door and jamb. "ComStar Precentor Marcellin at your service, Highness." The grave look on the man's face told Victor the news was woeful.

"Let's have it, Precentor. How bad is it on Deia?"

"Highness?"

"You have news of Deia, don't you? Tell me, tell me this instant." Victor nodded at Galen and his aide readied himself to translate the Precentor's news into numbers the simulation could use. "Come on, man. I don't have all day!"

"Y-yes, Highness." Marcellin blinked a couple of times, then composed himself. "The Zouaves took up defensive positions in Sector 3342."

"Burton's Redoubt. The Speke River gives it a moat. High ground, no easy approaches. Taking it will be trouble." Galen spoke haltingly as he typed information into the computer. The simulation redrew itself, the blue force being bolstered with green troops and rising above the red forces. A light blue river separated the combatants. "Approximate strengths?"

The Precentor started to tremble. "I don't know, sir. I am not a military man. Zimmer is supposed to have had a battalion, but that was the remains of the militia and his people. He lost a whole company in the jungle."

Galen hit some keys and the number of defenders dropped, but not so much as to make Victor lose all heart. "Galen, Zimmer's done it. Because the raiders are not working with missiles, taking this little fortification will be hell to pay. He can hold out here for days." The Prince looked up at the Precentor. "Have the Wolves arrived?"

"Yes, Highness."

Victor clapped his hands together. "Now we have them! They must have grounded behind the bandits to trap them. Where did they come down?"

"Sector 3342."

Victor's eyes narrowed. "The same sector? Was Zimmer that close to collapse? Did they come in to bolster it?"

The Precentor shook his head. "No, Highness, to conquer it."

"What!"

The ComStar man opened his hands helplessly. "I do not know any more, Highness. Please, believe me. The last message we had said the Wolves were fighting with Zimmer's forces at the river. The raiders have taken that opportunity to pull back, and they may be leaving the world. But, believe me, I know nothing more."

Victor hammered the table with a fist. "Those sons of bitches! What the hell is going on here? The Wolves were supposed to be helping Zimmer, not finishing him off!" His hands tightened down into fists and he raised them up beside his head. "Who the hell do those Clanners think they are? What do they think this is? If we'd been there, Galen, this whole situation would have been different."

The Prince jabbed a finger toward the Precentor. "I want you to send a Priority Alpha message over my signature to the ilKhan of the Clans. It is to read as follows: On 19 June 3055 your Thirty-first Wolf Solahma landed on Deia and destroyed the one unit defending that world against the bandits the Thirty-first was sent to hunt. Though it would require an error of a sort yet unparalleled in all of human history to explain, I will not order the immediate hunting down of the Thirty-first Wolf Solahma. That order will await your explanation of their action and your determination on how they will conduct operations in the future.

"Effective this date, the Tenth Lyran Guards will be the primary military force engaged in hunting the raiders. The Thirty-first Wolf Solahma should understand that it is a subordinate force and subject to my command. If it interferes in any way with operations, I will order it destroyed."

The Precentor nodded uneasily. "Y-yes, Highness."

"Galen, draw up the necessary orders to get everyone moving. Cancel all leaves, and mobilize the local reserve units to help with loading. We can commandeer merchant DropShips if we need them." The Prince closed his eyes. "We'll need basic supplies for a month in transit. We can pick up more along the way. We'll also load refit kits so we can bring everyone up current. Also, contact the base auxiliary and tell them to gear up their counseling network. Also General Order 4492 concerning mortgage and loan interest rate rollbacks is now in effect."

"Yes, sir."

Victor opened his eyes again and saw the ComStar official still standing at the other end of the table. "Why are you still here, man? I gave you a message to send."

The man swallowed hard. "Yes, Highness. I know."

"Then what is it?" Victor opened his hands. "I *am* busy here. You can see that."

"Yes, Highness, I know that." The man nervously clutched his hands together, wringing them spasmodically. "It is just that I came with a message and have not yet been able to deliver it."

Victor shook his head and leaned forward on the table. "Then tell me."

"Your mother, Highness." The man stopped for a moment, then continued. "It was a bomb. I am very sorry."

Victor felt as though his knees had been shot out from under him. He sat down, catching only the edge of his chair, and ended up on the floor. His toppled chair clattered down beside him and he angrily batted it aside with his left arm. *"Mein Gott!"* He began to shake.

"There is no doubt?" He heard himself speak, but felt utterly detached from the sound.

"The alert went out immediately, Highness. There were no details, but there was no h-hedging." The Precentor's voice became softer. "A bomb exploded in front of her as she spoke. . . ."

"He doesn't need to know that, ghoul!"

"No, Galen. . . ." Victor looked up as his friend dropped to one knee beside him. "Precentor, please continue."

"It was at the library dedication banquet. Dozens of people died in the blast, and many more were severely wounded. Your mother could have felt no pain."

Victor reached up and locked his left hand on the edge of the table. Galen helped him up and he leaned against the table. He clenched his jaw and tried to keep back the tears welling in his eyes. He failed and the tears rolled down his cheeks as he hammered his right fist into the table. "Dammit, dammit, dammit!"

The ComStar Precentor bowed. "You wish to be alone, Highness."

Victor shook his head and pushed away the throbbing pain in his hand. "No, wait. Galen, gather up all the information we've worked up on the bandits. Include the Geist file. Get it ready so the Precentor here can ship it out. Precentor, I will require you to send another message for me. Is my sister on Tharkad?"

"Katrina? Yes, Highness."

Victor used his left hand to wipe away his tears. "Tell Katherine that I am inbound. She is to conduct services as she deems appropriate. It is not likely that my mother's body"—his stomach clenched as the meaning behind his words slammed into him—"is in any condition for her to lie in state as our father did. If she thinks it best, she need not wait the funeral for my arrival. I want my mother remembered as she was when alive."

The Prince looked up toward the ceiling and squeezed tears out of tightly shut eyes. "I also want to be kept abreast of the investigation with Priority Alpha messages as I come in. And can you tell the Primus and the Precentor Martial that I would like ComStar's cooperation in locating any messages that might pertain to the assassination?'' Victor opened his eyes and wiped away more tears.

The ComStar Precentor nodded solemnly. ''It shall be communicated as you wish.'' The man raised a hand. ''And concerning the message to the ilKhan? Do you still wish to send it?''

Galen shook his head. ''Victor, there is no way we can go after the bandits with you on Tharkad.''

''You're right, Galen.'' The Prince looked over at the Precentor. ''Send it anyway, but we'll change the name of the unit.''

''Highness?''

''Zimmer's people were *my* people, so the bandits *will* be hunted down.'' Victor cradled his right hand in his left. ''Zimmer's people were also Kell Hounds' people. Fate has dealt me a bad hand here, but having the Kell Hounds angry and sent after them won't deal the bandits one that's any better.''

22

Tamar
Wolf Clan Occupation Zone
21 June 3055

Phelan Ward saluted as he entered the ilKhan's quarters. "Reporting as ordered, sir."

The slender, white-haired man returned the salute, then offered Phelan his hand. "Beta Galaxy seems to be coming along well under your leadership, Phelan," Ulric Kerensky said, sitting down in a camp chair and gesturing to Phelan to have a seat in the one opposite it. "Their scores were good before your return, and in the last month they have gotten even better. You are to be commended."

The younger man smiled. "I shall pass word of your praise on to the others. Star Colonel Athen Kederk has worked miracles since he came over from the 328th Assault Cluster. I thank you for letting him come. I also thank you for leaving us the Thirteenth Wolf Guards when Natasha took command of Alpha Galaxy. They, as always, know how to confront an opponent with all kinds of unusual tactical challenges."

Ulric laughed lightly. "The other units who trained against the Wolf Spiders tended to phrase their opinions in less flattering ways."

"I can imagine." Phelan sat back in the steel and canvas chair. Looking around the sparsely decorated room, it struck him that Ulric Kerensky had not much changed since the first time he had seen him. On the JumpShip *Dire Wolf* he had been invited to Khan Kerensky's quarters, where everything was either utilitarian or aesthetically simple. It occurred to him that many of the furnishings in the room here on Tamar were exactly the same ones that had occupied Ulric's cabin during the Clan invasion of the Inner Sphere.

Ulric stroked his white goatee a moment before speaking. "I asked you here because I have some disturbing news."

The tone of the ilKhan's voice surprised Phelan. It carried regret, but also sounded as if Ulric were uncertain how much information he should reveal. "What is it?"

"Two days ago, an assassin killed Archon Melissa Steiner on Tharkad. He did so by exploding a bomb at a banquet she was attending."

"Oh my God!" Phelan's jaw dropped open. "Who did it?"

Ulric shook his head. "I do not know, nor did the ComStar Precentor who communicated the information. He did say, however, that your parents were in attendance at the dinner. Your father introduced Melissa Steiner, and both your parents were seated on the dais." The ilKhan took a deep breath. "Your mother was killed by the blast. Your father was gravely wounded and is undergoing treatment."

The curious tone of Ulric's voice undercut the gravity of his news. Phelan wanted to deny what he had heard, and focused on the fact that because Clan warriors never knew their true parents, Ulric could not know how much the news hurt him. Ulric could not inject the right amount of sorrow and sympathy into his words because he could not understand sentiments he had never felt.

"Oh, God." Phelan slumped in the chair. "My mother . . . dead? It can't be, it can't. I just saw her a month ago." He looked up at Ulric and let a little laugh escape his throat. "With my father retiring, the two of them were traveling to Tharkad to get away from the unit and fighting and death for a while. She cheated death so often on the battlefield . . . how could it get her at a banquet?"

The ilKhan simply shook his head. "I cannot begin to understand what you are feeling, Phelan, yet I dearly wish I could."

"Forgive me, ilKhan, but you do *not* want to share these feelings."

"I do, and it comes not from wondering how this will

affect your performance in my command. You are a friend and I can see that this hurts you . . . deeply." Ulric looked down at his hands. "I have other unsettling news."

Phelan head bobbed with a snort. "In for a cent, in for a C-bill."

"At roughly the same time the bomb exploded, the Thirty-first Wolf Solahma made a combat drop on Deia. They dropped onto what was left of Zimmer's Zouaves and the Deia Militia. They ripped them apart, but in doing so allowed the bandits to escape. Because Conal bid away his air wing to win this assignment, he had nothing with which to pursue the bandits as they left the world."

"Conal dropped on a unit he was supposed to be helping?" Phelan sat bolt upright in his chair. "What in the name of hell possessed him to do that?"

Ulric exhaled slowly. "Conal claims that he told the mercenary commander to remove his troops from a defensive position that Conal wanted to occupy. That commander refused, and accepted Conal's challenge to fight for the place."

The younger man's nostrils flared as he took in a deep breath. He had no doubt that the actions of Conal—as slimy a weasel and a bastard as ever saw a sunrise—were exactly what any Clansman would have thought appropriate. He was just as certain that Conal had landed hard on the Zouaves for two main reasons. First, they were mercenaries, and the Clans generally considered mercenaries to be lower than the bandits Conal was meant to be chasing.

Second, the Zouaves were connected to the Kell Hounds, and that meant they were connected to him, Phelan. "You know why Conal did that, *quiaff?*"

"I think there is no question," Ulric said with a nod. "You know, of course, what I must do in return."

"I will have my Command Trinary ready to go in a week. We will take care of the bandits in short order. After I attend my mother's funeral, I will rendezvous with the Silver Keshik in Federated Commonwealth space."

"No."

"No?"

Ulric stood and stroked his goatee as he started to pace.

"I cannot send the Silver Keshik or any other part of your Galaxy. You forget one thing in suggesting that I send them. Not your fault, actually."

"What is it?"

"In the Inner Sphere it is possible, even probable, that an elite unit could be sent out to deal with a bandit problem." Ulric's blue eyes flicked up at Phelan. "As I recall, we captured you while the Kell Hounds were serving in just such a function."

Phelan nodded. "That is true."

"Within the Clans, though, bandit-hunting is not a task for true warriors. It is reserved for units made up of old or disgraced warriors who want to die with honor—"

"Or over-ambitious fools who make *big* mistakes."

"Exactly, but to think of Conal as a fool is to sink to his level. He *is* cunning and doubtless did go after the Zouaves because of their connection to your family unit." Ulric folded his arms across his chest. "Conal also knew it would force both me and the Federated Commonwealth into action."

"The FedCom cannot rely on us to hunt down the bandits. They will have to send someone after them." Phelan focused on the chair where Ulric had been sitting. "Ryan Steiner is already demanding that a Skye or Tamar unit be given the honor. Victor would want the assignment for the Tenth Lyran Guards. The Archon would likely have given the job to Ryan's choice and prayed Conal would deny Ryan the political boost. With the Archon dead, though, Victor now rules. He will not send the Tenth Lyran Guards, but he will not let Ryan fight, either."

Ulric smiled slightly. "I have received a message from this Victor. He said he would not order the destruction of the Thirty-first Wolf Solahma, pending an explanation of their actions. He also said that the Solahma would have to be subordinate to whatever unit he chose to put in charge of hunting the bandits down."

"That is Victor." Phelan frowned. "Conal will never agree to that. He will not follow orders given by someone from the Inner Sphere."

"That is precisely why you will serve as the liaison officer between the Thirty-first Solahma and the Inner Sphere unit." The ilKhan stopped behind his chair and leaned against the back of it. "Victor chose the Kell Hounds to destroy the bandits."

Phelan's surprise melted into a sense of dread. "Conal will not listen to me and he will not like orders coming from a mercenary unit. He especially will not like orders coming from *that* mercenary unit." Phelan gave it a moment more of thought, and his feelings shifted to a cold sense of satisfaction. "But then, Conal has to obey me because I am a Khan. And he will have to perform well or else be embarrassed because a mercenary unit did what he could not. This might not be so bad after all."

"Conal is already hedging his bets."

"How so?"

Ulric straightened up again. "He is suggesting that the bandits are not Clan renegades, as we all have assumed up until now. He says they are actually a group of mercenaries financed secretly by Ryan Steiner. He says the raids are staged to make the people of the border regions believe they are not safe and that the Davions have no intention of defending them. He suggests that our helping hunt the bandits jeopardizes the peace *and* might even show that I have been tricked into helping stabilize the Inner Sphere so they can oppose us when the truce runs its course."

"And I am the person who is tricking you, *quiaff*? With me as Conal's liaison officer, if he gets the bandits, he succeeded despite all I did to stop him, and if he fails, I prevented him from succeeding?" Phelan pressed his hands together. "It is Conal's loss that the Clans have no politician caste."

"It is indeed." Ulric walked over to the desk next to the wall and held up a holodisk in its protective sleeve. "I have here orders for you to head out immediately. You will link up with the Kell Hounds in Federated Commonwealth space."

Phelan stood up. "Why not just meet them at my mother's funeral?"

"There will not be a funeral just yet, or so I am given to understand." Ulric tapped the holodisk against the fingers of his left hand. "Your father decided to have your mother's body shipped to Arc-Royal and kept until the Kell Hounds can all be present. As nearly as ComStar knows, the Hounds are heading out from Arc-Royal now.''

''Business before mourning.'' The young Khan took the disk. ''The *Owl's Nest* is the DropShip I want to use—I cannot see depriving the unit of the larger ones.''

''I concur.''

''And the *Nest* will carry a Trinary each of Elementals, aerospace fighters, and BattleMechs. It should not travel empty.''

''True.'' Ulric half-closed his eyes. ''However, any troops you bring with you will feel disgraced because they are off to hunt bandits.''

Phelan countered easily. ''Hardly. I am a Khan. I am due an honor guard, *quiaff?*''

''Aff, but even I do not travel with three Trinaries.'' Ulric lifted his head. ''You may travel with a Point each of Elementals and fighters, and with a full Star of 'Mechs.''

''If the Khan of the *Wolf* Clan is allowed to travel with so few warriors by his side, the Jade Falcons will never let us cross their space. At least two Stars of each. That would total six Stars, the number I am entitled to wear as a Khan.''

''But you are the *junior* Khan, do not forget. Perhaps if you had your Star of 'Mechs and a Star of Elementals to accompany your Point of fighters, the Jade Falcons would find you acceptable.''

''They would find me dead if I only had two fighters to act as outriders. At least accord me a full Star of each branch.''

''So be it.''

Ulric would have ended the bargaining there, but Phelan held up his hand. ''As this *is* an honor guard *and* a liaison unit, I should have with me personnel who know how to act properly and who have some experience with people of the Inner Sphere. Star Captains Evantha Fetladral and Ranna should come with me. Evantha can command the Elemental Star. I would also like Star Captain Carew to command the fighter Star.''

''Carew is unblooded. The command of that wing should go to someone who is a Bloodnamed.''

''Or someone who is guaranteed of being offered a place in the next Trial of Bloodright for the Nygren line.''

Phelan watched the ilKhan carefully as he pushed his request. "The ilKhan should be able to exert some influence in that area."

Ulric nodded slowly. "He should. Have you other requests?"

"I do." Phelan clasped his hands behind his back. "I also want Ragnar with me. We have already adopted him into the warrior caste because of his actions on Arc-Royal. I want to assign him to a 'Mech in my honor guard despite his not having tested out yet. I also want Lajos in my Star."

"That is four. Do you want Vlad to make your fifth?"

Nicely done, Ulric. Phelan suppressed his reaction to the ilKhan's suggestion that his archrival be made to serve beneath him. "I think not, ilKhan. Delta Galaxy lost a great deal when Conal Ward was sent to the Thirty-first Wolf Solahma. Star Captain Vlad has enough to do just bringing his Trinary up to the levels of performance it knew on Tukayyid. I thought the ilKhan could suggest someone who would be suitable."

"You will take Alita of the Fourth Wolf Guards. She is of the Winson bloodline and would do well to learn about the Inner Sphere."

That suggestion struck Phelan as interesting. Of Alita he knew little beyond the fact that she had been wounded at Tukayyid. That Ulric chose her meant he expected her to be influential in the future. It also meant he expected her to win her Bloodname fairly soon. Phelan seemed to recall that she had not competed for the Winson Bloodname after Tukayyid because her wounds had not yet healed.

"Thank you, ilKhan. An excellent suggestion."

"Good. I grant what you request, but only because I have something to ask in return." Ulric's face hardened. "Phrased that way it sounds like a request, but it is, ultimately, why I am sending you and not Natasha."

"And that reason is?"

"These bandits threaten the ComStar truce. They make the people of the Inner Sphere feel vulnerable and they give the Jade Falcons an opportunity to point out the Inner Sphere's weakness. The fact that these bandits are doing so much damage has breathed new life into the

Crusaders' attempt to repudiate the truce and continue the advance toward Terra.''

"But hitting and running is much easier than a war of conquest.''

"Agreed, which is what I have used to hold them back.'' The ilKhan rested his hands on Phelan's shoulders. "Preserving this truce is your paramount mission. Do whatever it takes. If it means chasing the bandits back to the Clan homeworld of Strana Mechty, so be it.''

Phelan nodded. "And if it means stopping Conal from committing another atrocity?''

"Whatever it takes.''

23

Recharge Station, Thuban
Federated Commonwealth
26 June 3055

When Carl Ashe left the DropShip *Columbus* at the Thuban recharging station it was to await a shuttle that would take him down to Thuban. Ashe went directly to the First Orbital Mercantile Bank, where he was allowed into the vault of safety deposit drawers after being identified by a retinal scanner.

From his drawer he withdrew new identification documents and a magnetic keycard. Then he stuffed his old identification papers into it, and closed it up. He gave the drawer back to the clerk and left the bank.

Though space is at a premium on any space station, a premium price can save someone a piece of it. A corporate bank account paid the rent on a small suite of rooms in the Corona Hotel. It was purportedly for the use of executives passing through the system, but it had only been used once in the last year. That happened to have been when Carlos Negron first visited the station and Carl Ashe last left it.

Reversing the process he had used eight months earlier, the assassin went to his room without speaking to the clerk at registration. Using the keycard, he opened the door and stepped inside, then closed the door behind him. Everything looked as it had when last he'd departed, save for a light coat of dust over the room, but the assassin checked things carefully and did not touch anything until certain the room had not been disturbed in his absence.

Satisfied, he immediately stripped off all his clothes and walked into the bathroom. From a toiletries kit he took a bottle of what appeared to be allergy capsules and ate two of them. Returning to the main room, he set the alarm chronometer in the headboard for one hour, then lay down to nap. When the alarm went off, he got up and went back to the bathroom and turned on the sunlamp.

The capsules had contained a drug that stimulated his skin to produce melanin, and the sunlamp helped him darken up quickly. His pasty gray skin took on a healthy olive tone. Using hair dye he blackened the hair on his head and body. That job finished, he returned to the main room and dressed in the trousers and workshirt a merchant marine like Negron would wear.

It took less than four hours to complete the total transformation from Carl Ashe to Carlos Negron.

Carlos Negron, shouldering the duffel bag he'd left in the room eight months before, headed back out to the Merchant Marine Union Hall near the docks at the base of the station. He mixed in with a crowd of workmen like himself who had recently come in from a planetary shuttle, then entered the Hall and presented his dues card. The man at the door logged him in and waved him on through the door.

The assassin knew that the quick scan of the dues card would put him in line for an upcoming outbound job. Because Carlos' history showed him to be competent with loading equipment and even light construction 'Mechs, he would be chosen for jobs that involved such machinery. It also showed that he had done a fair amount of work on the Marik border, which meant he would be heading down and away from Tharkad, and that would take him eventually to his goal.

He left his duffel with an apprentice and headed into the bar. There, despite regulations, smoke filled the darkness. The crowd looked sparse, which pleased him for two reasons. The first was that it lowered the chances of his bumping into anyone who might remember him from his earlier visit. Second, and far more important, it meant that ships were harvesting crew at a quick rate, a good sign that he might be leaving Thuban for another world in short order.

He settled at the bar and ordered a beer. The bartender

delivered it with more head than liquid and slopped half of that on the bar itself. Carlos frowned and rapped his fist against the bar. "What's this?"

The bartender looked at what he had done, then shook his head and whisked the glass away. "Sorry, mate. The holovid's showing the disk of the Archon's funeral. I missed it the first time they ran it through the system. Here, this one's full and on the house. Drink it in the Archon's memory."

Carlos respectfully raised the glass. "To the Archon and her place at God's table."

A number of others in the bar joined his toast. A man in the back followed it immediately with another. "And God rot that scrawny bastard who calls himself her son."

That toast got more drinkers than the one he had offered, confusing the assassin. "What has Victor done?"

The bartender's expression became almost a snarl. "Not what he's done, but what he hasn't. Do you remember when his father died? Old Man Hanse lay in state for thirty-one days, a month and a day! What did his mother get? Two days! Even Jesus got three!"

"You can be sure Victor didn't offer her that much for fear she'd rise from the dead!" quipped the man in the back.

The bartender leaned forward. "The way we hear it, he sent a message to Katrina and told her, `bury the bitch!' Gave her an order, he did. He was coming in as fast as he could from the Dragon's border—will make it a week from now, I've been told by those what know—but couldn't have the funeral wait. Mind you, the other children came on a command circuit from New Avalon—over twice the distance Victor had to go—and they made it. Can you imagine that? Prince Victor didn't even want to attend his mother's funeral?"

Up on the holovid screen affixed in the corner of the bar, the assassin saw the camera focus in on a tall, slender woman dressed head to toe in black. Beside her on the left stood a tall man with blond hair, who the assassin recognized as Ryan Steiner. "That the Archon's daughter?"

"Spitting image of her grandmother—was named for her, too. Victor made her preside over the funeral. Those are her brothers Peter and Arthur, and the girl there is

Melissa's youngest, Yvonne.'' The bartender shook his head as he wiped away a moisture ring on the bar. ''Katrina's been defending Victor, pointing out that he's got a government to run. Most of the people feel sorry for her so they accept it, but deep down we know the truth.''

Carlos nodded and drank some beer. ''Been nothing but trouble since Melissa married Hanse.''

The man from the back of the bar came over and plopped himself down on the seat beside Carlos. ''You know it, brother. But you also know why Katrina gave Melissa to Hanse, eh?''

Carlos shook his head. ''Why?''

''Hanse told her that if she didn't, he was going to make an alliance with the Dragons. He would have married Constance Kurita. He would have forced his half-sister Marie to divorce Michael Hasek-Davion and would have married her off to Theodore. If he'd 'a done that, right now we'd all be drinking rice wine and speaking Dragon.''

The assassin, who was fluent in Japanese, decided it was no time to reveal his prowess with that tongue. ''I didn't know that.''

The man from the back nodded emphatically. ''Yes, part of the Davion plan, you know. You can see Victor keeping it up, too, the way he carries on with Omi Kurita. Why do you think the Tenth Lyran is stationed on the Drac border?''

''Hearing you tell it like that, it all begins to make sense.''

''Damned straight it does.'' The man's eyes narrowed. ''I can even tell you who did it, who set the bomb and why.''

The assassin made Carlos lean in closer. ''Who?''

The man glanced around the room, then lowered his voice. ''Victor had it done. Being so tight with Omi, he had some of her assassins, the *nekogami,* do the job. The thing is this—they missed the real target. The bomb wasn't meant to get Melissa.''

''No?''

''No. See, it was meant to get Ryan Steiner. Victor pledged to his father on his deathbed that he would kill Ryan. See, Ryan was supposed to be there. He was the one who was supposed to introduce the Archon that night, not Morgan Kell. It was meant to get him, it was.''

The assassin wanted to be cautious, but he knew Carlos would have pressed the point. ''But wasn't the explosive powerful? Didn't everyone on the dais die?''

The man shrugged. ''The Kurita character for 'enough' translates as 'overkill,' you know. Besides, not everyone died. Morgan Kell lived, though he probably wasn't meant to. Now, there's a patriotic family for you—they're waiting his wife's funeral so the Hounds can kill off bandits.''

''Patriotic?'' Carlos indicated that the bartender should draw two more beers. ''I mean, I know what the Hounds have done and all, and I appreciate that, but isn't Morgan's son a Khan of the Wolf Clan?''

''Aye, that's true, mate.'' The man beside him drained off a third of the beer. ''But you have to understand something. The son of my wife's cousin went to the Nagelring at the same time as bonny Prince Victor and this Phelan. He told me that Phelan wanted nothing to do with his high and mighty cousin. Makes him okay in my book, even if he was brainwashed by the Clans. And, here, look, Phelan came all the way back for his father's retirement, didn't he? You can bet that he'd have been there for the funeral if it was his father had died. And he *will* be there for his mother's.''

Carlos nodded as another man entered the bar. He had a clipboard propped against his belly. ''Anderson, Capetti, Chung, Negron, Watterman—*Woman Scorned* is heading out in six hours. Lamon is the destination, with stops at Chukchi, Ciotat, and Trant. Standard compensation plus a twenty-five kilo freight allowance.''

Carlos drained his beer and slapped his companion on the shoulder. ''Thanks for catching me up, brother. I always enjoy talking with someone who's no fool and knows how the universe *really* works.''

= 24 =

Victor Steiner-Davion pounded his fist against the bulkhead of his cabin on the *Barbarossa*. "What do you mean it will be five days before planetfall?" He spitted the station master with a vicious stare. "Why we were given clearance to come in here as opposed to the pirate point near Tharkad, I don't know, but *five* days to reach the planet?"

"Highness, please, try to understand. Even if you traveled at three gravities of acceleration, you would only shave a day off the time." The man clutched his hands together. "One and a half gravities is a much safer speed."

"I don't care about safety, dammit." Victor pointed at the porthole and the planet hanging like a jewel just beyond it. "That is my *home*. My mother died there and was buried there. I want to be there."

"Highness, there are government procedures . . ."

"I don't care about the procedures!" Victor's fist slammed into the bulkhead again. "Damn you, I *am* the government. Recharge this JumpShip and we'll jump in closer."

"I can't."

"And I say you *can!*" Victor wanted to launch himself at the man, but he held back. He could see the image of Phelan in his mind, grinning at him and shaking his head. Before he could do something to spite that image of his cousin, Galen returned to the cabin accompanied by an older man with steely eyes and a face that looked chiseled from ice.

The ice man tapped the station master on the shoulder. "Go."

Victor nearly ripped into the new man, but he saw Galen shake his head slightly. The Prince held back as the station master left the cabin and the ice man closed the hatch. Taking his own time, the ice man made certain it was secure, then glanced at a boxy apparatus on his wrist. He punched two buttons, punched them again, then looked up.

"I am with the Intelligence Secretariat."

Victor leaned back against the bulkhead. "You're very welcome because I've seen damned little intelligence recently."

The man ignored Victor's remark. "You're here and you're going in at 1.5 gees because of security concerns."

"I'm ordering this ship to recharge and jump in close so I can make Tharkad by tonight."

The ice man shook his head. "You're not."

Victor waved his denial away. "I am. I'm not concerned about an attempt on my life."

"Neither was your mother."

That *hurt!* Victor's hands knotted into fists. "You son of a bitch, who do you think you are?"

"I know who I am." The man's eyes sparked cold blue fire. "I'm the person assigned to make sure the maggots and vipers don't do to you what they did to the Archon. I'm part of the machine that is trying to find the animal who killed her. Right now, along with Kommandant Cox here and maybe your brothers and sisters, I'm the only person in this system who cares if you make it to Tharkad at all."

The man's directness and bloodlessness poured in through the hole in Victor's anger that the earlier remark had opened. The Prince bit back his desire to snap at the man and crossed to his desk. He sat down and pointed both Galen and this security man to chairs. "Fine, so you're doing your job. Does that include briefing me?"

The man remained standing. "Most is need-to-know basis."

"I need to know."

''He doesn't.''

Galen smiled. ''Excellent point, Agent Curaitis.''

Galen started to get up from his chair, but Victor shook his head. ''Galen can hear it as well. Whatever clearance he needs he has. If I can't trust him, I can't trust anyone.''

Curaitis looked at Galen, then shifted his gaze to Victor. ''The assassin used a very sophisticated plan to defeat the security around Archon Melissa. He realized, as we did later, that the one weakness she had was for *mycosia* flowers. He used the pots in which they were kept to get to her.''

As the man spoke, Victor sensed his anger, but it seemed unfocused. Mostly it was revealed in the rigid way he stood giving his report. It made Victor uneasy at first, but then he imagined that anger directed at those who wished him harm.

''We always varied your mother's schedule significantly to prevent an assassin from using a time bomb effectively against her. Whoever killed her knew that, and also knew that we use radio-frequency scanners to pick up RF modulations from the kind of computer chips used in a computer-controlled bomb. If the bomb's chips are shielded to prevent emission of RF mods, then they are also shielded from taking outside input through radiowaves. They have to be timers, but time bombs are unreliable.''

Because you varied my mother's schedule. Victor nodded as he realized that Curaitis was not going to explain everything twice, so he paid even closer attention to his words. ''How did the bomb work, then?''

''A plastic explosive—SX-497, manufactured on Hesperus II, in a lot lost in shipping—was shaped into a plant pot form. It was then baked to hardness and coated with an acrylic sealant to prevent sniffers from detecting it. The guts from four cellular visiphones were set up to start a magnesium-thermite fuse when a call came in to the number for which all of them had been programmed.''

The Prince sat back. ''But the cellular units must have given off RF mods, correct?''

''The pots were sealed with a semi-permeable rubber coating that allowed water through. The power supply to the cellular units was connected through a countdown timer that was itself powered by a water-conversion cell. When enough water leaked through the rubber to power the conversion cell, the connecting timer came to life and counted down. When it was done, the visiphones became live. All this happened after the last RF sweep on the room.''

''Why wasn't one done later?''

Curaitis stared at Victor. ''The digital watches, cellular phones, pacemakers, cybernetic limbs, and a number of the high-fashion gowns worn that night gave off RF mods. Sweeping later than five-thirty in the evening would have been futile. We believe the devices went live at six-thirty, half an hour after the doors opened and people started filing into the room. The assassin watched the speeches on the public-access holovid channel and made his call when your mother started to speak. Sometime thereafter the devices exploded.''

Victor's jaw fell open. ''You have the assassination on holovid?''

''Multiple angles. Review of the tapes are how we determined it was the pots that exploded and not the stand that held them.''

''I want to see the tapes.''

''Victor!'' Galen half rose out of his chair. ''Do you know what you're asking?''

''Galen, there might be something there that I—''

''No, Victor, no!'' Galen almost leaped from his chair. ''There is nothing on those tapes that Curaitis and the Secretariat specialists haven't already gone over. Just because you saw your father die does not mean you have to watch your mother die, too.''

''But, if there is something, Galen, I have to find it.''

''This is madness, Victor. You don't need to torture yourself.''

''I will have the tapes for you when we reach Tharkad,'' Curaitis said.

Galen turned on him. ''You can't.''

''Do you have a reason for not wanting the Prince to see them, Kommandant?''

Victor saw Galen stiffen and for a half-second wondered what Galen had to hide. *Why is Curaitis suspicious of Galen? Why did he want him out of the room? Does*

Curaitis have evidence to link Galen to my mother's murder?

Victor's aide straightened up and shook his head. "You're very good, Agent Curaitis. You see me as a risk and work to eliminate me. I applaud this principle, but not its application. The Prince is my friend as well as my lord and it is that which makes me think that perhaps, just perhaps, he is better off remembering his mother the way she always was, *not* after a bomb blew her to bits."

Galen turned to Victor. "I know you, Victor. I know you think nothing gets done unless you do it yourself. That works in a military command, but not in government. Your responsibilities are greater now and will go unfulfilled if you mire yourself in the details of your mother's death."

Victor looked up at his friend and heard the caution in his words. "You're right, Galen, but you also know I have no choice. I am who I am, and I cannot let her death go unavenged."

"Vengeance will come when men like Curaitis finish their investigations, Victor."

Victor nodded and shifted his gaze to the intelligence agent. "Do you know the assassin's identity?"

"We know who he became while on Tharkad. We know where he worked and what he did for the last six months of his life. His records beyond that seem complete, but are false. We are dealing with a professional who has been working on this mission for a long time, and appeared to be prepared to work on it yet longer, had the situation demanded." Curaitis' Adam's apple bobbed up and down. "We do not yet have him, but yes, we know he was a man."

Victor's eyes narrowed. "What has the public been told?"

"Deranged, disgruntled bomber. His record showed a mother who is in a home for the care of the senile. She knows nothing and lives in a world of dementia. A state subsidy pays for her care and the facility is not the best one could hope for. This has been used to explain what motivated the assassin. We believe he is already off Tharkad, but the public believes he committed suicide."

"If you think he's gone, then why the travel restrictions?" Victor saw Curaitis's head turn slightly. "I mean,

I assume trying to limit the speed of my ship is a general regulation to help you find the assassin by screening all outbound passengers.''

The security man shook his head. ''The public is very angry with you. Your mother lay in state for two days, as compared to your father's thirty-one day vigil.''

''But the bomb . . .'' Victor shook his head. ''She could not have been viewed as my father was.''

''You missed the funeral.''

''Not because I wanted to.'' The Prince looked at Galen. ''We left immediately and commandeered every JumpShip heading in this direction, and a few that were not. I am here as fast as I could be.''

Curaitis gave no sign of having heard Victor. ''It is said your sister cut the viewing short and had the funeral conducted quickly on your orders.''

''I told her to use her best judgment in the matter.''

''Word is you told her to 'burn the witch.' ''

''I never!''

''Peter, Arthur, and Yvonne made it to the funeral from New Avalon. They traveled five hundred and forty light years and made it faster than you made the two hundred-ten light-year run from Port Moseby.''

''Katherine thought it best that they be there,'' Victor snapped.

''Some people even believe you plotted your mother's death because she did not have the good sense to abdicate in your favor. It is said she refused to abdicate because you were secretly married to Omi Kurita on Outreach.'' The security man looked over at Galen. ''You must remember that one, for you are rumored to have been the best man.''

''That is outrageous!''

''It may be, gentlemen, but it is exactly what is being whispered in taverns and bars, laundries and stores, at social gatherings and over the visiphone.'' Curaitis' face remained dead. ''There is more. Did you know that you, Highness, actually tried to murder Kai Allard-Liao on Alyina because he advised you against pursuing your romance with Omi? It is becoming accepted as fact that he could have been taken off Alyina when you abandoned the planet but that you refused to wait for him. Men have sworn they heard his radio call but that you ordered the ships away.''

Victor slammed both his fists down on his desk. ''No! That is preposterous!'' He opened his mouth and tried to find words to express the extent of his disbelief and anger, but he could not. *Everything is perverted! Lies are being manufactured out of the truth.* ''How, who, why?''

Curaitis shrugged, for the first time the set of his shoulders easing a bit. ''I do not know, nor do I care. You have enemies, and you have allies. Kai Allard regularly dedicates victories to you on Solaris. Your older sister is your best defender. Peter, while very earnest, does not have the temperament to help your case at all. The first thing Morgan Kell wanted to know when he came out of surgery was if you had also been attacked. When the orders to the Hounds went out over your signature, he put off his wife's funeral so the bandits could be destroyed. You are not alone, but you *are* exposed and it is my job to make certain no one does to you what they did to your mother.''

Victor swallowed hard and stared at the picture of his family on one side of his desk. *My mother and father, gone. I feel so isolated. Is it too late to break through?* He looked up and narrowed his eyes. ''Agent Curaitis, you've mentioned my sister twice, but never called her by name.''

Curaitis looked at him but said nothing.

''What is her name?''

The security man's face remained unchanged. ''Katherine.''

''Good.'' Victor nodded. ''I am pleased to have you working for me. And I want to see those tapes.''

''I'll get them for you, but I want to correct one misconception.''

''Yes?''

''I don't work for you, I work to protect you.'' Curaitis smiled, but it was not pleasant. ''As we spend time together, you'll see the difference.''

''And if I don't?''

''You'll be dead and you won't much care.''

25

DropShip **Lugh**
Nadir Recharge Station, Great X
Federated Commonwealth
10 July 3055

Christian Kell pulled himself through the hatchway on the *Lugh*. "Came as soon as I could, Colonel. What's up?"

Daniel Allard waved Chris over to the communications console. "It's about time for Conal Ward to find something else to bitch about. I thought having a witness here to offer some input would be useful. You're drafted because Colonel Brahe has already threatened to kill him if they ever meet."

Chris laughed lightly, but he knew the Clansman must have been working hard if he succeeded in getting a rise out of the unflappable Akira Brahe, commanding officer of the First Regiment.

A commtech's voice came through the console speaker. "Message coming in from the *White Fang* for you, Colonel Allard."

Dan winked at Chris. "I can set my watch by him. Probably even has creases in his birthday suit." The Kell Hound commander punched a button on the console and the monitor filled with the image of a handsome man with a fierce scowl on his face. The anger in his eyes seemed to smolder from the depths of some dark, hidden place. "Good afternoon, Star Colonel Ward."

"Daniel, I have to break this prohibition you have placed on extra-system communications."

Dan Allard continued on as if he had not been interrupted. "I would like to present one of my battalion commanders, Major Christian Kell."

Conal Ward looked over at Chris from the screen, his expression darkening even further. "I should have expected it. You are the half-caste, freebirth bastard of Morgan Kell's brother, *quiaff?*"

Chris nodded. His face did not betray his shock at the words, but only because he knew Conal was trying to provoke him. Had the Clansman not added the word "freebirth" to his insult, Chris might have taken offense. That term, while a vile slur against any member of the genetically engineered Clan warrior caste, was meaningless in the Inner Sphere, where everyone was born "freely." *To react is to give him power over me, and that I shall not do.*

The Clansman looked back at Dan. "Colonel, I am required to make a report to my leader, the ilKhan. Since you have coerced the spineless ComStar bureaucrats into clinging to this fiction that their hyperpulse equipment is damaged, I am prepared to use my own hyperpulse generator."

Dan frowned, as if confused, but Chris knew from years of association with the older man that it was a mask of deception. "Star Colonel, a prohibition on communications is in place for a reason. I think your report can wait."

"And I think it cannot." The black-haired man pounded his fist into the palm of his other hand. "This is a military unit, Colonel. We have a chain of command."

Dan's head came up at Conal's furious tone. "And *this* is a military operation, Colonel. Your chain of command runs through me. Request denied."

"It was not a request, Colonel."

"It is still denied, Colonel Ward." Dan turned from the screen and nodded to Chris. "The reason I asked Major Kell to be present was to inform you of the reason we've been sitting at this recharge station with our tracking signals identifying us as merchant vessels. I know I have tried before, but you do not seem to understand. Major?"

Chris wanted to laugh out loud, but suppressed the desire. "Colonel, the desire for complete HP-communications silence is because we hope to make Great X a target for the raiders. We know what sort of information they were able to gather on Deia, and your transmission of the interrogation transcripts from the men you captured has been helpful. If we could debrief them, we think we could learn more.''

Conal shook his head. ''That is impossible. Those individuals have been destroyed.''

Dan blinked and came back around to face the screen. ''What? Destroyed?''

''That is what we Clans do with bandits. They are obviously defective.'' Conal became smug. ''We do not desire their presence in the gene pool, so we expunge it.''

Chris stared hard at Conal Ward's image on the screen. ''But in the transcripts they claimed that it was the Red Corsair who enslaved them and whose orders brought their release.''

''Disinformation. You can take nothing they said as fact.''

''But Hooper and Vandermeer both checked out as members of the Robinson Rangers. They were captured on Kooken's Pleasure Pit.'' Dan punched up data on an auxiliary screen. ''Voiceprints matched the men you had.''

''Then they were traitors and became even more deserving of death.''

Dan Allard shook his head. ''I think, from this point on, you will not be destroying any more prisoners. Consider that an order.''

Conal's face hardened. ''I will take it under advisement.''

''You will deliver all prisoners to the Kell Hounds, Star Colonel. You will maintain radio silence until such time as the raiders have committed their DropShips to a run on Great X Four.''

Chris marveled at how Dan kept his voice level and under control.

Conal seemed unimpressed. ''Or what, Colonel?''

''Do not challenge me, Conal Ward.'' Dan leaned forward and Chris saw his chest expand. ''I was on Luthien when we crushed the Smoke Jaguars and the Nova Cats. My 'Mechs are the equal of yours and my warriors are experienced in the ways of Clan combat. If you really want that chip knocked off your shoulder, I have six times as many warriors as you do, and every one of them would love to avenge the Zouaves.

"We're here to stop the bandits, Star Colonel. That comes first. When that's done, we can find some airless mudball where we can settle our differences. Until that time, you're under my orders, and those orders are to stick with the briefing we sent you earlier. Got it?"

Before Conal could reply, a new image filled the console. It was the regional traffic control scan of the solar system, showing little symbols and codes to designate all DropShips and JumpShips in the area. Chris immediately noticed a new symbol located at a pirate jump point two days out from Great X Four.

"Colonel Allard, we have a JumpShip arriving in-system. Prelim scan shows no IFF indicators and it seems to conform to previous scans made on the bandits."

Dan hit a button his desk and an alert klaxon began to blare throughout the *Lugh*. "This is it. To your machines. When the bandits commit, we make this their last raid."

Locked in the virtual world of the Red Corsair's base, Nelson Geist traveled alone with his thoughts. An internal conflict raged within him and it angered him because he knew that, on one level, the Red Corsair had engineered matters specifically to twist him up. That made him want to dismiss the whole lot and try to keep it out of his mind, but he could not.

She had remained good to her word and released some of the other slaves on Deia. She had summoned those captured on Kooken's Pleasure Pit and told them that *he* had chosen those who could go free. Then she had selected three men who had been with the Robinson Rangers and turned them loose. Though Nelson was glad for those men, it tore him up inside to see the anger in the eyes of Spider and the other Reservists, who believed he had betrayed them.

That, however, was a mere stone in the shoe compared to the other huge problem he faced. The Red Corsair had proved to be a voracious and skilled lover. She had kept him with her throughout the burn away from Deia and seemed almost drunk with happiness over having outrun the Wolves. In the intervening three weeks they had continued to spend their nights together, more often than not finally collapsing exhausted in each other's arms.

Nelson had never known such a sexual partner. With her there was no compromise, no surrender. Within days of their first encounter they had blasted beyond the envelope of what he had previously experienced, and never looked back. Their lovemaking seemed to rejuvenate him, even healing the damage his male pride had suffered because of the maiming of his hand. In bed they were equals and even partners, consuming and consumed by what they were and what they became together.

Yet when he awoke in her arms, the shock of where he was and who he was with would jerk him suddenly into crystalline consciousness. He was sleeping with the woman who had enslaved him. He was giving pleasure to the woman who kept his comrades in thrall and who forced him to kill others to prevent their deaths. He was drawing life from a woman who was a handmaiden to death, and finding rapture with someone who caused others to know grief and sorrow.

As much as he wanted to push her away, he could not. She was addictive and his only solace came from seeing that she seemed equally ensnared. They both knew that it could only lead to their mutual self-destruction, yet they laughed in the face of coming disaster. It was as if the paradoxes heightened the pleasure and the futility of it all made them hunger even more.

Then, as the bandits prepared for another raid, she began to distance herself from him in order to concentrate on the tasks they faced. He knew that the rejection was only temporary—she had said as much in words and deeds—but the hurt still surprised him. *All this time I've been wanting to be free of her because, deep down, I really do hate her, yet the separation is eating me alive.*

In an attempt to reestablish control over his emotions, Nelson descended to the deepest level of the main building, and headed for the corridor and doors that had caused him trouble on the eve of the Deia raid. *If I visualize her and get a shock, maybe I can start my own crude form of aversion therapy.* He smiled at the thought and turned the corner.

He braced for a shock, but none came. Instead he felt his head expanding like some cartoon character sucking on a compressed air hose. It grew larger and larger, with the world he saw before him splitting into two parallel views, then shrinking away to pinpoints. Bright white light surrounded the black dots and he tried to shut his eyes against the glare, but it seemed to feed directly into the vision centers of his brain.

As if drawn back into a slingshot and then released, the twin vision pellets shot forward. They expanded and rushed at him. He tried to duck away as they sailed in, but no matter what he did, they never deviated from their course.

He felt himself hit the right rail on the treadmill, then the moving rubber ribbon pulled his feet out from under him. He fell and slipped off the treadmill to the side. *What happened?* As he struggled to free himself from the goggles and earphones, he heard a siren signaling a call to battle stations.

He tried to roll up to his feet, but his head swam in familiar waves of nausea. *We jumped. We jumped into the next system. Where we are?*

As he lay on his back on the deck, the world stopped spinning. He tugged at his gloves and started to peel the markers off his body, but the siren died and three tones sounded. Hearing them, he reached out and grabbed one of the treadmill posts. *We're jumping again!*

The universe blew up like a bubble, then exploded. At once Nelson Geist saw himself as a quark in some ultra-large molecule and also knew that molecule was but a tiny part of himself. Those sensations fed back and forth, reflecting each other like facing mirror images repeating ad infinitum.

The hatch leading into the Red Corsair's cabin swung open and she lurched into the room. She laughed aloud, then crossed to where he lay, and kneeled to kiss him full on the mouth. "It was wonderful, Nelson. Almost perfect!"

"What?"

"They were waiting for us at Great X. They could have had us, too, had they waited until we'd committed ourselves to a raid." She lifted her head, baring her throat, and laughed again. "Trust the Wolves to be overeager. When we appeared, they immediately issued a challenge. We jumped to our secondary destination and left them wondering where we had gone!''

She lowered her faced toward his again and the fire in her beautiful eyes inflamed him. ''A narrow escape,'' he said.

She smiled devilishly. ''On the razor's edge, Nelson. To come so close to annihilation and to dodge it so handily. To be at the brink of death and get a reprieve.'' She reached out her hand and helped him to a kneeling position opposite her. ''There is only one thing that can make this day more perfect. Come with me and we shall both have it.''

Chris saw the JumpShip icon vanish from the screen. ''Where did it go?''

''They jumped again.'' Dan punched up a closed line to his JumpShip captain. ''Janos, get your navigators working on where a ship could have jumped from here. Correlate that data with our list of probable targets.''

''That will be a fairly long list, Colonel.''

''I don't care. If we're still sitting here when they hit a target, there will be hell to pay. Our lithium-fusion batteries are at 100 percent, so we can make two jumps if we have to, right?''

''Affirmative. We hit two stars, so does the *Bifrost* and that Wolf ship. That's six out of thousands.''

Chris nodded as Janos's statement sank in. A jump could take an FTL ship thirty light years in any direction, and the lithium-fusion batteries allowed each ship to store two jumps' worth of energy. Though the number of inhabited worlds within the jump range of Great X was limited to five, the number of uninhabited star systems approached triple digits, and the bandits could recharge their ship at any one of them.

''Colonel, it's not going to be an easy hunt. If they hit an inhabited world, we'll know and can react.''

''True, Chris, but what if they take a week to recharge for one jump and go. That could put them beyond our range.'' Dan shook his head and punched up the communications officer. ''Korliss, any clue as to why the bandits jumped out?''

"Nothing positive, sir, but I think they got a tight-beam message from the Wolves."

"Oh, really?" The surprised look on Dan's face melted into a deep scowl. "Lieutenant, do me the favor of getting Star Colonel Ward back in communication with me."

"Yes, sir."

Chris pointed to the screen's image of the system. "We have another ship in."

Dan nodded as the new icon flashed on the screen, then the whole system image vanished, to be replaced by Conal Ward's face. "Yes, Colonel Allard? What is it, I have to prepare for a jump."

"Oh, you do? And where would that be?"

"In pursuit of the bandits, of course."

"Of course." Dan's voice took on an edge that Chris had heard only once before and it gave him a start. "Star Colonel, we seem to have detected a broadcast from your ship to the bandits."

Conal nodded perfunctorily. "Yes."

"What would that have been, Star Colonel?"

"A standard combat inquiry, Colonel Allard. You must have gotten the same from the Smoke Jaguars on Luthien."

"We did indeed but we were not looking to ambush the Smoke Jaguars."

Conal's head came up. "Real warriors do not wait in ambush."

Dan snarled. *"Real* warriors follow orders."

"Another signal coming in, Colonel, from the new ship," announced Korliss' voice. "It's going to the Wolves, too."

"Split the screen." Dan continued to stare at Conal. "Understand these orders, Star Colonel—you stay where you are until *I* tell you where you are going."

"I take no orders from any mercenary!"

"Then you *will* take them from me, Star Colonel," a new voice commanded as Phelan's face joined Conal's on the screen. "The ilKhan sends you greetings, Colonel Allard. We are here to destroy bandits and we will do whatever it takes to accomplish our mission."

26

Caledonia
Federated Commonwealth
10 July 3055

The assassin abandoned his Carlos Negron identity at Lamon. At the planet's space station union hall, he sent messages that ComStar would eventually carry to his confederates. All similarly worded, the messages said that he had met a woman and would be staying with her for a while on Lamon. He asked that communications be sent care of the union hall, where he would pick them up.

That was a lie, of course, because he expected no messages. The few friends Carlos Negron had were among his fellow workers, who also liked to keep to themselves. Any messages to Negron would be from agents who had somehow tied him to the assassination, and those were communications he definitely did *not* want to answer.

On the Lamon station Carlos underwent a startling transformation from a hard-drinking, foul-mouthed longshoreman to a black-clad member of the neo-Puritanical Wildmon sect. Wearing a crisply starched black suit and black hat that hid most of his face, he boarded a DropShip for the short hop to Caledonia. Fearing a dressing-down for almost anything, no one aboard ship spoke to him during the trip, which he did not mind at all.

At Caledonia the assassin again changed his identity, once more using a room held for a dummy corporation. The fearsome Wildmon vanished and was replaced by Chuck Grayson. Grayson, bound for a gaming junket on Solaris, dressed in gaudy clothes that would have sent a

Wildmon member into convulsions. Chuck booked passage on the DropShip *Lady Luck,* stowed his gear in his cabin, and immediately headed for a lounge.

In the lounge his garish clothes were like tiger stripes in a jungle. Worming his way through a press of merrymakers, he ended up shoulder to shoulder with a stunning brunette wearing a sarong made from the same patterned cloth as his shirt. "You have wonderful taste in clothes, Miss. . . ."

Her green eyes studied him going up and coming down again. "Calley. I'm Judith Calley, but my friends call me Jude. And your taste is impressive, Mr . . . ?"

"Charles Grayson, and my friends call me Chuck." The assassin saw the bartender hand her two thick, slushy drinks with a paper umbrella stuck in each one. "Are those good?"

Jude nodded. "Delicious." She sipped one and licked her lips. "I'd give you one, but the other is for my cabin-mate. Join us over in the corner when you order."

As she moved away, the assassin told the bartender to get him one of the same, then pressed a thumb to the bar tab, which immediately logged the price of the drink to his account. Taking the drink, he cut back through the crowd and found the corner table. Jude moved over so he could sit next to her on the edge of the semicircular booth.

"Chuck, this is Ronda, my cabin-mate, and John and Toni and Georgie and Mike."

"Chuck Grayson. Hi." He sat down and smiled politely as he felt Jude's right leg press against his left. "You all seem to know each other. Did you just meet here, or . . . ?"

John, a tall, muscular man—the group's alpha male—leaned back and looped his arm over Toni's shoulders. "We all work for Fennic-Dobbs, in the electronics sales division. The figures for sales last Christmas finally came in, and our department had the highest sales *and* the highest collection rate. Because of it, we won a two-month junket to Solaris."

"Very nice." Chuck raised his glass and smiled. "Congratulations."

Ronda gulped a bit of her drink. "What do you do, Chuck?"

The assassin forced a blush on Chuck. "I'm a ghost writer. I work with celebs and other bigwigs and help them write autobiographies. I also do some of those instant-bio things on celebs who hit big."

John's dark eyes sharpened. "So is this trip business or pleasure?"

"It's supposed to be the former, but I hope for a bit of the latter." He smiled easily. "I'm going to see if I can get an interview with Kai Allard-Liao. . . ."

Ronda squealed delightedly. "Oh, he's such a *dream.*"

Everyone at the table laughed a bit and Ronda turned a brilliant shade of red. "Well, he is."

"I hope you're not alone in feeling that, Ronda. I could use the sales." The assassin tasted the fruity drink and immediately realized the thing was packed with alcohol. He set it back down and resolved to nurse the drink for a long time. "He's never talked about what he did on Alyina, and my publisher hopes I can get him to spill the story."

Ronda smiled like a cat that had caught a whole flock of canaries. "I heard that after Prince Victor tried to kill him, Kai led the planet in a revolt that threw off the Clans and that he killed the Clan leader in single combat—thereby becoming the ruler of the world."

Toni, the petite blonde beneath John's beefy arm, spoke in a quiet voice. "I don't think the Prince tried to kill Kai."

Mike laughed aloud. "Toni, you don't believe Victor killed the Archon, either."

"He didn't."

Jude leaned over and stage-whispered to him, "Toni met the Prince once, years ago. She grew up on Tharkad and went to one of the Nagelring dances."

Toni's head came up and her lower lip thrust out defiantly. "I did meet him, and I even danced with him. He's too nice to have killed the Archon. He wouldn't do it."

The assassin shook his head. "I've been buried in writing a book for the past couple of months. The Prince killed his mother?"

John waved the assertion off. "Nothing official."

"You think they'd say if there was?" Ronda asked.

Mike pushed his glass of beer aside, and began to draw on the table with his left hand. "It's like this, Chuck. Victor ordered his sister to let his mother lie in state for only two days and then had her buried in a funeral he didn't attend. Now they say he's personally working at directing the investigation of his mother's death and that he keeps viewing all the films about it. If his sister Katrina wasn't running interference for him, the whole Federated Commonwealth—or at least the Lyran part of it—would be in chaos."

Chuck nodded thoughtfully. "Mind you, I'd not put it past any ruler of the Inner Sphere to kill his predecessor. Face it, the average person lives to be a hundred, but if you're a ruler, you die at least twenty years shy of that mark. I also seem to remember some very short-lived rumors that the Archon had her husband knocked off so she could rule the Federated Commonwealth, but those proved groundless."

Ronda shook her head. "Yes, but remember—it was Victor who found his father. Who's to say old Victor didn't kill Hanse, too?"

"With his mother in line to rule?" John frowned. "No motive."

"Hanse was going to strip the Tenth Lyran Guards from Victor because of a confidential report from Kai Allard saying that Victor had tried to murder him on Alyina. Besides, Hanse was going to disown his son because he couldn't stand the fact that Victor married Omi Kurita while he was in Drac space."

Georgie rapped her knuckles on the table top. "You're wrong about Victor, all of you. The Archon was killed by a member of the Nature First movement. They killed her with the *mycosia pseudoflora* to protest the warping of genetics for human whim and pleasure. That official line about a nut is just a diversion."

"If you're right," Ronda challenged, "then why are so many questions still not answered?"

"Because the government doesn't want folks to know how widespread Nature First really is. It would cause a panic."

Jude gave him a little nudge. "They'll go on about this for hours. I want to stretch my legs. Care to tour the ship?"

The assassin nodded. "My pleasure."

"That can be arranged." Jude took his hand in hers and turned to her friends. "We'll see you later, *much* later."

27

Victor's steady hand and practiced manipulation of the holovid remote control slowed the image to near immobility. The picture of his mother remained clear, as if, cell by cell, it had been etched on the inside of the holovid viewer screen. With every little movement or shift in her facial expression, a horde of memories surged up into his thoughts. *You are too young to have died, Mother.*

Victor cringed as she raised her right hand to emphasize a point. Like a signal to someone outside the picture, her gesture seemed to call forth an intense brightening of the light in front of her. It burned away all the shadows and fatigue lines, the next moment burning away her whole image, leaving the screen filled with only fire and destruction.

Hearing a sharp rap on his door, Victor hit the Pause button. "Enter," he said impatiently.

Galen Cox opened the door, then closed it behind him with a military crispness that Victor had not seen in the man since their first meeting. He snapped his hand up in a salute and held it until Victor returned the gesture. "You sent for me, sir?" Galen remained standing at attention like a cadet braced for a dressing-down.

The Prince nodded and swiveled away from the screen and toward the spread of folders on his desk. He picked up a single sheet of paper. "What is this supposed to be, Galen?"

"It's a Form 342881-A, Request for a Transfer of Duty, sir."

"Enough of that, Galen." Victor wadded the request and tossed it into a wastebasket. "Request denied."

"In that case, sir, I will resign my commission immediately."

Victor's head came up, realizing from Galen's tone that this was not some joke. "What's going on here, Galen? You're my friend. I need you."

The blue-eyed MechWarrior looked down at his commander. "Permission to speak freely, sir?"

"As always, Galen."

"No, sir, not as of late." Galen's stiff posture shifted and his hands settled on his hips. Victor knew his friend was preparing to blast him, and though he wanted to forestall it, something made him hold his tongue.

"Highness, with all due respect, you don't need me at all. You're not listening to my advice, nor that of anyone else. You're not doing your job and you're headed for disaster. I like you too much to want to hang around and see that."

Victor felt the sting of Galen's words and knew his criticisms echoed doubts stuffed away somewhere in his own mind. "What are you talking about?"

"Highness, in the years we've known each other I've seen two things in your personality that identify you as accurately as any retinal pattern. The first is that you're incredibly judgmental. You look at a person and think you've got him or her pegged after hearing a few sentences out of the person's mouth. And ninety-nine times out of a hundred you're dead right. That sometimes makes you a bear, and coupled with your willingness to speak your mind, it also makes you a diplomatic nightmare."

"I have to judge people. I need to know who is using me and who isn't."

"I know that better than you, Highness, but the problem is that you're not perfect. That one time out of a hundred when you botch it up is when you hurt people. Worse yet, you can overlook treachery that's well-hidden."

The Prince's head came up. "Name me one case. . . ."

"I can't, dammit, but that's not the point."

"What is, then?"

"The point is that you are more than capable of developing blind spots." Galen jabbed a finger in Victor's direction. "And coupled with the second trait, it's getting you into trouble right now."

Victor fought to keep his temper under control. "And that second trait is?"

Galen laughed lightly. "Polite folks say you're driven, others say you're overcompensating for the fact that you're not tall. I'd probably say you're goal-oriented, but it all boils down to the same thing—you have an unequaled capacity for obsessiveness."

Victor waved Galen's assertion off angrily. "I don't have to listen to this."

"Yes you do, dammit. You owe it to me because I've bloody well saved your life. I got your butt off Trellwan and I was ready to die with you on Alyina. You owe listening to me to all the men and women who died so you could live. If you don't listen, if you don't change, you're going to be a laughingstock and history will say those who sacrificed were a bunch of clowns."

Galen wouldn't let Victor interrupt. "You're obsessing on the damned murder of your mother."

"You would too, if—"

"No, I wouldn't." Galen shook his head slowly. "My parents died in the War of 3039. Dracs killed them. Call it collateral damage, whatever, it doesn't matter. They died at the hands of Kurita soldiers. My desire for revenge sent me off to the military, but I *grew up*. I realized that my parents had their counterparts in Combine civilians who also died when we hit their planets. Fate hadn't singled me out for the destiny of leading a crusade to destroy the Draconis Combine.

"Looking at reality in the cold clarity of mature thought, I realized my job was to protect the people of the Federated Commonwealth. I'm not here to avenge my parents, but to make sure no one else loses theirs. Since I met you I've gained a greater perspective and I realize the well-being of the Federated Commonwealth affects billions and billions of lives. If my role of protector means I have to tell you that your head is so far up your ass that you could bite off your own tonsils, I will." He glanced down. "Until last month I could have, but I haven't needed to until now and it *is!*"

The Prince had started to build up a head of steam, but Galen's one-two punch knocked it back out of him. *I never knew his parents were dead. . . . Why didn't I? He is a friend, a close friend. Why didn't he ever tell me?* Victor realized in an instant that he had always treated Galen like a faithful retainer, not a real human being. Galen Cox had become for him what Ardan Sortek had been to his father—an aide and a bellwether. It dawned on him that Galen was Horatio to his Hamlet, and that comparison sank a dagger into Victor's heart.

Am I obsessing? The moment he asked the question, he knew the answer. He also felt compelled to defend his action. "I'm just trying to find out who killed my mother."

"That is nonsense and you know it, sir." Galen walked over to the screen and rapped it with his knuckles. "You've been torturing yourself because you imagine that you could somehow have saved her. You're thinking, *dreaming*, that if you'd been there you could have prevented her death. You would have spotted the bomb. You would have prevented the blast from killing her.

"Grow up!" Galen shook his head slowly and with a finality that killed Victor's wildest "what if" fantasies. "The Intelligence Secretariat has gone over the tapes again and again. I know you've seen their frame-by-frame analysis hundreds of times. They know everything that happened and how it happened. There is nothing more you can learn, yet you persist. If you don't deal with the problems that is creating, you're going to wish you had been there and within the blast radius."

"What are you talking about?"

Galen folded his arms across his chest. "You never get out, but I do. The way rumors have been running rampant in the city, I'd guess they're probably spreading across the whole Federated Commonwealth by now. The stories range from the ridiculous to the truly vicious. People are saying that you have taken charge of the investigation to cover for your mother's murderer."

The Prince's eyes narrowed. "And who would that be?"

"An agent working for you." Galen glanced at the screen again. "Morgan Kell."

"What!" Victor hit the Rewind button, then punched another that switched the read-laser to a different section of the holovid disk. Instead of the close-up front view, the scene appeared as shot from a profile camera that showed Morgan Kell and his wife sitting with their chairs half-turned toward the podium. As Victor punched the Play button, the scene began to crawl forward.

Morgan turned back toward the camera to smile at his wife. As he did so, his napkin dropped from his lap. Twisting around, he half-ducked down to retrieve it. At precisely that moment the flowers exploded and the whole scene dissolved into static.

Victor popped the viewpoint over to another camera, which presented an elevated three-quarters view. Thick smoke billowed up and out from where the podium had stood and little flames licked at the corners of the semi-circular hole blown in the dais itself. From the right side of the screen a nightmare creature emerged. What was left of his dress jacket hung in smoldering tatters on his body. Blood streamed from his nose and ears. His broad chest hid his right arm from view until a security man leaped up onto the dais and tried to grab him.

Morgan Kell pushed the man way with his left arm, flinging him into the air and out into the crowd. As he did so, his torso twisted and Victor saw a skeletal arm hanging from Morgan's right shoulder. The mercenary knelt where Melissa had been standing and reached his left hand out toward her body.

The Prince killed the picture. "How can they suspect Morgan? He lost his arm."

"And you bought him a new one, Highness."

"My God, Galen, the man went to help my mother even before realizing the blast had killed his wife! If that were not enough, he is one of my closest living relatives." Victor looked up, appalled. "How can they believe such things?"

"They do so, Highness, because you give them nothing else to think about." Galen shook his head. "You are now the ruler of a star-spanning empire. You are not some amateur detective. You have many more duties to attend to than to see if you can spot the vital clue concerning your mother's death. I can tell you, I don't think that clue exists. I think Curaitis has it right—a professional did the job and even *if* you were to find him, you might not be able to learn who hired him because he might not know.''

The Prince nodded as Galen reminded him of his greater responsibilities. ''How bad are things out there?''

Galen shrugged his shoulders. ''I'm not a political advisor, but people are angry. You and I both know why you told your sister to use her best judgment about your mother's lying in state and the funeral, but it doesn't play well to the masses. To them there is only one reason that you did *not* attend the funeral and that your brothers and sisters *did*—they think you didn't love your mother.''

''But that's not true.''

''Again, you and I know that, but *they* don't.'' Galen opened his hands in a gesture of helplessness. ''You need to do things. You need to have memorial coins struck and memorial bills printed. You need to give money to charities your mother supported and you need to endow some scholarship funds in her name.''

''But those are gestures, they mean nothing.''

''You might see it that way, but the people do not. Sure, you're a war hero, but your most daring exploit involved a mission to save the heir to the throne of a sworn enemy. Then you invited Phelan to Arc-Royal, a man they see as a traitor to the Inner Sphere. Then this same traitor had the gall to arrive here with a captured Inner Sphere prince in bondage, and you did nothing. Finally you have allowed a Clan Cluster free access to Commonwealth space. None of this goes over well with the people you rule.'' Galen reflected for a moment, then nodded. ''I tell you what, if I were you, I'd keep your mother's face on the money and delay putting your face on it for a year or so.''

Victor was surprised at his own reaction to that suggestion because he'd never have thought having his face on money—a sign of his accession to the throne—would mean so much to him. Part of him realized that he had always subconsciously looked forward to it as an affirmation of his right to rule, but another part of him saw the wisdom of Galen's words.

''For someone who disavows any political acumen,

Galen, you have some skill in that area." Victor made a note on a slip of paper. "Consider those suggestions implemented. Have you others?"

"One. Give some interviews."

"I don't have time to talk to reporters and media folk."

"You don't have time not to. People already see you as your father in miniature. They're afraid you're going to start a war, and in many ways, they think your father didn't do enough to stop the Clans. Yes, I know that's stupid, but they don't. All they see is the former Federated Suns untouched by the war, while their worlds are dotted with refugee camps."

Galen chuckled. "Look, I know you're not comfortable with the media, but why not talk to Katherine about it? She knows how to handle them and she can probably give you some pointers."

The Prince frowned, then nodded. "All right, I'm willing to do that, but I want something from you in return."

"What?"

Victor pointed at the black screen. "I still want the people who killed my mother. That means the assassin and whoever hired him. If I accept that you're right and that I've been obsessing about this, I also accept that I'm too close to it. What am I doing wrong?"

"I don't know. I know the intelligence folks have put together a psych profile of the assassin, but they're trying to follow whatever trail he might have left. They're as much interested in learning why and how he got through their security as they are in catching him. And even catching him won't tell you who hired him."

"You're saying I have two problems, right?"

"Hard lock and fire." Galen's hands again rested on his hips, but the set of his shoulders was no longer belligerent. "The assassin was a professional and had to be working for money because no political groups have claimed responsibility for the assassination. Tracking him down is likely to be frustrating and full of dead-ends, but at least we know what could bring him out of hiding."

"Money."

"Yes, that and an assignment worthy of the man who killed the Archon of the Federated Commonwealth. Taking the time and the care he did to get to your mother means that he thinks of himself as a virtuoso, whether he's aware of it or not. I doubt he would be willing to risk himself on a job that was less a test of his skills than your mother was.''

Victor nodded slowly. ''The Intelligence Secretariat has said that assassins of that caliber have been known to base themselves on Solaris. With the traffic there and the relatively open nature of the world, getting in and out and laundering money is easy. We could put the word out on Solaris.'' Victor smiled slowly. ''In fact, I think I know just the person to do the job.''

''Good, then maybe you'll get the assassin.'' Galen frowned. ''But that still leaves his patron.''

''That won't be easy. From what you say, most people think I'm the person who had the most to gain from her death.''

Galen nodded. ''True enough, but you have an advantage because you know you didn't do it. Make a list of who else benefits besides you, then weed them out by process of elimination.''

''What do I do when I get down to the finalists?''

Galen Cox shook his head. ''That question is precisely why uneasy rests the head that wears the crown.''

28

Cue Ball, Moon orbiting Yeguas III
Federated Commonwealth
30 July 3055

The stark contrast between the chalky white dust of the canyon and the black vault overhead struck Nelson Geist as the difference between life and death itself. The Red Corsair's JumpShip had entered the Yeguas system at a pirate point close to the third planet. Waiting for them at the system's apex jump point was the Thirty-first Wolf Solahma.

The Wolves immediately issued a combat challenge to the raiders, which the Red Corsair just as promptly accepted. She offered to meet them on Cue Ball, but told them that if they didn't make it there within six days, their window to stop her was closed, because she was leaving then.

The jump point where the Wolves had been waiting was seven and a half days out at a normal one gravity burn. The Wolves pushed their acceleration to two gravities, thereby shaving two days off the transit time. Nelson was with the Red Corsair when she got the report, and he thought she would be displeased because it meant she would finally have to face the Wolves.

"Hardly, Nelson," she purred. "I look forward to fighting the Wolves. The Clans send scum to fight bandits, and I will bloody their scum for them."

The Red Corsair grounded her BattleMechs on Cue Ball and took advantage of the waiting time to give her troops a chance to become accustomed to the reduced gravity. With far less mass than a normal world, Cue Ball had .47 standard gravities. BattleMechs could move faster and jump further, but their ability to stop and turn was also affected. In the exercises she conducted, the Red Corsair had Nelson backseating her and she turned fire control over to him while she mastered the delicacies of movement on the airless moon.

Leaving her bandits on the lunar surface, the Red Corsair had sent her DropShips in at Yeguas. Radioing ahead, she told the world's government that she would not feel the need to attack if they would send shuttles out with "tribute." What she asked for was fairly conservative and consisted mostly of food and inexpensive baubles. The government decided in very short order that paying the tribute would do fine, probably believing they would get it back after the Wolves trashed the bandits.

Waiting in the high gunnery seat of the *BattleMaster,* Nelson watched on his auxiliary monitor as two Wolf Clan DropShips grounded and began to disgorge BattleMechs. "It looks like three Trinaries of fifteen 'Mechs each and a command Star. That's fifty to our seventy-five. Their commander must be insane."

The Red Corsair shook her head. "Not at all. He holds us in contempt. He will pay." She started her *BattleMaster* walking down to the mouth of the canyon that opened into the vast crater where the Wolves had deployed. According to her plan, the other bandits should be all around them, making similar approaches through the cracks in the crater's walls.

The image on Nelson's auxiliary screen showed the Wolves deploying in attack groups and moving forward in a haphazard way. "I don't understand. . . .They should be good troops." A light laugh from the Red Corsair made him realize suddenly why the Wolves looked and moved so oddly. "Coming in at two gees' acceleration, compensating for the reduced gravity is even more difficult here. The contrast is even greater because of the fatigue from coming in that fast."

"Very good, Nelson." The Red Corsair hit a button on her console and a holographic display with a gold crosshairs in the middle materialized in front of him. "Fire control is yours."

"Do my friends go free if I kill Wolves?"

"No, but neither do they die if we do." Her voice sank

to a throaty whisper as she worked the *BattleMaster* around a corner. "You have no love for the Clans and I have no love for the Wolves. We are allies in this fight."

Nelson hesitated an instant, then nodded. "Fire control accepted."

"Get ready." She stepped the *BattleMaster* into the mouth of the canyon and raised both arms above the 'Mech's head. Opening a broadbeam radio channel, she offered the Wolves a challenge of her own. "Welcome, you freebirth whelps of a mangy bitch cur. It is time to show you why you are fit for nothing but bandit bait."

Her words had an immediate effect on the Clanners, and Nelson knew that the Wolves had lost the battle even before the first shot was fired. Two light 'Mechs thrust forward, one arcing into the dark sky on twin jump jets. The 'Mech looked like a *Stinger,* hardly a threat. The other one, which the onboard computer identified as a *Hermes,* struck him as more dangerous, so he covered it with the *BattleMaster*'s targeting crosshairs.

It was in trouble even before he shot at it. The pilot, unused to the light gravity, had pushed the 'Mech to full throttle. The 'Mech's speed built faster than normal, taking it from a steady, pumping gait to long, leaping strides that dangerously unbalanced the BattleMech. The *Hermes* pilot lost control of the war machine as it came down in a small field of boulders.

Nelson had managed to keep tracking it and began to punch the *BattleMaster*'s firing studs without remorse. The first PPC bolt clawed its way through the *Hermes'* right chest, taking with it all the structural supports in that side of the 'Mech's torso. The second PPC bolt speared the 'Mech's right arm. The *Hermes* shed armor on the limb like dead skin, then the arm itself withered away to white fire and black smoke.

The PPC bolts actually contained enough energy to slow the *Hermes* and straighten it up for a second. They started it twisting back around to the right, then its legs ran out from under it. The 'Mech flew ahead, legs first and bent at the knees, with its left hand clawing at the stars. A boulder sheared its shins off. The torso hit hard, then bounded up above the planet's surface, trailing the dust that the hole in its chest had scooped out. It hit again and rolled into a house-sized rock, then bounced off and lay dented and dead, staring at the stars.

As the *Stinger* started to come down, Nelson shifted his aim up to where it intersected with the 'Mech's gentle trajectory. If the pilot had been smart, he would have hit his jets again and changed course, but he did not. Nelson figured that the pilot, unnerved by how far he had actually flown in one jump, wanted nothing better than to be grounded again. *We aim to please.*

One PPC bolt missed high, but the other hit the *Stinger* in the right knee. The azure lightning stabbed straight through the joint, exploding armor and amputating the lower half of the leg. The lesser portion of the limb started to spin backward while the *Stinger* began a slow, rolling somersault.

Nelson next hit the *Stinger* with the *BattleMaster*'s center-mounted large pulse laser. The green energy darts peppered the *Stinger*'s torso and actually stopped the forward roll. The laser fire blasted away all the armor over the 'Mech's heart and melted away some internal supports, but it failed to put the 'Mech out of commission.

But Nelson had allies in inertia and the moon itself. As the *Stinger* slammed into the ground on the right side of its chest, the medium laser in its right hand flew up and away in pieces. The 'Mech itself, with armor shards dropping away like scales from a lizard, rebounded from the collision and almost became upright again. The pilot, had he remained alive or conscious after the landing, might have been able to stabilize the 'Mech and brace it against the dolmen into which it had sailed. As it was, the 'Mech smacked straight up against the huge rock, then both rock and machine wavered and fell down, toppling onto their backs like mirror images.

Throughout the crater Nelson saw other bandits shooting at Wolf Clan 'Mechs. Some of the Wolves had advanced, but most had ended up like the two that charged at the Red Corsair. One core group of heavy 'Mechs was shooting back without moving, but only their beam weapons had any effect. The missiles and projectile weapons, not having been recalibrated for the lower gravity, consistently shot high.

The Red Corsair hit a button on her console. "Corsairs, pull back."

Nelson hit his intercom. "Pull back? The battle hasn't even begun."

"Unless the Wolf commander is even stupider than *you* could imagine, the battle is over." She stepped her 'Mech backward into the canyon as a missile impacted against the crater walls high above her. "I am turning now. Watch our back."

Nelson used a round dial to spin the holographic view so that their rear area appeared dead-center on the display. "Covered. Both rear lasers operational. But why is the battle over?"

"The commander knows that we will pick his forces apart if he follows us into the canyons. This is not the sort of battle he bargained for. He has lost some light 'Mechs, but they can be repaired. If he presses the attack, he might lose more substantial machines *and* we might even sneak in and take some of the damaged machines away from him. He could never stand to have that happen."

"It sounds like you know the Wolf commander well."

She shook her head. "Never even heard of him, but I know his type. We tricked him here. We will not get the better of him in this way again, but we will best him. He will be wondering what we are up to in the future, and that will count for a very great deal."

29

DropShip **Lugh**
Apex Recharge Station, Santana
Federated Commonwealth
3 August 3055

Khan Phelan Ward frowned at his cousin. "I think I am missing something here, Chris. Your reaction to my denying your request to send your battalion to Yeguas is grossly out of place."

"Is it?" Chris pointed to the holographic display of the Yeguas system hovering above the briefing table. "When the bandits arrived, the Wolves reported that they had showed up at a pirate point near both Cue Ball and Yeguas III. You yourself said they were going to be burning in too fast if the bandits should decide to skip out instead of letting the Wolves ground for a battle. Had you permitted, my battalion could have jumped in and kept them from getting to their JumpShip. It seems like you don't want the bandits caught after all."

Phelan said nothing and forced down his anger. When he spoke, the words came in a neutral tone, but he bit them off sharply, giving both Dan Allard and Christian Kell ample warning of his darkening mood. "First off, cousin, I did not prevent you from going. I am not in command of this operation. Colonel Allard made that decision, but he gave weight to my request to let the Thirty-first handle most of the problem. When we drew lots to see *where* we would station ourselves, they got Yeguas. Had you gotten Yeguas, I am certain the Thirty-first's request to help you would have been similarly denied."

The Wolf Clan Khan rose from his seat and stared at the other man across the table. "I do not like the implication that I am not anxious to catch these bandits. I want them destroyed more than you know."

"That is not apparent by your action, or *inaction*, cousin." Chris folded his arms across his chest. His shirt sleeves were rolled up to his elbows, revealing a riot of tattooed colors decorating his left forearm, but Phelan could not make out the full design. "I think you are operating from a hidden agenda that will ultimately culminate in the resumption of war between the Clans and the Inner Sphere."

Phelan shook his head vehemently. "That's ridiculous. I am here to do just the opposite."

"Are you?" Chris turned to where Dan Allard remained seated at the head of the briefing table. "Fact: the bandits are making our military units look stupid. Fact: they're using tactics against us that we used against them with great success. Fact: all that's needed to reignite the war is for a Clan unit to pass over the truce line, and these bandits are halfway there—with another Clan unit hot on their tails."

Phelan slapped his right hand flat against the table. "There is no proof the bandits are a Clan unit."

"Ha! Look at their equipment. Look at their tactics."

"If we look at equipment, Chris, the Kell Hounds are more of a Clan unit than the bandits. Unity, the Hounds have better equipment than the Thirty-first Wolf Solahma." Phelan leaned forward and the computer painted part of the Yeguas system on his throat. "You yourself said the bandits employed Inner Sphere tactics, which makes them highly atypical of any Clan unit. I'll not deny there are Clan renegades among the bandits—and they may even be running the operation, but this pirate band is no Clan unit."

"Is not, or just that you don't want it to be?"

Chris's question caught Phelan off-guard and sent a little jolt through him. *Could the Red Corsairs be Clan and on a covert mission to disrupt the truce? If so, why masquerade as bandits?* Even as he pondered the question, an answer slowly formed in his mind. If the unit pretended to be bandits, they could continue their raiding spree while the rest of the Clans built up a desire to fight against the Inner Sphere again. When the unit crossed the line they could openly declare themselves Clan, fracturing the peace. The Inner Sphere would respond *en masse,* never believing the fake bandits had operated on their own. If, on the other hand, the bandits had come in as a straight military unit, the ilKhan could have repudiated them and forced the offending sponsor Clan to disown them or else face trouble in the form of a Grand Council.

And the Jade Falcons say the bandits originated in Wolf Clan space. If the raiders are Clan, the Wolves will be blamed and the ilKhan's efforts to keep the peace will look like the most hideous betrayal of the Precentor Martial and the Inner Sphere.

Phelan shook his head. "Your question has no meaning, Chris. The bandits have not declared themselves Clan, we have no evidence they are Clan, nor has any Clan claimed them. To decide, in absence of fact, that they *are* Clan is to complicate matters unnecessarily."

"I don't believe that is true. Look, the raids are helping promote the general impression that Victor Davion is not effective as a ruler and that he cares more about the Federated Suns than he does the Lyran Commonwealth. Ryan Steiner is gathering together a coalition able to exert considerable pressure on Victor. There is nothing that would better serve the interest of the Clans than instability in the government of the Federated Commonwealth."

"Chris, listen to yourself." Phelan sighed heavily. "With the evidence you've just presented, we should surmise that Ryan Steiner is behind the bandits because *he* benefits more from their raids than even the Clans do. In fact, with the bandits making the Wolves look like morons, you'd think that would bolster up the morale of the Federated Commonwealth and its people."

"Gentlemen, I think you are ranging far afield here, and it does us no good." Dan waved both men back to their chairs. "Chris, Phelan had good reasons for denying the request. Because of the movements of the other moon around Yeguas III, the nearest pirate point you could have jumped into was two days out at a two-gee burn, and that's only if your navigator could have sold Janos on letting a ship try for that one. And even if you could have gotten in, you couldn't have jumped back out for a week after that. The safer and better site would have been four days out, but in either case, the bandits could have returned to their ship and jumped out without you ever getting a shot at them.''

''Chris, it would have been worth a shot, *if* the Thirty-first Wolf Solahma had not been there to see you get tricked.''

''Our being there might have prevented them from being chewed up.''

Phelan shook his head and laughed, ''Chewing did them some good.''

Chris stared at him and Phelan wondered if he'd suddenly grown horns and a tail. ''My God in heaven, you have truly become one of them, haven't you?''

''What are you talking about?''

''You. You're one of the Clans.'' Chris shivered. ''You let warriors die on Cue Ball as though their lives were worthless.''

''The Thirty-first only lost two pilots.''

''But you couldn't have known that going in.'' The mercenary looked at his cousin with disbelief. ''Do they know you consider them disposable?''

Phelan stiffened. ''Certainly, in just the same way you told Zimmer's Zouaves they were meant to be flypaper.'' He saw Chris wince as the remark hit home. ''I don't consider the men and women of the Thirty-first Wolf Solahma expendable any more than you see any of your people that way. Yes, they may be warriors reduced to hunting bandits, but they are people. Even if they believe dying in combat is a fitting end to their lives, I do not.''

''Then how can you say gnawing is good for them.''

''You are right, Chris, I misspoke.'' The image of Conal Ward floated before Phelan's mind's-eye. ''Their commander is an old adversary of mine. All the things you attributed to me a moment ago you can tattoo on him and he would not mind at all. He did everything he could to prevent me from winning a Bloodname, including cheating in a sacred Clan ritual. As a result he was forced to resign from his position as Clan Loremaster, and had to accept duty as the head of a bandit-hunting unit. Because his hatred for the Inner Sphere nearly equals his hatred for me, he was assigned to destroy the Red Corsair and I was assigned to be his immediate superior.''

Phelan chewed his lower lip for a moment. "I doubt that Conal learned humility from being embarrassed by the Red Corsair, but I can hope. What is important is that he had his shot and he missed." He took in a deep breath and looked at Chris. "So, if you think I'm working with a hidden agenda, I guess I am. I want to see peace maintained. And the best chance for it is if the Kell Hounds dust these bandits while Conal's folks prove ineffective. That will weaken his position and help discredit his allies—all of whom oppose the peace."

Chris frowned in puzzlement. "I am not sure I understand."

"It is simple, actually. The Clans are split into two factions—the Crusaders and the Wardens. The Crusaders want to take over the Inner Sphere and become its rulers under a reborn Star League. The Crusaders are a minority in the Wolf Clan, but Conal is one of them. The Wardens, on the other hand, believe their mission is to protect the Inner Sphere. Though we predominate in the Wolf Clan, we are the minority in Clans such as the Jade Falcons and Smoke Jaguars."

"For all that your ilKhan is a Warden, he seems to have almost accomplished the Crusader goal." Chris punched up a larger star map that showed the wedge the Clans had driven down into the Inner Sphere. "The Wolves were the cutting edge."

"And the ilKhan negotiated the peace with ComStar. He had to be in front to stop the juggernaut, and he succeeded." Phelan traced the border area between the Federated Commonwealth and the Jade Falcon occupation zone. "The same kind of unrest you report here in the Commonwealth is happening within the Clans. The ilKhan faces pressure to abrogate the truce and press the attack. The bandits seem determined to show how weak the Inner Sphere is. If the Kell Hounds can crush the bandits, we'll put a lie to the myth of the Inner Sphere's vulnerability. It may not be enough to stop the pressure, but it will bleed much of it off."

Chris looked at Phelan curiously. "You said 'We'll put a lie to the myth.' Does that mean you consider yourself one of the Inner Sphere now?"

"By 'we' I meant those who realize the insanity of renewing the war." Phelan offered his cousin his hand.

"And, just so you know, joining the Clans did not include repudiating my family. You can trust me, Chris, as I trust you."

Chris shook the offered hand, but Phelan still saw doubt in his eyes. *You're too suspicious, Chris, but maybe that is what kept you alive in the Combine.* Phelan thought for a moment and nodded to himself. *If Conal is playing some sort of game, your suspicion might keep us all alive.*

Dan Allard smiled as the two men broke their grip. "I assume, Phelan, that you had more in mind than a family reunion when you originally asked for this meeting."

The Wolf Clan Khan nodded. "Aside from giving us solid readouts on the Red Corsair's 'Mechs, Yeguas showed us two things. The first is that the bandits don't seem to have aerospace assets. They did not use any to cover their DropShips headed out to get the tribute, nor did they use any to maul the Thirty-first. That leaves them very vulnerable, especially if we can ambush them as they come in on a run on a system."

Chris nodded, but his expression changed to a frown. "We could hide aerospace fighters in a DropShip in an asteroid field or behind a moon, but that would require knowing in advance where the Corsairs are going to be and where they will appear in that star system."

Phelan smiled triumphantly. "That's the second thing. Using the data we've collected concerning their arrival points, cross-correlating it with system data and the catalog of their pirate points that Janos Vandermeer has put together, we've isolated what is probably the program they are using for navigation. By running selections through a copy of that program, and selecting targets based on the parameters they appear to have used before, the list of candidates for their next attack gets damned tiny."

Dan leaned forward. "How tiny?"

Phelan stabbed a finger into a star in the starfield map. "Zanderij is their next target. And when they come in, we'll be waiting."

= 30 =

The assassin briefly debated whether or not he would have to kill Judith Calley. Though she knew him only as Chuck Grayson and apparently suspected nothing amiss, she might have picked up unconsciously on clues that could come back to haunt him later. After the time he had spent as Karl Kole, keeping so much to himself, the intimacy of their relationship was a welcome contrast. All the passions he had kept pent up as Kole erupted in their affair.

He realized that continuing to spend time with Jude was dangerous, but he forced his worries away and locked them in the dark recesses of his mind. He was not working, so his normal level of caution was not necessary. He could fully devote himself to becoming Chuck Grayson. He got pleasure and a sense of belonging unlike anything he had ever known when he made his approach to Kai Allard-Liao's managers and was rebuffed. Ronda slowly began to sour on Allard-Liao because of the way they treated Chuck, and John accepted him into the fold once his failure meant Grayson was no longer a threat to John's domination of the group.

He felt normal and even more than that. He could, of course, never forget who and what he was, but it was becoming easier to distance himself from it. He willingly engaged in heated debates about who had really been behind the death of the Archon and whether or not Prince

Victor had killed his father. After seeing the first of a series of interviews Victor gave the media, he even took to defending the Prince. This did not make him overly popular with some folks from the Lyran sector of the Federated Commonwealth, but those from the Federated Suns area often bought him drinks and invited him to visit them in their homes if he ever got out that way.

For nearly a month he thought very little about work. Indeed, he had earned enough from the hit on the Archon that he'd never need to accept another assignment. That had, in fact, been his motivation for taking on the Archon's assassination, but as time went by, he began to feel the urge to work again. He was definitely enjoying his time as Chuck Grayson, but he was *not* Chuck Grayson and the person he was *needed* another job.

The same part of him that had urged caution at his slipping into the Grayson persona shifted and immediately began to argue that he should not look for a new job. The assassin realized that part of his urge came from all the theories concerning Melissa's death that were running wild. Everyone, from a mad florist to organized crime, to Kurita assassins to Recom-terrorists, had been credited with the kill—everyone except for *him!* That buffeted his ego, yet revealing his identity to soothe his bruised ego was a short road to ending up dead.

On the other hand he knew that performing another hit might give those in the know, the Intelligence Secretariat and other similar governmental bodies, enough clues to realize that a very good assassin was at work. Actually, he told himself, it wouldn't be the clues, but the lack of them that would key them to the fact that the Archon's assassin had struck again.

Ego overruling logic, and thumb covering the camera lens that would record his picture, he called a message drop from a payvis. He'd compiled an identification code based on the combined date, time, and temperature divided by a constant that only he and the computer at the other end of the line knew. He punched in that code, then hit two buttons on the visiphone console, feeding the computer the access number for the booth where he sat. He then severed the connection, looked at his chronometer, and waited.

If he had any messages, the computer would call back. He would have to enter a new check code and he would be given the message or be connected with one of his contacts who could give him details of any prospective employment. If no call came within five minutes, either he had no messages or it was not possible to make a connection with the other party wishing to speak with him.

He glanced at his chronometer, then read the public access newsbytes scrolling up on the idle screen. Kai Allard-Liao had successfully defended his title yet again. His string of victories had long since eclipsed the mark set by his father and even the one established by his father's mentor, Gray Noton. As with almost all the stories concerning the Solaris champion, the writer speculated that he might be leaving the Game World soon to pursue other endeavors.

When the visiphone suddenly bleated at him, he covered the camera before hitting a button to accept the call. A face appeared on the screen that he recognized as Kevin Chen—a contact who had gotten him one job in the Capellan Confederation that had turned out well. "A man wishes to speak with you. It will pay as well as your last job and offers some of the same perks without the same risks. A week?"

The assassin frowned. Jude and her group would be leaving in a week. In the past he would never have pushed a meeting back because of something like a final party with friends, but then he'd never really had friends before. It could wait. "Eight days."

"Done."

"Who will I be meeting?"

"Don't worry, he checks out."

"I worry. Who?"

Chen looked uneasy and dropped his voice to a whisper. "Fuh Teng."

"Message me details."

The assassin broke the connection and opened the door to the booth. *Fuh Teng.* He had been Kai Allard-Liao's manager ever since the warrior first came to Solaris, and had managed the family's stable of fighters on Solaris since his early partnership with Justin Allard. *Whoever he wants dead will not be easy to kill.*

The assassin smiled to himself and laughed in a way that would have made Chuck Grayson shiver. *But with me doing the job, whoever it is will die well.*

=== 31 ===

DropShip **Tigress**
Pirate Jump Point, Zanderij
Federated Commonwealth
20 August 3055

Knowing the Red Corsair was planning to jump soon, Nelson Geist did not fully seat the earphones for his journey into the computer-reality. He wanted to be able to hear the three-tone signal warning that jump was imminent beyond the sounds of the artificial world. When it came suddenly, he braced himself on the treadmill railing and moved his feet to the sides of the rubber tread.

He pulled off his helmet and hung it on the corner of the railing, then swung under and sat down on the ground. Hugging his knees to his chest, Nelson concentrated on breathing. *In, out. Jumping isn't that bad.* He screwed his eyes shut and felt his stomach lurch as the ship entered hyperspace.

The universe compacted itself into the size of a pinhead, which then seemed to lodge at the base of his skull. He saw visions of everything happening at once, as if time had been stripped away. In those visions he suddenly grasped the key to all of reality. For a single nanosecond he and the universe were one, and realization of that fact brought with it a glimmering of hope that he had not known since his capture.

Then the universe exploded back to its full dimensions and he felt pain as the explosion lasered up and down his spine. For the barest of moments he feared the ship had made a misjump and ended up in whatever ethereal limbo waited for starships with faulty jump drives. But opening his eyes he realized that all was well, and somewhere at the back of his mind, he caught and held on to a wisp of the hope he had discovered in the moment of the jump.

The whole *Tigress* remained eerily silent for a short time. Because of the near ambushes at Great X and Yeguas, Nelson knew that the Red Corsair was not going to commit her DropShips to a run on the fourth planet unless she could determine what threat, if any, the enemy could offer.

A solar system being a rather huge place, hiding a JumpShip or DropShips full of 'Mechs should have been a simple thing, but Nelson knew from his years as a warrior that it was not. Because gravity could rip a JumpShip to pieces as it entered or left a system, the ship had to be stationed either well above or well below the plane of the elliptic. That usually put it at either solar pole, but pirate points—little windows in the dynamic gravitational matrices near the planets and moons—made it possible to come in dangerously close to planets at certain times and at certain points.

The JumpShip *Fire Rose* had come in at just one of those pirate points and that it had not jumped back out immediately meant the initial scan showed no danger. As seconds passed into infinity, Nelson steeled himself against the possible jolt of another jump. *Not so soon*, he pleaded silently because he knew that with another jump, despair would replace the hope he had glimpsed.

Klaxons rang through the ship and he heard the whirring clicks as the two *Overlord* Class DropShips pulled away from the *Fire Rose*. Nelson felt himself get heavy as the *Tigress* began accelerating away from the *Rose*, and as he struggled to his feet, he realized the Red Corsair meant to go in hot. *We're pushing 1.5 gees. She wants to be in and out before the Wolves can react to a distress call from Zanderij.*

Caitlin Kell keyed her radio as she saw DropShip separation on her secondary cockpit screen. "Raven Leader to Raven Flight, we have separation. ETA fifteen minutes." She punched another button on her console and switched over to the command frequency. "Vulture Leader, we have separation."

"Roger, Raven Leader," Carew responded. "We pick them up in ten, and you close the door on them."

"Roger, Vulture Leader. Good luck." Caitlin shifted her radio back to her own tactical frequency and realized she was smiling. She was proud that her brother's plan had worked out. The asteroid field just outside Zanderij IV had provided ample hiding places for her fighter wing. The asteroids, while a nasty hazard for fighters going full-bore, were much more dangerous for the larger DropShips, and forced them into some fairly specific and narrow channels.

The ambush plan was simple and would have been perfect had there not been two equally accessible pirate points in the Zanderij system. Two of the three Kell Hound fighter squadrons had been stationed at a point roughly 1.6 million kilometers away. With her, Caitlin had the First Fighter Squadron and the ten Clan fliers in the Honor Guard Star that had come with Phelan.

She knew that twenty-eight fighters were insufficient to engage two *Overlord* Class DropShips, but the DropShips' transit through an asteroid field made them especially vulnerable. The Red Corsair's ships would have no choice but to run the gauntlet. She would hit them as they went in, but if the Corsair failed to reverse and jump out, the Hounds would join them in-system and engage on the ground. The key for Caitlin's fighter group was to do the DropShips as much damage as possible. If one or both of the DropShips smashed into the asteroids and died, everyone would consider that a bonus.

Caitlin watched the video feed coming from the sensor pod mounted atop the abandoned mining office on the asteroid where her aerospace squadron had been stationed. The two DropShips were coming in fast and dangerously close to each other, with the ship designated the *Tigress* coming first. The *Lioness* lingered behind a bit, but their port and starboard fields of fire overlapped. The zone between them, instead of being a death zone, would be fairly open because neither ship could fire for fear of hitting its sister.

"Raven Leader, prep launch in 1.5 minutes. Velocity adjustment for run to plus fifty-two percent."

"Acknowledged, Vulture Leader." Caitlin relayed the information to her Raven squadron and knew that Crow and Blackbird squadrons were getting similar orders from Carew. The Kell Hounds were in command of the overall operation against the Clans, but Phelan and Dan Allard had agreed that having Carew command at least this part of the ambush would give Conal Ward less to complain about. The assignment would satisfy the Wolf Clan's sense of honor.

She punched up her engines and let them build up to 110 percent of military power. They came online quickly and pushed power to her *Stingray*'s wing-mounted large and medium laser pairs and the PPC mounted in the nose. She vectored the thrust up so it would keep her on the asteroid, but she knew that the second she shifted it the other way, the asteroid's vestigial gravity would release her fighter and send it out into the fray.

The clock on her auxiliary screen counted down to zero. "Raven Flight, go!"

As Caitlin pulled the stick back and eased the throttle forward, the *Stingray* leaped from the asteroid like a falcon freed for flight. Punching both feet down on the overthrust pedals spiked the power output and jammed her back into her command couch as the fighter shot up and away. Glancing at her holographic combat display, she saw another *Stingray* pull in beside her. "Glad you're here, Mulligan."

The pair of swept-wing fighters threaded their way through the asteroid field and broke into the cylinder the DropShips had used to make their passage in toward the planet. Caitlin kicked her fighter up on its right wing in a looping turn that centered her in the cylinder. As the craft's nose pointed in at Zanderij IV, she spotted the two bright dots that were the bandit DropShips.

"Bandits at twelve o'clock," she radioed her squadron. "Fire at will."

Nelson stumbled against a bulkhead as the *Tigress* shuddered with the first hit. The blaring klaxons summoning bandits to battle stations had already told him something was wrong, but the hit confirmed it. *Fighters. They jumped us with fighters.* He hit the button to open the hatch to the corridor and stepped through it as another explosion rocked the DropShip.

In the corridor he could feel the thrumming rhythm of

the *Overlord*'s autocannons coming into play against the fighters. The ship swayed as gunners activated missile launchers and unleashed their clouds of missiles. The *Tigress* started to spin slowly and Nelson realized that it was doing so to bring all its weapons into play. *We're too close to the* Lioness *for a full sphere of fire.*

As a MechWarrior, Nelson felt a mixture of joy and dread concerning fighters. He knew they could easily devastate ground-bound forces and even cripple Drop-Ships. Though such an action would mean his death, the idea made him happy because it would also bring the Red Corsair's predations to an end. That fed into the optimistic feelings in his heart, and spawned a desperate plan.

I don't have to die. Nelson knew it was true with the conviction of a madman or a prophet, and he knew two other things without a doubt. The first was that he would survive whatever happened at Zanderij.

The second was that he would finally be free of the Red Corsair!

"Watch it, Raven Deuce, open up," Caitlin snarled into her radio as Mulligan's *Stingray* strayed in close to her fighter. Seeing his fighter jerk ahead as he hit the overthrusters, she dropped back to cover him in case the bandits launched fighters of their own. Spinning asteroids whirled strobelike through sun and shadow, reducing the channel to a surreal tunnel with a firestorm at the far end.

"I'm in!" Mulligan's words echoed through her helmet as he flipped his *Stingray* up on its canopy in a tight roll, and made a run on the *Lioness*. His wing-mounted medium and large lasers flashed out with competing red and green shafts of energy, raking like claws through the armor of the egg-shaped DropShip, then the PPC in the *Stingray*'s nose jolted the larger ship with an azure bolt of artificial lightning.

Caitlin had less than a second to appreciate Mulligan's handiwork before her own attack run started. She dropped her golden crosshairs onto the ship and immediately got the gold dot in the center, confirming a target lock. She punched her thumb down on the joystick's firing stud, and heat spiked colorfully on her auxiliary monitor. The PPC sent a jagged blue line of lightning into the *Lioness*.

Hitting the trigger under her index finger, Caitlin next fired both large lasers, pushing her ship's heat higher. The fighter's green beams bracketed the PPC blast and melted away yet more armor on the DropShip's hull.

"Nice shooting, Cait!" Mulligan corkscrewed his fighter down through the death alley between the two DropShips, and she followed in his wake. "Another run?"

"Roger, Raven Two." She remembered Phelan's instructions to the pilots. "Whatever it takes."

Nelson ran as hard as he could through the corridor, the klaxons harrying him like hunting horns after a fox. *I will escape!* He threaded his way through the ship, running counter to the ship's rotation. Glancing at letters stenciled on the wall, he knew he was only two segments away from his goal.

Suddenly a huge explosion rocked the *Tigress,* smashing him against the interior bulkhead. He saw stars when he hit his forehead, then rebounded and sprawled on the deck. Darkness wanted to close around him, but he forced it away. Pushing himself to a sitting position, Nelson felt blood dripping down from the gash on his head, but his adrenaline and sense of urgency blocked any pain.

The *Tigress* tipped on its axis, pitching the deck up. Nelson grabbed a structural girder and held on, then pulled himself forward. Sinking to his hands and knees, he scrambled uphill, then somersaulted forward as the ship violently righted itself. A wave of dizziness passed over him, then he regained his feet and started running forward again.

Around the curve of the ship he saw the access hatch to the escape pod. He ran to it and slammed his right palm down on the panel switch to open it. The hatch irised open, revealing the dark interior of the womblike pod.

As he started to step into it, a bandit grabbed the upper part of his left arm and pulled him away. "Where do you think *you're* going?"

Nelson slumped his shoulders in defeat, then balled his maimed fist. He swung it down in a short arc that terminated in the bandit's groin. As the man squealed and bent over, Nelson brought his right knee up. The man's nose shattered in a spray of blood, then he dropped to the deck.

Nelson pulled the pistol from the bandit's holster and pumped two bullets into him. Clutching the gun and scanning the corridor in both directions, he backed into the pod. He used the gun barrel to punch the button that closed the hatch, then he felt his ears pop as the pod pressurized. He reached out with his half-hand and hit the launch sequencer.

"Countdown commencing. Ten, nine, eight . . . ," droned a computer voice.

Nelson heard a thumping on the pod hatch, followed by the sight of a face pressed against the glass. He pointed the gun at it. "Override. Launch immediately."

"Affirmative."

Heavily padded panels slid down over the hatch and the controls. Three small explosions rippled through the pod, then he sank deeply into the padding as one final blast hurled the pod out and away from the *Tigress*. The rocket motor's roar filled the pod, rattling Nelson's teeth and making his ears ring, but he couldn't have been happier.

I'm free. I can go home again. The pod's viewport pads retracted, giving him a central view of the space battle raging around the DropShips. *I can go home again, but only if I survive the attempt to kill the Red Corsair and all her people.*

Caitlin had a bad feeling as Mulligan turned around to make the second run. He pushed his speed for going back, which did not make much sense because the DropShips were coming toward them. She knew Mulligan was addicted to velocity and he obviously thought that the DropShips were not a danger. "Careful, Raven Deuce."

"Roger, Raven Leader. I'm going in."

Despite the excitement in his voice, Caitlin knew Mulligan was being careful and she had come to respect his abilities ever since they'd been paired in the squadron. He brought his ship over and around in a barrel roll that lined him up perfectly on the *Tigress* and then onto her sister ship.

She smiled and pushed her fighter after him as Mulligan burned in close and skimmed the surface of the *Tigress*. Their laser and PPC shots burned parallel paths through the ship's armor, and she saw one autocannon turret flame out as their PPC beams met at its location.

"Deuce, your nine!"

The escape pod looked like a comet as it streaked up and away from the *Tigress*. Mulligan rolled down and away from it, but sailed directly into the spreading debris cloud from the autocannon turret they'd taken out. Caitlin saw something hit his *Stingray*, then he spun away and flashed on toward the *Lioness*.

For an instant or two as she chased him, Caitlin thought Mulligan was in command and just finishing up his attack run. As she came around onto his aft, however, she saw damage to his left wing and a jammed vector-thruster. "Clear, Mulligan. You've lost maneuvering on port."

Getting no response, she pushed herself forward just enough to see that his cockpit was gone, then she pulled up and away from the *Lioness*. She popped up on her left wing, then came down and through in a loop that shifted her perpendicular to her previous course. She let the change stand for three seconds, then rolled up on her right wing and reversed the maneuver to take her in a circular course outside the *Lioness'* lethal perimeter.

Mulligan's fighter arrowed into the *Lioness* near the ion engines, and went from being a small pellet of steel and ceramics to a boiling ball of plasma. At first the bright blossom of fire seemed far too small to have affected the ship, and even the amount of debris that geysered out into space through the hole it left behind hardly seemed fatal. Caitlin shuddered, thinking her friend's death should have counted for more.

Then one of the DropShip's four ion engines winked out, making the *Lioness* begin to spin faster and start to wobble in its course. The rotation picked up speed, which smoothed out the course irregularities, but when the directional rockets fired to bring that back under control, the ovoid craft twisted in its axis and the two ends began to circle out of sync with each other.

Caitlin knew the *Lioness* was in trouble as it fired maneuvering rockets in sequence to somersault the ship around to reorient the boosters for a retreat. The wobble transformed that maneuver into a spinning, skidding tumble through space that was utterly out of control. Jets pulsed out energy to try to regain control, but merely lit the ship up like a meteor hitting atmosphere.

The *Lioness* caromed off an asteroid twice its size into the thick of the asteroid field. Miraculously it sailed between two whirling giants, and for a moment Caitlin wanted the ship to survive. Then the *Lioness* impaled itself on a smaller asteroid that punched a hole right through it. The ship's hull surrounded the asteroid like a corona for a moment, then split apart into glittering fragments that shattered and spilled through space like droplets of quicksilver.

Poised on his hands and knees, Nelson saw the *Lioness* career into the asteroid field. The first collision crumpled the ship, and debris trailed after it. He winced when it hit the final rock, the metal running like water over the asteroid's surface. Frantically looking to spot any 'Mechs, any people, any*thing* that had survived the crash, he felt both victorious and horrified when he could not.

Looking up from the viewport in the pod's belly to the one at its head, he caught sight of the *Tigress*. It had been damaged, but compared to the other ship, it was pristine. As he watched, the ship executed a forward roll that reversed the main thruster position. The ion jets pulsed brilliantly, then the ship slowed, beginning the sharp ascent back up toward where the *Fire Rose* waited.

The fighters swarmed in at the lone DropShip, but the *Tigress* no longer had to idle part of its awesome firepower. To make things even worse, the *Fire Rose* used its large laser batteries to strike at the fighters that flew ahead of the *Tigress* and waited to attack.

As much as Nelson wanted the *Tigress* and the woman who ruled her to die, he admired them both as they fought off the enemy fighters. Before the *Tigress* had completed half the distance back to the *Fire Rose*, the fighters broke off their attack. The DropShip completed its rendezvous with the JumpShip and then the mated ships winked out of existence.

Nelson watched them go with relief and sadness. Though happy to be free, he regretted that it meant abandoning his comrades, who remained captives of the Corsairs. He knew that he was still responsible for them, even if they hated him for his association with the Red Corsair.

Seeing two aerofighters heading his way, each deploying a pod capture net, he smiled and made a solemn vow. "I'll find a way to get you guys back. I'll do it, or die trying."

32

The thick, sweet scent of the steaming green tea took the assassin back nearly ten years to an assignment he had successfully carried out within the Capellan Confederation. Looking around the small, ramshackle hut that arrogantly proclaimed itself a restaurant, all he saw now were old Liao expatriates hunched over steaming bowls of noodles. His sources had said this place was a cover for an opium den, and the urgency on the faces of those who gravitated toward the back doorway gave the assassin confirmation of that story.

The *déjà vu* he felt was not at all pleasant. An agent of Romano Liao had hired him to murder a minor noble who displeased her, and then the Chancellor of the Capellan Confederation had tried to have him killed, too. He had needed every drop of the cunning and resourcefulness that made him so good at his work to get away from her hired killer. Diving back into the crucible did not arouse happy memories.

A shiver ran up his spine, but he flicked it off with a quick roll of his shoulders. Dressed in a dark long coat, the assassin felt secure with a needle pistol hidden at his back and another secreted in a boot top under the wide legs of his woolen trousers. No one knew better than he that it was impossible to make himself invulnerable or invincible, but he counted on his wits to get him out of any unforeseen trouble.

Spotting Fuh Teng in a back booth, the assassin approached him slowly and carefully, then slid into the seat across from him. He studied the room, then settled his gaze on the aged oriental man sitting opposite him. "I am here."

Fuh Teng smiled and bowed his head, upsetting the few white strands of hair lying across his tanned pate. "You will have tea?" The old man poured from the pot on the table, filling the two porcelain cups set out between them.

The assassin accepted the dark liquid and joined Fuh's toast to his health. He tasted nothing odd in the tea, but he knew very well that dozens of poisons that could cripple or kill him in an instant were undetectable by taste. He also knew that if, for some reason, Fuh Teng was setting him up, he'd be dead already.

The old man kept both hands clutched around his cup. "There is a story I would tell you."

"That is not necessary. I do not require to know why you seek my services."

"I will tell it anyway, because you are a businessman, as am I. You see, there was an old man who worked all his life for a noble family. He slaved and made a great fortune for this family, but they did not reward him. The old man was happy in his ignorance of how he was being treated, but then his life changed. In his old age he discovered the youth-giving gift of love, and his lover pointed out the injustices done to him."

The assassin suppressed a smile. *So the old man has a gold-digger who wants him to make her rich.*

"This old man wished to make up for the years of poor treatment, and began to help himself to greater compensation for his services. Meanwhile his old master died and his master's son has become his employer. His new employer wishes to pension the old man off, but the old man will be exposed when someone is brought in to replace him."

The assassin nodded. "So the old man would like his employer. . ."

"Distracted." Fuh Teng met the assassin's gaze with an unwavering stare. "The old man loves his employer like a son and is ashamed of having hurt him. Had he wished his employer dead, given his employer's line of work, that could easily have been accomplished. He only wants him distracted."

Fuh Teng slid his left hand forward, then pulled it back. On the table lay revealed a large golden coin with Chinese characters encircling the perimeter and impressed into the edge. More important, though, the assassin recognized the profile on the coin. "Candace Liao."

The old man nodded and the pieces began to fit into place for the assassin. If Candace were killed, the blame would immediately fall on her nephew, Sun-Tzu Liao, her sworn enemy and the Chancellor of the Capellan Confederation. Kai, her son, would be forced to assume his role as ruler of the St. Ives Compact, and might possibly even be forced to launch a war that would result in the reunification of the Capellan Confederation and the Compact under his rule.

"It can be done. When?"

"Four months?"

That would make it a quick hit, which he preferred to avoid, but it was possible. "As with anything, it can be done either quickly or cheaply, but not both."

"If you are able to prove to me that the assignment should be yours, and then accomplish the job successfully, you will be paid 3.5 million C-bills worth of corporate stocks, including shares in TharHes Industries and Defiance Industries."

The equal of what I got for the Archon, and paid in defense stocks. Obviously, he wants to ignite a war. "Impressive. You are ambitious."

"Frugal. I have been supporting Candace's brother in his posturing and threats against the Confederation for years. He has done nothing but grow fat on my charity. You are a stone with which I can kill two birds."

The assassin nodded. "How should I prove myself to you?"

Fuh Teng shrugged. "On Solaris a man is judged by his last battle."

The assassin shrugged. "That is too bad, because my last job had me working as a florist."

Fuh Teng nodded. "Candace does not like flowers." The old man stood up, exited the booth and bowed. "May your endeavor of the next four months prove fortuitous."

The assassin sipped tea calmly while he waited for the old man to leave the restaurant. He picked up the gold coin and ran his thumbnail over the characters incised into the edge. *Candace Liao. She will prove a challenge.* He snapped the coin down on the table and left the booth. *A worthy challenge.*

By the time he reached the door and saw the light drizzle beginning to come down, the assassin had almost completed the transformation to Chuck Grayson. He pulled his collar up and hunched his shoulders against the cold rain. He stepped out into the night, and started across the street.

A sudden shout from his left made him begin to turn that way just as a car on his right squealed on its brakes. The assassin hesitated, part of him refusing to believe that he could be taken down in a simple traffic accident. As the car clipped his right leg, fracturing the thigh and shin, a bolt of agony shot up his spine and exploded out the top of his head.

As he hit the ground, echoes of the pain rippled through him, but he smiled in spite of it. That pain was not enough to hide the sting of the dart he felt in his shoulder, or the knowledge that the pain had been dulled by the drugs in his tea. He had been taken, and taken by professionals.

Unconsciousness did not wipe away his smile. The realization that he had, in fact, proved a worthy challenge to someone else made his sleep quite pleasant.

══ 33 ══

Arc-Royal
Federated Commonwealth
25 August 3055

Nelson Geist held his head high despite the fatigue making every muscle and bone of his body ache. Though he was not in chains and the Kell Hound infantrymen leading him down the corridor did not handle him unkindly, neither was he being treated as a free man. In some ways he had known more liberty with the Red Corsair, and with that thought the steel band on his wrist began to chafe.

He had given the Hounds everything they had asked for, both under normal interrogation and again when some nameless bastard who stank of the Clans started using chemical interrogation techniques. Nelson had a sneaking suspicion that the Clanner would have resorted to physical torture had he not been restrained because the man so obviously did not like the answers Nelson had given him.

The guards split apart as they approached a set of double doors that swung open and admitted Nelson to a briefing room. At the head of a long oaken table sat Colonel Allard and at his right was a young man in Clan leathers. Seated on Allard's left was the Clanner who had interrogated him. A couple of other officers took up places at the far end of the table, including one who reminded Nelson of the statue of Patrick Kell he had seen during his stint at the Nagelring twenty-seven years before.

Dan Allard pointed at the lone chair at the nearer end of the table. "Please be seated, Kommandant Geist. We apologize for putting you through an ordeal, but our need is urgent.''

Nelson lowered himself carefully into the chair, resisting the desire to slump in exhaustion. ''I appreciate your concern, Colonel. For the most part I have not found the experience unpleasant, but I would not want to repeat it.'' He leaned forward and rested his elbows on his knees. ''I want to help, and I've told you everything I can. Give me a 'Mech and I'll repay my debts to you and the Red Corsair in full.''

As Nelson looked around at the men and lone woman seated in front of him, the MechWarriors among them shied from eye contact—*even the Clanners.* ''You're not going to do that, are you, Colonel Allard?'' Full realization of what was truly going on hit him. ''This is a trial, isn't it?''

Dan shook his head. ''No, Kommandant, this is not a trial. It is an informal hearing, convened to let you know where you stand and to explain why we have reached the decisions we have made concerning you.'' Dan glanced at the man to his left. ''Star Colonel Ward fervently believes you are a Trojan horse full of disinformation designed to cripple our efforts to stop the Red Corsair. Conversely, Major Kell here is willing to make a place for you in his battalion.''

Chris Kell's warm smile shielded Nelson from the icy glare the older Clanner gave him. ''And you, Colonel, and the rest of you?''

Dan shook his head. ''I am undecided. I think you are a fine warrior and I would be happy to have someone of your caliber in my command. Conal Ward, Khan Phelan Ward, and Dr. Kendall have reservations that make me approach you cautiously.''

Nelson's gaze flicked past Khan Phelan and settled on the petite, black-haired woman sitting around the corner of the table from the Khan. *I remember her.* Dim recollections of the woman visiting him while he was still in the throes of a chemical interrogation returned slowly. *She said her name was Susan. I thought she was a dream.*

She adjusted her glasses and met his stare. ''In our interview I learned some things that concern me, Kommandant. Mind you, none of these matters are pathological, and with proper therapy, I think you should recover fully. . . .''

''The only therapy I need, Doctor, is to be strapped into a 'Mech with the Red Corsair in my sights.''

Nelson's growl reinforced the smile on Chris Kell's face, but that did not stop Doctor Kendall. ''The Stockholm syndrome was first identified nearly eleven hundred years ago as a hostage's identification with his captors. It is a form of adaptation that is quite normal in a highly stressful situation like the one in which you found yourself.''

Nelson leaned back and raised his right fist. ''This manacle marked me a slave, Doctor, not a hostage. This kept me apart from the bandits. There was no *identification* with them.''

Conal Ward's head came up. ''Is that so, Nelson? You were the Red Corsair's lover. I hardly see a wall there.''

''That was different.''

''Was it?''

''Yes.'' Anger and rage shook him. ''She was an obsession. I hated her, yet I could not resist her. I'm sure the doctor here can tell you that I was punishing myself or compensating for my half-hand or something like that. I don't know and I don't care. All I know is that I still hate her and if she's ever in my crosshairs, she will become only a memory.''

As he finished speaking, Nelson realized he was gripping the steel link on his wrist and rotating it with his maimed hand. Glancing down, he saw blood begin to seep up through the abrasions. When he looked up again, he saw Kendall shaking her head.

''You obsess about more than the Red Corsair, Kommandant Geist. That manacle, for example.'' She glanced down at the small noteputer in front of her. ''You have steadfastly refused to let us remove it from your wrist.''

''It's not what you think. I do not cling to this as a way of identifying with the bandits.'' Nelson dropped his gaze, then continued in a subdued voice. ''When it hit me that I had abandoned my people—Spider and the others—when I escaped from the *Tigress,* I decided to continue to wear this constantly as a reminder of my obligation to them.''

He looked up and straight at Colonel Allard. ''You can

understand that, can't you? In a moment of madness I forgot about them. I got away, thinking only of myself. But I owe it to them to help free them, which is why I need a 'Mech.''

"I understand, Kommandant, and I understand your rejection of Dr. Kendall's assessment of you." Dan frowned, then shook his head. "As much as I want to believe you, and *do* believe you, I cannot give you a BattleMech.''

Anger jolted through Nelson. "Forgive me, sir, but if you believe me, and if I have convinced you that I am not in thrall to the bandits, why not? I'm able, very able." He held up his left hand. "Don't let this fool you. I can handle a 'Mech.''

Khan Phelan leaned forward slowly. "We are well aware of that, Kommandant, which is precisely why you will not be given a 'Mech.''

"I don't understand.''

The Clan Khan's eyes narrowed. "Computer, play back 55.04.30, Yeguas 3.1, Slot 7.''

The computer complied, and above the polished surface of the table a holographic display of a battle took shape. Nelson recognized the surface of Cue Ball, but realized he was seeing the engagement from the Wolf Clan perspective. As he watched, the viewpoint 'Mech went bounding forward toward a *BattleMaster*. The holographs began to waver as the 'Mech began to have trouble. When the *BattleMaster* fired its PPCs, however, the diagnostic subtrack started to report incredible damage.

"Isolate and magnify *BattleMaster*'s gunner.'' At Phelan's command, the battle froze and the perspective zoomed in until Nelson saw himself hovering over the table. The Khan stared at him through the ghostly green image. "We have similar battle ROMs from Deia. You did the Red Corsair's killing for her, Kommandant Geist. You will never again pilot a 'Mech, and if what you have told us *is* disinformation, you will face a court-martial and execution for your acts of treason.''

"That is a fair bit down the road, Khan Phelan.'' The white-haired Kell Hound leader turned back to Nelson. "You are under house arrest for the time being, Kommandant, but anything you require, within reason, will be made available to you.''

"But not a 'Mech?"

"I'm sorry, no."

"Why not just take me out and have me shot?" *If I cannot get a 'Mech here on Arc-Royal, I will never be rid of her.*

Conal's head come up. "That is *my* recommendation, quisling."

"Soon there will be killing enough for us all." Dan glanced at the Clansman on either side of him. "You *are* a security risk, Kommandant Geist, but not one that figures high on my list of worries. Soon this will all be behind you. You are dismissed."

"With all due respect, Colonel Allard, you don't understand." Nelson's hands balled into fists. "Don't send me away, don't cut me out. You need me. I know how the Red Corsair thinks. I can help you figure out where she will strike next."

Khan Phelan leaned back in his chair. "We already know where she will strike. And when."

Nelson blinked his eyes. "And you are here, on the ground? Are you fools? You will never be able to react fast enough to get her."

"We do not need to react." Phelan steepled his fingers. "The Kell Hounds and the Wolf Clan hurt her. There is only one place she can hit where she can hurt both entities." The young Khan's smile reminded Nelson of an expression he had often seen on the Red Corsair's face. "We have sent our JumpShips and DropShips off to guard other worlds, and that is information she will stumble across easily."

Nelson's mouth went dry. "Which means she'll be coming here."

Phelan nodded as solemnly as an undertaker. "And on Arc-Royal her career ends."

BOOK III

The Killing Time

34

Arc-Royal
Federated Commonwealth
5 September 3055

Khan Phelan Ward looked out the window of the office meant for the Grand Duke of Arc-Royal. Down below two dozen people were picketing, slowing traffic and attracting a small crowd of the curious. Phelan's eyes narrowed, but the half-smile never left his lips.

"I would have them all shot." Conal Ward stood away from the window, like a vampire dreading the sun's warm kiss. "The ruling caste of Arc-Royal has decided to let you remain here, yet these people commit treason and you tolerate it." The Clansman sniffed. "But then you have become used to abiding treason."

Phelan whipped around and skewered Conal with a cold stare. "I tolerated it in your case."

Despite his efforts to show no reaction, Conal's cheeks reddened. "I was referring to the decision to let Nelson remain alive."

The Clan Khan suppressed a smile. He knew that Conal refused to use Nelson's surname of Geist because, to a Clanner, it would have meant conferring the honor of a Bloodname on him. Instead, he tried to put all his disgust into the word Nelson, yet somehow that name couldn't carry the weight of so much vitriol. Geist, on the other hand, would have suited the purpose perfectly, but Conal could not unbend enough to see it.

"I find him still worthwhile and valuable as an information source. I do not believe he is a traitor. His compatriots were probably innocent, too, but you did not wait long enough to find that out."

"You deny him a 'Mech."

"I do." Phelan walked from the window to the massive mahogany desk that had been his grandfather's. "That I do not think him a traitor does not mean I believe him capable of handling a 'Mech now. I will admit, though, that the battle ROMs of Cue Ball show him to be an able gunner."

"That was a trap."

"One you fell into."

"As would you, had you been there instead of cowering with these mercenaries." Conal's eyes smoldered in the black pits of his eye sockets. "How can you stand it? These people are sheep."

"Then I am a shepherd."

"You are a Wolf!" Conal jabbed a finger at him. "Or, by this time, you should be. You and I, we have political differences, but at the heart, we are the same. We are warriors and the people should respect us. Look at those people down there—instead of glorying in the honor of having the Wolves hunting down the bandits that attack their homeworld, they protest it! How can you permit that?"

Phelan shook his head. "How can I permit it? I can and do because they have their right to be afraid and to show it. I do not relish the idea of war coming to my homeworld, but I accept that it must happen if the Red Corsair is to be stopped. That people express their fear and their worries is not disloyalty—it would be disloyalty to have them arrested."

He glanced toward the window. "Is it any wonder they protest my presence on this planet? Those who have not lost their worlds to the Clan invasion have lost kin and lovers to the war. To them I am a traitor, but they suffer my presence out of respect for my family. Were my father dead and I attempting to exercise my legal inheritance here, you would see a civil war. Besides, you can bet that if I were still a man of the Inner Sphere, I would be *leading* the fight against a Clanner inheriting Arc-Royal."

The Khan looked at the leader of the Thirty-first Wolf Solahma and slowly exhaled. "At the heart you and I are not the same. We *are* warriors, but you live for battle.

You are an irresistible force that devours all before it. I am an immovable object that wants what you do to stop for all time.''

Conal's eyes narrowed. ''You know that by framing matters in those terms, we cannot coexist.''

''Not so. We can, but you will have to change.'' Phelan's head came up. ''Ultimately, though, *Star Colonel,* I do not care what you do as long as you follow my orders.''

Conal's face screwed up with anger, but before he could snap out a retort, there was a gentle knocking on the office door, then the Grand Duke's executive assistant opened it partway and poked his head through. ''Forgive me for interrupting, sir, but the commander from the Home Defense Force is here.''

Phelan nodded. ''Send him in. Star Colonel Ward was just leaving.'' He looked at the Clansman. ''You have your orders, Star Colonel, follow them.''

Conal bowed his head deferentially. ''My Khan's will be done.''

As Phelan watched him go, he knew that despite Conal's polite remark they were still on a collision course. *If it can only wait until after the Red Corsair is dead!*

Christian Kell poured steaming coffee from the thermos into a mug and handed it to Ragnar. The Clan warrior tipped his yellow hardhat back on his head and nodded in thanks. Chris blew on the cup he had poured for himself, then took a sip. ''Not too bad.''

Ragnar yawned. ''Deuterium to a fusion engine. I have been up for six hours, which is four more than the sun. Still, I am not complaining. Work is going well.''

Chris nodded as he looked out at the vast city being constructed on a flat plain forty kilometers south of the Kell Hound base at Old Connaught. In the center of it was the small town of Denton and the McKiernan Power Company. When Denton had been created five years earlier as a planned community, the area had been graded, and roads, sewer, water, and power installed. All was going well until the Clan invasion made investors become conservative with their capital; the project collapsed and languished in the oblivion of bankruptcy.

Phelan, acting for his father, had nationalized it and

paid off the creditors. In less than two weeks the community came alive again as legions of carpenters, masons, electricians, and landscapers descended on the place. Where tract homes could not be constructed fast enough, mobile homes were hovered or coptered in. The construction activity took on an almost carnival atmosphere and the public responded to it with heartfelt enthusiasm.

The greatest response came from the exiled Rasalhagians. Ragnar had told Chris that they felt it was their way of repaying the debt to the world that had adopted them. By joining the defensive effort, the exiles began their final integration into Arc-Royal society.

Chris smiled as he watched two construction 'Mechs lift up one prefab chunk of a building. "You know, it's a pity we won't actually be able to occupy this base." He winked at Ragnar and pointed toward one brand-new house set on a slight rise. "I was thinking I would like that house there. The view is nice and it's not too far from the 'Mech bays."

Ragnar returned the smile. "I will see that it is wired last. If we run out of time . . ." He shrugged.

The mercenary nodded. "I don't think land values will be that high after we're done, my friend."

The former Prince of Rasalhague nodded and smiled again. "True enough, but your view will be unobstructed and the neighborhood will be very quiet."

"Construction continues on the new Kell Hound base at Denton," said the radio announcer's tinny voice. "Flushed with their stunning victory over the Red Corsair at Zanderij, and confident that the Red Corsair has gone off to lick her wounds, the mercenary regiment has launched into an ambitious building program that is scheduled to be finished before Grand Duke Morgan Kell leaves his sickbed on Tharkad and returns home."

The security officer with Nelson Geist turned the radio off and stopped the hovercar. The gull-wing doors opened at the touch of a button. Nelson swung out of the vehicle and scratched at the area behind his right ear, which was tight and dry around the site of the incision made a week earlier.

The security man shook his head. "Leave it alone and it will stop itching."

Nelson gave the man a surprised look. "Ah, you are a doctor now, too, I take it, Bates?"

Bob Bates laughed lightly. "Not hardly, but I remember when I had my locator implanted."

"But you could turn yours off when you went off-duty." Nelson frowned. The Kell Hounds had been most civilized concerning his incarceration. Having implanted a locator chip in his mastoid bone, they could determine where he was at any time. Though they preferred him to remain on their base, he was allowed to make accompanied trips off-base and into Old Connaught. Still, the constant itch behind his ear reminded Nelson that he was not trustworthy in their eyes.

Bates held his left wrist up near his mouth and activated his wrist recorder. "Friday, six June 3055. Subject: Nelson Geist. In accordance with a request filed two days ago and approved by Major Kell, I have taken the subject to the Finian Library of Astrophysics at Old Connaught University." Bates mounted the steps to the library and opened the door for Nelson. "Don't know what you expect to find in here, Kommandant, but I don't mind the change of scenery."

Nelson smiled. "When I find it, Mr. Bates, I'll let you know." *I'll let everyone know because it will mean the beginning of my revenge and an end to the Red Corsair.*

Phelan hit the answer button on the visiphone. "I am here, Colonel."

Dan Allard nodded and gave Phelan a brief, welcoming smile. "They're on schedule. You said they would be here between the tenth and the fifteenth. They just arrived in-system and should touch ground tomorrow."

The Clan Khan nodded. "The eleventh. Is the Hound Pound ready?"

"I gave the word and it's being evacuated now." Dan frowned. "There is one thing we didn't expect, though."

Phelan raised an eyebrow. "Yes?"

"The Corsair has *two* Overlord Class DropShips coming in."

"Two!" The Clansman shook his head. "That is not possible. We destroyed the *Lioness* at Zanderij."

"Tell that to the Red Corsair." Dan's expression darkened. "It gets worse. Remember how we had a positive identification of the JumpShip *Fire Rose* as being *Congress* Class?"

"Yes. It used large lasers to keep our fighters at bay while it recovered the *Tigress.*"

"Right, well, that ship out there now is *Black Lion* Class. It's still called the *Fire Rose* and has the same identification module, but it's definitely a *Black Lion.*"

But Black Lions have no energy weapons, so it couldn't be the same ship as before. "*Lion*s carry fighters."

Dan nodded. "My thoughts exactly."

Phelan sat back in the chair from which his greatgrandfather and grandfather and father had ruled ArcRoyal. The ability of the Red Corsair to re-arm herself so quickly and so expensively confirmed what he already knew: she was no ordinary bandit. She was working for someone else, and the easy answer to who that was happened to be the answer he didn't even want to consider.

He shook his head. "Let her bring them all. It doesn't matter." A predatory smile tugged up at the corners of his mouth. "She's come to us, to *our* battlefield. It is her first big mistake and she will pay for it with her life."

35

Arc-Royal
Federated Commonwealth
11 September 3055

Phelan hooked his thumbs into his gunbelt and smiled as he monitored the communications link between the Red Corsair and the Kell Hound base at Denton. His nephew Mark looked suitably nervous in what was obviously an oversized uniform. "What do you mean asking me what we have to defend our base? The Hounds aren't here."

"You wear the uniform of a warrior, child," the Red Corsair snarled. "Which are you: a coward soiling a noble uniform, or a warrior who will defend what is his."

Mark's eyes blazed with an anger Phelan knew was not feigned. "We'll meet you. The Scouts have two light lances. We'll meet you on Denton Flats." Mark shook a fist at her. "You'll be sorry."

The Red Corsair laughed from Phelan's auxiliary monitor. "I doubt that, pup. Corsair out."

The auxiliary went dead for a moment, then a system traffic display filled it. The Red Corsair and her two DropShips were burning into Arc-Royal at a fairly leisurely pace that would leave her warriors rested and ready to fight. Estimated time of arrival was two hours away, which meant Phelan and the rest of the Kell Hounds had to stay under cover until the ships had grounded.

Phelan touched the keypad on his *Wolfhound*'s command console and got a troop-strength estimate for the Red Corsair. The DropShips definitely had a fighter screen that consisted of eighteen aerospace fighters. Preliminary data analysis suggested that their flight profiles precluded the inclusion of bombs. That meant the Hound Pound could still work, but the fight would be nastier by half than they had originally anticipated.

He opened a land line to Dan Allard. The laser-based signal went out over a fiber-optic cable running through the dark recesses of the National Defense bunkers in the Clonarf Mountains. "Things look good for the moment from here, Colonel. We need to have our fighters on standby."

"Done. I've integrated what's left of your honor guard into the First Fighter Battalion. That brings them up to strength. Star Captain Carew suggested it."

Phelan smiled. *He is doing his best to earn his shot at a Bloodname.* "Good. What is the word on Geist?"

"Security reported in about ten minutes ago. He's still going over the material he got from the university. Bates says the man's seen more stars than all the prize fighters in history." Dan smiled. "In return I guess I should ask you if Star Colonel Ward has stopped complaining yet about his assignment."

You believe I don't trust Geist and you don't trust Conal. Little do you know, Dan, that our feelings about both men are closer to your position than not.

Old Connaught, though only forty kilometers north of Denton, was separated from it by the foothills of the Clonarf Mountains. The mountains themselves, which formed a semicircle around Denton to the south and west of the settlement, were where the Kell Hounds remained hidden. North of the foothills stretched a broad river valley. Through the middle of it ran the kilometer-wide Kilkenny River. Twenty kilometers north, up a gradual and well-wooded incline, Old Connaught sat on the shore of Lachlan Lake.

Conal and the Thirty-first Wolf Solahma had been placed in the woods. They were close enough to the M-5, the major highway running south of Old Connaught, and the bridge crossing for the Kilkenny, that they could be brought into play if the Red Corsair landed north of the mountains and south of the river. Ideally, though, she would ground both her DropShips in the Denton area, leaving them out of the fight entirely.

"Conal has taken some satisfaction in the fact that he

is defending the city, but only because I told him that a weapons subassembly plant was located there.'' The Clan Khan laughed lightly. ''I would not worry, Colonel, the Thirty-first Wolf Solahma will not be a problem.''

''I hope not, Phelan.'' Dan let the concern in his voice bleed out through his eyes. ''I remember what they did to Zimmer's Zouaves. I won't let that happen here.''

By the time the Red Corsair's DropShips had become visible, eight light 'Mechs had moved out of Denton and taken up battle positions in the Flats. Harry Pollard kept his *Valkyrie* out in front and raised the 'Mech's left hand when he thought he was far enough outside the fabricated town. ''This is it, guys,'' he said into his microphone, but he knew none of the others could hear him.

The suicide squad pilots were a mixed lot, none of them spectacular, but all of them experienced. Three were old pilots who suffered from inoperable cancers. They had traded their service in the Hounds for payment of their medical bills and the care of their survivors. It was their chance to go out with dignity instead of dying by pieces in a hospice somewhere.

The other five were, like Harry, former pilots who had been serving long sentences in Arc-Royal penal institutions. The trade they wanted to make was more simple: survive and get pardoned. Any kills would be paid for with a 10,000 C-bill bounty—all of which would go to pay back their victims. It wasn't so much, but it was preferable to rotting in a cell.

Harry licked his lips. He'd jumped at the chance to get back into the cockpit of a 'Mech. Even though his lawyer had defended him against a manslaughter charge with a plea that Harry had killed while under the influence of alcohol, Harry knew it was a lie. He'd rationalized the defense because the guy he had stabbed was a idiot and anything was better than being locked up in a cage that denied you your freedom. He jumped at the deal Phelan Ward offered him because it got him out of one cage and into another—a cage Harry thought of as freedom itself.

Clark, a rat-faced man who had once used an ice pick on someone who owed him some small change, had put the chances of their surviving longer than fifteen seconds at one in a thousand.

The odds were right, but the time was a gross over-estimate.

Harry saw the Red Corsair's fighters roll out of their formation and set up on an attack run. With his left hand, he turned his 'Mech toward the incoming fighters. He swung his crosshairs skyward, but aimed below the line of attack on which the planes had set up. He watched the range counter as it rapidly reeled off the meters. When range dropped below a kilometer he punched his feet down on the *Valkyrie's* jump-jet pedals and launched his 'Mech skyward. At the same time he saw a gold dot light up in his crosshairs and he hit all his triggers.

A suffocating blanket of heat cocooned around him in the 'Mech's cockpit as gravitational forces pounded him down into the command couch. He smiled as the LRMs streaking out of the left side of his chest corkscrewed into the lead fighter. The missiles exploded as they walked up and over the *Rogue's* nose and cockpit, but he knew they had not crippled the craft. Still, the boxy *Rogue* broke off its run and Harry counted that as a victory.

Triumph quickly soured in his mouth as the second *Rogue* and the pair of *Tridents* following it stayed on target. None of the other 'Mechs attempted his maneuver. As he watched from his vantage point, they did nothing while the fighters came in on their strafing runs.

The *Rogue* launched two flights of LRMs that arrowed in on Clark's *Panther*. Thirty explosive rockets converged on the BattleMech and detonated. A bright ball of fire consumed him while shards of armor and missile casings spat out in every direction. With its edges curling up into itself, the fireball rose into the sky, then imploded into greasy black smoke, leaving a charred and battered *Panther* in its wake.

Somehow Clark managed to keep the 'Mech upright, though the left arm hung useless at the 'Mech's side. The *Panther* raised the PPC mounted on the right arm and fired back at its tormentors, but the blue lightning missed and sizzled impotently into the sky.

The *Tridents* punished the *Panther* for its pilot's insolence. The medium lasers mounted beneath each wing and in the lead craft's nose created a wall of ruby energy that burned more armor from the *Panther*. As it swept on and savaged the other 'Mechs in the suicide squad, the second aerospace fighter pounced on the *Panther*. Its assault burned away the left arm and sent the 'Mech crashing to the ground.

Harry laughed as Clark went down. "Serves the stupid bastard right. Serves all those stupid bastards right."

Only when he began to bring the *Valkyrie* back to solid ground did Harry notice that the first *Rogue* had come back around for him. He glanced at his heat registers and saw that they were reading much higher than they should have. If he fired his jets again, he knew that the whole 'Mech might overheat and shut down. It dawned on him, as he landed the *Valkyrie*, that the Kell Hounds must have removed several of the cooling devices from his 'Mech, probably not wanting to waste heat sinks on the suicide squad.

Beyond the incoming fighter, Harry saw two *Overlord* DropShips preparing to land just outside Denton. Pointing his weapons at the nearest one, he got a weapons lock.

"Can't hurt, might help." Harry smiled and hit his triggers. "Better to die a man than live a rat in a cage."

Khan Phelan Ward saw the DropShip *Lioness* settling down on the outskirts of Denton and the fighters circling around for another run at the heavily damaged 'Mechs. The *Tigress* looked to be headed for the north side of the plains, right at the edge of the foothills. Things were not going as well as he'd hoped, but they were not the worst case either.

He hit a key and Carew's face appeared on his auxiliary monitor. "Carew?"

"Yes, my Khan?"

"Launch your fighters now. Engage over Denton." Phelan hit another key combination and switched to a frequency Ragnar was monitoring. "Ragnar, stand by." The Khan watched the bandit 'Mechs begin to disembark in Denton. "It is time to reap the whirlwind."

══ 36 ══

Harry Pollard's shining moment of glory ended when the returning *Rogue* launched thirty long-range missiles at his *Valkyrie*. First he saw his own medium laser actually hit the landing *Overlord* DropShip and his LRMs scatter flames over its hull, then his world erupted into flame. His head slammed back into the command couch and stars danced before his eyes as titanic forces shook the *Valkyrie*.

Warning klaxons blared inside the cockpit and Harry tasted blood on his upper lip. He felt his 'Mech spinning and saw the *Valkyrie*'s right arm whirl away through the fire curtain around him. The left-arm armor had also been breached, but the chest armor still held. Loss of the right arm meant that his laser had gone the way of his compatriots.

I still have missiles! Harry clung to that hope as his *Valkyrie* tottered and fell. Extending the 'Mech's left arm, he tried to post off the ground, but the machine had become too unstable for him to accomplish such a miraculous maneuver. He did manage to alter his fall so that he did not land face-down. *I can still punch out!*

The *Valkyrie* hit the ground with the considerable force that might be expected of a thirty-ton object propelled by copious amounts of high explosives. Its most important yet fragile component rattled around in the command couch like a lone pea in a can. Before he could hit the ejection system, Harry's head slammed again into the command couch, hitting with enough force to crack the neurohelmet and the skull beneath it.

Harry Pollard died in a cage, but he died happy.

Nestled in a dark room, with the bowl of the sky simulated above him in glittering detail, Nelson Geist heard the Kell Hound aerofighters scream skyward from the Old Connaught base. His fingers curled into fists as a *need* to be part of the fight burned in his veins. *They deny you the chance to fight, but they will need you yet.*

A bright rectangle opened on the horizon and Nelson recognized Bates's silhouette. "Kommandant Geist, we've got direct gun-camera feed here. They've got Red right where they want her. Want to see the end to it?"

The gaunt man shook his head mechanically. "No, thank you. They'll need my work when she escapes."

"She's not escaping. We have three regiments to oppose her one. She can't get away."

Nelson waved the door shut. "When she escapes, they'll need my work."

Bates shrugged. "Suit yourself."

He closed the door, leaving Nelson in his perforated darkness. "I am." He hit a button on the keyboard of the computer display unit he was using and constellations shifted as he centered himself on another world. *Just because they won't let me help them doesn't mean they don't need me. And it doesn't mean, when the time comes, that I won't be ready to help them.*

The forty kilometers from Old Connaught to Denton passed in 3.25 minutes for the Kell Hound fighters. Caitlin would have preferred flying higher and faster, but remaining on the deck gave them a shot at surprise. The foothills, though not terribly high, provided enough of a radar-shadow that fighters with their radar in air-to-ground mode might not notice them until too late.

A minute and a half out Raven Flight shot over the Kilkenny. Caitlin used the bridges as a check against her computer-generated map, smiling to see that they were dead on course. As the land sloped back up toward the foothills, she nudged the throttle forward. Only thirty seconds from Denton she began to pick up passive radar tracks from the enemy fighters.

e flipped her weapons-control on and saw all four
er lasers and the PPC in the nose go green. *All
used up and someplace to go!* The secondary monitor
showed another flight coming in behind her and she knew
from the designation that it was the Clanners. "Luck,
Carew," she breathed cautiously. Opening her radio
channel she brought her *Stingray* up and over the foothills. "Go, Ravens, go!"

Caitlin dropped her crosshairs on the boxy shape of a
Rogue rising lazily out of a strafing run. Kicking her rud-
der right she slipped into his six and let him have it with
everything her *Stingray* had to offer. From his lack of movement she knew she'd hit him before he knew he was hunted.

The PPC strung a blue line from the *Stingray*'s nose
to the ship's fuselage. Starting just behind the cockpit
and ripping back along the craft, the hits bisected the
stabilizer between the halves of the split tail. One medium pulse laser pumped more fire into the scar while
the other chipped away at the armored engine cowling in
the aft. One of the two large lasers pulsed a green energy
rod into the left wing, melting armor into a ceramic rain
that fell on Denton while the other cored the engine.

A brilliant shower of sparks shot out of the engine as
a drive unit failed, sending the *Rogue* into a slow roll
that marked its loss of power. The craft began to pull
back to the starboard side, then it simply disintegrated.
It happened so slowly and carefully that it almost looked
to Caitlin like a computer diagram being exploded to
show what the *Rogue* looked like inside.

A wall of heat hit her. She glanced at her auxiliary
monitor and saw the heat spike up into the red zone and
remain there despite her heat sinks coming on line. She
shook her head to fight off the desire to faint in the heat
and she overrode the fighter's computer-mandated desire
to shut down. *Too much, too fast. Gotta watch it, kid.*

She pulled up and came over in a looping turn that let
her bleed off some heat and build up some airspeed.
Gotta be more careful, Caitlin. She smiled as she saw
the *Rogue*'s fragments continue to fall. *But that was one
hell of a first impression we made.*

With the fighters' arrival imminent, Dan Allard gave
the order for the Hounds to move forward out of the

Clonarf bunkers. Huge doors cranked open and the 'Mechs best suited to antiair operations came out first to take out any unwelcome bandit pilots on a strafing run. Once they had secured the canyons and draws where the openings to the mountain bases had been hidden, the scout units headed out.

Phelan headed his *Wolfhound* straight north, and saw from ground level what had been fed to him from watching stations on top of the mountains. One *Overlord* had grounded on the edge of Denton, while the other had moved out toward the foothills and the M5 leading north to Old Connaught. As the first of the fighters withdrew, both ships disgorged their armies. One flew north, beyond the foothills, while the other shifted south and landed in Denton.

Phelan started a search program on his onboard computer, and it locked on to a target in the furthest group of bandit 'Mechs. He ordered up magnification on his holographic display and was rewarded with the image of a scarlet *BattleMaster*. Punching up a tightbeam radio configuration, he focused it on that 'Mech.

"In the name of the ilKhan of the Clans and in the name of Prince Victor Davion, I order you and your people to surrender now. If you do not, your command will be destroyed."

The return message came immediately as a picture filled his secondary monitor. He saw red hair splayed out over the shoulders of a cooling vest and bright eyes peering through the triangular viewport of a neurohelmet. "Those better than you have already tried, wolfling."

Phelan shook his head, "There are none better than I am. There are none better than the Kell Hounds. We outnumber you three to one. Surrender."

"Only a Wolf would offer surrender, and only a Wolf would accept it." Her eyes narrowed. "Though you do not deserve it, I will grant you a warrior's death."

Her confidence, though strong and angry, seemed unnatural to Phelan. *She cannot believe what she is saying. She is covering surprise, but how solid is that cover?* "I do not offer you surrender for myself," he started slowly, "but I offer it at the request of Nelson Geist."

Her eyes widened for a moment before the image went dead. *That hit home!* He shifted over to Tac One. "Colonel Allard, it's a fight to the finish. No quarter asked or given."

"Never expected it to be anything else." Dan's voice began to fade as more frequencies were opened. "Defend your home, Hounds."

Chris Kell's *Thunderbolt* led Alpha Battalion from its position in the west and out into the sunlight. He had the northwestern flank of the Kell Hound position, his battalion serving as a screening force to pick up the bandit unit near the foothills. Chris knew the Red Corsair had grounded a force there to defend against troops coming down from Old Connaught, which was the most logical location for reinforcements.

As his troops moved out, Chris saw the battle plan that Phelan and Dan had outlined beginning to unfold. The foothill group of bandits, designated the Sidhe, began to withdraw into the hills. The other group, the Baile, moved into Denton. Though it looked as though the Sidhe were abandoning the Baile, to make their way across the plain north of Denton and into the town, or out of it, would have meant marching across a killzone and the death of the bandits making the trip.

Chris opened a radio channel to Dan Allard. "Colonel, the Sidhe are into the hills. Alpha is in position and awaiting your order to pursue."

"Roger, Major. Stand by."

Chris saw a long line of the red and black Kell Hounds 'Mechs form a semicircle around Denton to the south and west. The BattleMechs to the south, with a star of black 'Mechs from the Wolf Clan at the far end, began to move forward. In Denton, the scarlet and gold bandit 'Mechs spread out and assumed defensive positions that promised nasty urban fighting.

"Alpha Leader?"

Chris nodded. "Yes, Colonel?"

"Go. The Sidhe are yours."

Caitlin pulled back on her stick and pointed the *Stingray*'s nose at the sky. She punched her feet down on the overthrust pedals and felt gravity pull her down into the command couch as she rocketed away from Arc-Royal. The keening sound in her cockpit told her the maneuver had not shaken her pursuit, and as she dropped her crosshairs into her aft arc, she saw the range between them dropping off.

Damned Hellcat can out-climb me. Still, it's a flying wing. Yaw has to be a problem! "Raven Leader, I have a *Hellcat* in my six. Who wants him?"

"I will oblige you."

Caitlin smiled as she heard Carew answer her call. "Okay, he's yours!" She jammed her stick forward in a maneuver that started her in a loop that put her cockpit on the outside of the circle. She began to see red as the forces of gravity rushed blood to her head. She knew, as did every pilot who had ever flown, that the loop she had started was slow and stupid and almost guaranteed to make the pilot "red-out."

Before she could lose consciousness, she cranked the *Stingray* around in a tight roll centered on the left wingtip. Pulling up on the stick, she regained some altitude and managed to flash past the nose of the *Hellcat*. Twin green laser beams passed through a point on her six, but they missed her by a hundred meters.

"Get him, Vulture Leader." Caitlin popped her *Stingray* into another roll and lined a *Trident* up in her sights.

"Wilco, Raven Leader," Carew growled as he pulled his *Visigoth* up into a steep climb. His aerospace fighter had nowhere near the power of the *Hellcat,* or the *Stingray,* for that matter, but it packed more weaponry than either of them. Closer in shape to the flying wing design of the *Hellcat* than the *Stingray,* the dual rear stabilizers and the elongated weapon pods running parallel to and in front of the fuselage eliminated the faster fighter's yaw problem.

The Clan pilot watched the *Hellcat*'s nose begin to dip as the *Stingray* went into the negative-G loop. He smiled as she inverted and shot back up in a teardrop loop above the *Hellcat*'s nose. The *Cat*'s pilot rolled to get back on Caitlin's tail, and started a long dive to pick up air speed. When he saw Carew, he punched his overthrusters, sending long flame jets out the back of the *Hellcat*'s tail.

In his panic, the *Hellcat* pilot hit one pedal a second

before the other, giving the fighter's engine a momentary burst of energy before the other engine kicked in. In most aerospace fighters this would have resulted in the start of a power turn, but in the *Hellcat* it created another problem. The leading edge of the right wing began to inch forward as the fighter started a rotation around its vertical axis.

It took a second or two to correct, and in that time Carew rolled his *Visigoth* in right behind the *Hellcat*. When Carew punched his thumb down on the stick's firing stud, the nose-mounted particle projection cannon loosed a bolt of synthetic lightning that chopped into the *Hellcat*'s left wing and nibbled away at the vertical stabilizer. As Carew also hit the missile launcher, the *Hellcat* juked to the left, pulling the wing out of harm's way.

Thirty LRMs streaked from the *Visigoth* and peppered the *Hellcat*'s fuselage. Carew saw two green-gray clouds from missile clusters that told him heat sinks had been destroyed. One set of missiles had pulverized thrust vector nozzles while another three LRMs had blasted away at the armor over the engine. None of the hits were fatal in themselves, but taken as a whole, they doomed the *Hellcat*.

The flying wing, unable to use the port thrust vectors, remained flying straight and level for what must have seemed an eternity to the pilot. Carew, riding close behind the craft, felt time slipping away incredibly fast, but his heat monitor showed the *Visigoth*'s temperature dropping back to normal ranges, so he fired again.

The PPC's blue lightning raked through the armor over the fuselage, and another heat sink exploded in a spray of greenish liquid. A pulse laser lanced red darts into the engine cowling and another blew more armor from the fuselage, again destroying thrust vector nozzles.

Carew glanced at his secondary display. The *Hellcat* had lost three of its fifteen heat sinks. The armor on the fuselage had been damaged but not breached. The pilot had to want to disengage, but his thruster damage prevented that and the loss of his heat sinks meant overthrusting would make him overheat. Still, the fighter was operational and—as the laser from the after turret reminded Carew—it was still dangerous.

How much damage will you take before you die? Carew

dropped the crosshairs on the plane's outline. *And how long before one of your comrades scrapes me off your tail?*

Phelan hit his radio as he brought his Star up at the extreme edge of what was likely to be the bandit's range. "Ragnar, we have to let them know we are serious. We need an example. Try the DropShip."

"As you will it, my Khan."

Phelan's eyes narrowed as he gazed at the *Overlord* DropShip sitting on the pristine ferrocrete of the landing pad. A reality of warfare in the thirty-first century was that it had become incalculably expensive. Over the previous three hundred years the Inner Sphere had managed to all but blow itself back into the Stone Age. Recovery of a memory core from the Star League era had begun a renaissance that brought with it more factories to produce the materiel of war, but most BattleMechs were still being cobbled together from bits and pieces salvaged after battles.

The Kell Hounds had been rebuilt after the battle for Luthien from just such salvage. The bandits would be stopped, but if the Hounds could convince them to surrender before their machines were destroyed, not only would it save lives on both sides, it would also enrich the mercenaries above and beyond the compensation promised by Victor Davion.

The DropShip *Lioness* was a masterpiece of lostech—the Inner Sphere term for any item whose technology had been lost for so long. The robotic factories in the Inner Sphere turned out less than a thousand DropShips a year, making each one incredibly valuable. While the *Overlord* Class ship represented a staggering sum of money if it could be captured, it also represented the Baile's only way off Arc-Royal.

The ferrocrete of the landing pad had been poured over a metric quarter-ton of plastic explosive shaped in a cylinder and centered beneath the circle at the heart of the pad. When Ragnar hit a switch on the command console of his *Viper,* the plastique detonated. It blew up and out with a force that would have registered 5.2 on the Richter scale, vaporizing the ferrocrete and shooting a fiery plume half a kilometer into the air.

The *Lioness* had landed somewhat west and north of

center. The explosion crumpled the aft-starboard quadrant, rupturing the vessel like a hammer smashing a *naranji*. The ship lifted up off the ground and started to tumble, then came down again, bounced through a building, then started to come apart. Weapon magazines began to explode, spraying out armor and weapons, then the ship landed on a second building, creating an explosion that ripped the *Overlord* DropShip apart.

Phelan felt the shockwave of the detonation and steadied his *Wolfhound* against it. In Denton windows shattered and 'Mechs toppled. As he watched, most of the machines got back to their feet and braced themselves for the Kell Hound attack.

Phelan saw a light start to blink on his radio control panel and he punched the button beneath it. A bandit stared up at him from his secondary monitor. "Treacherous dog. Come to your monument and we will show you how real warriors die."

"If you *were* real warriors, I would." Phelan's green eyes narrowed. "You are bandits. You will die like bandits and you shall be remembered as bandits." Then he broke the connection and reopened his link to Ragnar. "The school, then the municipal building. Drive them south so they won't harass Alpha Battalion."

When the plan was first proposed, Chris and his people had not liked the idea of being sent into the foothills after the Sidhe. The hills were a bonus to the defender, both because the aggressor had to attack uphill and because the defenders could arrange ambushes by lying in wait. The Red Corsair might be leading bandits, but in that terrain, even bad pilots could amass kills.

A blue light flashed on Chris's command console as telemetry began to scroll up his secondary screen. He opened a radio channel and sent the data out to his fire support lances. "The fix is in. Fire at will."

Deep in the foothills, hidden halfway down a wooded ravine that ran north to south, Evantha held the laser built into the right arm of her Elemental armor steady on the *Vindicator*. The bandit 'Mech's red and gold color contrasted sharply with the surrounding foliage, but it did not matter because she watched him on the infrared setting of her armor's holographic display. In addition to the normal heat radiating from the charging coils of the PPC that replaced the bandit 'Mech's right forearm, a small dot rode on the junction of its torso and right hip.

It came from the invisible infrared beam of her laser. She had not been at all comfortable with the idea of sacrificing one of her main weapons for a spotting laser, but the Khan had approved the plan, so she accepted it. Each of the five Elemental Points had one member acting as spotter, with the rest ready to pick off any survivors.

She saw a blue flash at the lower corner of her viewplate. *Incoming.* Holding her arm rigid, she braced herself for the blast. She knew it would not be long in coming and would be devastating when it hit.

To Evantha it looked as if a volcano had opened up beneath the *Vindicator's* broad feet. One moment the 'Mech was walking through a forest and the next it had become a black silhouette in the center of a fire spout. Missile after missile pounded the *Vindicator,* crushing armor into sharp ceramic shards, stripping the right arm of armor, and mangling both the shoulder and elbow joints. The PPC twisted out of line with the 'Mech's flank and pointed down toward the ground.

Amazingly, as the smoke cleared and burning trees toppled, the *Vindicator* remained standing. The armor on its body and both legs had been damaged, but the pilot had managed to keep the war machine upright. Evantha knew that meant he was very skilled—better than any bandit should be.

Evantha kept her laser trained on him. Glancing at the row of icons beneath her holographic display, she triggered one and sent out another burst of telemetry. *Hit him again, Chris.*

As Carew covered the *Hellcat* with his crosshairs once more, the warning klaxon started to blare. *Someone has a lock on me!* He glanced at his display and saw a *Trident* swooping down on him in his four. He rolled his *Visigoth* over on its right wing, then pulled back on the stick and came up into an Immelmann. As he headed back toward the *Trident* and passed beyond it, he again hugged the stick to his stomach and completed the full loop.

The *Hellcat* came up into his sights again, so he punched the PPC off and added in twin medium pulse lasers. The PPC blasted away at the engine cowling while one of the lasers smoked another heat sink. The second laser ripped up the armor on the right wing, burning away some of the paint job.

Carew blinked as the *Hellcat* came up and over on its left wing. As it whirled away to his port, he got a good look at the insignia previously hidden by the bandits' burning red and gold paint. *No, that could not have been! No one would be so bold. No one would be so insane.* The flames consumed the insignia, but Carew could not forget it.

Before the true import of what he had seen could sink in, the warning klaxon again sounded in his cockpit. *Damned* Trident! Carew fixed it with his rear lasers and was about to trigger a blast when three energy beams shot up from beneath the *Trident* and raked through it like shrapnel through fog. A PPC beam opened the fuselage from nose to tail like a giant blue can opener, while twin large lasers scissored through the right wing. The wing folded up and in toward the cockpit, then snapped off and dropped away as the smoking fighter began to spiral down toward the ground.

"Eagle Leader says thanks."

"Not a problem, Eagle Leader," he heard Caitlin answer him. "Just returning a favor."

Under the cover of his fire support lances, Chris and the rest of Alpha Battalion entered the foothills. The paths left by the bandits were easy to follow. Radio messages from the Elementals made locating the enemy 'Mechs easy, and the first ones he saw were the burning, smashed hulks of those the LRM-equipped 'Mechs were destroying from afar.

Bringing his *Thunderbolt* around a hillock, Chris saw an improbably slender BattleMech move into the meadow from another little valley off to his right. He swung the *Thunderbolt* to the right and centered the crosshairs on the *Ostsol*. He kept the sights on the 'Mech's torso, and when he got the dot confirming a weapons lock, he fired.

The large laser mated to the *Thunderbolt*'s right fore-arm sent needles of green energy through the *Ostsol*'s right arm armor, stripping it completely and even chipping away at the ferro-titanium bone beneath. But Chris knew better than to take comfort in that damage. The *Ostsol*'s arms were used only for balance and, apparently, absorbing damage that would have been more harmful elsewhere.

The trio of medium lasers mounted in the *Thunderbolt* did more damage. Two melted away armor in the *Ostsol*'s chest, and the third savaged the left leg armor. Another shot or two in those places and he could cripple the enemy 'Mech.

The *Ostsol* gave back better than it got, however. The twin large pulse lasers mounted high in the torso superheated armor over the center of the *Thunderbolt*'s chest and on the left arm. One of the medium pulse lasers in the 'Mech's belly added more damage to that on the *Thunderbolt*'s chest, reducing its armor to 40 percent of the original, while the other one burned a nasty gash in the armor on the *Thunderbolt*'s left thigh.

The *Ostsol* had burned off more than two tons of armor plating, and the *Thunderbolt*'s gyros sought to compensate for the weight loss. Chris managed to keep the 'Mech upright, tracking the *Ostsol* with his sights. The assault had left him running hot, but he could see that his enemy had also pushed his heat high in hopes of scoring a crippling blow.

In a split-second Chris decided not to push his heat again. He knew his 'Mech was better-suited to a slugging match than the *Ostsol*. He triggered his three pulse lasers and felt a heat spike gush hot air into the cockpit. Sweat covered his exposed flesh, but he was concentrating too hard on the damage his shots did to worry about heat.

The medium pulse lasers all hit, but they failed to punch through the *Ostsol*'s armor. Two continued his assault on the center and right sides of the chest, but the third burned armor from the 'Mech's vestigial left arm. The pilot kept his 'Mech upright and returned fire with a vengeance.

The *Ostsol* pilot had decided to take no chances. One of the two large pulse lasers he directed at the *Thunderbolt* missed high, but the second burned almost all the way through the armor over the 'Mech's heart. A medium pulse laser followed it up and melted away some of the center torso's internal structures. Warning klaxons screamed throughout the cockpit, then more of them sounded as the second pulse laser blasted into the *Thunderbolt*'s head, vaporizing virtually all the armor.

Chris reflexively shied away from the brilliant headshot, and his *Thunderbolt* recoiled with him. It stumbled and went down to one knee. Chris jerked forward, held in his command couch by the restraining belts, then arched his back and pulled the *Thunderbolt* upright. Its right leg kicked out to stabilize it—dirt clods flying and trees falling as the foot dug into the dark loam for solid traction.

My chest armor is breached! Chris looked at the glowing circle of red on the auxiliary monitor's picture of the *Thunderbolt*. He knew a shot there or to the head with anything the *Ostsol* carried would finish his 'Mech and likely kill him. He swung his large laser over to cover the enemy 'Mech, prepared to trigger everything. *Now is no time to be cautious*.

As he dropped the crosshairs on the *Ostsol*, he noticed it was not moving at all. Shifting his holographic display over from vislight to infrared, he saw the machine glowing like a supernova. *It's overheated. The computers shut it down*.

He tightbeamed a message to the pilot. "Pop your canopy now and surrender. The fight is over for you."

Chris got a reply, but not the one he expected.

As he watched in horror, the canopy exploded outward in a shower of smoky glass fragments. A fireball ignited in the cockpit and he expected to see the command couch shoot out on an ejector rocket. He knew that ejecting into the woods was suicidal because the trees would crush any escaping pilot against their boles before the couch could correct its course. Instead of the command couch and pilot, the fire spat out bits and pieces of both. The spherical head plumped at the edges, then the top of it blew clean off.

The *Ostsol* fell forward, spilling burning sparks from its cockpit like glowing coals bouncing from a toppling barbecue.

Chris's mouth went sour. He knew that what he had seen *could* have been a failure of the escape rocket to ignite properly, or else the failure of restraining bolts to pop free on the command couch. Deep down he *hoped* that was what he had witnessed, but he knew it was not.

That pilot committed suicide to avoid capture. Chris swallowed hard. *We've always known these bandits were unusual. Just how unusual we underestimated by a parsec.*

Phelan acknowledged the radio call from Dan Allard with a nod. "Roger, Colonel, the Sidhe have broken and are heading north. I will have Conal's people move in and cut them off from the DropShip out there to pick them up." Phelan twitched his right hand and brought his crosshairs onto a *Rifleman* lining up a shot at Ranna's *Warhawk*. He punched his thumb down and sent a large laser beam slicing through the *Rifleman*'s exposed knee joint. The beam melted away the ends of the ferro-titanium bones, pitching the big 'Mech to the right and spoiling its aim at Ranna.

The Clan Khan keyed his radio to Tac Three. "Star Colonel Ward, the Sidhe are headed in your direction. Stop them."

"They will not pass, my Khan."

Conal's reply bothered Phelan briefly, but then a bandit *Vindicator* took notice of him. The 'Mech's PPC swung into line with the *Wolfhound* and let fly with a bolt of cerulean electricity. The energy whip flayed all the armor off the *Wolfhound*'s right arm and started to work on the pseudomuscles and bones. Phelan rocked back in his command couch and felt a static tingle over his arms and legs.

A glance at his auxiliary monitor told him that the 'Mech's arm still functioned and that its large laser mounted was still useable, but not whether the *Vindicator* had hit it again. *Can't take that chance.* He gritted his teeth and spitted the *Vindicator* on his crosshairs.

The combination of the Clan targeting computer and Phelan's steady hand kept all the *Wolfhound*'s weapons tight on target. The green beam of the large laser punched into the left side of the *Vindicator*'s chest, reducing more than 60 percent of its armor to vapor and liquid droplets. Then the trio of medium pulse lasers sent a hail of red energy darts through the armor steam. Flames jetted back out through the quintet of LRM firing ports in the 'Mech's left breast and a greenish tinge in the smoke told Phelan that a heat sink had been blasted away. The 'Mech's left arm sagged as the shoulder girdle evaporated.

The sheer violence of the assault against it twisted the *Vindicator* around and dumped it on the ground. As the pilot tried to lever the 'Mech back up, pushing off the ground with its PPC, two green energy spears passed through it, one reigniting the fire in its chest and the other obliterating its head. Decapitated by the beam, the 'Mech flopped onto its back, with twin smoke plumes drifting upward.

"Thank you, Ranna," Phelan gasped as heat shot into his cockpit. His heat sinks labored to purge it, and brought the temperature down quickly, but the burst of heat from his attack left him breathless for a moment. "Good shooting."

"It would not do for the Khan's Honor Guard to allow him to die."

Conal's face appeared on Phelan's secondary monitor. "The bridges have been blown. Old Connaught is safe."

"What? What are you talking about?"

"I have blown the bridges, as you ordered. Your home is safe." Conal's image vanished and was replaced with a gun-camera feed showing the two bridges over the Kilkenny sagging into the river. "The bandits will not cross!"

"What have you done, Conal?" Phelan's slammed one fist against the arm of his command couch. "I told you to stop them, not blow the bridges!"

"And I have. You placed us here to guard Old Connaught. I have made certain they will not reach the city."

"I wanted you to prevent the Red Corsair from reaching her DropShip, Conal! Quickly, get there before she does."

"We cannot, we are north of the river. We cannot cross it."

"Why would you blow it before you had crossed?"

"She has access to a DropShip. She could have gotten to Old Connaught had we crossed before blowing the bridge."

I know you are not so obtuse, Conal. Did you suffer brain-fade, or are you out to tarnish my victory here? Phelan's hands tightened into fists. "Pull back to Old

Connaught at full speed, Conal. If the Red Corsair *does* reach her DropShip and gets behind you, I will meet you in a Circle of Equals and rip your heart out with my bare hands, do you understand?"

"Aff, my Khan. It will be as you desire."

Phelan stabbed the commlink button to Tac Two. "Eagle Leader, can you get at the Red Corsair's DropShip and stop it?"

"Negative, Wolf One." Carew's voice carried a note of caution. "The *Tigress* apparently carried with it a Point of *Stukas*, a Point of *Transgressors*, and a Point of *Corsairs*. They are flying CAP for the DropShip and we are all running light on ammo. They seem content to let us strafe stragglers, but I am not confident we can get through. If it is what you desire, I will try."

Phelan knew that he had only to give the order and Carew would give his life trying to accomplish the task. "Stand by, Eagle Leader." Phelan switched to Tac Four. "Star Captain Fetladral, report on the Sidhe."

"Less than a Star running. The Red Corsair is one of those in retreat. They are within a kilometer of the *Tigress*. Alpha Battalion has the rest of them under control or dead."

"Roger, Star Captain. Wolf One out." Phelan reestablished the link with Carew. "Eagle One, initiate ground-support operations. Let the DropShip go . . . mop up. No reason for more of us to die today."

Bates again broke the darkness of Nelson's improvised planetarium, but that was fine with him. "The battle is over, Kommandant. The good guys won."

Nelson smiled unconsciously. "She escaped, didn't she?"

Bates hesitated, then nodded. "How did you know?"

The maimed MechWarrior curled his half-hand into a misshapen fist. "There are times, Mr. Bates, when God *does* answer prayers."

37

Tharkad
Federated Commonwealth
12 September 3055

Victor Davion looked up with relief from the crop reports as Galen Cox entered his office. The smile on Galen's face raised a cousin on Victor's lips despite the late hour and his fatigue. "You have heard some good news?"

Galen nodded and a laugh escaped him. "Report from Arc-Royal. The Corsair's raiding days are finished."

"Yes!" Victor slapped the top of his desk and gave Galen a thumb's-up. "That's the best news I've had in months. Did they get her? Will we have a trial?"

"No, she escaped with a half-dozen or so fighters and two other 'Mechs." Galen frowned slightly. "The rest of the bandits were killed, to a man. The Hounds are hedging their estimates of salvage. . . ."

"Who cares? They can have it all." Victor allowed himself a half-smile. "The Hounds were created with money my grandfather gave Morgan and Patrick Kell, and doubled in size with a bequest from my grandmother's will. Given their success rate and their loyalty to the Steiners, I should pay them enough to establish two more regiments."

Galen shook his head slightly. "I believe your mother would applaud that decision, but I do not think it is a good public relations move. It reinforces your image as a cold militarist."

"We wouldn't want that, now, would we?" Victor sighed and glanced at the agricultural printouts stacked on his desk. "On some worlds we have to protect the price of grains because they are so abundant and on others we have to discount the grain we import so people can afford to buy bread. And I thought the logistics of running a military unit were bad."

"I shall leave you to your work, then."

"No, not so fast. You're not getting off that easily." Victor stood up and stretched. "What did today's briefing from Curaitis say?"

Victor saw a spark of annoyance in Galen's eyes, but his aide acquiesced and sat down heavily in a wingback chair. Galen had offered to filter reports on the investigation to Victor, and the Prince had taken him up on it. It freed Victor for the important business of running the Federated Commonwealth, but sentenced Galen to informal daily briefings.

"Curaitis says that they have completed the third round of narco-interrogation of the assassin. It was, by far, the most satisfactory of the rounds because they are no longer giving him medication for the fat embolis."

"The assassin will live, then?" Initially the doctors had feared that the assassin would not survive because the fractures to his leg had released bone marrow into the bloodstream. The fat from the marrow had clogged the man's coronary arteries, resulting in a massive and very unexpected heart attack. The fat embolis had come very close to killing the assassin and had delayed his interrogation for what, to Victor, was an intolerable amount of time.

"Yes, the angioplasty cleared up the problem with his heart, and the doctors do not expect a brain embolis. His death won't become part of your conspiracy to hide your involvement in your mother's death." Galen smiled sardonically. "In this interrogation Curaitis learned about the assassin's connections and how he was given assignments. It seems fairly clear that the man was not working for House Liao or Kurita."

Victor frowned. "That leaves someone from the Free Worlds League or the Federated Commonwealth as his employer. And I know which one I'd wish to be the correct one."

"It is possible that someone did strike at your mother because of the perception that Joshua Marik is being held 'hostage' at the New Avalon Institute of Science, but Thomas Marik cannot deny that the leukemia treatments are keeping the boy's disease in check. Chances are, however, that any strike from that quarter would have been carried out by an agent of the ComStar splinter group now based in the Free Worlds League.''

"And this guy had no ComStar or Word of Blake ties," Victor said. "That means it's someone here, someone from the Federated Commonwealth. But who?"

Galen shook his head. "If I knew that, you would have his head on a platter desk."

"What about that list of people who purchased tickets to the banquet? Have they all checked out?"

"The list is still being compiled. The assassin's capture shifted some of our assets in that direction." Galen frowned. "I'll make sure it gets finished."

"Good. When it's done, I want to see it." Victor leaned forward in the red chair opposite the one where Galen sat. "Any improvement in public opinion?"

The slender blond man nodded. "You're no longer the demon they were painting you three months ago. The interviews you've given have been drawing bigger audiences as they move from world to world. Your approval rating has climbed a bit—and the end of the Red Corsair should help that even more."

Victor nodded. "I was thinking I might attend Salome Kell's funeral on Arc-Royal."

Galen hissed. "I don't know. How would it look if you went to her funeral after not attending your own mother's?"

"But won't it look worse if I don't acknowledge the service the Hounds have performed for the Federated Commonwealth?" Victor frowned. "I'm damned if I do and damned if I don't."

"Such are the rewards of your office."

"I suppose." Victor suppressed a yawn. "I think I'll send Katherine to the funeral and have her carry a message to Morgan and the Kell Hounds from me. The same day that Salome is buried, I will lay a wreath at my mother's grave and make a large contribution to the orphanage fund she supported." He sighed. "It all seems like a game of hollow gestures. I would rather be there. I hope Morgan will understand."

"I am sure he will, Highness."

Victor nodded slowly. "Good. At least that's one who will."

38

Kell Hound Headquarters
Old Connaught, Arc-Royal
Federated Commonwealth
18 September 3055

Seated alone and in the dark, Phelan Ward stared at the image frozen on the computer screen on his desk. Isolated from Carew's gun-camera battle ROM, the digitized image showed what looked to Phelan like a green raptor bearing a katana in its talons. Phelan had constructed the composite picture by layering on the frames as the logo was revealed and then consumed by fire.

There was no mistaking it. *The fighters belonged to the Jade Falcons.*

Phelan felt a chill run to the marrow his bones. It was the conclusion that satisfied Occam's razor—the simplest answer was most often the correct one. Assigning past ownership of the aerospace fighters or of *that* aerospace fighter to the Jade Falcons limited the enormity of the problem he might have uncovered.

That simple answer brought dozens of questions with it. It was possible that the Red Corsair, with her one DropShip, had staged a raid on a Jade Falcon world from which she got fighters, another DropShip, more 'Mechs, and a new JumpShip, but it was inconceivable that he would not have heard about it. The Jade Falcons would have screamed about such losses to the ilKhan, using the failure of the Thirty-first Wolf Solahma and the Kell Hounds against Ulric like a club. The ilKhan would have told him about the attack, both to stress the urgency of stopping the Red Corsair and to warn him that she had new assets.

Phelan could think of only one reason why he would not have heard about a raid on the Jade Falcons: the raid did not take place. That, in turn, meant that it was the Jade Falcons who had been resupplying the Red Corsair. Yet the Falcons had never acknowledged the bandits as their agents and, in fact, would never disgrace such a good fighting unit with that label.

What began to unfold in the young Khan's mind was the outline of a conspiracy so bold and well-executed that he could not prove a bit of it. Had it succeeded, the Inner Sphere and the Clans would have once again been pitted against each other in a war of conquest. The truce would have been a memory and the ilKhan would have been disgraced and swept from power in a silent coup by the Jade Falcons.

In many ways it made more sense the more he thought about it. The Jade Falcons had suffered gravely in the war against the Inner Sphere. Kai Allard-Liao had almost singlehandedly defeated them at Twycross, frustrated and then humiliated them at Alyina, and then worked with them to liberate the planet from ComStar. Besides, no matter that they came off as the second-best of seven Clans fighting ComStar on Tukayyid, they were so far behind the Wolves' performance that they looked hardly better than the rest. Once an influential and powerful Clan, the Jade Falcons had lost both strength and political influence in the course of the invasion of the Inner Sphere.

The truce of Tukayyid had helped them more than they wanted to acknowledge because it forestalled any Federated Commonwealth counterattack along their border. Both sides raided above the truce line. The year before, a combined Federated Commonwealth/Wolf's Dragoons force had thrown back a big Jade Falcon push at Morges, but real gains were few and temporary at best. But the Jade Falcons were resilient and might still have expanded at the Commonwealth's expense but for one thing.

That one thing was the resumption of interClan raiding. The invasion of the Inner Sphere had brought the Clans together, providing a unifying focus that led to a gradual reduction in internecine battles. With the signing of the truce the other Clans had begun trying to nibble away at the Falcons, whose Inner Sphere holdings were sandwiched between the Federated Commonwealth and the Wolf Clan.

If the bandits had managed to raid their way over the truce line and then had proclaimed themselves as Jade Falcons, two things would have happened immediately. The first was that war with the Inner Sphere would have resumed instantly. That would have pitted the Wolves against ComStar, and the other Clans against the Draconis Combine. Once again the need to vanquish the common enemy of the Inner Sphere would have postponed the internal fighting that threatened the Jade Falcons.

More important, though, the Jade Falcons would have proved that even a bandit outfit could best the Inner Sphere. The various Clan forces opposed to the truce would have immediately swung their backing to the Jade Falcons and could have challenged Ulric to a Trial of Refusal to repudiate the truce. Even if Ulric succeeded in defending his position, the challenges would come so quickly that he would be forced to repudiate the truce himself as ComStar renewed hostilities. Precentor Martial Focht would have been forced to attack because he would no longer have been able to control the radical elements within ComStar.

Until the Jade Falcons succeeded, however, they had to travel incognito because the ilKhan would have forced their recall before they could get anywhere near the truce line. That would have resulted in the Jade Falcons losing even more power and prestige, and possibly embroiled them in a war with the Wolf Clan had they disobeyed the ilKhan's directive.

It occurred to Phelan that if the Jade Falcons *were* backing the Red Corsair, revelation of that fact could tear the Clans apart and transform interClan raiding into an all-out civil war. Such internal division would be an unhoped-for boon to the Inner Sphere, all but guaranteeing an end to the hostilities.

I wonder how much ComStar knew about the raiders when the Precentor Martial forced the ilKhan and the Archon to have Victor and me agree to hunting the Red Corsair down? Had a Jade Falcon unit discovered this renegade Falcon plot during their battle against the raiders, they would have suppressed it and the Clan would have dealt with it internally. This would have removed the plotters from their midst, but would have weakened the Jade Falcons and created a serious split in their ranks. ComStar would have loved that.

As a Wolf Khan who was committed to maintaining the peace, Phelan's knowledge of the raiders' possible backing was as good as not having discovered it at all. His appointment as liaison, and the selection of a Wolf Clan unit to hunt the bandits, were the best possible outcome of ComStar's plan. *At the least the ilKhan is cautioned about duplicity within the Clans, and at the most, the Clans will devour each other, returning to the very divisiveness that spawned them three hundred years ago.*

But, if ComStar knew enough to guess at all that . . . Phelan shivered. *Stop! I have conspiracies on the brain!*

A message scrolling across the bottom of his screen told him that the Thirty-first Wolf Solahma had linked up with their JumpShip and were headed home. Phelan knew he should have sent a message up to the ship, bidding his people farewell, but he did not because it would have meant seeing Conal's face again. He was happy to be rid of him because he was certain Conal would have applauded the Falcon ploy and even suggested they finish the bandits' mission.

Phelan shrugged. *It matters no longer. They are gone. The Red Corsair is gone.* Phelan realized that someone might give her more men and materiel, but it was unlikely. This foray had cost her backers more than 20 fighters, 103 BattleMechs, and 2 *Overlord* Class DropShips. *The gamble had been worth it, but repeating it was not. He'd have liked to have her in his hands, though, to learn who else was involved in this conspiracy.*

Phelan's thought vanished as the door to his office burst open. He looked up and saw Nelson Geist standing in the doorway. Pressing a key to wipe the screen, the Khan brought his head up. "The stellar hermit emerges from his celestial lair?"

Geist's eyes blazed with zealous fervor. "I can give you the Red Corsair."

Phelan raised an eyebrow. "What?"

"I know where she's going." Geist held up an optical data disk as if it were a holy relic.

"How?"

The man laughed aloud. "Not how, Ward, but how much. How much is the information worth to you?"

"I won't be blackmailed, Geist."

"And I won't be left behind." Nelson ran the fingers of his half-hand back through his hair. "You know I am not a traitor. You know I hate her. Promise me I go too."

"Bargained well and done." Phelan stood. "Where is she?"

Nelson Geist's lungs pumped like a bellows. "When she had me, she ran me in a computer simulation of her base. She made me learn it and promised me that I would live out the rest of my days there as her slave." The MechWarrior tapped the disk against the steel manacle he wore. "I learned my lessons well, very well. I outfoxed her."

The man tossed the disk to the Khan. "While there I spent time studying the night sky on her world. I picked out and named constellations. It has taken me two weeks of reviewing star charts from worlds you Clans have taken. I saw them all, season by season, hemisphere by hemisphere."

Nelson Geist smiled for the first time in Phelan's memory and it was not a pleasant thing to see. "Elissa. That's where we'll find her." Geist's smile broadened. "And that's where she'll die."

Arc-Royal
Federated Commonwealth
19 September 3055

Looking skyward, Nelson Geist could just barely make out the four DropShips the First 'Mech Regiment was using for transport to the waiting JumpShips. He dropped his half-empty dufflebag and gave Phelan a smart salute. "Kommandant Nelson Geist reporting as ordered, sir."

The tall, slender Khan nodded curtly. "You will be billeted aboard the *Owl's Nest*, sharing a cabin with Mr. Bates."

Nelson felt his heart sink into his stomach. "Bates? But I thought?"

"You thought what, Kommandant?"

"I thought you trusted me."

Phelan's eyes hooded over and Nelson felt a chill run down his spine. In an instant he knew that the Khan trusted no one outside his circle of advisors or the Kell Hounds. The Red Corsair had gotten to him that much. That kept Nelson an outsider, but he knew it also made them kindred spirits.

"You have provided me information that is very useful, Kommandant. I am bringing you with me because that was our agreement in trade for your information." The edge in Phelan's voice eased a bit. "And you do know the Red Corsair. But *trust*? Trust in this matter is a very volatile commodity."

Nelson's head came up. "When we get there, I will get a 'Mech?"

''No.''

''No!'' Nelson's jaw dropped. ''But . . .''

''You bargained to come along, nothing more. I hold you to your bargain. You can come or not, your choice.''

The fantasy Nelson had nurtured since his escape, the vision of facing the Red Corsair in a gigantic Circle of Equals vanished. *Who was I kidding?* He tried to ball his hands into fists, but his half-hand mocked him. *He is Clan, she is Clan. The conflict is beyond me.*

Nelson looked up at the Wolf Khan. ''She still has my men. I'm going.''

Phelan drummed his fingers impatiently on the arm of the chair in his cabin aboard the *Owl's Nest*. Dan Allard, sitting next to him, smiled. ''Phelan, you'll have worn your way through the arm by the time we get there. Patience is a virtue.''

''True enough, Colonel, but I fear this is one race that will go to the swift.'' Phelan tugged at the restraining belt as he watched the timer on his commlink computer tick down. After the initial jump from Arc-Royal, both JumpShips immediately made another hop to Yeguas. There they wasted a week charging their Kearny-Fuchida jump drives' coils from their solar sails while recharging the lithium-fusion batteries aboard both ships at the recharge station at the star's apex jump point.

The older man shook his head. ''I think we must be ahead of her already. We have no word of her raiding a recharge station in the Federated Commonwealth for a recharge, so she's probably still in our space. I don't think your Clans are going to be any more charitable to her than the Feds will be. We will reach her base and inhabit it a month before she comes home.''

Phelan kept his face expressionless. *Unless she reaches the Jade Falcons and they speed her on her way.* He drummed his fingers some more. ''I hope you're right, because I do not want to give her the chance to rebuild and re-arm, then come back. Elissa is a planet settled by a pacificistic sect known as the Inheritors. Its members have given up on technology. They live as simple farmers, scattered in little villages across the planet. Clan Wolf doesn't even have a garrison on the world. But it is possible that a Star League depot still exists there and the Red Corsair has tapped into that as a source of supply . . .''

Dan smiled. ''We fall back on your secondary plan. We use the Kell Hounds to blockade the world and you summon up your Galaxy to destroy her. Either way, she's done.''

Three tones sounded throughout the *Owl's Nest*. Phelan forced himself to relax as the timer clicked down to zero, and the universe suddenly collapsed in on him. Blackness curled upward and around in a bowl starting at his feet, like the trough of two black waves headed at each other. They continued to pull back and grew higher and higher until they closed over the top of him.

The bubble in which he had been trapped began to thin at the walls as the first jump ended, but it imploded when the second kicked in. The black water roof fell in on him. He felt himself drowning and watched images of the Red Corsair, Ulric, Conal, Victor, Ranna, and Vlad swirling around him. Millions of conspiracy plots swam through the darkness, and the urgent need for speed thundered through his head.

The second jump ended and Phelan shook his head to clear it. The commlink on his desk showed a Jade Falcon logo, then dissolved into the face of a Clanner who looked bored with his duty. ''Alyina Recharge Station.''

Phelan sat up, releasing the restraining belt. He tugged at the base of his tunic. ''I am Khan Phelan Ward of the Wolves. Recharge both of these ships immediately.''

The commtech looked surprised, then his face darkened. ''I do not have you scheduled here, Khan Phelan.''

''We are on an urgent mission for the ilKhan. Do as I have commanded.''

That brought the man's head up, and Phelan instantly knew he had overplayed his hand. ''The ilKhan and I do not correspond, and the authorization you seek is not mine to grant. I will switch you.''

The screen returned to the logo and Phelan slammed a fist into the arm of his chair. ''Dammit.''

Dan arched an eyebrow. ''Is that bad?''

Phelan shrugged. ''That man is a member of the technician caste. He should have obeyed me. His superior is no doubt a warrior.''

The logo again vanished and was replaced with a man's

face. From the thickness of his neck and the massive set of his shoulders, Phelan knew he was an Elemental. "I am Star Colonel Taman Malthus. I am in command of Alyina and its resources."

"I am Khan Phelan Ward and I need . . ."

The man held up a huge hand. "The nature of your demand has been made known to me, Khan Ward. I am afraid the Jade Falcons have ships coming through that will require the charges you desire."

"We are on a mission for the ilKhan!"

The blue-eyed Elemental shrugged. "I have no orders to assist you and I am not one of your pups to comply just because a wolfling demands it."

Dan Allard leaned over to Phelan. "Perhaps if we could meet with the Star Colonel to explain . . ."

Malthus frowned. "If you are thinking of invading Alyina, I will defend with all I have. My first action will be to cripple the recharge station, so you will not gain by it."

"Easy." Phelan held both his hands up. "What Colonel Allard meant was . . ."

"Allard?" Malthus' blue eyes narrowed with suspicion. "He is an Allard?"

Phelan hit a button on the commlink that zoomed the lens back to bring Dan into the picture with him. He looked at the older man and jerked a thumb at the commlink.

Dan gave Malthus a disarming smile. "I am Colonel Daniel Allard of the Kell Hounds."

The Elemental stared out from the flat screen for a moment. "Do you know of Kai Allard-Liao?"

Dan's smile broadened. "I do. He is my nephew, my late brother's son."

Malthus nodded. "I know him. I hunted him. I fought beside him."

"He has not spoken much of his time on Alyina." Dan's expression grew grim. "It was not an easy time for him."

"But it was one of which he should be proud," said Malthus. "I have seen an Allard fight. On the chance that what he knew he learned from you, I will bargain away the ship charges you need in return for your promise of peaceful passage away from Alyina."

Dan smiled. "Bargained well and done. I will tell Kai that we spoke."

The Elemental nodded. "Tell him I said I am proud to consider him a comrade."

Of all the people in the task force, Nelson Geist knew that he alone was happy at the week added to their schedule when Phelan detoured through Jade Falcon space and into the Wolf Clan occupation zone. The detour forced an added pair of jumps that gave Nelson the one thing he wanted: time.

During the delays Chris Kell worked with him in combat simulators to bring him back into training. The schedule Nelson set himself was grueling and both Bates and Kell had to urge him to get more sleep and to eat regularly. He knew they thought him obsessive, but they had become his allies, working hard to help him hone his skills as a pilot.

Together they hatched a plot that was as elegant as it was simple. Nelson prepared a document in which he resigned his commission in the Kooken Militia. Chris Kell then offered him a contract with the Kell Hounds and convinced Dan Allard to sign off on it. Kommandant Nelson Geist became Major Nelson Geist, a tactical advisor with the Kell Hounds.

When the papers were signed, Nelson could not keep a smile from his face. "My grandsons would be overjoyed to know I have signed with the Hounds. I will have to find them a playmate so both of them can command little armies of Kell Hounds."

Chris nodded in agreement. "You will have to bring them to Arc-Royal. They will find plenty of children there to play with—though I would say *all* of them will be partial to the Hounds."

With the paperwork out of the way, Nelson's training went into high gear. If any opening came up in the First Regiment, Chris vowed to push him as the man to fill the empty slot. Chris even suggested that he would trade slots with another man in the unit so he could get a *Battle-Master* and let Nelson backseat him.

Nelson repaid Chris's faith in him during the times when they were not training or he was not napping. Throughout the trip, repairs continued on the BattleMechs of the

First Regiment. Nelson, Bates, and Chris all labored long and hard to refit the *Thunderbolt* with armor and to re-inforce the skeletal structures damaged on Arc-Royal.

The repairs were pronounced finished just in time for the last jump to Elissa. Chris joined the other mercenary officers in the Khan's cabin for a final meeting. Chris said he would be pushing the case for Nelson's participation in any battle that took place on Elissa, so it came as only a slight surprise when the Khan summoned Nelson into his presence.

When he entered the cabin he knew immediately that Chris's request had been denied. The Khan had no trouble meeting Nelson's gaze while Chris shied from it and shook his head. "You sent for me, Khan Phelan?" Nelson stood at ease, with his head proudly raised.

"I applaud your effort, Kommandant, and I wish more warriors had your heart and drive. Your request to serve in a 'Mech has been denied." The Khan's hard expression softened a bit. "That does not mean, however, that I do not recognize your skills. I will communicate them in a letter to Prince Victor Davion and urge him to re-instate you in the regular army." The Khan looked at Dan. "That is, *if* Colonel Allard decides to give you up."

"Thank you, sir." Nelson choked down the lump in his throat. "Is that all, sir?"

"No." Phelan leaned forward on his desk. "We will be jumping into Elissa in less than two minutes. Is there anything you have not told us?"

Nelson shook his head. "You know all of it."

"Very well." The Khan pointed him to a chair. "Be seated. We are about to jump."

Nelson and the Kell Hound officers strapped themselves into their chairs. Chris reached out and squeezed Nelson's shoulder. "I'm sorry. I tried."

Nelson nodded. "I know. I hope the training you did against me allows you to finish what I cannot."

"My finger will be on the button, but your spirit will be pushing it."

Three tones sounded, with the last one echoing into the eternity that swallowed Nelson when the ship jumped. He felt himself stretched out until he was only an atom in thickness, then feared he would be torn apart. That fear died amid the regret he felt at being unable to avenge himself against the Red Corsair. Suddenly he reconstituted himself around his need for revenge and as his atoms returned to flesh him out once again, he knew he had escaped oblivion for only one purpose: to kill the Red Corsair.

Nothing and no one can stop me from that.

His vision cleared and he saw the Khan concentrating on his commlink screen. "Incoming message from Elissa, Khan Phelan," he heard a commtech say.

The Khan looked at the officers in the room. "It seems we are anticipated. So much for the advantage of surprise." He hit a button on his computer. "Run it in here."

Oh, there is an advantage in surprise, but they have it! Nelson saw the blank screen fill with Conal Ward's face. "Khan Phelan Ward, with what forces will you attack Elissa?"

Phelan sat back, clearly stunned. "If this is your idea of a joke, Conal."

"With what forces will you attack Elissa?"

Nelson's mind reeled with the repetition of the question. *The Thirty-first Wolf Solahma left Arc-Royal before I told the Khan where the Red Corsair maintained her hideout. Conal could only have gotten that information from her, which means he is in league with her. But his Khan opposes her. How can this be?"*

Nelson heard the fury in the Khan's voice. "Star Colonel Conal Ward, I am your Khan. I order you to abandon Elissa and to turn the Red Corsair over to me."

"No."

"You realize you are committing an act of treason, Star Colonel."

Conal shook his head. "With all due respect, my Khan, it is you who are leading a force from the Inner Sphere to conquer a world held by the Wolf Clan. I am defending it against your treason."

Phelan leaned in toward the screen. "Is this really how you want to play this out, Conal? If so, I will see to it that all your offspring are slain and your DNA is expunged from all breeding programs."

Conal lost a bit of his color, but his face hardened into a mask of hatred. "*If* you defeat me, Khan Phelan, you *might* be able to carry out your threat. I will be defending Elissa with the Thirty-first Wolf Solahma. I would ask you to refrain from using your aerospace fighters.''

The Khan shook his head. ''No, Conal, you made your bed, now you can die in it. We will attack with everything we have. You have grossly overstepped yourself, Conal, and you will pay.''

The other Clan warrior managed a sarcastic smile. ''Winners write the history, Khan Phelan. Remember that, and hope that I will be generous when I write your epitaph.''

40

Elissa
Wolf Clan Occupation Zone
25 October 3055

Phelan shrugged on his cooling vest and snapped it up. He pointed to the holographic map of the valley for which they were headed. "Conal will be waiting for us here, at the north end of the valley. The settlement here, near the south, looks empty. We do have indications of an extensive underground network—both from our sensors and from what Geist told us about the virtual world in which the Red Corsair had him running around." He glanced up at Christian Kell. "Geist confirmed the layout of the town?"

Chris nodded. "He said it matched."

Evantha pointed at the map. "What are the chances Conal will have rigged this settlement the way you booby-trapped Denton?"

"Good question." Phelan belted his pistol on and bent over to tie the holster down to his right leg. "I would say they are slim. He wants us to land close to him, which precludes our running to the city to get trapped. It also makes me think there will not be an ambush from a force hidden there."

The young Khan looked over at Carew and Caitlin. "If there *is* any force coming out of the city at us, that is when you hit them. Conal did not want you in the fight. I want you flying CAP in case we need you. I want you up to preoccupy him."

Chris frowned. "Why not just strafe the hell out of his troops?"

Phelan ground his teeth. *He's right, it would be easier.* "Because those troops are still members of the Wolf Clan. I do not want to have to kill them if it can be avoided."

Dan Allard passed a hand through the mountains at the rear of the Wolf Solahma lines. "These mountains are a warren of mines. If Conal takes his people in there, it will be nasty infighting to root them out."

"Then we will let them starve in there. My main concern is to get the Red Corsair." Phelan pulled his pistol from the holster and jacked a round into the breech. Easing the hammer down, he returned the weapon to its holster. "We are going to defeat Conal, get the Red Corsair, and get out."

The *Owl's Nest* jerked a bit as it entered the atmosphere. Phelan looked at the men and women filling the small briefing room. Young and old, they all knew what they were getting into and he sensed no fear, only impatience. "We are about an hour away from touching down. Any last-minute questions?"

Chris raised his hand. "Are you going to commute Kommandant Geist's sentence?"

"Chris, he switched sides. He shot at *our* people." Phelan shook his head. "I cannot give him a 'Mech."

"Seems to me, cousin, that he is not the first man ever to shoot at forces from his own nation."

The bitter acrimony in Chris's voice squeezed Phelan's heart. He acknowledged the observation with a nod. "True, cousin, I switched sides and shot at people from the Inner Sphere. Were I in his position, would you give me a 'Mech?"

Chris started to answer, then caught himself. "Touché, Phelan. I think you're wrong, but it is your decision."

Phelan gave his cousin a quick smile. "And I think you're right. I also know I'd rather regret not having armed a loyal man than regret putting a traitorous man into the cockpit of a 'Mech."

"Point."

"Battle stations, everyone." Phelan hit a button and the planetary tableau vanished. "We have found our quarry, now we need to kill it."

* * *

Nelson Geist held his hand against his forehead to shade his eyes. "Where? I don't see her."

Standing beside Geist on the nose of the stationary hovercar they had borrowed from the *Owl's Nest*, Bates pointed through a gap between Alpha and Beta Battalions of the Kell Hound regiments. "There she is. It's a red *BattleMaster*."

Nelson squinted his eyes and tried to make out something through the waves of heat blurring the dust cloud raised by the advancing Kell Hounds. "I can't see anything." He dug an elbow into Bates's ribs. "Let me use your binoculars."

Bates ducked his head to get the strap off his neck and handed the heavy field glasses over. Nelson wiped the sweat from the edge of the viewing lenses, then raised them to his eyes. Holding them as steady as he could with his half-hand, he focused them with his right index finger.

The Kell Hounds, with their BattleMechs painted black on the legs and red on the body and arms, had their backs to him. In their center he saw a knot of black 'Mechs that were the Khan and his Star. Half-hidden by the dust cloud that the titanic war machines had raised were the Elementals of Evantha's command reinforcing the far left portion of the mercenary formation, its western flank.

Beyond them, through the gap Bates had pointed out earlier, Nelson focused on the Thirty-first Wolf Solahma. Their 'Mechs had been painted a drab olive green that Nelson thought was suitably martial, but decidedly unremarkable. He knew that the Thirty-first Solahma, though a Clan unit, was despised by the Khan and his people. If the Thirty-first Solahma were judged by the amount of work put into the decorations on the 'Mechs present, they would have come out at the bottom of the heap.

Nelson guessed that they sank even lower in the Khan's estimation because they had with them four other BattleMechs. Three of the machines he did not recognize, though their scarlet and gold markings were appropriate for the bandits. The last machine he did know, and know very well. *So, she is there. I wonder if she is wondering where I am?*

"See her now?"

Nelson nodded, losing sight of her for a moment, then finding her again when her 'Mech began to move forward. As the *BattleMaster* closed with the Kell Hounds, he thought he noticed hesitation. The 'Mech did not move with the fluid grace the Red Corsair had always shown. *What's going on? She* has *to be there. That* has *to be her.*

Nelson lowered the glasses and rubbed at his eyes. Raising them once more he saw the *BattleMaster* swing its right PPC toward the Kell Hound line, then bring it back as it overcorrected the first targeting maneuver. *My God . . .*

Nelson held the glasses out for Bates. ''Yeah, I see.''

The security man reached for the binoculars and never saw Nelson's right knee come up and around. The knee caught Bates in the groin, doubling him over, then Nelson brought the binoculars down and clipped him behind the right ear. Bates toppled from the hovercar and landed unconscious on the ground.

Nelson jumped down beside him and laid the glasses on his chest. ''Sorry, my friend, but you wouldn't have understood.'' He hopped into the hovercar and freed the shotgun from the scabbard on the left side of the vehicle. Laying it on the seat beside him, he started the car and sent it speeding toward the settlement.

Phelan knew that when the first exchange came his 'Mech would be targeted for destruction. Though well-armored for a light 'Mech, it was nothing in comparison to the *Man O'War* Conal piloted. That 'Mech was an OmniMech—top-of-the-line Clan war materiel like the *Warhawk* in which Ranna fought. A single hit by almost any of Conal's weapons would be enough to tear a limb off the *Wolfhound.*

The rest of the Thirty-first Solahma had BattleMechs that were equal to or slightly less than what the Kell Hounds had arrayed against them. Because the Thirty-first were intended to be fighting bandits, the Clans wasted none of their new 'Mechs on them. Conal's OmniMech was a relic of the glory he had once known.

The battle lines were drawn just over a kilometer apart. Ready reports filled Phelan's secondary monitor. The Hounds were ready. He adjusted his pistol and decided he was too. He keyed his radio.

"Conal Ward, you are hereby stripped of your command of the Thirty-first Wolf Solahma. You are to report to me immediately. You will be placed under arrest, pending a court-martial for insubordination and disobeying a superior officer. All those in your command are hereby offered amnesty if they leave you now."

He watched his holographic battle display, but, as he expected, none of the Wolves on the other side moved. He spotted Conal in the center of the enemy formation and saw the Red Corsair coming up beside him. "It does not have to end this way, Conal."

Conal's derisive laugh burst into Phelan's neurohelmet. "I was wrong when I said you were a Wolf before, Phelan. You are still an Inner Sphere weakling. No Wolf would have offered me a second chance to surrender. If you were a true Wolf, one of us would already be dead."

Phelan flipped his radio over to Tac One. "It is time."

Nelson Geist steered the stolen hovercar through the streets he had wandered ages ago. The town was not as neat and clean as it had been in the simulation, but he instantly recognized every aspect of it. It sent a shiver down his spine and started him sweating. He stopped the vehicle, got out and vomited.

He remained on his hands and knees, his chest heaving as his stomach tried to purge itself. He mentally demanded that it stop. *I am here for a purpose.* He wiped his mouth on his left sleeve. *She had contempt for me. She saw me as weak. I am* not *weak!*

Reaching up, he grabbed the edge of the hovercar and pulled himself to his feet. From the car he took the pump shotgun and jacked a shell into the chamber. The weapon dangled from his right hand by the pistolgrip as he stalked across the empty plaza toward the main building. "I know where you are. I have you. You are mine."

The Kell Hound close assault lances entered the gap between the two forces as their fire support lances sent flight after flight of missiles arcing up and over them. Chris Kell fought the leftward rotation of his charging *Thunderbolt* when its shoulder-mounted LRM launcher sent a flight of fifteen missiles at the enemy. Keeping his crosshairs steady on the *Clint* that was his target, he let go with his extended range large laser and the trio of medium pulse lasers in his arsenal.

Two of the pulse lasers missed at that range, but the third slashed open the armor on the *Clint*'s right arm. Semi-molten armor plates dropped to the ground, exposing metal bones, synthetic muscles, and the complex mechanism of the 'Mech's particle projection cannon. The *Thunderbolt*'s large laser thrust a green energy beam into the *Clint*'s chest, melting away all but a thin armor veneer.

Four of the missiles Chris had launched slammed home in the same spot, blasting away the last of the armor and causing some internal damage. When another set of missiles savaged the armor on the 'Mech's right leg, Chris thought the machine had wobbled a bit, but it stayed upright.

The *Clint*'s return fire hit the *Thunderbolt* hard, the PPC devouring nearly a ton of armor on the left side of the 'Mech's chest. The two pulse lasers mounted in the *Clint*'s torso converged on the *Thunderbolt*'s midline. They cut bubbling furrows in the armor over the big 'Mech's heart, but failed to breach it. Chris successfully fought the unbalancing effect of losing so much armor, and kept his 'Mech charging forward.

Nelson Geist spat on the tile floor of the dimly lit corridor. Down below the surface of the planet the heat was intense, and he felt sweat soaking his shirt. Droplets of perspiration also ran down his temples and speckled his upper lip. He licked it off, then wiped his half-hand on his pants before returning it to the shotgun's pump.

As he crept down the hallway toward the forbidden corridor, a nervous smile stole over his face. *If I were in a 'Mech, I would have a cooling vest and I would be bone-dry in a cockpit five times as hot as this.* He glanced down and checked for the hundredth time to see that the gun's safety was off.

Turning the corner Nelson felt a constriction in his throat. He nearly panicked, imagining for a second that somehow the shock-collar had been again fitted around his neck. His half-hand clawed at his collar, but when he felt only flesh and the burning rake of his fingernails, he leaned back against the wall. *This time there is nothing to stop you.*

He wiped stinging sweat out of his eyes and resumed his trek to the end of the corridor. There, just as he had seen in the simulation, stood two closed doors. *Almost closed*, he corrected himself. A thin bar of yellowish light separated the doors. His smile returned, but his teeth clamped down to stifle any cry of triumph that might escape him.

Step by step, meter by meter, he paced his way forward silently. He forced himself to breathe through his nose, searching the musty dry air for any hint of her, but the only scent was the stink of his own vomit and perspiration. As he exhaled, the droplets of sweat that had collected around his nostrils sprayed down over his hands.

Nearing the doors he heard a pair of clicks. He glanced back the way he'd come, fearing the approach of guards armed to cut him down on the threshold of his goal. He saw no one and nothing behind him and realized that the noise had come from the room. He ran the sounds through his mind and could think of no weapon that sounded quite like that when cocked. *Sounded more like the latches on a briefcase being opened.*

Nelson took one last deep breath as he pushed the left door open noiselessly. In his time on the *Tigress* and in countless nightmares afterward he had imagined incredible and horrible things in the room beyond those doors. Torture chambers, a hall of horrors, a trophy room decorated with bits and pieces of individuals the Red Corsair had defeated, with the missing half of his hand featured prominently. Yet whatever he had imagined in fevered, malevolent dreams, none of it approached the malignant reality.

As he entered the room, the Red Corsair twisted the head of the cylinder she had inserted into the blocky device built into the wall. The yellow and black safety tabs came away as her motion locked the cylinder in place. She tossed the tabs aside, then smiled as she looked up and saw him. "I thought it might be you."

Nelson looked from her to the briefcase on the desk in front of her and then to the thing on the wall. The warning symbol on the back of the briefcase was one he knew from his cadet training so long ago. Though he could not see into the case, he knew it had a soft foam bed with a cutout to hold the cylinder in place because, as his instructor had said, "nuclear mine triggers are not built to be banged around."

A nuclear mine? This whole valley, everything, will be destroyed. She is mad!

"It's me." Nelson motioned with the gun and the Red Corsair raised her hands. "It's over for you."

The Red Corsair shook her head. "You will not kill me, Nelson Geist."

"I won't? You're here assembling a nuclear device that will wipe out everything in this valley, save those in the bunkers built into the mountains. You're beyond mad, you're evil. There is nothing you could say that would stop me from killing you."

She smiled carefully. "I love you, Nelson Geist." Her hands slowly fell to caress her stomach through her cooling vest. "I am carrying your child."

From the first exchange the battle began to go exactly the way Phelan knew it had to. The Thirty-first Wolf Solahma had begun to retreat before the gap could be closed. Their goal was obviously to pull back into the mountain stronghold and fight from there, but Conal had established his line too far forward. *He must have forgotten that the Hounds are equipped with weapons like ours—weapons salvaged from the Smoke Jaguars and Nova Cats after the battle for Luthien.*

Phelan smiled as he realized that was the solution to the mystery of how Conal had been caught away from his cover. He had expected that a couple of long-range exchanges would slow the Hound advance, then he could withdraw in good order to the mountains. Because he had been too arrogant to coordinate with the Hounds during any of the bandit-hunting operation, he had never learned what they could do. *Your stupid arrogance is the reason the truce must remain. If we do not learn to respect the Inner Sphere, they will swarm over and destroy us.*

The Khan saw Conal's 'Mech pulling back, but he stopped as a hailstorm of LRMs brought the Red Corsair's *BattleMaster* to its knees. The *Man O'War* inter-

posed itself between the downed *BattleMaster* and the
Kell Hound lines.

The *Man O'War* raised its two arms and crossed them
above its head in a clear Clan challenge. "I am untouched, Khan Phelan. Will you be the one to finish me?"
Behind him his lines crumbled and the Thirty-first broke
running for the bunkers.

Phelan opened his radio and folded in all the tactical
frequencies. "What do you offer me if I win?"

"My people surrender."

"They will abide by this?"

"They will, Khan Phelan."

Phelan's eyes narrowed. *You are a cheating, treacherous bastard. You cheated during the last fight for my
Bloodname and you have done almost as much damage
in the Inner Sphere as the Red Corsair.* Phelan saw a
signal indicator flicker, and his secondary monitor reported that a coded tightbeam message had gone out from
Conal to the settlement. *You have something up your
sleeve, but I have Carew and Caitlin's pilots in the air
to forestall an ambush.* Phelan set his computer to beep
if an answer came back on that narrow frequency, then
nodded.

"Bargained well and done, Conal." The Khan smiled
to himself as his 'Mech started to move away from the
Kell Hound lines. *You have your trick, and I have mine.
Who will fool whom?*

"My child?"

As Nelson spoke, the Red Corsair lunged for the briefcase. Nelson thrust his gun in her direction and yanked
the trigger. The first cloud of lead pellets caught her in
the left shoulder, twisting her around. As she swung back
to the left, her right hand come up out of the case with
the machine pistol that had been concealed there.

Without thinking Nelson pumped another shell into the
gun and fired again. Her machine pistol lipped flame back
at him, then his second shot hit the gun and destroyed
the lower half of her right arm. Her body slammed back
against the wall, then slid to the floor, leaving bloody
streaks to mark her passage.

Nelson felt himself gasping for air and thought it was
because of the shock of such close combat, then he tasted

blood on his lips. He looked down and saw two holes in his shirt. The pain started when he dropped his gun and pressed his right hand and forearm against the wounds. But when he pulled his arm away, the pain became even greater.

He took a step forward, then another. The world began to grow dim, but Nelson refused to pass out. Hugging his arm tight to his body, he reached out with his maimed hand and stumbled forward to the desk. He batted the case aside, toppling it to the floor, then worked his way around the corner.

When he saw her, he fell to his knees and knew he'd never stand up again. She was dead—pellets from the first burst had blown her throat out yet somehow left her face untouched. He reached out with his left hand and closed her staring eyes. He bent his head for a moment, mourning what might have been were black changed for white in the universe. Then he began to look for a place to die.

The radio handset on the Red Corsair's belt beeped, and a voice said, "They are in position. Do it now."

Nelson spat out blood and plucked the black box from her belt. He clutched it in his left hand, waiting for what seemed like a lifetime to build up the strength needed to raise it. He heard air slowly hissing out of his lungs, but he forced himself to lift the device to his face. He pressed the red switch down.

"You're on your own." He stopped and caught his breath. "When you get to hell, she can tell you where it went wrong."

Phelan knew his only advantage lay in the speed of his 'Mech. While Conal's *Man O'War* could have nearly matched him in a foot race, the *Wolfhound* could sometimes be almost impossible to hit because of its agility. If Conal was not careful about the heat buildup in his 'Mech—a tall order for a 'Mech that handled heat as efficiently as the *Man O'War*—his targeting circuits would start to fry.

Phelan had to wait for Conal to falter. Moving fast would make him a difficult target, but it also made it damned hard for him to hit anything either. *Push him, make him push himself, then take him!* The Khan started forward and worked to his own right, keeping as far as possible from the *Man O'War*'s right arm.

Conal shifted the 'Mech right and thrust the right arm at the *Wolfhound*. Twin ropes of crackling blue energy shot out from the over and under PPC muzzles. Both gouged great furrows through the ground behind the lithe *Wolfhound*, flinging half-molten chunks of rock into the air. The *Man O'War*'s left arm also tracked Phelan, but its large and medium pulse lasers scattered their energy darts high over the 'Mech's head.

He missed high? What is he doing? Phelan shook his head as he watched the *Man O'War* move awkwardly. *Conal is being sloppy. What is his game? Does he think he can lure me in close? He moves so I cannot kill him, but he is not putting out his full effort to kill me. Why not?*

Phelan flipped his holographic display over to infrared and was rewarded with a glowing outline of the *Man O'War*. Conal had already succeeded in pushing it, but the heat was not *that* high. It would not take enough of an edge off Conal's aim to make any sort of approach possible. As he hesitated, then pushed the *Wolfhound* forward in a burst of speed, he had the sinking feeling that Conal—no matter how sloppy he got—would never give him the opening he needed to win.

Suddenly his computer beeped, informing him of the reply to Conal's tightbeam. Phelan looked up and saw that Conal had stopped tracking him for the moment. The *Man O'War* missed a step, then two, and the weapons dipped half a meter toward the ground.

Phelan cut left with the *Wolfhound* and closed the gap between the two machines. Continuing his circle, but drawing it tighter, the *Wolfhound* slipped beyond the forward arc of the *Man O'War*'s weapons. Coming around into the slowly turning 'Mech's aft, Phelan dropped his crosshairs onto the OmniMech's broad back, then cut loose with everything.

The large laser mounted in the *Wolfhound*'s right arm used the green beam like a scalpel, ripping a huge hole in the armor over the other 'Mech's back. The three pulse lasers then poured scarlet needles of pulsed laser energy into the heart of the *Man O'War*. The lasers shattered the gyro casings, spitting bits and pieces of them out through the gaping wound in the 'Mech's back.

Stabilizing the giant war machines was simply not possible without the gyros, even with the direct feed from Conal's neurohelmet. The *Man O'War* landed in a cloud of dust, its limbs smashing against the ground and disintegrating, leaving the downed 'Mech broken and helpless.

Nelson Geist realized that he had dropped the radio when he heard it shatter on the ground. He smiled, then leaned back against the desk, chiding himself for being so clumsy. He continued to stare at the black plastic and bright transistors, even though it was painful to have his head in that awkward position. He knew the pain would not last much longer and he told himself that staring at a broken radio was much better than having the last thing he ever saw be the Red Corsair.

41

Tharkad
Federated Commonwealth
25 October 3055

Victor Davion sat alone in the Archon's office and studied the slip of paper in his hands. *So, this is what it comes down to.* After months of exhaustive investigation, he had a list of four names. They were the four people who had purchased tickets to the Frederick Steiner Memorial Library dedication banquet but who had not attended nor given their tickets to someone else.

As far as Victor was concerned, the first name on the list was the only one that needed to be there. *Ryan Steiner*. Ryan had been a thorn in his father's side from the moment he had wedded Melissa Steiner. Ryan was heir to the ambitions of Alessandro Steiner, the man his grandmother had deposed and who had allowed Ryan to start his own career by betraying Frederick Steiner, another rival for power.

Ryan thrived in the swamp of politics, and Victor knew he *had* to be the man behind the assassination. Ryan had married Morasha Kelswa, heir to the title of the Tamar Pact. Since their marriage he had become a tireless champion for the independence of the Tamar worlds. The fact that Tamar had been all but swallowed up by the Jade Falcons had done nothing to quiet him.

Ryan also controlled the Skye separatist movement that had almost set off a civil war fifteen years earlier. Steiner had provoked a revolt, then stepped in to smooth things over when Victor's father had sent troops to put down the rebellion. The little bloodshed that did occur was blamed on Hanse Davion. If not for Melissa's popularity with the Lyrans, the incident might have precipitated all-out civil war.

Ryan Steiner had the most to gain from my mother's death. Victor's nostrils flared as he thought about all that had happened since her death. If his sister Katherine had not pushed her role as a media darling to make peace between him and Ryan, their respective camps would no doubt already be on the brink of open conflict. Victor was certain that Ryan was behind the continuing campaign of whispers blaming him for his own mother's assassination.

He looked at the second name. Anastasius Focht, the Precentor Martial of ComStar, had purchased a ticket, but had not attended and had not assigned the local Precentor to attend in his stead. Though Victor had never met the man, Focht had been the one who directed the defeat of the Clans at Tukayyid. Melissa had also spoken highly of him. Still, old suspicions about ComStar died hard, and the lack of an apparent motive did not exonerate Focht—no one had ever been sure of the Precentor Martial's true motives and Victor suspected no one ever would.

The third name struck him as equally absurd: Katherine Steiner-Davion. He tried to reconcile his view of his sister with that of a ruthless conspirator arranging the cold-blooded murder of their mother. *If she were Romano Liao's daughter, perhaps, but Katherine? Never.* No matter that he knew she could never be part of an assassination plot against mother, his sister's presence on the list chilled him. *Since when did Katherine miss a party?*

The last name deepened the cold sucking at his marrow. *Victor Ian Steiner-Davion. I was supposed to have been there. I would have been seated within the blast radius.* Victor tasted sour bile in his mouth.

He knew how his name had ended up on the list. The banquet had been a charity event. An invitation had been transmitted as a matter of course and he had purchased tickets without a second thought. The invitation had come through in a whole stack of papers that he'd signed before leaving Port Moseby for Arc-Royal. The Secretariat had found the sheet and had verified his fingerprints and signature and even Galen's prints on it.

Victor had the advantage of knowing he had not murdered his mother, but he also knew others were seeing it differently. His absence condemned him. Had he attended the banquet, he too would have died. Because he was still alive, he had inherited the throne of the Federated Commonwealth instead. If it weren't bad enough that he profited from his mother's death, people pointed out that he hadn't even attended her funeral.

The Prince sat back in his chair. *If I had died, Katherine would now be in my place and Ryan Steiner would be that much closer to taking over the Commonwealth. Did he think I would be at the banquet? Had he hoped to get me, too and Katherine as well?*

His mouth went dry. *Or did Katherine expect me to die with our mother?*

Victor crumpled the paper and tossed it on the desk. *My father would have arrested Ryan in an instant, and the Secretariat would have broken him. Justin Allard would have arranged an insidious intelligence operation to ferret out the truth. My mother?* Victor smiled as he remembered her. *Smooth as silk but hard as steel. She would have managed to squeeze Ryan economically and politically until his power base evaporated. She would have charmed his allies away from him and left him isolated and alone.*

The Prince stood and leaned on his desk. *But this isn't about how any of them would have handled it. They are dead and I must do it on my own. What do I truly know? What do I have to work with? How will Victor Davion handle this problem?*

He smoothed the paper out again, picked up a pen, and drew a line through his own name. "I *know* one person on this list is innocent." He drew a star beside Ryan's name. "And I know I want to think one person is guilty. And what I have to work with are two men I can trust and a man who kills for hire."

Victor hit the intercom button on his commlink console. "Please find Galen Cox and Mr. Curaitis and have them report to me immediately."

The five minutes it took for the pair to make their way

to his office was enough for Victor to finalize his plan. *This is how Victor Davion handles the problem.*

Galen Cox handed Victor a yellow slip of paper. "Picked this up on my way in here. Thought you'd want to see it."

Victor read the brief message that had been sent Alpha Priority through ComStar. "Red Corsair is dead. Full report to follow. Dan Allard."

The Prince smiled. "This is excellent news, and ties in with what I wanted to tell you, Galen."

"Sir?"

"Pack your bags, you're going to Arc-Royal." Victor kept the smile on his face. "I want you to represent me there with Katherine when the Kell Hounds bury their dead. I also want you to keep an eye on my sister for me." He saw Galen's expression begin to darken, but waved away any misgivings his friend might have. "Don't spy on her, Galen. Just make sure Ryan and his people don't try with her what they did with Ragnar. Consider it a vacation and your chance to get linked with my sister in the scandal vids."

"A vacation? I guess I can handle that sort of temporary duty." The blond officer did not even try to hide his pleasure at being asked to accompany Katherine. "Thank you, Victor."

"You've earned it, my friend." Victor waved him out of the office. "Go pack. You'll have to leave immediately to reach Arc-Royal by the time the Hounds return."

Galen saluted, Victor returned it, then the man left the office.

Curaitis's eyes sharpened. "What didn't you want him to hear?"

The Prince nodded. "I hope you are even better than your remark suggests you are."

"I am."

"Good. The assassin has survived his fat embolis?"

The security man nodded. "He will be fit enough to hang, though it is a waste of rope."

"Waste not, want not." Victor folded his arms across his chest. "I want him taken to the old leprosarium on Poulsbo. I want him kept up to speed on anything and everything that would enhance his performance as an assassin. Give him nothing that truly works, but let him log all the computer simulation time he wants.''

Curaitis nodded stiffly. ''It is a dangerous game you are playing. If word were to get out that you were 'keeping' the assassin who killed your mother. . . ''

''That's why you are acting as my agent in this, Curaitis. I do not expect word of his existence to get out. Period.'' Victor took a deep breath, then exhaled it slowly. ''Someone else defined the rules of this game and I'm just learning them. Once I've mastered them, I will be ready to destroy my enemies. And when that day comes, it will be my distinct pleasure to use their best weapon against them.''

42

Elissa
Wolf Clan Occupation Zone
26 October 3055

Phelan Kell rubbed at his eyes. The insides of his eyelids felt like they were coated in sandpaper, but that was to be expected after hours of staring at a computer screen. Still clad as he had been in the cockpit of his *Wolfhound*, he had left the battlefield and immediately taken command of the Red Corsair's office. What he had planned as a cursory examination of files turned into an hours'-long plunge into a conspiracy that left him feeling shaken and hollow.

He looked up from the desk as someone knocked at the door. "Enter."

Two Elementals in gray jumpsuits and bearing side-arms led Conal Ward into the spacious office. They hustled him along, dragging him when the chain hobbling his feet kept him from matching their stride. Holding him upright on the white marble floor, they let him get his feet under himself.

Then the Elementals took a step back, but stood ready to restrain the prisoner. Phelan gave them a smile, then held out his right hand. "Please give me the key to his shackles. You may leave. We do not want to be disturbed." One of the Elementals hesitated and the Khan added, "We will not have trouble, will we, Conal?"

The prisoner shook his head.

The Elementals complied with Phelan's order and withdrew. As the door clicked shut, Conal's head came up. "Figured it all out, did you?"

Phelan's fist tightened on the key, then he flipped it to Conal. "These documents leave little to the imagination. I would not have believed you hated me so much."

"Do not flatter yourself." Conal freed his legs and started working on his manacles. "Yes, I hate you, but even more I hate the way you Wardens have crippled the Clans. We live for war and we are the ultimate army. Ulric and Natasha and others like them have stripped us of our true nature."

"I would not have thought treason was part of a Clansman's true nature." Phelan rested his left hand on the computer console. "I have read how the atomic mine was to be used to destroy this base and leave no clue if the Red Corsair's mission failed. You could have set it and been clear long before we arrived."

The Khan shook his head. "I wondered why you didn't press me when we fought. You should have ripped me to pieces, but you were looking beyond that immediate pleasure to a greater revenge. No one from outside the Clans would believe you were willing to die in a nuclear blast just to get at me and the Wolf Clan. But then they would not understand how the Clans work. They don't know their history."

Conal sneered at him. "And you do?"

"I know enough to realize that your plan would have cost more lives than all the other wars mankind has known. You would have destroyed all the Wolves, you know, not just the Wardens." Phelan shivered. "The last Clan that dared use atomics was utterly destroyed. They were hunted down—men, women, and children—and all slain. The Clans barely even acknowledge that they ever existed, and their crime . . ."

Conal shook his head. "The Wolverines used a nuclear blast to destroy a genetic repository. They deserved to die. Here things would have been different. Many of my people would have survived and the conclusion they would have drawn was that a nuclear weapon brought in by the Kell Hounds detonated prematurely. You would have been blamed, and Ulric along with you. The Wolf Clan would have been destroyed just like the Wolverines, but our bloodlines—good *Crusader* bloodlines—would have passed into other Clans."

Conal laughed in the face of Phelan's horror. "Yes, I

would have died in the blast along with you, but I would have died a hero because I opposed you. My genetic material would have contributed to legions of sibkos, and battles would have been waged for its possession."

"You are a monster!" Phelan stood and ripped open a desk drawer. He pulled out a black grease pencil and tossed it to Conal. "Use it. Draw a circle. I will give you the honor of dying in a Circle of Equals."

Conal batted the pencil out of the air and defiantly rested his fists on his hips. "I may be a monster, but I am not a stupid one. You are my Khan. You have a duty to me and the Clans. As is my right, I demand a trial before the Grand Council."

Conal's request took Phelan's breath away. "What?" he whispered hoarsely.

The elder Clansman smiled triumphantly. "You heard me correctly, Khan Phelan. I demand a trial before the Grand Council. I want my fate decided before a Council of all the Khans."

"You *are* insane, no doubt about it." Phelan shook his head, hoping to banish the start of the headache pulsing out pain at his temples. "Were *I* you, I would have no desire to see my treason paraded before the Khans."

"But you are not me, and you do not have my understanding of Clan politics." Conal's smug expression made Phelan's heart begin to sink. "What you have determined about the nuclear mine and our fight is just supposition. You have no proof."

The Khan rapped his knuckles on the computer console. "The Corsair's evacuation plan for the base is here. It talks about using the nuke to destroy everything."

Conal shrugged. "So the Red Corsair stumbled upon a device hidden by the pirates who used to inhabit this place, and she decided to use it. She was a renegade."

"No she wasn't." Phelan frowned heavily. "She was being aided and abetted by the Jade Falcons. They gave her ships and BattleMechs both before and during her campaign."

"You will find no record of such things in Jade Falcon files." Conal shrugged. "Besides, she is dead and what was given to her is immaterial to my trial. It will not, in fact, affect how my trial turns out. Innocent or guilty, I will win."

"I don't understand."

"I know." Conal held out his left hand. "If I am found innocent, you and the ilKhan will be viewed as having entered a treasonous alliance with Victor Davion to retake Elissa. Ulric will be challenged, as will you. Natasha will be challenged, too, and you will see the Crusaders replacing you within the hierarchy of our Clan. A new ilKhan will be elected and the truce will be repudiated."

Conal's right hand came up. "Even if I am found guilty of treason, my act of treason will have been in the name of defending a woman who proved what we all know to be true: the truce is a sham that protects the Inner Sphere from us. With only a poorly armed and supported force, she was able to raid at will within the Inner Sphere."

Phelan swallowed hard. "The truce is again questioned, Ulric is challenged, and the peace dies."

"And that is just from the Clan side of things." Conal pointed back toward the door. "If even a hint of this gets out to the Inner Sphere, the demand for war on their part will shatter your precious truce. And you can be assured that word will get out, because I will demand testimony from the Kell Hounds and other Inner Sphere witnesses."

Conal folded his arms across his chest. "Sooner rather than later, the truce is dead and we return to doing what we do the best—war. If you were really of the Clans, you would see that and would have joined me. You know I am right—I can see it in your eyes—I have won! You have lost, the Inner Sphere has lost. You know now what my trial will make manifest to everyone."

In one smooth motion Phelan drew his pistol, aimed, and pulled the trigger. The bullet caught Conal over the right eye and blew back out the rear of his head. His body twisted around and fell to the ground, dead before it hit.

The Khan of the Wolf Clan came around from behind the desk and picked the grease pencil off the floor. Grasping it firmly in his left hand, he carefully drew a black circle in the middle of the floor. It surrounded the body.

He finished the circle and placed the pencil on the desk. "Guards!"

The two Elementals, anxiety showing on their faces, burst into the room with their guns leveled. They looked from Phelan to the body and back up.

"He preferred a Circle of Equals to a trial on charges of treason." Phelan holstered his pistol. "He lost."

Epilogue

Kooken's Pleasure Pit
Federated Commonwealth
13 November 3055

Christian Kell smiled at the two boys playing in the yard when he stopped the Rover he had rented in Dobson. He climbed out, then pulled his black cap from beneath the shoulder flap on his red fatigue shirt. He settled it on his head with a tug on the bill, then walked toward the house. By that time the two boys, clones of each other, stood in his way, craning their heads back to look up at him.

"You're from the Kell Hounds, aren't you?" one asked.

Chris squatted down to meet them at eye level. "I am and I would guess you are Jacob and you are Joachim." The twins looked at him in awe, and Chris smiled, thankful he had been lucky with his guesses. "Your grandfather told me all about you."

"Boys, come inside."

The blond twins turned to look at the woman standing on the porch, holding the door open. "Mom, he's a Kell Hound. He knows Grandpa."

"In the house. *Now!*" Her stance and her tone promised no reversal and no mercy, so the two boys trudged listlessly under her arm and into the house. She released her grip on the door, then let it slam shut behind them. Hugging the folds of a thick sweater around her, the woman stood ready to defend her sons against the threat he represented to them.

The mercenary straightened up. "I am Major Christian Kell."

"I know who you are. I remember you from when you tried to visiphone." She looked up at Chris and the blue of her eyes sent a jolt straight through to his soul. "I told you then that I didn't want to talk to you. I meant it."

"I knew you did, at the time. I thought. . . ."

"You thought wrong, *if* you thought at all." A shiver shook her skeletal form. "First Jon and then the Kommandant. I won't have it happen to my boys. Please leave."

"Mrs. Geist, Dorete, I'm here to discharge a debt to your father-in-law." He coughed lightly. "You're not making this easy."

"His dying doesn't make it very easy on me." Venom pumped like blood through her words. "Nelson Geist is dead. He lived and died by the sword. You owe him nothing."

"Wrong!" Chris re-exerted control after his initial shout. He could see she wanted to provoke a reaction. "I owe him my life. Every one of the people we brought back here to Kooken owes Nelson Geist his life. The fact that the Inner Sphere is not again at war with the Clans is because of Nelson Geist. Just hear me out, give him that much, then you can tell me to leave."

Dorete remained silent and stone-still. The breeze tugged at the hem of her floral print dress and whipped a few wisps of blond hair across her face, but she did not move a muscle. She didn't even blink and Chris wondered if she was going to faint. When she did not, he took her silence as permission for him to continue.

"Nelson Geist resigned his commission with the militia and joined the Kell Hounds before he died. He was given the rank of major. Because of that you—and your sons—have certain rights and privileges that we accord the survivors of our fallen members."

Her head came up and Chris saw a tremor in her lower lip. "I have memorial flags and apologetic holovids enough, thank you, Major."

Chris shook his head. "I understand that, ma'am. This is different. We're taking Major Geist to Arc-Royal to be buried with the other Hounds. We'd like you and his grandsons to come along. You'll have a place there. We have programs that will get the boys an education.''

''No!'' She bunched the sweater in her hands as she balled her fists. ''I won't have my boys turned into soldiers.''

''That's not what we're talking about, Mrs. Geist.'' Chris pulled off his cap and clutched it in his hands. ''We're talking about a chance for the boys to grow up to be whatever they want: doctors, lawyers, whatever. No obligation to the Hounds: we'd be repaying our debt to Major Geist.''

''Nelson Geist is dead.'' Her face hardened. ''I don't want anything from him.''

''That's too bad, Dorete, because you already have it.'' Chris let an edge creep into his voice. ''Nelson Geist gave you a future. That's why he died, to give a future to you and to your children and to their children and to theirs.'' Then he softened his voice again. ''And, yes, they *might* decide to be soldiers, but if that happens, you know as well as I that, short of killing them yourself, you could do nothing to stop them.''

A tear splashed down her cheek and her mouth opened in a soundless scream. Chris mounted the steps to the porch and put his arms around her. She fought him for a moment, then relented and clung to him. ''Why?''

Chris shrugged. ''That is the question no one can answer. Right now, though, Nelson's death means you and the boys don't need to face the future alone.''

He looked down and saw the two boys framed by the screen door. Their mother's sobs had tears brimming in their eyes. ''Who are you, mister?''

Chris gave them as brave a smile as he could muster, but then words failed him.

''He is a friend.'' Dorete shifted within his arms and looked at her sons. ''Your grandfather sent him. He's taking us home.''

CRUSADER

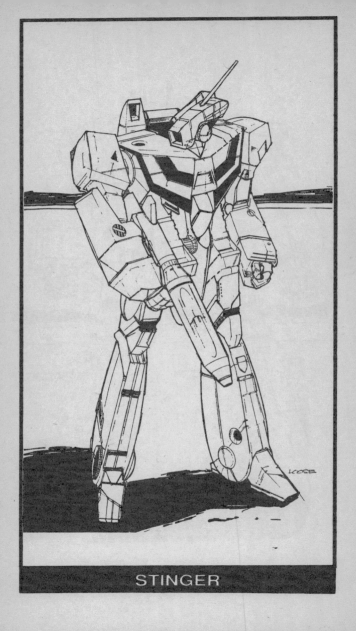

STINGER

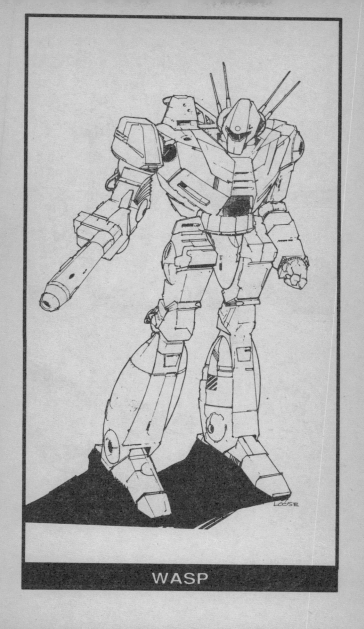

WASP

LOCUST

RIFLEMAN